Killing Secrets

A Thorne's Thorns Romantic Suspense Novel - Book One

K.L. Docter

ABOUT THE BOOK

Some secrets are better left dead.

When Rachel James's ex-husband walks out of prison, he's determined to reclaim everything he lost, especially Rachel and their little girl. Terrified, Rachel runs to Denver, desperate to keep her daughter safe. But the child hasn't spoken a word since her father's arrest, and Rachel's running out of places to hide.

Contractor Patrick Thorne isn't looking for redemption or another chance to fail someone who needs him. Haunted by the loss of his wife and unborn son, he's focused on saving his business from a ruthless saboteur. He can't protect the frightened woman and her child, who are being sheltered by his parents.

Little do they know, danger has already found them. Can they trust each other enough to escape a serial killer's hit list and save a little girl from her silent prison?

DEDICATION

For Mom
I learned my love of suspense from you.
Thank you for setting me on the road.

&

For Jan
You were right.
I wish you were here to say, "I told you so."
I love and miss you, my friend, my sister.

PROLOGUE

Four Weeks....
Two Days....
Sixteen Hours....
...'Til death.

The first time he laid eyes on her, he stood on the threshold of a doorway he dare not cross. He fell into her fathomless dark gaze, unable, *unwilling* to shake his soul free and, in that one moment, he knew.

She was meant for him to love.

Untouched by the sordid life that flourished around her, she was sunlight in a gray existence. A smile in a dingy room. A joy such as he'd never known. She was a gift from a cold, unforgiving God. Forever innocent.

Why God would give him such a precious angel, he hadn't a clue. But he suddenly knew what he was willing to die for. What he'd kill for.

In that instant of clarity the monster that lurked in the dark recesses of his mind was freed. A creature designed to kill. To live and die. Over and over again. Until his angel ascended once more to her place in Heaven at God's feet where he couldn't reach her.

'Til death parted them, she was his and his alone.

Certain she'd been lost to him, the shock of spotting her again in LoDo, a lower downtown section of Denver, nearly brought him to his knees. His brain tried to tell him he was mistaken. She had more curves than he remembered. Her hairstyle and clothes were different.

The others were different, too.

He shook his head against the monster's treacherous whisper. He refused to listen. Couldn't listen. His angel smiled at him. His soul recognized her. Somehow, some way, his fractious God had been appeased and given him yet another chance.

The past seven days were hell. Watching her. Wanting to take her. He couldn't screw up and lose her again. Tonight, his preparations in place, she'd return to his side where she belonged.

Breathing slow and measured through the full-face ski mask he'd bought at a thrift store, he sucked in a lungful of musty stench. In this uncommon late-May heat wave, he was sweating bullets, but the wool soaked it up before it could sting his eyes. The itching would drive him insane, though, if she didn't come home from work soon.

The LoDo sports bar where she waited tables closed almost an hour ago. She couldn't have gone on a date at two o'clock on a Thursday morning, could she?

Three times he'd entered her ground floor apartment after she'd left for work, and he'd seen no sign she was involved with anyone. No jockey shorts mixed with her panties in the hamper. No extra razor. The food in the refrigerator wasn't enough to feed a cat, let alone her and a boyfriend, and the only scent on her pillows was floral. The sole message from a male on her answering machine had identified himself as a special research librarian from the Denver Public Library reminding her to pick up the copy of "The Warwick Genealogy" she'd requested.

That doesn't mean she isn't still involved with him, *the almighty scion of Thorne Enterprises. She's probably crawling into his bed like a whore right this minute, letting him do things to her, making her scream....*

Screams.

Blood.

Death.

"No! Stop!" he whispered. "That was a mistake!"

Was it? The insidious question lashed him from the dark place in his pounding skull.

He rejected the smirking voice, the vivid images. Think of something else. Anything else. Forgetforgetfor—

A car alarm screamed at an outlying parking lot and dragged him out of his fugue. His eyes cleared. The pain behind them eased to a level he'd learned to carry over the years.

Soon, he would kill the nightmares forever. Patrick Thorne would die and the secrets with him. But the contractor hadn't been punished enough yet. Before he finished, he'd ruin Thorne's reputation, his livelihood, destroy everything he loved most in the world.

Just as Thorne destroyed our lives. The man must die! Now!

Restless to escape its bonds the monster thrust knife-hot pain in his brain, but he wrestled it back into the shadows and locked it down. Retribution was almost at hand, but not tonight. This night was about her.

Where was she?

There! Her tennis shoes slapped the sidewalk as she approached. He caught a flash of uniform—shorts and sports shirt, both too tight for decency. Then she walked out of the weak light that pooled across the commons into the dark well that led to her door. Her building superintendent had replaced her broken porch light this morning, but he'd smashed it again. He smiled when she cursed someone named Ronnie.

With a jingle of keys, she passed the niche he'd carved for himself in the shrubs. A bunch of adrenaline surged through him, made him light-headed with anticipation. He shook the buzz from his head and crashed out of the bushes with more noise than he intended.

Her head snapped left. She shot a glance over her shoulder. Her eyes widened. She lunged for the safety of her door.

He chased after her, grabbed her by the throat. A squeeze of her windpipe cut off her scream. He didn't want to damage her too much. He just needed to get her alone.

To atone. To give him another chance.

With her body crushed against him, he groaned with pleasure. It had been so long! For a moment he forgot his purpose, lost in the new scent of her, in the innocent softness of her curves. Her breasts were full beneath his forearm. The sweet curve of her ass cradled his stiff penis. With another groan, his grip relaxed.

She screamed. Struggling, she broke loose of his hold.

Shit! Reaching out, he snagged her long ponytail and yanked her back hard. With his other hand, he strangled her next scream into a whimper. "Do that again," he grated, "I'll use my knife." The honed blade was secure in his pocket but she didn't know that.

"I have money," she croaked. "Three hundred. Tips. In my pocket. Please! Don't—"

"Shh. Don't fight me. Shh," he crooned into her hair. He tugged a chloroform-laced rag from his pants pocket and fitted it over her face. "Just give me another chance, Angel, and everything will be fine."

This time she'd make the right choice because, God only knew, he'd truly go insane if he had to kill her all over again.

Kolthern Ranch, outside Dallas, Texas.

"Til death us do part, darlin'. I keep what's mine!"

Rachel James jolted awake in her apartment above the Kolthern carriage house, the harsh words scraping her nerves as if there weren't six months and fifteen hundred miles standing between her and her ex-husband's threats.

For a long moment, their last night together flayed her mind with sickening memories. Punishing sex. The pain of his whip, blows that cracked one rib. Two. But it was the vicious threats that cut her to the heart, those scars never healed.

Eyes squeezed shut, she smothered the nightmare, sucked air into her lungs and ordered her body to unlock from its fetal position. Her pulse stampeded as she flipped on a table lamp and slid off the sturdy rough hewn daybed that doubled as her sofa. Shaking with fatigue, she reached for the suitcase she'd half-filled before dozing off.

"If you don't finish packing and get your fanny out of Texas," she muttered, "your worst nightmare's going to walk right through your front door." A too brief reprieve, divorce, name change, and concerted efforts to wrest some measure of control over her life meant nothing now that Greg had somehow manipulated his release from jail. Dallas suddenly didn't feel quite far enough from San Francisco.

It took less than ten minutes to finish packing her little girl's belongings. Rachel was topping off a second suitcase with her own clothes when she heard someone moving in the half-empty five-car garage beneath her. She froze. The line between her nightmare world and the real one blurred. Blood thundered in her ears.

Why hadn't she left yesterday?

She cocked her head to listen for another sound that might reveal the intruder's exact location. She only needed forty-two seconds to run the length of the apartment, wake Amanda, and climb down the emergency ladder fixed outside the bedroom window. She'd timed it. Had she missed the squeak on the first two steps? Greg wasn't scheduled to be released for several more hours and it would take him time to locate her, but for all she knew, he could already be standing outside her flimsy door preparing to kick it in.

Squeak.

Thump.

Squeak.

Thump.

Her knees almost buckled when she identified the familiar sounds. Cane thumping the wooden risers in counterpoint to her footsteps, Katherine Kolthern, Rachel's landlady, boss, and friend began her slow climb up the interior stairs. Rachel leaned her forehead on the doorjamb and listened to the maddeningly independent woman make her way to the small landing on the other side of the door.

Rachel gritted her teeth against an impulse to rush out to help her. Finally, she unlocked the door with a smile. "I'm sorry, Katy." She invited her into the apartment with a small wave. "Did my lights wake you?"

"I don't sleep much. I looked out my bedroom window and saw you were already up and about." Her sharp gaze fell on Rachel's mussed bed, her open suitcase. Making a rude noise, she thunked her cane on the wood plank floor. "I have a good mind to march myself down to little Danny Johnson's office to tell him he has no call to upset you like this."

A genuine smile tugged at Rachel's lips at the thought of Katy waiting in her nightgown, robe and snakeskin boots on the D.A.'s doorstep when he arrived for work later that morning. With her long, gray hair floating in wild disarray around her shoulders the woman looked fierce. Or she would if one discounted her five-foot three-inch frame. It might be worth sticking around Dallas to see Katy shake a chastising finger at the six-foot-six descendent of a reputed gunslinger.

"Daniel did me a favor warning me about Greg's release," she said. "I'm grateful he kept in touch with his friend at the FBI." No one in San Francisco bothered to warn her the evidence in Greg's case—evidence *she'd* supplied the FBI—had disappeared, forcing them to withdraw their felony fraud and theft charges before they could go to trial next month.

With one look at the digital clock on the side table, Rachel's heart sank to the handwoven rag rug beneath her bare feet. She'd planned to be long gone by now. Arranging for Katy and the nurseries to be looked after once she'd gone had taken most of the last thirty-six hours. If she didn't leave soon, she might as well throw herself at her ex-husband's feet when he showed up and beg for mercy.

Not if she had anything to say about it!

"Confronting the Devil is hard, child," Katy said, "but I wish you wouldn't run away. You said it yourself. He won't expect to find you here."

Rachel was startled to have her own words thrown back at her. When she ran home to Dallas after Greg was hauled off to jail, she'd had to convince Katy to let her take care of her. The sixty-year-old woman was too fragile from her heart attack and she was the closest thing Rachel had to a mother since she was a child. She'd been without a parent altogether after her father walked out of her life ten years ago. Katy was family. She loved her.

She also owed her. It was Rachel's fault Greg got close enough to the older woman to decimate her livelihood, along with the others he'd conned across two states. The authorities had only found a small portion of the money he'd scammed, so her friend might yet be forced to sell off a chunk of her family's homestead. She'd lost so much already.

It broke Rachel's heart that she couldn't stay to fix everything. "I have to go, Katy. I'm sorry."

Katy thunked her cane on the floor again. "Has it occurred to you that maybe you're being paranoid and he's not coming at all?"

Her frustration palpable—they'd argued her decision to leave since the D.A.'s call—she reminded herself that Katy wasn't in San Francisco in those days before Greg's arrest. She hadn't seen the obsessive rage in his eyes when he'd beaten Rachel before trying to escape prosecution. Her friend was in an ICU ward fighting for her life after a heart attack provoked by Greg's con. Another charge to throw at his feet.

Rachel's laugh came out rusty. "He's coming. Take my word for it." Hurrying across the room to the battered sideboard that served as her dresser, she grabbed her mama's silver mirror, comb and brush set. She carefully rolled the precious items in a wad of white cotton panties in one corner of the suitcase.

Katy pushed the bag out of reach and perched on the side of the daybed. She patted the cleared space beside her. "Sit, child. I get that you're spooked. But you can't let it gnaw at your soul like snails on a lettuce patch. You're not alone any more. Let me help."

Too antsy to sit, she paced the long, narrow room instead. Twelve steps to the front door in the kitchenette. Twelve in the opposite direction to the hallway. "I'm supposed to take care of you, Katy, not the other way around."

"Bah! You've spent the past six months nursing me back to health. You've worked yourself to the bone from dawn to dusk to single-handedly save Kolthern Nurseries. Stop beating yourself up for what that no good, no account polecat did to me. We were both fooled, girl. None of this is your fault." She grabbed Rachel's hand as she passed, stopped her in her tracks. "Rachel, you're the daughter Henry and I could never have. Please let me do something. I'll never forgive myself if you and Amanda gets hurt again."

As she hugged the other woman, tears threatened to slide down Rachel's cheeks. She'd not heard such a declaration of love from anyone since she was ten years old and her mama died. Except from Amanda. But her daughter, tucked in the single bedroom down the hall, didn't tell Rachel she loved her anymore. She didn't speak at all. Not since the horrible night her daddy almost killed her mama.

Rachel walked to the open window where the cool breeze fluttered the muslin curtains she'd made late one night in a fit of sleeplessness. She craned to hear the Kolthern cattle lowing in the field a quarter of a mile away. Rain-washed essences drifted from the family herb garden situated by the back porch near the big house. She inhaled the aroma-rich air, redolent with blossoming honeysuckle and freshly turned garden soil, hoping to gather enough memories to give her strength to do what she knew was necessary.

She'd gotten a lot of practice leaving her life behind thanks to her nomadic father but this was different. This had become her home! "We were supposed to be set free the day Greg went to jail," she whispered.

Katy heard her. "He should rot for an eternity for what he did to the two of you, honey."

There was no arguing that point. Katy was the only one in Dallas who knew Greg as more than a consummate con artist. Her friend had seen the scars he'd whipped into Rachel's belly and back. That one fit of rage would haunt her forever. However, the last thing she wanted to think about was the brutal end of her sham marriage. Her daughter needed her mama to be strong.

With the trial, she'd hoped to remove Amanda from her father's sphere of influence before he could hurt her, too. They hadn't escaped soon enough. Amanda didn't carry her mother's physical scars. She'd buried her wounds inside a prison of silence. The physical pain Rachel carried out of her bedroom six months ago was nothing to the agonizing grief she'd experienced when she discovered her four-year-old daughter in the hall curled into a ball around her new baby doll.

Guilt tore at her conscience. Her poor daughter must have heard everything through those closed doors. She suspected Greg said something to the child before he left them alone in the house, too. Amanda wasn't saying. PTSD, Post Traumatic Stress Disorder, according to the specialist Rachel found upon their arrival in Dallas. The label didn't matter. Her little girl was hurting and she required more than a handful of sessions with the therapist to break through her trauma.

They'd run out of time.

She placed a protective hand over her stomach. The noose Greg held around Rachel's neck for so long had loosened these past months of freedom, but he still had the power to yank her back. All he had to do was get his hands on Amanda again.

"What I don't understand, Rachel," Katy said, dragging her away from her dark thoughts, "is why you're suddenly tearing up the roots you've planted here. You have friends who can help you stand up to Greg. Your great-aunt's estate will be finalized in a few months, no matter what your mother's family tries to do to break the will. You'll have all the money you need to surround yourself and Amanda with the best security money can buy. What aren't you telling me?"

The temptation to tell the truth was overwhelming. Her friend was amazingly adept at picking at a problem until it unraveled into an untidy little mess, and Rachel had revealed a lot to Katy since her return to Dallas. God help her, she didn't dare trust anyone with *this* secret. All she'd ever wanted was the little girl sleeping in the other room. She couldn't lose her!

"Rachel?"

She looked her friend straight in the eye and lied. "There's nothing to tell. I just can't take the chance Greg will come here."

"Let him come! You and Amanda can move back into the main house with me. I'll get half a dozen guard dogs. We've got an army of employees between the greenhouses and the nurseries to make sure you're never alone. I can—"

"Stop! Please, Katy...just stop." Sick at heart, Rachel went to the dresser for a few last items to tuck into her bag. "Don't you see? You and Amanda are the only family I have left. If I'm not here, maybe Greg will leave you alone.

"I'm not certain what he'll do, though, and that worries me. If you weren't going to your brother's dude ranch, I'd be dragging you with me.

I'll rest easier knowing you're safe in Abilene helping him get ready for his next batch of guests." She smoothed away another tear at the thought of leaving Katy. "As soon as I find somewhere safe to hole up, I'll call so you won't worry."

"Child, I'll always worry about the two of you. It's what family does, blood kin or not." Tears running freely down her weathered cheeks, Katy stared at her a long time before rising slowly to her feet. She reached into her robe pocket and pulled out several sheets of paper.

Rachel skimmed through the documents thrust into her hand and found two airline e-tickets made out for herself and Amanda, a car leasing agreement, and detailed driving directions that outlined a direct path from Denver International Airport to an address somewhere in the sprawling city. At the bottom of the stack was an envelope addressed to Mrs. Evelyn Thorne. "What is all this?"

"A place to hole up. Evelyn and I were in college together. She's one of my best friends. Even better, Greg knows nothing about her. I confirmed everything with her last night. She and her husband, Ross, are expecting you. They're heading out of the country for a few weeks, but you'll be safe at their place with their five strappin' boys protecting you until you can come home."

Rachel thought her heart might break when she saw the resignation shadow Katy's expression. Neither would say it, but they were both aware they might never see each other again. Not for the first time she thought of staying, of fighting for her life. For Amanda's. But it was too risky. She was too scared of losing everything that mattered to her. "Katy. I-I—"

"I love you, too." Katy smiled brightly through her tears and reached up to pat her cheek. "Okay, let's get you on that plane before I go with my impulse to lock you and Amanda in the potting shed so I can watch over you myself. I'm too danged eager to pull Henry's shotgun off the mantle rack and shoot me some polecat!"

"Rachel's never going to forgive me for manipulating her like this," Katy said several hours later, jockeying her cell phone between her ear and her shoulder. She pulled a pair of worn jeans from the suitcase the girl lovingly packed for her and jammed them back in the dresser drawer. "I hated lying to her about going to Abilene." Regret chewed on her conscience. "You'd think I'd be used to that. I've been lying to her one way or another since the day we met, haven't I?"

"It was necessary," the man on the other end of the phone line assured her. "That girl's just stubborn enough to jump in front of a charging bull if it means protecting someone she loves. She loves you. She'll forgive you anything."

Katy heard the pain lining his gravelly voice and knew the ache was as much emotional as physical. She wasn't so sure he was right. Rachel hadn't forgiven her own father in the past ten years. "Tell her why you left, Dixon," she said. "Just give her a chance and tell her the truth."

"It's too late. I made my bed." He coughed a snort of self-deprecating laughter into her ear. "Now, I'm sleeping in it."

"But don't you think—"

"Let it ride." A heavy sigh revealed his weariness. "I only called to make sure she's on her way to Denver."

She looked up at the ceiling and cursed the stubborn man. The acorn hadn't fallen very far from *that* tree! The only person more stubborn than Dixon and his daughter was Rachel's mama, Katy's best friend. Criminy, but she still missed her! "Rachel and Amanda will be tucked away at Evelyn's this afternoon." It would be a serious test of their friendship if Katy told him about her attempts to talk Rachel out of leaving Dallas. She hadn't succeeded, so it didn't matter.

"You're a good woman, Katy. I'm sorry, well, I'm sorry about a lot of things." A coughing fit took all of his air. When he spoke again, his voice was raspier. "You're sure you'll be okay if that ex-husband of hers shows up? If you won't let me hire someone to protect you, maybe you *should* go to your brother's for a couple of weeks. Just until we see which way this snake is going to break once he's set free."

Anticipation rose in Katy's breast. "Just let him step one foot on my property. Henry's shotgun hasn't had a real challenge since the last time you two went duck hunting." It had been only days after that hunting trip she'd lost Henry to a massive heart attack. Her loss was as fresh today as it had been fifteen years ago when this man helped her to lay her husband to rest.

"Be careful. You know what he's capable of."

She knew, all right. As did Dixon. Rachel would be devastated if she knew Katy had told her father everything Greg had done to her, hoping the revelation might make him reach out to his daughter at last. It hadn't. "When Rachel gets to Denver, call her. You have the numbers. Some secrets aren't good for anyone. You need her as much as she needs you. They *both* need you."

Silence met her suggestion. Then, it was broken. "It's not time yet," he said before the phone line went dead.

Denver, Colorado.

"Tell me again why I filed another police report if Denver's finest are going to sit on their collective asses and do nothing. Are you guys re-papering the men's room with my complaints in triplicate?" Patrick Thorne glared across his kitchen at Detective Jack Montgomery, irritated enough to push one of his foster brother's hot buttons.

"We ran out of toilet paper." Jack's green eyes flashed. He poured a cup of black coffee, then leaned back on the counter and studied him. "What do you want me to say? You filed the report five hours ago. You think we've got nothing better to do than send everyone out on a vandalism report?"

Patrick snorted. "Vandalism is spray paint and tagging. Vandalism is pouring sugar into gas tanks. Tearing through entire floors of sheet rock with a claw hammer like a possessed maniac is sabotage," he argued. "This isn't an isolated incident, and the attacks are getting vicious. I'm being specifically targeted."

"By whom?"

"If I knew that I'd take care of the bastard myself!" Gritting his teeth, he stalked out of the kitchen down the hall to his office at the back of the house.

Jack followed, setting his coffee down on Patrick's desk when he sat in front of him. "I may agree with the sentiment, Patrick," Jack said, "but start talking about taking the law into your own hands and we're done here. You can't go off half-cocked and threaten retribution in front of me. I'd have to toss your sorry ass in jail. Then, Mom would lop off my dick and, damn it, I'm getting married next month!"

The warning cut off Patrick's outburst as effectively as it had when they were both seventeen and bent on kicking the crap out of each other. Jack always won hands down despite the fact they'd stood eye-to-eye, even then at six-foot-two. In truth, the only person who'd ever cowed Jack was mom. Even their tough and burly street cop father toed the line rather than disappoint her.

It was one of the reasons she'd made such a great foster parent. Patrick might have been the only natural-born child of Ross and Evelyn Thorne, but he'd grown up with five brothers thanks to a slim bird of a woman who'd wielded an enormous influence on them all, an influence that hasn't abated in the years since her "boys" had grown into manhood. Patrick certainly hadn't wandered far from her homemade casseroles and old-fashioned homilies, not for long.

He glanced out the open office window at the six-bedroom Victorian next door where he'd lived until he'd enlisted in the army at eighteen. Days before he was scheduled to sign his Rangers re-enlistment papers, a parachuting accident forced him into permanent retirement. Giving in to his parents' repeated offers to float him his first loan to get Thorne Enterprises off the ground, he'd bought the neighboring house and converted most of the lower floor of the Victorian into office space for his construction business.

"Dad would understand my desire to catch this man," he said bitterly. "I refuse to stand by and do nothing."

"You are doing something. You're patiently filing reports and allowing the department to catch your vandal," Jack replied, more a warning than a reassurance.

"I've only filed three police reports, but I'm sure I can lay half a dozen more attacks at this bugger's door." He ran his hand through his hair to corral his frustration. "What about fingerprints on the hammer? Have you identified anything in the clothes left behind?" Somehow, the single untouched wall with women's clothing stapled all over it like some kind of macabre trophy wall was more disturbing than the vicious holes his saboteur left everywhere else.

"It's one of your own hammers kept in a tool box with a broken lock. Anyone could have handled it. I'll be surprised if they find a viable print, although the clothes might reveal something." Jack heaved a long suffering sigh. "We've barely had time to catalogue the evidence since you called us this morning. We're not exactly sitting on our thumbs, no matter what you think."

"What I *think* is it's becoming more and more difficult to keep my problems under wraps."

"You couldn't tell after reading that sweet, full-page feature the <u>Denver Post</u> ran on you yesterday." Jack picked up the newspaper section sitting on the corner of Patrick's desk and read the headline aloud. "'No Thorns in Thorne Enterprise's Rosy Future'. According to this you're," he scanned the article, "'a new contractor barely in his thirties with a Midas touch who's made it to the major leagues with the multi-million dollar, up-scale Villas at Three Oaks Ranch'." Jack grinned. "You must have really schmoozed that reporter, bro."

"The headline would have read something radically different," Patrick replied sourly, "if she'd dug a little deeper and uncovered the truth."

Angered again at the thought of what he stood to lose, he reached across the desk, snatched the newspaper out of Jack's hand, and threw it into a wire basket for his office manager, Jane Brown, to file. "You know what I've been dealing with these last few months," he said. "Vandals tag building sites. Supplies go missing. Equipment breaks down."

"But this is different, Jack. You saw those walls at Southgate. This isn't kids on a lark, pissing out territorial boundaries."

"I agree. But as my captain pointed out, I'm a little close to the situation and I'm not on the case."

Patrick barked a harsh laugh. "What does this guy have to do before the department takes this seriously? Leave a dead body?"

"It might take just that," Jack retorted. "We're up to our armpits in what's rolled downhill from the mayor's office after the kidnapping of that councilman's daughter last week."

If it weren't for the radios blasting all day on his sites Patrick wouldn't keep up with local events. Yet he'd heard about the coed who'd disappeared while he was in Cheyenne. "She's been gone, what, four days? Do you have any leads?"

"We don't even have a ransom note. After a coworker dropped her off at her apartment complex, it's like the girl disappeared into thin air."

Patrick saw Jack's jaw tighten, a sign of the increasing stress he'd been under in recent months. "You think she's a victim of the Angel Killer, don't you?" The local news media had dubbed the serial killer with the name because of the angel tattoo he'd burned into each of the girls he brutally killed. He remembered Jack's fury, as one of the detectives on the task force, over the leak of that critical piece of information.

"Unless her body shows up we can't be certain, but yeah, we think she may be the fourth." Jack grunted. "This guy has one hell of a cooling off period after each one. He's like a phantom. He disappears, only to pop back up several months later. His third victim was just last month. So if this girl does show up dead, his timetable's seriously escalating."

Jack paused and reached for his coffee cup. After drinking half of it in one swallow, he returned to their original conversation. "The point is, your vandalism isn't high up on our 'To Do' list."

Finding the missing girl was critical. It didn't, however, resolve Patrick's problem. "I'll stop wasting your time filing reports," he said.

Jack's eyes narrowed. "I *will* arrest you if I hear you're pursuing this on your own," he warned. "This is a criminal investigation. The last thing we need is a hotheaded civilian charging in and mucking things up."

"I won't—"

Holding up his hand, Jack cut him off. "I'll find whoever's doing this if I have to investigate myself. Just give me time."

"Time is one commodity we may not have." He railed at the uneasiness that had begun to gnaw on him. "The attacks have gotten worse the past few weeks. Something tells me they're leading up to something."

"Let's hope you're wrong."

Patrick knew he'd pushed Jack as hard as he dared, but he couldn't let it go. "We're heading into the height of our construction season. I'm juggling several luxury homes and remodel jobs, not to mention the Southgate and Mortenson condo sites. The dirt work starts on the first three villas next week.

"What am I supposed to do? Shut down my entire operation? I have more than fifty employees with families to feed." He waved a hand at the schedule posted on the wall above the wainscoting next to his desk. "I'm going to be screwed if I start losing subcontractors because they can't rearrange their schedules to accommodate these delays."

"Hire night security," Jack suggested, "at least until we find this guy."

"Already done." Acid churned in his gut at the thought of how much his saboteur was costing him. "Find him, Jack. Fast. There's a reason my business office is still here in my home. I'm stretched to the limit. None of my crews will have jobs if this goes on much longer."

Jack leaned forward in his chair. "Patrick, I get that you're frustrated. The best we can do is increase patrols around your sites for a while to see if that will help. There will be an extra patrol here, too."

"That's not necessary. Just protect the sites and my crews."

Jack didn't say anything. Reaching for his coffee cup, he emptied it before he set it back on the desk with a slight grimace, like the coffee had suddenly turned bitter. "I had an unofficial chat with the police shrink and showed him the pictures the forensics team took at the condo," he said. "He agrees with you. Whoever your vandal is, he's channeling some serious rage. The doc also believes this may be personal. He thinks buttoning down this guy's playground might make him take a more direct route to you."

"You think I'm under a personal threat?"

"For all intents and purposes, you are Thorne Enterprises. If you attack one, you attack the other. I'd feel better if you keep that in mind the next time you walk out the door."

The chill of mortality that crawled under Patrick's skin was ugly and familiar—one of the few things he remembered about those moments after wind shear caught his parachute and threw him into a tangle of trees, ending his Ranger career. "It's a good thing I have you to watch my back then, huh, big brother?" he said.

"Damn straight, runt." Jack was only four months older than Patrick but his descent into the familiar adolescent name-calling underscored his concern. "So don't go off half cocked like the Lone Ranger. Mom and Dad will be really ticked if you get yourself killed."

Patrick's Lone Ranger days ended when he buried his wife and child. "It's just as well Mom and Dad are gone until your wedding next month. We won't have to worry about them."

"Maybe not. But we have no idea how far this perp will reach into your life, so I need you to keep an eye on Mom's and Dad's houseguests while I work on the problem. Rachel James has had her own brand of trouble, and I promised Mom I'd check on her and her little girl periodically."

Had Mom asked *all* of his brothers—excluding Ben living in California—to look in on the willowy blond house-sitting their mother's flourishing greenhouse next door? For some reason, the thought of four single men traipsing up the flower-laden front path to the divorcee's door like a herd of rutting bull elk pissed him off.

Not that he had any interest in racing his brothers up that path toward sure destruction. "I have enough problems," he grumbled. "The last thing I want is to take on another of Mom's special projects. I don't rescue her broken wings anymore."

Jack looked askance at the term their brother, Cole, had given to the troubled women their mother sometimes counseled. "How do you know what Rachel's like? She's been here more than three days, and you haven't bothered to meet her."

"I've been kind of busy since I left your bachelor party on Thursday," he said in his defense. "I had to meet with the architects and bankers for the Villa project, remember? With the economy the way it is, they wanted my personal assurances the project is moving forward and on budget." If he didn't keep to the schedule they'd hammered out, Thorne Enterprises was finished. Everything was riding on this project. "Maybe you don't remember. You were pretty drunk when I left your place."

"I was not drunk. Much." Jack shrugged. "Anyway, you could have made an effort this morning."

"Holiday or not, I work. If I hadn't inspected the sites this morning, I wouldn't have discovered the condo destruction until tomorrow." He stared at his brother. "Why are you pushing this woman on me?"

"I'm not push—" Jack paused. Then his eyebrows rose. "For God's sake, Patrick, I just thought you should meet her before you start making assumptions about her. No one's asking you to marry this one!"

Air lodged in Patrick's lungs under the onslaught of harsh emotions that welled up with the breach of the forbidden subject. Pain. Torment. Anger. They cut through him with all the speed of a buzz saw.

"I'm sorry. I shouldn't have—" Jack stopped in mid-apology. "No. I'm not sorry! I don't care what everyone says. I'm tired of pussyfooting around Karly's memory and what she did. It wasn't your fault. She's dead. You're not. It's been almost two years, Patrick. *Two*. When are you going to stop punishing yourself?"

"This has nothing to do with Karly." Except his hands, clenched on the arms of his office chair, called him a liar.

"Tell that to someone who didn't spend four days putting you back together last year." Jack studied him a moment too long. "Should I arrange a short vacation soon? The anniversary of her death is coming up again in, what, a few weeks?"

Three weeks, five days, and six hours, give or take a few numb minutes. But who was counting?

"Save your heroic impulses for your fiancée, Jack." Patrick forced his hands to relax against the arms of the chair. Jack had dragged him from the black hole he'd crawled into last year without a word about it after it was done. He'd earned the right to probe the one topic Patrick refused to discuss with the rest of his family. That didn't mean he intended to talk about it now. "I won't be drowning my sorrows this year," he said with studied calm.

This year, he was avoiding the family homestead in the mountains where Karly was buried. With the rigid construction schedule he'd laid out, he had no time to battle his personal demons. He'd come to terms with the circumstances of Karly's death, and his part in it, set that part of his life in concrete where it would remain undisturbed. "I plan to be chin deep in Spanish tile and mural painters for the rest of the summer."

"Well, I'll be! Sam was right. Joe was positive—"

His eyes narrowed at the mention of two of his other foster brothers. "Sounds like I missed a family meeting while I was in Cheyenne. Was I the only topic under consideration or did you take turns psychoanalyzing each other?"

"Just you." A familiar, crooked grin spread over Jack's face. "Our time was limited, and we do try to do a thorough job."

"And your conclusions?"

Jack opened his mouth, but Patrick stopped him. "No, don't bother. Let me guess."

He considered his family members. "Cole's prepared to take me on one of his bachelor excursions so he can drown me in wine, women and song. Sam thinks I should do what he does, bury all the emotional baggage under a clinical façade and hours of work. Joe, the only one of you with psychological training, believes I should wallow in my misery until I come out the other side of the pit whole and happy. And you, Mom and Dad agree I should get married again and lose the rest of my sanity in the arms of another woman."

With a long whistle, Jack confirmed his evaluation. "You must have been that fly on the wall Mom shooed outside, although you're wrong about a couple of things. Cole wasn't there. He's kayaking somewhere in South America again. Ben called from San Francisco, though, and said pretty much what Cole would have said. I didn't say you should get married either. I just said you should get laid." He looked down briefly before he spoke again, all traces of humor erased from his expression. "Patrick, we're family. We're...concerned.

As much as he loved his brothers, when they ganged up on him like this he sometimes wished he'd remained an only child. Patrick could see his mother's nudging hand behind them. She probably wrote down a list of instructions for everyone before she left the country as she'd done for him. *Trash cans on curb for Monday pickup.* Speak to your stubborn brother, Patrick, on Tuesday. *Help Rachel deliver seven flower baskets to Sunset Pines on Saturday.*

At the thought of whom he was supposed to help with his mother's flower deliveries, he stiffened in his chair. "Tell me you didn't dissect my sex life in front of that woman!"

"That woman has a name, Patrick. Rachel and her daughter ate breakfast with us before going to mass." Jack snorted. "And don't get your shorts in a wad. You know how Mom is about manners, especially on Sunday. We didn't talk about your limp dick until they'd left."

"I don't have—" He stopped, making a mental note not to miss any more of his family's Sunday morning breakfast powwows. "There's no reason to march me off to the psychiatric ward, on vacation, or into some strange woman's arms. I've got a business to run. I don't have time for anything else."

"Fine, I'll leave you alone." Jack stood and walked toward the office doorway before turning back to face him with a crooked smile. "But I still think you should get laid."

Despite his irritation, Patrick smiled. "So speaks the man who's getting married next month. If there were more women out there like Maggie, I'd consider it." If Karly had been half as strong-minded as Jack's fiancée, he'd not only still have a wife but a toddling son playing at his feet.

Don't go there or someone will *have to clean you off the floor again this year.* Patrick never wanted his family to learn all that was lost when Karly jumped in front of that bus. It was bad enough he knew how miserably he'd failed her and their unborn son.

"They broke the mold when they made my Maggie," Jack said, effectively sidetracked from Patrick's inner turmoil. "I just wish we'd run off to Vegas like I wanted. Between the hormones from her pregnancy, her old man's reservations and her mother's expectations, this high society wedding is giving me an ulcer. I'm surprised Mom didn't go nuts sooner about being left out of all of the arrangements. I'm glad Dad dragged her off to the islands. One less thing to worry about."

"They should have stayed and taken care of their house guests," Patrick said. There was no hiding his irritation with the situation he'd found upon his return from Cheyenne. "Why can't one of the others do it? I don't have time to babysit."

"We're all checking on Rachel when we can, so you'll just have to make time in that busy schedule of yours. You're right next door. Her daughter, Amanda, is already running in and out of your office all day with Suze so Jane can keep an eye on both of them." Jack pinned him under a baleful eye. "Stop being a pain in the ass. I can't be here 'round the clock, and you promised Mom."

Patrick shifted in his seat. "I remember what I promised." The trick was to figure out how to keep that promise without spending every spare moment hanging out his office window with his tongue brushing the ground while he waited for a glimpse of the ethereal blond, as he'd done since he spotted her last night.

On his return from Cheyenne around midnight, he'd walked out his back door to dump the garbage. He would have missed her sitting on the lounge in the shadows of his parents' side porch if she hadn't sighed, something low and wistful, sounding so lost. There was enough moonlight to capture the curve of her face, a riot of short honey blond curls, and the lean lines of long legs and thighs barely covered by a pair of cutoffs, stretched out to rest on the wicker ottoman.

The moment she spotted him, he knew. She stilled. Gasped. He'd felt the heat of her gaze on him. For an eternity, he kept still, afraid to scare her off. Then she slipped off the lounge and disappeared inside the house. He was left with a raging hard-on and the wild thought he'd imagined the woman, that he'd inadvertently caught sight of one of the magical fairy queens his office manager's granddaughter insisted lived in his mother's gardens.

A brief glimpse this morning through his mother's kitchen window revealed Rachel James was real, and there was no question he'd keep an eye on her. Not because he'd made any rash promises to do so, but because he couldn't seem to *not* watch the blasted woman. He just planned to do it from his side of the property line that separated his parents' home from his own.

He could handle lust...from afar. If that made him a craven coward, so be it. The last thing he wanted was another needy woman in his life. He didn't do relationships, didn't dare step over that line again.

Whatever Rachel James' problems might be, he'd only make them worse. He'd learned a hard lesson trying to help Karly. Broken women can't be fixed, not by him at least. He didn't rescue damsels in distress anymore. There was nothing—no one—who could induce him to stick his neck out again. Two deaths on his conscience were enough.

Hills near Sausalito, California.

Greg Bishop made no attempt to cover the sound of his footsteps once he broke into the Pointeview Clinic for Reproductive Sciences. The muted gray carpet was plush and no one but his quarry remained in the rambling single-story building at this hour. He'd watched to make certain.

Why Simon Vanhouten was working late on Memorial Day despite his successful fertility practice Greg would never know. However, in this case, the doctor's propensity for burning the midnight oil worked in his favor. Interruptions weren't acceptable. Greg had important business with the good doctor, and he didn't have any more time to waste.

He faltered in the middle of the trendy waiting room decorated with bold colors and modern furniture, rage searing a hole in his gut. Two days he'd wasted attempting to access the money and IDs he'd ferreted away for emergencies. Two fucking days! What did he find? Two of his three safe deposit boxes had somehow been accessed and closed leaving him nothing. Chasing down suppliers for replacement IDs swallowed another day. He'd spent most of today sweltering in his car, then in the bushes like an animal, where no one could see him as both clinic parking lots emptied.

All the while, his real prey had scurried away.

Like all of his plans, though—with the exception of the one *she* would soon pay for—this one was coming together. If there was one thing he'd learned over the years, it was to take his time and wait for the right moment.

Forcing himself to concentrate on a stylized bronze sculpture of a mother with her newborn infant that stood in one corner he blew off his residual tension and anger. Only when he was once again centered solely on his immediate purpose did he resume his path through the building.

He followed a wedge of fluorescent light that spread down the wide corridor from the suite of support offices in the front of the clinic toward the examination rooms at the back. The next time he paused, he stood in the open doorway of one of the two large operating rooms where hundreds of women received the benefit of Vanhouten's expertise over the years. As Greg's wife had benefited.

It was his turn to reap the rewards of the biggest con of his life. But, first things first.

His quarry within his sights, he watched the lean, balding man with his back to the door manhandle a large oxygen tank along the far wall where several other tanks were housed. It escaped his grasp, falling to the floor on its side with a reverberating clang.

When the man bent down to examine the crack he'd made in the floor tile and uttered an ineffectual curse, Greg smirked. "With the obscene amount of money you charge seeding the upper echelon, Simon," he drawled, "you should consider hiring someone to do your grunt work."

Vanhouten straightened, whirled around on one loafer-shod heel, and gaped. "Bishop! When did they, how did you...?"

He enjoyed the flash of alarm he saw in Simon's blue-gray eyes. No matter how long it had been since their last meeting, fear kept the man under Greg's thumb where he could be squeezed. Hard. "I was released from jail Friday, thanks for asking," he said conversationally. "As for how I got in here? Breaking into this ornamental boutique for the childless was a piece of cake thanks to Tank, the bad-ass burglar and murderer in the cell next to mine."

Although Greg smiled at the sick expression on the doctor's patrician face, deep inside he felt the same horror at what he'd been forced to endure these past six months. "Something else my loving wife will pay for," he murmured.

Mentioning his wife had a visible effect on Simon. "Felicia's not here. In the Bay area, I mean. I-I haven't seen or heard from her since the day you—"

His lips thinned before he finished in a rush, "Since the day I treated her for what you'd done to her. Even if I knew where she went, I wouldn't tell you."

Greg now knew who'd helped his wife to flee California, to escape him. He'd suspected Simon's complicity from the beginning. The holier-than-thou prick had taken it upon himself years ago to step in as her knight in shining armor. Her protector against him, her own husband. Greg resented it. It reminded him she and Vanhouten were of a kind, blue-bloods through and through. While he, born in a Los Angeles tenement he'd barely escaped at the age of twelve, wasn't good enough to spit shine their shoes.

It gave him immense pleasure to have them both shaking in those fancy-ass shoes. "I know exactly where my wife is," he said his voice calm.

"She's taken her mother's family name back. So it looks like I'm one up on you...as always. That's not why I'm here."

Greg saw trepidation return to Simon's expression, though he tried to disguise it as disinterest. He turned his back on Greg, struggled to lift the fallen tank upright, and began to examine the connections and fittings. After several long moments, Simon looked over his shoulder. "So why are you here?"

Entering the room, Greg wandered aimlessly, relaxed. He was in his element now. This was a game he'd mastered. "I need money for a project." He stopped to peer into a boxy machine that looked like a microwave but probably cost several hundred thousand dollars. Money he would have put to better use.

"Don't touch that!" Simon rushed toward him but stopped abruptly four feet away.

Pleased the man was more worried about getting too close to him than the possible loss of his equipment Greg picked up a large bottle of ethyl alcohol from a corner shelf and scanned the flammable warning label. Looking up, he repeated his demand. "I want money."

"I'm not a freaking bank, Bishop!" He shook his head. "I won't fund any more of your cons. Return to a life of crime on your own dime."

"Ah! I see the gloves are off." Hefting the alcohol bottle absently in one hand, he set it on the counter and studied Simon like he was an odd new specimen that defied logic. The man had grown a set of balls since he last saw him. An interesting development. Not that it made a bit of difference. "Who said this is for a con?"

It didn't take long for enlightenment to hit. "I won't give you money to go chasing after Felicia either. Leave her alone. Haven't you done enough damage?"

"I'll say when it's enough!" Rage rose like a tsunami inside him again. Huge. Uncontrolled. He picked up a metal tray and threw it at a nearby wall so hard it dug a chunk out of the plaster before it fell to the floor, scuttled partway under a piece of equipment, and lay still.

"For God's sake, Bishop!"

The shock on Simon's face was just what Greg needed to calm down. *Get the money. Stick to the plan.*

He eyed the large bottle of alcohol on the counter with renewed interest. One of the first things he'd learned growing up was that intimidation went a long way when opponents were unevenly matched. Simon Forrester Vanhouten the Third had never faced anything more traumatic than arriving unfashionably late to one of his wife's political dinners. He had no idea what a man was capable of when it came to survival.

Picking up the bottle, Greg broke the seal. He tossed the cap onto the empty counter beside him and poured a ragged line of colorless liquid the length of it. The room immediately filled with an astringent smell strong enough to make his eyes water.

"What's wrong with you?" Simon lunged at him.

Greg shoved him away. He splashed alcohol over a five-foot area of corner shelving stacked with linens, hospital gowns, and miscellaneous supplies that bisected two peach-colored walls. Then he tossed the open bottle on the floor where the liquid spread in a widening arc in the direction of a wall of storage cupboards.

Incensed, Simon came at him again. "If that alcohol gets into any of my equipment——"

He grabbed the doctor's Armani polo shirt in his fist, and dragged the man close enough to smell the cinnamon candies Simon favored. "You're not getting the message, Simon," he growled in the man's face. "I don't give a rat's ass about your opinions, your objections, or your equipment."

The doctor scraped ineffectually at Greg's grip. "You will if you spark a fire and blow us to kingdom come, you idiot! There's enough O2 and nitrous oxide in the tanks behind us to level this building."

"Then give me what I want!" Blinking furiously against the noxious fumes, he yanked Simon out of the examination room down the hallway to the brightly-lit room two doors down. "Let's not pretend you have a choice here." He thrust the man into his office. "You will give me every last dime tucked away in that safe behind your desk."

"Or what? We won't be friends anymore?" Simon snorted with derision, straightened his shirt with a tug, and quickly put the desk between them. "In case it's escaped your notice, Bishop," he continued harshly, "we were never friends. The only reason you were allowed in our inner circle at college was because——"

"I kept quiet!" The knowledge he'd never fit in with Vanhouten's disgustingly rich fraternity friends never ceased to enrage Greg. Even after he'd acquired a wife descended from their rarified gene pool, they'd treated him like a reject from the projects.

"Blackmailers aren't friends. They're parasites on society, leeches, and never welcome in any circle."

"You're breaking my heart." He sneered. "Call me all the names you want. It doesn't change the fact I've had nothing to do in jail the past six months, but twiddle my dick and follow a particular congresswoman's illustrious career. Laura's become quite the people's darlin', hasn't she? Being so strident on the abortion issue and all."

That barb dug deep and hit a raw nerve. Simon blanched. "Leave my wife out of this."

"Laura's up for re-election in November, isn't she?" Greg smiled. "It would be a shame if your dirty little secret came out. Her adoring public might forgive her if she cheats on you. But cheat on *them*? Once they hear she had an abortion in college, an abortion performed by a medical student without a license to practice, her congressional career will die a fiery death." He had the man by the short hairs, and they both knew it. "Of course, those juicy headlines won't do your baby-making career much good either."

"You're a bastard."

He laughed. "Since my mother was a cheap whore who'd fuck anyone for a line of coke, I am. But I intend to be a rich one." He took a step forward, forcing Simon to step back, even though a desk stood between them. "Just give me the money. I'll go collect my wife and the kid, and leave you and yours alone."

Simon didn't do anything for several moments. Then, without comment, he turned to the original Cézanne hung behind his desk. He took down the painting from the wall and opened the safe Greg knew from experience was hidden there, filled with money for those times the doctor's bleeding heart was tapped and he funded some stupid girl through an unplanned pregnancy.

The moron didn't keep track of the money he gave away for tax purposes. It was free for the taking. Greg figured he was as entitled to that money as some slut who couldn't keep her legs together. At least he wouldn't piss it down the drain on some worthless brat created in the back seat of a car alongside an empty six-pack of beer.

After pulling straps of $100s from the safe, Simon faced him. "I'll make a deal with you." He had the gall to flick a thumb through one stack of bundled cash.

It took everything he had to keep from punching the man's superior expression off his face. "You're in no position to make deals tonight, Simon."

"That's where you're wrong. I have twenty thousand here." He reached into the pocket of his Levi's, drew out a set of car keys and threw them in the middle of the desk. "Those are the keys to my new Lincoln Mark LT four-by-four pickup parked in the back lot. It's fully loaded, worth over sixty thousand. I'll sign over the title and write you a check for another fifty thousand if you'll walk out of here and never come back. And, I mean never." He held up his hand before Greg could respond. "You also have to leave Felicia and Amanda alone."

There was no way Greg would agree to his terms, but the memory of his empty safe deposit boxes waved a bright red flag in his mind. He had to have an immediate infusion of cash. "Write the check for half a mil."

"Are you insane? I'm not a——"

"'Freakin' bank', I know." He shrugged. "That's the deal." For that kind of money he'd delay his departure until morning and hang around the Bay area until the banks opened so he could cash the check. The doctor was good for it. He knew better than to stiff Greg with a stop payment.

As expected, Simon caved. "Whatever it takes!" He pulled his checkbook from the desk drawer, wrote the check, and set it on top of the cash and keys. Then he reached back into the safe, pulled out a vehicle title, signed it and tossed it in the middle of the pile on the desk. He silently watched Greg pocket everything. Keys and truck title wadded in his left front pants pocket. The check and straps of cash distributed between his right front and back pockets.

The desk surface was empty again before Simon spoke. "Now, get out of my clinic and out of my life once and for all, Bishop. And if I ever hear of you getting near Felicia and Amanda again, I'll——"

"What? Go to the police?" Greg laughed, no longer willing to humor the idiot. "I don't think so. You can't afford to reveal your secrets."

"There are records."

The power in the room shifted with those three simple words. Greg felt it deep in his gut. "What are you talking about?"

"What we did, what you blackmailed me into doing," Simon paused, shrugged. "I'm a doctor. I have to keep medications, procedures straight. I wrote it all down. If you break our deal, if you come back here again or go after Felicia or Amanda, I'll hand those records over to Felicia. Then your little house of cards will come tumbling down."

Anxiety and desperation uncoiled in Greg's chest. The first time he'd experienced the ugly emotions was when he was a skinny five-year-old squeezed behind his mother's dresser hiding from one of her more violent Johns. Exposure could kill him now, as easily as it would have then. His entire future was built on his haughty wife's shoulders. "If you had records, you'd have used them before."

"I'm using them now. I won't allow you to hurt Felicia and Amanda ever again." Something flickered in his eyes. "How does it feel to be on the receiving end, Bishop?"

Greg stared at him, trying to gauge whether Simon had grown a conscience or was simply blowing smoke up his ass. "You're bluffing."

Simon actually looked down his patronizing nose at him. "I may not want to expose my wife to your blackmail. That doesn't mean I won't reveal you to yours. Once Felicia hears the truth, your power is gone. You'll lose all that glorious money that means so much——"

Before he could finish his taunt, Greg reacted. Scrambling over the desk, he grabbed Simon's head in both hands and smashed it against the open safe door. Over and over, unable to stop, he beat the doctor's head bloody on the metal surface until, his blind rage subsiding, he let the man fall to the floor.

Staring down at the body bleeding out into the muted gray carpet, Greg sucked air into his lungs. Huge noisy gulps that sounded suspiciously like sobs.

Was he dead?

Jesus!

Served the prick right.

Christ! He shuddered at the sight of gore on his hands and clothes. The metallic scent of blood mixed with the smell of his own sweat and the rubbing alcohol he'd spilled on his hands. His stomach heaved.

Focus.

Think.

Plan.

His insides grew ice cold as the lifelong mantra settled him. His brain kicked into overdrive as he sifted through everything he'd ever learned. He never knew what he could use in a future con so he'd spent his life soaking up information like a spong——

He knew just what to do.

Stepping over the body, he walked into the attached full-sized bathroom Simon used when he occasionally ran late for one of his wife's political functions. After showering Simon's blood off, Greg changed into the clothes he found hanging in a closet, switching the contents of his pockets. Then he left the building to turn off the water to the fire sprinklers.

Back inside, he located the Records room, kicked the locked door open, and tore files at random into several piles to which he added hospital gowns soaked in flammable chemicals he found in a storage closet. He opened up all of the oxygen and nitrous oxide tanks in the two operating rooms before wending his way through the building, splashing chemical cleaners and any other flammable liquids he could find, from Simon's office to Records and back again to his starting point at the operating rooms.

Minutes later he knelt near Simon's office doorway across the hall, cigarette lighter in hand, when he heard the doctor moan. He listened for a heartbeat. Two. There wasn't another sound. "Simon says," he murmured, touching the slim blue flame to the chemically soaked carpet, "absolutely nothing."

With a distinctive whoosh, a flickering line skated over the tips of the saturated carpet fibers down the hall in two directions. Wallpaper caught fire and curled. As Greg watched, a large spray of woody stalks and silk flowers went up in a flash of snapping blues and greens, reds and yellows. The self-renewing fuel gave birth to another line of flames that crawled along the ceiling tiles overhead. Within minutes, he could hear a growing roar in the examination rooms, popping sounds as glass and electrical components exploded. Smoke billowed from the Records room.

Time to go!

In the increasing pall of noxious smoke, he doubled over and worked his way toward the far back corner of the building. Coughing, his lungs burned as he pushed his way through an emergency exit. He ignored the blare of the door alarm. There was no ignoring the powerful force that suddenly rushed up behind him, scooped him off his feet and slammed him into the grass twenty feet behind the building.

Stunned, he gasped for air and stared up at a ball of fire dissipating into the night sky, followed by a ringing silence that seemed to last for an eternity. Scrambling for safety he topped the berm separating the clinic from the employee parking lot thirty feet away. He dug keys out of his pocket as he ran toward the lone truck parked in the doctor's reserved parking space.

In seconds, the truck was unlocked and he sat inside patting himself down. Still in one piece despite how close he'd cut his escape, he looked through the windshield at the broken silhouette of the fertility clinic. He coughed smoke from his lungs, watching what was left of the building burn fiercely across the moonlit California sky.

Vanhouten was right. There had been enough oxygen and nitrous oxide in those tanks to level the building. There was no way anything could survive that! The doctor and his records were history. Greg's secrets were safe forever now.

Reaching into his right pocket, he pulled out the wadded title to his new truck and threw it into the glove box. Then he emptied his pockets of cash, skimming the stacks of Ben Franklins before he tossed them on top of the title. Good. All here. It would have been a shame if any of it had fallen from his pocket and been blown to smithereens along with the doctor. It wasn't like Vanhouten could use it anymore, and the tracker Greg had sitting on Felicia—or Rachel as she was called—didn't come cheap.

He stared at the half-million-dollar check with disgust. He didn't dare stick around long enough to cash it. This was one cavernous, money well he hadn't completely tapped. It was gone. Up in smoke and flames. With a decisive movement, he shredded the check and scattered the pieces out the truck window in the brisk coastal breeze.

The debt to be laid at Felicia's feet had grown substantially in the last hour. "I think it's time," he muttered, leaving the truck's headlights off when he spotted a police cruiser squeal around the corner of the intersection down the hill, "to settle that debt with my darlin' wife." There was no one standing between him and his wife's millions now.

Denver, Colorado.

At the first crack of gunfire, Rachel dove headfirst into the garden she was weeding. Listening for the second report she expected to follow, she prayed Amanda stayed at Patrick Thorne's house where she'd gone an hour ago to play with her new friend, Suze.

Gasping for air, she inhaled the rich, spicy scent of freshly turned soil and crushed nasturtiums instead. Dirt and grit bit into her cheek and the bare flesh exposed by her cutoffs and T-shirt. The mid-afternoon sun beat hot on her shoulders and legs, and all she could do was lie there and watch a fat bumblebee dip into a russet blossom three inches from her nose.

Had she run almost nine hundred miles only to die like this, grubbing alone in the dirt like a spineless worm?

A surge of anger gave her the impetus to lift her head. She peeked over the flimsy wall of twelve-inch annuals between her and the street. A second gunshot rang out, belched in a cloud of black smoke from an ancient Volkswagen bus that disappeared around the corner.

Backfire?

She groaned, more relieved than embarrassed by her overreaction. Her chin dropped. Taking several deep draughts of the thin Colorado air, she worked to calm the pounding of her heart inside her ribcage. Her efforts made her head swim. A minute later she was able to push herself out of the three-foot section of the garden she'd mown down.

Her nerves had been on edge since she fled Dallas on Friday, five days ago. If she weren't so overwrought it would have occurred to her Greg would never stand at a distance and take potshots at her. No. Greg liked to look into her eyes when he meted out his punishments.

An icy shiver skimmed her skin. Each day that passed without his appearance should have reassured her she'd made the right decision to accept Katy's arrangements with the Thornes. As long as Greg didn't track her and Amanda to Denver, they were safe.

Problem is she hadn't felt safe since Amanda was born and she discovered what kind of man she'd married. She couldn't pluck enough weeds from Evelyn Thorne's gardens by day to tear the anxiety from her heart at night. Her growing sense of trepidation kept her awake long after the morning stars dimmed above the mile-high city's cloudless skies.

How could the justice system simply hand Greg a "get out of jail free" card? She'd always suspected the man had connections in high places, but how had he arranged for the evidence in his case—evidence she'd risked everything to provide—to disappear before he went to trial? If he'd accomplished that feat while behind bars, how in the world was she and Amanda going to stay out of his clutches?

She felt like there was a giant bull's-eyes painted on their backs, that it was only a matter of time before Greg tracked them down. During their marriage the man would spend weeks, months, laying meticulous groundwork for one of his cons. He'd had six months to plan dozens of new punishments for his betrayer.

"'Til death us do part, darlin'."

His words echoed over the expanse of time and distance, ringing a fresh peal of dread in Rachel's breast. With one hand, she swept clumps of soil off her tangerine T-shirt and whispered a small prayer. *Please don't let him find us!*

She tossed her worry as well as a forgotten fistful of dandelions clutched in her hand into the metal bucket at her side. She flicked cotton dandelion seeds from her fingertips and rubbed at an ache in her lower back.

Examining the flowerbed she'd weeded before lunch, she sighed with satisfaction. She'd made it her mission today to eradicate every weed in the nasturtium bed that ran the length of the house. As missions went, it wasn't much. But it was something she could control, and the very least she could do for the woman who'd given her another hole to crawl into, saving her from running one more mile.

There weren't many people who'd hand over their home and greenhouse to a total stranger for a month. Evelyn Thorne was either a saint or naive as sin. Exactly the kind of mark Greg specialized in conning out of their life savings.

Her insides twisted at the thought of how many innocents had suffered at Greg's hands. But it was the last innocent, the little girl who'd built an impenetrable wall around her world that tormented Rachel most.

Amanda hadn't said a word when her mother pulled her out of bed on Friday and drove her away from the sparse home they'd built with Katy. Just as she hadn't spoken that awful night when Rachel's doctor friend, Simon, hustled them out of their house to his clinic where he tended Rachel's broken body. In pain, sedated, she hadn't registered that her daughter had gone completely mute until the next morning when she woke up in the hotel room where Simon had stashed them. The child just stood there at the side of the bed, her doe-like brown eyes fixed on her mama, clutching the doll her father gave her a week earlier to replace her puppy savaged by a rogue coyote.

Simon hadn't missed the signs though and, when he gave Rachel money to escape San Francisco, he'd given her enough to take Amanda to a doctor when they got settled. Now that they were on the run again, Rachel despaired of helping her little girl back to normalcy.

Suddenly appearing from nowhere, the precocious child from next door who'd been first to welcome the new arrivals hunkered down beside Rachel. She pointed at the garden. "What happened to them flowers?" Suze Brown asked in a voice designed to wake the dead.

Rachel's pulse jumped back into the stratosphere. She managed to smile at the five-year-old and then at Amanda, who squatted down in imitation of her newfound friend, her doll tucked under one arm. "I had a little accident," Rachel said without explaining her ignoble dive into the dirt.

"Looks like Mr. Donovan's big slobber dog rolled all over 'em." Suze squinted at a bent stem. "Miss Evie's gonna be sad you broke them pretty flowers."

"They're not all broken," she reassured her. "See those little ones? They're baby nasturtiums. I'll move them, and they'll grow bigger and fill in the space."

"That's a funny name. Nasty-shamus."

Amanda giggled.

Rachel was more startled by that natural burst of sound than the back-fire made by the Volkswagen minutes earlier. Hope filled her heart as she searched her daughter's face. "Can you say nasturtium, too, Amanda?"

She used to say so much more, her vocabulary even at three far beyond her years. Yet she said nothing, hugging her doll like it was an impenetrable shield she'd placed between herself and her mother.

Rachel's hopes died. It was only then she noticed the doll her daughter clutched in a death grip was not the one her father gave her. "Honey, where's your baby?"

"She's taking a nap in my playroom." Suze pointed next door at the dormer window attached to the second story bedroom where the children liked to play. "We traded."

"Suze, you have to give it back. Amanda doesn't like anyone else to play with Becca." An understatement. She'd cried painfully soundless tears the one time Rachel took the toy away, ostensibly to wash the dirty clothes, but hoping to throw away the constant reminder of the child's father. Amanda was so upset Rachel gave it back to her to avoid causing her further trauma.

"Is that the baby's name? It's pretty," Suze said. "My baby's name is Susan, like me, but I wish it was Becca."

"I understand you like Becca but you can't keep her."

"But we shared!" The little girl rounded on Amanda. "We're blood sisters!"

With only a small hesitation, Amanda nodded her support of Suze's claim. She hugged the new doll fiercely in a display her mother couldn't misunderstand.

Rachel wished she knew how to proceed. How had a five-year-old, in less than three days, broken through the barriers she and a trained psychologist hadn't breached in six months? "As long as you are both okay with this, I guess you can trade for a while. But what's this about being blood sisters?"

"There was this cowboy and Indian. Ya know...on T.V." Suze shrugged a shoulder. "They traded and cut their hands with this big ol' knife. They shared secrets and stuff and was blood brothers. Kinda like that."

Rachel frantically searched the parts of their sun-kissed bodies not covered by shorts and T-shirts. "Where did you cut yourselves?"

"Ew!" Suze screwed up her face. "That part was yucky! We make-believed."

Vowing to monitor their friendship more carefully in the future, Rachel examined Amanda's expression for clues to her feelings. "So now you're sisters and keep each other's secrets. What if you want to trade back?"

Suze answered for Amanda. "We can't be sisters, if I'm mean and don't give it back. It's tem-tem—"

"Temporary?"

"Yeah." She stood abruptly. "Grandma has cookies and milk so's we can play tea party. Ya want some?"

"Grandma" was Suze's grandmother, Jane Brown. The older woman worked next door as office manager for Evelyn Thorne's son and had accompanied her granddaughter over that first day to make sure it was all right for the little girls to play together.

Thankfully, the big boss hadn't tagged along. Try as she might, Rachel couldn't get over her one unnerving glimpse of Patrick Thorne. His mother had pointed out the eighteen-year-old wearing an army uniform in a family photo when she'd shown her around the house, telling Rachel she could count on him for anything while they were in the Virgin Islands. She'd promptly forgotten the young man with the goofy grin, holding rabbit ears over one of his brother's heads...until he'd walked out of his back door Sunday night to toss a couple of bags in the trash.

She wasn't prepared for the man in the flesh. He was at least ten years older than she'd expected, a virile man in his prime that drew a woman's gaze and made her forget the necessity to breathe. With one look, her heart hammered too hard for comfort. She'd felt an overwhelming urge to sneak off the side porch where she'd gone to calm her restless thoughts, and lock all the doors behind her. She avoided most men these days. If they exuded a blatant masculinity that made her pulse skitter, she ran in the opposite direction quicker than a wind devil on a Texas prairie.

Rachel would have bolted, too, if she'd thought she could do it without alerting him to her presence in the protective shadows. Left with nothing to do but watch the shirtless man walk through the moon-washed night, she'd allowed herself the pleasure. His naked chest and back, broad and muscular above the waistband of his jeans, gleamed in the moonlight. Iron tight abs and powerful legs carried him across the backyard with an almost feral grace. His biceps barely straining under the weight of two thirty-gallon trash bags, there was no question the man's occupation had made him fit. Raw power in motion.

"You want some?"

Startled, Rachel stared at Suze. "Some what?"

The child rolled her eyes and sighed with exaggerated patience. "Cookies."

"Um, no, thank you." She turned to Suze. "Won't you be in your grandmother's way when she's working?"

"Naw. We have tea parties when Grandma's s'posed to rest."

"When she takes a break?"

"Yeah." Suze fidgeted. "Mr. Patrick said he might eat a cookie, too, but we gots to ask him."

"You *have* to ask him," Rachel corrected. It was a struggle to visualize the man perched on a tiny seat at a child's tea table wearing his construction helmet, pinkie raised, a fragile porcelain teacup balanced in his hand.

No. The muscular contractor oozed testosterone. She'd recognized it two nights ago from yards away, still felt it right down to her bare tingling toes. Patrick Thorne would be more at home in the overtly masculine surroundings of his building sites, or in a darkened bedroom, naked, tangled in damp sheets with a woman writhing beneath him. Her skin heated when she realized the woman she'd visualized beneath him looked too much like her.

"He'll prob'ly say yes if he's done 'spections." Suze sighed again. "Can we go now?"

Shaking off the impossible image of Patrick Thorne in her bed—sex in real life was not as pleasurable or satisfying as fantasy—Rachel jammed her rebellious hormones in a mental hole where they belonged. "Okay, but only for a small tea party." She turned to Amanda. "Honey, come back after that because we have to go grocery shop—"

If she hadn't looked straight at her daughter at that moment she might have missed the abrupt change in her demeanor. Her eyes widening, Amanda stared at something over her mother's shoulder. Her smile faltered. Disappeared.

The fine hairs on the back of Rachel's neck tickled a warning, alerted her to imminent danger. Once she inhaled, she didn't have to look over her shoulder to know who stood behind her. She'd always be able to identify that particular brand of designer men's cologne. It still nauseated her.

Greg.

He'd found them!

"Hello, darlin'. Miss me?"

Her heart stalled. She started to rise and face her ex-husband. But she hesitated when she saw a shudder wrack Amanda's small frame, followed quickly by another, precursors to one of her anxiety attacks if Rachel didn't distract her...and quickly.

Grab Amanda and run!

The voice in her head reminded her she was all that stood between the two little girls and a conscienceless monster. She smoothed the back of her knuckles over her child's cheek and dredged up a steady smile. "Run along with Suze and have your tea party with Ms. Jane and Mr. Patrick. Stay there until Mama comes for you."

"She's not going anywhere!"

A coldness that always lined Greg's voice when he was crossed told Rachel she didn't have much time to get the helpless children out of harm's way. "Run along, baby," she whispered. "Go!"

Tears welled in Amanda's eyes. She opened her mouth as if, at last, she wanted to say something. Then she grabbed Suze's hand in hers and dashed off, leaving Rachel to stand and face her ex-husband alone.

The children disappeared safely from view around the front corner of Patrick's house as Rachel fought to dampen her own gut-wrenching terror. She wanted to run after the children to find a hiding place of her own.

Too late.

The stench of Greg's cologne smothered her senses. His hand clamped around her wrist. "You may have chopped off all of your hair and stopped wearing the makeup I like," he muttered next to her ear, "but I see some things haven't changed while I was gone. You still mollycoddle that kid like she's something special."

"Amanda *is* special," she said, goaded as much by his sneering words as his revolting touch. She tried to pull away, but his hand tightened until she was sure her wrist would snap in two. "She's your daughter," she said quickly. "She's the one good thing to come out of our marriage." How this man could produce such a wondrous child in the first place was a miracle.

His grip tightened further and she knew his bruising fingerprints would ring her wrist by morning like some kind of slave bracelet, a reminder of what she'd been forced to pay over and again for that miracle.

"You've obviously forgotten how good it was between us, darlin'." He rubbed his erection on her hip. "I've been thinking about it for six long months, about all the ways I want to refresh your memory. Do you have any idea what it felt like sitting in that jail cell wanting you, knowing you stabbed me in the back only to make me pay for messing with your home-wrecking friend?"

Swallowing back the urge to retch, she winced when she thought of Katy. Her friend hadn't been the only reason she'd done something to escape the untenable situation she'd lived for four years. Katy had simply given Rachel hope. That she could leave Greg. That she could escape without losing Amanda. The older woman had offered her old job back, reminded her of the peaceful joy of landscaping, a settled place for her heart and dreams that didn't include a man who controlled her every waking moment.

Righteous anger stiffened her spine. She suddenly tore free of Greg's grasp, staggered away and sucked clean air into her lungs. "You're lucky they only arrested you for theft and fraud. If Katy had died from the heart attack you caused, you'd have been charged with murder too."

On a roll, she said more than she'd ever dared before. "As for how good it was between us, *darlin'*, my memory's a lot different than yours. I stayed to protect Amanda, and you know it. Do you think I've forgotten what you did to me?"

Her laughter overflowed with bitterness six years of marriage had left seared on her battered soul. "You're deluded if you think I'll ever let you touch me again. I never wanted you after I knew you for the snake you are!"

She regretted her final words the moment she uttered them because snakes strike when provoked. Greg's handsome face mottled with familiar fury. She didn't see his hand move, but she felt it pass through her blessedly short hair where he used to grab the waist-length strands, heard his growl of frustration when he didn't snag anything. Before he could try again, she jerked away. Her legs tangled up beneath her and she sprawled flat, her head snapping backward to hit the ground with a sickening thud.

Dizziness swirling through her mind, the taste of blood on her tongue, she stared at the metal weed bucket she'd forgotten at her feet. She shook her head, then looked up at Greg, debating the wisdom of rising.

"Get up," he ordered.

Staying put sounded like a better idea. "You can't tell me what to do anymore. We're divorced."

He laughed. "You think a piece of paper means a fucking thing to me? To us? You're mine 'til the day you die, darlin'."

Maybe it was the blow to her head messing with her good sense, but she couldn't stop baiting him. "If you want to kill me," she said, "you're going to have to come down here and get your hands dirty. I'm not moving."

"Killing you isn't in the plan." His expression twisted. "But don't force my hand."

Trepidation centered in her midsection beneath her scars. "How did you find us?"

"I know a tracker."

"You've had me watched? Followed?" She'd thought it was her imagination, sheer paranoia, the few times she'd felt unseen eyes upon her these past couple of days. "How long?"

"Since the day I discovered you turned me over to the FBI. My plan was foolproof," his smile held no humor, "except for the knife my darlin' wife thrust in my back."

Six months? He'd been keeping tabs on her the entire time he was in jail? Dear God, hadn't she paid enough when he beat her that night? Her answer was burning through his ice-blue eyes. *Killing you isn't in the plan.*

No. She hadn't paid nearly enough.

Why did you allow Katy and Evelyn to convince you to stop running? It's harder to shoot at a moving target. Had she learned nothing at her own daddy's knee?

She moaned as a series of sharp stabbing pains began to creep around the back of her head like a filigree iron band. Exploring the area behind her left ear with one hand, she discovered a large goose egg. One light graze of her fingertips over the tender knob sent more streaks of pain radiating in all directions. When she yanked her hand away and looked down, her fingertips were smeared with blood. She'd knocked her head harder than she'd thought!

The reality of her situation hit her full force. How could she be so stupid thinking she could handle Greg alone? And Amanda! Greg knew where she was now. What was she going to do?

"Get up and go inside," he ordered. "You've got ten minutes to pack. Then we'll get your precious brat and hit the road." He glared at her bare legs and feet below her favorite cutoffs. "And put on a dress and heels. No woman of mine is going to embarrass me looking like filthy white trash."

She bit her tongue so she couldn't blurt out what she'd done with the walk-in closet full of designer clothes he'd forced her to wear. The FBI had frozen all of their assets with the exception of her personal clothing. She'd asked Simon to get rid of it all. Greg would not appreciate learning he'd clothed a dozen women housed in an inner city domestic violence shelter. What Rachel had kept could be wadded into one suitcase in five minutes less than the ten he'd given her to pack.

In the mood he was in, he just might decide to kill her here and now.

Rachel would go inside to do as he'd ordered, the moment she figured out a way to climb out the bedroom window without this man on her heels. She'd only gain a five-minute head start and a climb down Evelyn Thorne's rose trellis would be precarious, with or without a head injury, but the risks were worth it if she could somehow get her emotionally fragile daughter to another safe place out of her father's reach.

Was there such a place? Assuming she successfully gathered up Amanda from next door and made it to the rental car still gassed up behind Evelyn's greenhouse, where could she go? It was an exercise in futility if Greg hadn't called off his watchdog once he'd arrived in Denver.

Panic won't help you. Chances were good Greg sent her shadow on his way. *The man's arrogant enough to think he can handle you alone.* The challenge is to keep him from following her upstairs. *One step at a time.* "I'll go with you. But I must make arrangements—"

His lifted hand cut off her words. "Don't give me any more crap unless you want one of these. I didn't come all this way to go away empty-handed."

Hope fled with the realization he'd never leave her out of his sight long enough for her to escape. No one could save her.

Except, possibly, the large man jumping over the dwarf cranberry hedge that delineated the property line between the two Thorne households.

Rachel's heart began to pound as she looked across the yard into Patrick Thorne's furious brown eyes.

Patrick stalked across his parents' lawn past the woman he'd promised to watch over, lying on the ground like a negligent child's broken toy. He didn't stop moving until he'd slammed Rachel's attacker back into the painted wood siding of the house. "Hit her again, pal," he gritted out, pressing his forearm down on the man's windpipe, "and you won't have any hands at all!"

The man clawed ineffectually at Patrick's arm, his lips moved. All that came out was a gurgling noise.

"Wait! Stop!" Rachel said from behind them. "I-I fell!"

Patrick froze. That wasn't the impression he got running out of his house on the heels of Suze's interruption of his planning meeting with overwrought pleas to "save 'Manda's mommy from the bad man". All he saw was Rachel sprawled on the ground, a strange man looming over her with a raised fist. In Patrick's experience a man didn't raise a hand unless he were a hair's breath away from using it or already had, but he slowly backed off and released the stranger.

The man scuttled quickly around him to the middle of the yard, his hand rubbing his neck as he gasped for air. Blond, handsome in that cookie-cutter, preppy way many women couldn't seem to resist, at first glance he didn't look like a bad man. But Patrick had to give Suze credit for her ability to spot the mean look in his eyes. Pretty boy or not, this man was capable of violence.

"Preppy" stiffened. "How dare you come between me and my wife?"

As far as he knew his parents' houseguest was, in fact, a divorcee. Yet Patrick would have ignored the querulous question anyway. He walked over and reached out a hand to assist Rachel to her feet...and nearly dropped her again.

When her fingers slid across his calloused palm, a ragged edge of aware-ness zipped through his bloodstream, awakening something inside him he'd buried long ago. Craving. White hot and mind-numbing desire. He couldn't release Rachel fast enough. She swayed unsteadily, and her slender frame tumbled into his arms. The top of her head came to just below his chin and, damn it all to hell, she smelled like his mother's Persian lilacs after a spring rain. Lush. Potent.

He gave himself a mental shake. He had no business wrapping his starved libido in the scent and feel of this woman! Lifting a pale honey curl away from her cheekbone, he worked to reestablish his distance. "You okay?" he asked, the words like gravel in his throat. His gut knotted as she simply gazed back at him with those liquid brown eyes so like the mute, blond cutie that had traipsed through his house and office on Suze's heels these past few days.

"Let go of my wife."

"Screw you." It wasn't often he threw his bulk in another man's face, but for reasons he didn't want to acknowledge, he was spoiling for a fight. No matter what he'd told himself earlier about Rachel being on her own, he couldn't allow any woman to be threatened under his nose. He didn't think she "fell" all by her lonesome either. All of his protective instincts primed, he tucked her under his left arm.

The ages-old display of masculine possession wasn't lost on the stranger. His face turned the color of Mrs. Steinbecker's new dining room walls, a sickening shade of puce. "Who do you think you are?"

Rachel's Southern-laced voice punched through Patrick's senses like a double shot of raw whiskey, but it was the words she uttered that robbed his speech. "Patrick's my boyfriend, Greg."

"Preppy" laughed, although he didn't look the least bit amused. "You're joking."

Patrick didn't question how she knew who he was, much less contradict her. Her declaration did the weirdest thing to his objectivity though. Rather than immediately discounting her claim as the blatant lie it was, he felt a Neanderthal urge to puff up his chest and carry his prize off to his cave. He hadn't felt this possessive about a woman since...well, never.

Like they were the only things holding her up Rachel's fingers fisted in the folds of his work shirt at the base of his spine, a trembling reminder the woman was terrified and likely to grasp at anything to throw between her and the ex. Even a fake boyfriend would do.

Rachel's declaration gave him tacit permission to act as one. "You didn't expect Rachel to remain alone for long, did you?" he challenged.

"Is that what she told you her name is? Rachel? You must be rolling in dough." Her ex-husband curled a lip in a first class sneer. "I have to tell you, *pal*, Felicia's quite the con artist. She may look like some kind of ingénue, but she'll have you laid out to dry the second she gets her hands on your fat bank account."

For all he knew, the woman *was* a con artist. Her fabrication about their imaginary relationship had tripped off her tongue easily. She'd certainly insinuated herself and her daughter into his parents' good graces fast enough. However, he didn't like the way "Preppy" looked at her so he stifled his reservations. For now. "Rachel can shave her head, call herself the Dali Lama, and spend every penny I have," he said. "I have no problem sharing what I have with her and Amanda."

The man didn't say anything for several moments. Then, like he'd drawn four aces in a game of five-card stud, he smiled. "You may have somehow wormed your way into my frigid wife's bed, but that's about to end. You can't have my daughter. She's mine." His gaze shifted to Patrick's left. "And you're a package deal, aren't you, Felicia darlin'?"

Felicia darlin', Rachel, whatever her name truly was separated from Patrick's side. "Greg, please. Don't do this."

He said nothing.

Words, it seemed, were unnecessary. By the slope of her shoulders, the resignation that shadowed her expression when she glanced at Patrick, it was easy to see her emotional reserves were tapped. He didn't like the odd hold "Preppy" seemed to have over her. He wanted him gone.

"Rachel and Amanda aren't yours anymore," he informed him. "This is private property and it's mine, too. You've got ten seconds to clear out before I call the cops."

"Preppy's" blue eyes narrowed. "You have no right to—"

"*Nine,*" he said with implacable resolve.

"This isn't over!"

"Yes, it is. Unless Rachel wants to press criminal charges." Patrick glanced at her and gave her one last chance to reveal the real reason she "fell", but she shook her head. He frowned before turning back to the man. "Lucky you. *Eight.*"

"Felicia! You're going to regret—"

"*Seven.* Better run before she changes her mind. Before I do." Patrick took two purposeful strides forward and almost grinned with satisfaction at the flicker of unease that crossed the man's expression. "*Six.*"

Out of the corner of his eye Patrick saw half a dozen of his crew, left cooling their heels in his parlor, conference room, walk around the front corner of his house. His brother-in-law and assistant, Skip Davis, called across the yard. "Jane called the cops, Patrick."

John Branson, one of Patrick's foremen, crossed his arms over his two hundred and eighty-pound linebacker frame and planted his feet wide. "I told her not to bother. We all know how to take care of pansy-asses who beat on defenseless women."

Patrick wondered which alarmed "Preppy" more, the massive wall of construction workers ranged alongside them in an intimidating line or the threat of imminent police intervention. With a vicious curse, he turned on his silver-tipped cowboy boots and fled. He was seated in a swanky, smoky gray Lincoln pickup parked at the curb and squealing tires in thirty seconds flat. He left behind the smell of burnt rubber, the last wafts of some noxious cologne, and a peaceful hush broken only by the squabbling of two squirrels in a nearby cottonwood tree.

Nodding his thanks to his crew, Patrick turned to the woman they'd just rescued. "He'll think twice before bothering you again now that he knows we're here and you're protected."

He expected to see relief, a little gratitude, maybe, but Rachel just stood there and stared at him with wide, horrified eyes. Her head still shook back and forth. "If you believe that," her husky voice burned along his nerve endings, "I've got two thousand acres of dry farmland in the Louisiana Bayou to sell you."

Before he had time to respond, her angel-soft brown eyes rolled up and she crumpled into a faint at his feet. That's when he saw the glistening trail of blood. It trickled from the base of her skull down the vulnerable curve of her neck and back to soak into the fabric of the form-fitting, tangerine T-shirt he'd been admiring earlier that morning like a bull in heat.

He heaved a sigh. So much for staying on his own side of the property line.

He's going to kill you.

Kill you.

Kill....

The litany echoed louder and louder in Rachel's head with each of her husband's angry thrusts. But she was helpless to stop him, her wrists caught above her head in his relentless grip. Finally, he shuddered to a stop and glared down at her.

Her punishment over, she allowed her eyelids to close to block out the cruelty in Greg's gorgeous, blue eyes.

"Open your eyes and look at me," he snarled, tightening his hold on her wrists until she cried out in pain and did as she was told. "I should kill you for what you've done," he said. "But this," he twisted her nipple in his free hand, "is mine." He ground himself into her. "All mine!"

Her insides turned to ice when she realized he hadn't calmed down like he usually did once he found his release. In fact, his anger was building.

She couldn't bear the thought of him punishing her through the night! Why had she thought she could get through his arrest and trial without him finding out her part in helping the FBI to put him behind bars? "Greg—"

"When are they coming for me?"

Shocked, he knew his arrest was imminent, her eyes widened. How did he know? The FBI only called an hour before he came home to warn her they would have their warrants in the morning. "I don't—"

"Don't!" He grabbed her long hair in his fist and yanked her head back. "When?"

Not soon enough to save her. "I-In...the morning!" she croaked out. A hot tear ran from the corner of her eye across her temple to join the others in her damp hair.

"Plenty of time." His laugh was thin. "You think you've won, don't you? You think you won't have to pay for what you've done." His tone was conversational but the rage suffusing his handsome face was ugly. Deadly. "Well, my darlin', backstabbing wife, you haven't begun to pay."

Dear God, she prayed silently. *Help me!*

God didn't answer. He'd abandoned her to Greg for all her sins. "Greg, please!"

"I love it when you beg," he said, a smile softening his features. He climbed off her and stood at the side of the bed looking down at her naked body. He didn't hurry because he knew she didn't dare move before he told her she could. He reached down and spread her legs to his gaze.

All of the bedroom lights blazed, as they always did when he had sex with her, exposing every inch of her to him the way he liked. She gritted her teeth against her squirming compulsion to cover herself, and watched him reach back to the dresser behind him. She didn't react until she saw him raise his horsewhip over his head, and then it was too late.

The whip ripped across the flesh of her exposed belly. She screamed. She automatically curled into a fetal ball, but the next blow lashed at her spine. He whipped her and didn't stop, each blow punctuated with ranting words she could barely hear over her own screams, until black waves of nauseating pain swamped her senses.

Barely conscious, she didn't realize the beating had stopped until Greg leaned down and whispered harshly. "You're mine, Felicia, and don't you ever forget it. You'd better be here when I get back. If you aren't, I'll chase you down. And next time, I won't stop with you. You hear me?"

She moaned but couldn't push past the agony to respond. He punched her in the ribs and her world began to dim into blessed oblivion.

"'Til death, darlin'," he spat in her ear. "You'd better get it because, next time, it'll be your precious brat. And, next time...I...won't...stop."

6

"Amanda!" Rachel screamed with rage. She flailed her way out of the black abyss and attacked the demon threatening her child. Her fingernails tore into his warm flesh.

"Rachel, stop!" He cursed. "Open your eyes. It's me. Patrick!"

Her wrists caught in a firm grip, Rachel woke up and looked into Patrick Thorne's brown eyes. Not a demon. Not quite an angel either, judging by the scowl on his face.

A tormented sound escaped her throat as all of the fight rushed out of her. She collapsed onto her back. Patrick rose from her side and left her lying on the pile of daisy white and yellow pillows that decorated the vintage, black wicker couch on the side porch of the elder Thorne home.

Where she and Amanda had hidden.

From Greg.

He'd found them!

Rachel frantically scanned the yard. Twice. But Greg wasn't waiting impatiently on the lawn for her to come to her senses, so he could drag her off to her doom. Instead, half a dozen strangers wearing Thorne Enterprises hard-hats and varying degrees of curiosity on their faces stood nearby.

She relaxed. Eyes closed, recent events marched through her mind alongside the throbbing pain in her head. Everyone must think she was insane.

Evidence was on their side.

She'd claimed Patrick as her boyfriend! *Her lover.* What possessed her to say such a stupid, dangerous thing? She knew before they married Greg had a jealous streak a mile wide. Initially, his possessiveness was appealing. For the first time since her mother's death, she'd felt truly treasured. Loved.

It was on their Caribbean cruise honeymoon that belief was first tested. Greg decked a fellow passenger for simply talking to her at dinner, and then turned on her, accusing her of encouraging him. The incident was dropped when the man's wife suggested to officials her husband might have had a little too much to drink, and apologized for his actions. Rachel had paid the price. That night, when Greg had sex with her, he didn't consider her comfort or her feelings. She'd hesitated to call it rape, but that night made her ultra-aware of how she should interact with other men. She hadn't dared expose anyone else to Greg's possessiveness.

Until now.

Why did she blurt that bald-faced lie about Patrick being her boyfriend? The man had only tried to help, and she'd thrown him directly across Greg's destructive path. "What was I thinking?"

"Since you probably have a concussion that question is certainly up for grabs."

Her eyelids flew open at the severity in Patrick's tone. Was he still upset about the confrontation with Greg or with her for setting him up like a brazen hussy? If the blue-bloods in her mother's family were there to see what she'd done, they'd feel justified in their abandonment of her, at last certain only her father's bad blood coursed through her veins. Even Great-aunt Amanda, God rest her gracious, forgiving soul, might have raised a silver eyebrow at her goddaughter's blatant disregard for—

"Amanda!" Familial disapproval meant nothing if Greg got his hands on her great-aunt's namesake. "Where is she?"

"She's safe next door with Jane and Suze," Patrick assured her. When she tried to sit, he placed a hand on her shoulder and stopped her. "Don't move. You have a head injury."

Pushing his hand aside, she sat up. Dizziness washed over her, but she ignored it. "I have to see her."

He shook his head. "That's not a good idea right now. If the sight of all these strangers doesn't scare her, seeing her mother covered in blood will."

She was tempted to tell him what he could do with his orders until she looked down at his hand and saw the bloodstained washcloth he must have been using to clean her injury. The last thing she wanted was to traumatize her further, but...she shook her head, trying to think around the fuzziness in her brain. Her thoughts scattered. For several moments, Patrick's form undulated in front of her eyes like a horror movie carnival mirror.

Fighting to push the roiling image aside, she looked instead at the dried, reddish-brown smear on her fingertips. "I hit my head," she said, the weak explanation as much for her benefit as Patrick's.

"Evidently. Skip," he nodded toward the group of construction workers standing across the yard, "found blood on one of the stone garden figurines near where you fell."

She eyed the streaks of blood on Patrick's work shirt, evidence that he was the one who'd carried her to the porch, her gaze settling on the four angry scratches she'd carved into his muscular neck. "I'm sorry that I, that you—"

Nausea welled up and stopped her apology. "I-I think…I'm going…to be sick." Could she make this situation any worse than to throw up all over the man's work boots?

Snapping an order at his men to find the ambulance, Patrick tossed aside the washcloth in his hand and dumped a large bowl of pink-tinged water into a nearby flower bed. Setting the empty bowl on the side table next to her, he took a seat on the couch, cradled her face in his large hands, and examined her pupils.

"Breathe slowly through your nose," he suggested quietly. "We'll get a better idea how bad your injury is once the paramedics get here. My brother's on his way, too."

His calloused thumbs stroked her temples, a light touch, she felt low in her belly. Only it wasn't nausea skipping through her stomach now.

Maybe it was the atrocious hammering at the base of her skull or Patrick's disconcerting proximity that disoriented her. Her head fell forward until it rested on his broad chest. She concentrated on filling her lungs with the thin, mountain air, then letting it escape. Each time, she inhaled more of Patrick's clean, masculine scent. So different from any other man of her acquaintance, it was a mixture of soap, sweat, fresh-cut pine shavings, and Patrick. No aftershave, no cologne…an honest scent.

When was the last time you were this close to an honest man?

Bewildered by the urge to nuzzle until she found naked skin, she jerked her nose out of his shirt and looked at him. "Your brother," she murmured, "the doctor is coming?"

"You're thinking of Sam." He shook his head and continued to rub her temples, oblivious to the strangely erotic impulses his touch evoked. "No. Jane called Jack."

Her pulse stuttered at the thought of the detective with the probing green gaze. "I don't want—"

What she wanted was lost in a cacophony of noise that announced the arrival of what appeared to be the entire available Denver police force, followed by an ambulance. Quickly surrounded by a sea of authority figures, the scene conjured unnerving memories of the day the FBI had cornered her outside a grocery store seven months ago, throwing her life into a tailspin.

She fought a childish impulse to curl into a defensive ball. She had nothing left to hide.

Well, almost nothing.

Patrick rose from the couch as his brother strode through the crowd. Rachel knew exactly when the detective spotted the bloodstains on his brother's shirt. His jaw tightened. "Dispatch didn't say you were injured." He shouted over his shoulder. "Get those paramedics over here!"

"It's Rachel's," Patrick explained. "This isn't about me, Jack. Not this time."

One sandy-colored eyebrow quirked as he pointedly examined the ragged welts Rachel's fingernails had left on Patrick's tanned neck. She could have sworn the brothers communicated without uttering a word. Something else was going on here.

There was no time to sort it out. One of the paramedics stepped behind her to examine her head injury. From her seat on the couch, she distractedly fielded questions by the second paramedic taking her vitals and, peering over his shoulder, she watched a pair of police officers escort Patrick's crew back to the neighboring yard to take their statements. Jack spoke to several of the other officers, and they soon returned to their cars and pulled away.

She wished she could hear the animated conversation taking place several feet away between Patrick and his brother, especially when the detective lost his temper. "For God's sake, Patrick, why didn't you...?"

His voice lowered, the rest of his words were lost. But he glanced at Rachel and she had no doubts they were discussing her and the problem she'd brought to their door. She'd stupidly thrown Patrick in Greg's face. She might as well have painted a target on the poor man.

It didn't help he'd provoked Greg further by threatening to have him arrested. Now the authorities were involved. What a disaster! They might as well have kicked up a nest of rattlesnakes between them because it was a sure bet Greg was going react. And it wouldn't be pretty. He was at his worst when deprived of something he felt entitled to and, God knows, she and Amanda were property in his eyes.

Property he was determined to reclaim.

"I'd rather be thrown buck naked into a snake pit," she murmured. The urge to put the entire country between her and her ex-husband pushed her to her feet. Her knees felt like bread pudding. They refused to hold her up. She sat back down with a plop, white shards of light flashing behind her eyes.

"If you can sit tight a few more minutes, ma'am," the first paramedic said quickly, "we're not quite finished here."

The buzzing in her head gained strength. "Y-yes, you are."

The man exchanged a look with his partner. "Ma'am," he said in a reasonable tone, "you should go to the hospital for x-rays. You lost consciousness for several minutes. With that contusion behind your ear, a concussion is not out of the question."

"I'll sign whatever waivers you—"

"What are you doing?" Patrick's sharp question hit a second before Rachel registered that he and his brother had rejoined them on the porch.

Jack hung back, while Patrick loomed over her like some kind of dark avenging warrior.

Over six feet tall, he easily had thirty pounds on her ex-husband so the man's sheer size should have intimidated her. Yet all she could think about was how safe she'd felt tucked under his arm when he confronted Greg on her behalf. Another, saner voice in her head reminded her she'd thought to find safe haven with Greg at one time, too. She didn't give in to such self-delusions anymore. "I'm leaving."

"You mean you're going to the hospital to get checked out."

"No," she said. "I mean, just as soon as I'm packed I'll come get Amanda and we're gone."

"Ma'am, please reconsider," the paramedic tried again. "A head injury's nothing to play around with."

"I know you're only trying to do your job." Her voice rose alongside her growing anxiety. "But you don't understand. There's no time!"

"Shh, Rachel, I'm sure we can work this out," Jack said before addressing the paramedic. "Just tell my brother what to do, what to watch for and, if she decides later to go to the hospital for x-rays, he'll take her."

"I don't think—" Patrick began.

"I don't want—" she sputtered at the same time.

"If you're dead set against going to the hospital, Rachel, they need to make sure someone's taking care of you." Jack scowled at his brother. "And Patrick's not going anywhere."

Patrick's jaw flexed. He clearly wasn't any happier than she was to have decisions made for him. However, he didn't argue and, in a matter of minutes, the two paramedics shot a flurry of instructions at him, packed their equipment and left the scene.

The moment she was left alone with the two brothers, Rachel summoned a weak smile she was afraid conned no one. "I want to thank you both for your help, but I've got to go. You can't keep me here."

"No one's keeping you against your will—" Patrick started.

Jack quelled him with a look. "I get that you're scared," he said to Rachel. "But you can't keep running. You and Amanda are better off here than anywhere else."

Her heart skipped a beat. "You...know everything?"

He nodded, then glanced at his brother. "Well, I do. No matter how generous Mom is with her assistance, neither Dad nor I could allow her to invite a complete stranger into their home unless we'd confirmed your story with Katy Kolthern and the authorities in San Francisco."

Rachel hated to think about what they'd learned. She relaxed when she realized they couldn't possibly know everything.

They didn't know about Amanda.

God help her if Greg used his ace card and demanded his child back. These people could simply wrest Amanda from her, and Rachel would be helpless to stop them. Only one thing kept her ex-husband from doing just that. He needed Rachel, too. She and Amanda really were a package deal...more so today than he knew.

She refused to look the detective in the eye, afraid he'd uncover the one secret only she and two others knew. "Greg's here in Denver. We're leaving."

In the quiet after her definitive statement, the ring of a cell phone sounded loud and strident. Excusing himself, Jack pulled the phone out of his suit jacket pocket and walked out of earshot to a corner of the yard. She forced herself not to look at Patrick propped against a porch pillar, still silently watching the proceedings. Still looking tense with some strong emotion she couldn't decipher.

A sliver of uneasiness crawled up Rachel's spine as she watched a myriad of expressions chase across Jack's face at whatever the caller was telling him. When he hung up, he stared across the yard at her. He dragged a hand across the back of his neck, turned away and made a phone call with a single push of a button. Evidently, the call didn't go through to whomever he wanted because he hung up quickly after speaking to someone. Then he squared his shoulders and strode across the yard to the porch.

Uh-oh. Something was terribly wrong. The man's official demeanor scared the daylights out of her, but it was the authoritative words that made the blood rush from her head.

"I can't let you leave, Rachel," he said.

"You can't force me to stay here!" she retorted. She winced at the pain in her head, her next words quieter. "I've done nothing wrong."

Patrick, silent until then, stepped away from the pillar and inserted himself into the discussion. "What's going on?"

Jack studied his brother for a long moment. Then, he heaved a heavy sigh and motioned him to one of the wicker chairs before he took the one closest to where she sat on the couch. He leaned toward her, his expression grave. "I can't let you leave, Rachel. It's too dangerous," he waved his hand toward the street, "out there. In fact, we must get you and Amanda under a 24-hour watch until we can locate your ex-husband."

He thought it was dangerous *out there*? She bit back a hysterical laugh. "I told Patrick he didn't hit me. I'm not pressing charges so—" *Jack didn't want to find Greg for what he'd just done.* Her eyes widened. "What's wrong?"

Jack answered her question with one of his own. "Do you know a man by the name of Vanhouten?"

She leaned back on the couch, bewildered by the abrupt change of subject. "Simon?"

The detective's head tilted, reminiscent of a predator that just caught the scent of its prey. "Dr. Simon Vanhouten. You do know him then."

Of course, she knew Simon. He'd given her Amanda.

Dear God, he wouldn't, didn't—

Her heart a chunk of ice, she fought for calm. "Yes. He's a friend of the family."

An exaggeration. He'd been one of Greg's cronies. Yet, after all Simon had done for her, she owed him so much. Their friendship was forged the day he planted the seed of her child in her womb. Greg's child, with another woman's ovum, but still her child. At least, in her mind. Simon had been the only person she could call, the only one she could trust to help her that awful night....

"Look, I don't know what all of this has to do with Simon. I haven't talked to him in months. But—" She lunged to her feet despite the fact the motion made her stomach flip-flop like a dying carp. A mistake. "But," she gulped the bile rising in her throat and tried again, "if I-I don't...put a hundred miles between me and, and...." Her head spun. She swayed under the onslaught.

"Whoa there, sweetheart!" Patrick's voice sounded urgent, hollow, in her ear when he wrapped his arms around her. "Better sit down before you fall down."

She locked her knees, wondering how he'd gotten to her so fast. "I-I can't—I won't—" She could hardly think with Patrick this close. "Please," her hand, trapped between them, pushed at his warm bulk, "let me go."

He stared down at her a long moment, the concern in his eyes making her feel dizzier. Then he allowed her to sink back to the cushions on the couch. "Rachel," he said, his hands slowly releasing her upper arms, "Jack wouldn't say you can't leave unless there was a very good reason." He looked over his shoulder. "Jack?"

His brother nodded.

When Patrick took a step back and resumed his seat a couple feet away, she settled back in her chair to clear her head. She might as well listen to what the detective had to say. "What does any of this have to do with Simon?"

"Your friend's in the hospital." Jack frowned. "He's in a coma. It doesn't look good."

"How—I mean, God, what happened?"

"Someone tried to kill him on Monday."

She could barely process what the man was saying. *Simon, dear Simon with his cold hands, dry wit, and warm heart might die?*

Jack cursed. "Rachel, listen. Can you think of a reason why your ex-husband might want to murder Vanhouten and burn his clinic to the ground, almost before the ink is dry on his prison release papers?"

Could she think of a reason? Even dazed and confused, she could think of several hundred million reasons. And they all led to little Amanda.

A band of terror tightened around her lungs and squeezed. She shook her head. The buzzing noise grew ever louder in her ears until the rush of blood in her veins dragged her down into blessed darkness.

7

He should have stayed on his own side of the fence, not run straight into the dangerous territory he instinctively knew surrounded Rachel James.

Thunk! Patrick punched the nail home with a satisfying bang, having ditched the nail gun more than an hour ago in favor of a good, old-fashioned hammer. He had to hit something to beat yesterday's confrontation out of his head.

Patrick's my boyfriend, Greg.

Thunk, thunk!

I have to tell you, pal, Felicia's quite a con artist.

Thunk. Thunk. Thunk!

The woman certainly hadn't felt like a con artist. Patrick still remembered the way her full breasts felt grazing his chest, the tremble of her slender fingertips buried in the folds of his work shirt, the heady scent of lilacs on her sun-warmed hair weaving through his senses. He groaned at the memory of her silky skin beneath his calloused fingertips. Was she that silky smooth all over? She'd felt like pure sin in his arms.

No. She'd felt like trouble.

Why hadn't he heeded his own advice? When he'd agreed to keep an eye on Rachel and her daughter, the plan was simple. Watch. From a distance. It hadn't seemed much of a challenge with Amanda trailing in and out of his home and office as Suze's shadow. The little blond cutie from next door was so quiet, he hardly noticed she was there unless she inadvertently got close enough for him to get sucked into her wary brown-eyed gaze.

Just as he'd gotten sucked in by the little girl's mother. From his office window Rachel James was a delectable temptation Patrick could resist, *had* resisted for two entire days. He'd been unaware of the haunted look in her soft brown eyes, the smudges beneath her lashes that spoke of too many anxious days and sleepless nights. He hadn't realized her willowy frame would feel so fragile and so right, beneath his big hands.

One minute, he was maintaining his distance from a woman in trouble. The next he'd stepped, no, he'd run between Rachel and her ex-husband, crossing a line he'd promised never to bridge again. He could hardly stand by and allow Rachel to be abused. Yet it wasn't until he'd gotten up close and personal he realized her pull on his protective instincts might actually be as strong as his physical desire for the woman. He could fight the latter, maybe the former, but both at the same time? He didn't rescue needy women anymore!

He couldn't retreat back to his side of the cranberry hedge fast enough last night after driving her to the emergency room and leaving her in the hands of his capable brother, Sam. Yet he'd dragged her dilemma home with him, unable to forget the way she trembled when her ex-husband threatened to take Amanda. The look of devastation on her face when Jack hit her with the news about the attack on her doctor friend. How agitated she'd become when Sam admitted her to the hospital so he could monitor her concussion and the altitude sickness no one knew she'd been fighting since her arrival in Denver.

All Patrick could think about was that he would see her again in less than two hours when she was released from the hospital and he picked her up to bring her home.

Home?

Thwack.

Listening to the sharp tap-tap-tap of the nail gun in use one floor above him, he wiped the sweat off his forehead before he examined the hole he'd inadvertently hammered into the new sheet rock he'd been hanging since dawn. Between yesterday's incident with Rachel, all of the gouged drywall he had to replace, and a shade temperature hovering in the upper nineties, he was ready to tear a strip off someone.

He didn't have time for this unwelcome barrage of self-analysis.

Rather than taking out his frustration on the drywall he should be making phone calls to locate a new source for the bathroom sink fixtures for the Mortenson condos, mistakenly shipped to Ohio. He had no time to wait for the supplier to straighten out the shipping mess, and he had an entire crew to replace damaged walls here at Southgate.

He glared at what was left of the bedroom he was working on. It wasn't enough to spray paint obscenities this time, something a fresh overcoat would quickly fix. No, his saboteur punched vicious holes through eight units on the second floor. The loss to Thorne Enterprises, both in time and money, was substantial. This was his third major claim this year, and the year wasn't half over. His insurance agent was having kittens.

Patrick pulled a bottle from a nearby cooler. The icy water did nothing to cool his anger for his unseen nemesis. "Okay. I get the message you're pissed," he muttered. "Just face me like a man when you rip my guts out, you miserable coward."

"There you are!" John Branson, the Southgate foreman entered the room with an odd expression on his face that set off Patrick's internal alarms.

"What's wrong?"

The man grinned. "I hear you're having slumber parties at your house, and I didn't rate an invitation? What's up with that?"

He almost groaned out loud. Was it too much to hope Jane hadn't broadcast to the world she and Suze had stayed overnight at his house after Jack insisted he keep an eye on Amanda so Rachel would stay in the hospital? "Tell me Jane only shared details with you," he growled, "so I don't have to fire her."

"Well, as long as everyone's radios were like yours, *off*," John said pointedly, "I'm the only one who heard you had a pizza party with Suze's teddies and dollies." He grinned. "There was also something about building Barbie a ski chalet with Popsicle sticks?"

Patrick did groan, then. Every Thorne employee carried a radio to ease communications among the crew, which meant more than fifty men and women could have heard about his impromptu slumber party for Amanda. He hadn't known what to do with a four-year-old, especially a girl who didn't communicate. Asking Jane and Suze to stay overnight in one of the five spare bedrooms had been his only line of defense.

He hadn't expected to be drawn into their game plan for the evening, though, so now he was in for it. He'd be finding dolls, bears, and Popsicle sticks stuffed into the crevices of his truck for the rest of the summer. A few of his crew could be evil pranksters when inspired. Nothing inspired them more than a show of alpha-male slippage.

With a shake of his head, he glanced down at the radio clipped to his belt. The yellow battery light blinked back at him. "Sorry you were pulled off the job, John. I forgot to charge my radio yesterday after returning from the hospital. Did Jane say what she wanted...beyond ruining my macho image?"

John chuckled. "She wanted me to give you a message. Guess Amanda's mama checked out of the hospital already. Jane said to tell you she picked her up so you don't have to cut out early. Said she'd stay with her and the girls at your folks' house with the security alarm set until you get home tonight."

Patrick told himself he was relieved to have that chore off his plate. Between the sabotage, a construction schedule in danger of imploding, and his dinner tonight with the Landers to go over spec changes on their dream home he didn't have a minute to spare today.

Why, then, did a pang of disappointment wrench through him?

It didn't. That was heartburn from the roast beef, fried onion, and hot pepper sandwich he'd slammed down when the roving food truck stopped at ten o'clock. He didn't *want* to spend any more time with Rachel of the luscious brown eyes and fragrant skin. That way was a pipeline to disaster.

"Thanks, John." He forced himself to turn to other, more pressing concerns. "How did inspections go this morning?"

The man grimaced. "I understand why it's necessary to kick in new security procedures after this latest," he waved at the remaining damaged wall in the bedroom Patrick was working on, "but conducting detailed inspections of all of the sites before the crew clocks in every day is cutting deep into our schedule. Took me an hour and a half just to check Southgate. Chavez wasn't able to do much better with the Mortenson condos. I hate to think how long it will take once we break ground on the villas next week. Add in all of the time it takes to travel between sites and we've got us a mess of hurt."

"I know." The saboteur hadn't seriously damaged the integrity of any of Patrick's structures. Yet. It didn't mean he couldn't. "But crew safety comes first. So, until I say otherwise, no one walks onto a Thorne site until it's thoroughly checked out."

Patrick rubbed a hand over the back of his neck like the gesture would wring out another solution to his dwindling options. "If it will speed things up, team yourself and the other foremen with supervisors. I'll okay overtime for two man inspection teams to come in an hour before regular shift. Concentrate your efforts only on whatever sites are active that day." Problem was, most of the sites were active and they both knew it.

John nodded his approval. "Teams and an earlier start might help keep our noses above water for a while longer."

"I'll tell Skip to radio the other foremen. Have you seen—"

"Here, boss!" Skip Davis poked his head around the doorjamb like a jack-in-the-box.

Patrick shook his head, amused by how often his lanky brother-in-law showed up exactly when needed, just like Radar on the old M.A.S.H. reruns. Skip had come aboard Thorne Enterprises almost two years ago after he was discharged from the army on the heels of Karly's death. Skip was so devastated to have lost his sister, felt so guilty at not being there to save her from herself that Patrick found a comrade in arms. It was easier to deal with Skip's grief, rather than his own.

When Jane couldn't continue with site work after she took on Suze full time, he'd hired Skip as his personal assistant. Even with limited construction knowledge, his trusty notebook in hand to combat the memory losses he occasionally experienced since his return from Afghanistan, Skip had become Patrick's invaluable set of extra hands. "Did you—"

"Heard you comin' in. Already in my notebook." He waved it in the air. "And before you waste time on the phone, the sink fixtures will be here tomorrow. All two hundred sixty of 'em. The new supplier I found is so happy to get in bed with Thorne Enterprises he shaved off an extra fifteen percent. So, I went ahead and ordered the fittings you wanted for the Caston job. All the supplier needs is your authorization on the invoices, and we're good to go." He barely paused. "I also called the plumbing sub-contractor to tell him we're back on schedule. He'll be at the Mortenson site with his crew day after tomorrow."

The day was definitely looking up. Patrick smiled. "I'm going to have to give you another raise, aren't I?"

Skip grinned at John. "You're my witness!" Then, he sobered when he turned back to Patrick. "With the stuff going on lately I'm just grateful to have a job. Which reminds me, Morgan radioed from the trailer. Jack is waiting to talk to you."

Patrick nodded. "I'll head that way soon as we're done here."

After a few last instructions for John and Skip, Patrick put away his tools, took a final draught on his bottle of water, and poured what was left into a rag to clean construction dust off his face and hands. Then he left the building and walked across the site toward the trailer. Jack told him last night he'd check in as soon as he had an update on the arrest of Rachel's ex-husband. With any luck, he'd also learned who was out to destroy everything Patrick had worked so hard to build.

With the number of challenges his crews had experienced these past ten months, they all deserved raises. Yet it was all he could do to make their current paychecks. Each attack on one of his jobs poked another hole in his bottom line and he was sinking. Fast.

He had to keep his priorities straight.

That meant no more rescuing doe-eyed blonds with felonious exes on their heels. As Jack pointed out at the hospital last night that became his job the moment authorities in California put out an APB on "Preppy" for grand theft, arson, and attempted murder. If Rachel's doctor friend didn't come out of his coma and died, Greg Bishop would be facing murder charges.

Patrick handled the situation all wrong with Bishop yesterday. If he hadn't let the man get to him, the police would have arrived and Rachel's ex-husband would be in custody today. Rachel and Amanda would be back on their side of the hedge, and he on his side. He'd screwed up, so now he was stuck babysitting the pair of them until Jack could arrange for official protection. Who knew how long that would take? The department's manpower was already overextended with their search for the missing coed.

Patrick was shaken from his reverie when he walked into the air-conditioned trailer and collided with his brother pacing in front of the door. "Whoa! Sorry you had to wait, Jack. I was finishing up—"

A cold knot of uneasiness developed in his gut when he saw his brother's severe expression. "What's wrong?"

Jack's scowl deepened. "They've identified some of the clothing your saboteur left behind," he said without preliminary.

"And...?"

"It's bad, Patrick. There are traces of semen and blood on everything. Sondra Manning's blood type."

The feeling of imminent danger he'd felt as a Ranger about to enter a hot zone stirred in his chest. "The councilman's daughter that went missing last week?"

His brother nodded.

Patrick quickly worked through the implications staring him in the face. "You think there's a connection between my saboteur and the Angel Killer."

"Yes. Your saboteur just hit the top of our 'To Do' list." He reached into his pocket and pulled out his keys. "Let's go. We'll take my car."

Three Weeks....
Three Days....
Two Hours....
...'Til death.

Sondra Lynn Manning yanked hysterically on the thick chain that led from a centralized eight-by-eight inch pillar to her cuffed ankle. Then she sagged to the floor of her prison and sobbed in defeat. A line of blood that was sure to upset her captor trickled from a new tear on her ankle down her foot to seep into the rug beneath her, but she didn't care. She suddenly understood why a fox would chew off its own foot to escape a trap.

Her trap had been well laid. The pillar, chain and cuff that confined her were made of strong steel. The bed and lone chair were bolted to the concrete floor in the middle of a windowless room large enough she could use the furniture, but couldn't reach any of the padded walls or ceiling that blocked the sound of her screams. The only thing not bolted down was the camp toilet, and the floor lamp that glared twenty-four, seven in the corner well beyond her reach.

Her days had run together. At least she thought it had been days since she returned home from work and fell into her kidnapper's hands. His visits were irregular. She'd been drugged at least twice, and she had no natural light to give her body a sense of daily rhythm.

At twenty-one years old, she'd never once given a thought to her death. Until Death gained a name and a face, and locked her in this godforsaken place. Now she had time to think of nothing else.

With a gasp, she shifted position to ease the pain of the tattoo her captor had burned into her left butt cheek when she regained consciousness the first time. She looked away from the stain darkening the concrete two feet away—not quite covered by the rug she sat on—unwilling to acknowledge she wasn't the first to be kept in this prison.

She regretted the day she'd moved out from under her father's protective roof. Regretted they'd argued and both been too stubborn to resolve their differences in the three months since. Now, when she was certain it was her fate to die here, she wished she hadn't declared her independence from their gated community and security systems quite so completely.

Did her father know she was missing? She hadn't talked to him in weeks thanks to her moratorium on his nightly phone calls to check on her. And her jailer told her there was no ransom note.

Until he'd told her she wasn't kidnapped for the ransom her lawyer father could pay for her release, Sondra had held out hope. Ransomed, she at least stood a chance of surviving this...whatever *this* was. But, though she knew deep down who her kidnapper was, she didn't understand what he wanted from her.

He ranted. He raved. He talked about people she'd never met and, every time she tried to tell him he'd mistaken her for someone else, he became enraged and threatened to kill her. To kill everyone she loved.

When he wasn't acting crazy, he brought her presents. A book. Perfume. Clothing. She hated the last, not because the girlish blouses and skirts were awful or didn't fit, but because he insisted she strip in front of him and give him everything. The first time, she'd refused. Dragging her by her chain to the bed, he'd cut everything off her. And he'd not been gentle. She still had several cuts from the knife he'd used. Since then, she'd swallowed her humiliation and done as he asked.

Thank God, he'd taken each change of clothing and his disgusting hard-on with him when he left her alone again. But she was terrified of the day when he didn't. "Daddy, please," she sobbed, praying into her knees. "Bug me. Smother me. Make me move back home. Just come get me before it's too late!"

Her tears stopped abruptly when she heard the only sound that ever reached into her prison from the outside world, the scrape of a key on the door lock. Scrambling across the floor to the armchair, she settled into it and hid her bleeding ankle by tucking her foot under her bottom. She arranged her skirt hem over her bare legs just in time.

The door opened and her captor walked in.

Fear gripped her senses. She frantically searched his expression as a barometer of his state of mind. Last time he'd left her, he'd been infuriated by her refusal to open the present he'd brought her. She'd forced herself to open the package. But it was too little, too late. With a growl that sounded more animal than human, he'd leveled her with a vicious backhand that threw her several feet onto the bed and stalked from the room. Her head ringing from where it struck the brass bed frame, she'd almost pitied the poor sap that crossed his path before he cooled down. She hated even more thinking about him coming back and turning that monstrous rage on her.

"Ah, Angel," he frowned, "you've been crying again." He emptied his jeans pockets, setting coins, candy wrappers and what looked like a walkie-talkie or radio alongside his keys on a shelf next to the door just like he was returning home after a long day at work. "I think I've got something here that will cheer you up."

All he had to do was approach her with something with which she could hit him. *That* would cheer her up! Not that it would do her any good with the key to her ankle cuff dangling from his key fob three feet beyond the length of her chain.

Reaching around the doorjamb, he picked up something. When he turned around, he had a deli sack and a small box she recognized from her favorite cheesecake store. Hope surged. She'd wondered how far her kidnapper had taken her. She was still in or near Denver!

If she could just escape this room—

The air froze in her lungs when he crossed the invisible line delineating the real world and the end of her chain. "Your favorites, Angel," he said, approaching her chair. "Ham, turkey and pastrami sub with brown mustard, low-salt chips, whole milk and a double slice of chocolate mousse cheesecake."

She hated that he knew such intimate details about her. He must have been watching her for some time to have learned so many of her preferences. She knew he'd been in her apartment because the pillow on the bed was hers and he'd given her books to read off the shelves in her living room. With the exception of the schoolgirl clothes he'd forced her to wear since she'd awakened the first time and the name he called her, she could almost believe he knew who she was.

The distinctive aroma of spicy pastrami and mustard permeated the air and her mouth watered with anticipation. The box of dry, honeyed oat cereal he'd left her was long gone and she was hungry enough to wonder how many meals she'd missed since his last visit. But she couldn't eat it. The last time he'd brought her something she couldn't resist, it was laced with drugs. She'd passed out on the bed with him holding her close enough for her to feel his erection beneath her bare bottom, brushing her hair like some sick pervert.

Never again! If the asshole intended to rape her she wasn't going to make it easy for him.

"N-no," she said, turning up her nose. "I'm not hungry."

He scowled. "Angel, you must eat."

"My name's not Angel."

"Of course, it isn't." He smiled. "But it was always my special name for you. Just as you've always called me Robby. You know that."

Her sense of defeat raced through her and loosened her tongue. "How am I supposed to know that? I'm. Not. Angel!" she shouted for the hundredth time. "I keep telling you I don't know who you are, or why you kidnapped me, or what you want."

She moderated her voice when his expression darkened. "Please," she begged, "let me go. I won't tell anyone. I just want to go home!"

Without warning, he threw his food offerings on the floor beside her chair and wrapped his hands around her bare arms. "Your home is with me," he said, punctuating each word with a shake. "Say it! Your heart is with *me*! You love me! Me!"

Terrified of the rage she'd provoked, she swallowed against the pain of his fingers digging furrows into her arms. "M-my heart," she stammered, "is with you. I-I l-love you, R-Robby."

His brown eyes searched her face. She stared back for five seconds, ten, trying to decide if he believed her or not, before her gaze dropped to the tick in his jaw.

"Liar." His accusation came out flat, with no inflection whatsoever. "You still want Thorne."

She cried out when he unexpectedly lifted her from the chair so that her ankles and chain dangled in the air. "No, please! I don't want anyone. I mean, I don't want *him*!" Heaven help her, she didn't know anyone named Patrick Thorne!

Robby tossed her on the bed. He stared at the blood drying on her ankle and his expression closed down altogether, which she found more disturbing than his fury. It was like he was staring at her from a distant room, leaving her alone with a soulless husk of a man. "But you'll hurt yourself trying to get back to him, won't you?"

"Robby. Please. Tell me what you want me to say. I'll say it. I'll give you whatever you want. *Please*!"

Something changed in his expression. A new light entered his soulless eyes. An evil, monstrous light that scared her to death. He leaned over her and smiled. "You should have given him what he wanted," he said, his voice changed, "because now you're mine."

"I-I-Robby, please!" she stammered.

"Robby has left the building," he said, with an awful chuckle that curdled her blood.

If she ever had a doubt that she was in the hands of the Angel Killer, she had no doubt now. Hysteria beat at her senses. She could barely breathe.

Then she couldn't. Her killer wrapped his cruel hand around her throat and squeezed until she saw bright flashes of light behind her darkening eyes. When he eased up, she gasped. And then her real terror began.

Hot pain tore into her belly. Her breasts. Between her legs. Over and over. Every part of her ripped and torn until she screamed for death. And through it all, she heard nothing but the gleeful laughter of a vicious monster.

Until she heard no more.

9

Patrick was exhausted and frustrated when he let himself into his parents'
front door after six o'clock that night. Five hours at the police station being
grilled by the Angel Killer task force, to no avail. They were no closer to
figuring out the connection between him and the serial killer than when
he walked into the station with Jack this afternoon.

All he wanted to do was pop the top on an ice cold beer and kick up
his feet. But that wasn't an option tonight. He had to relieve his office
manager, Jane, who'd been babysitting Rachel and Amanda since picking
up Rachel from the hospital before lunch.

Who was he kidding? He was looking forward to taking over babysitting
duty. Just thinking about seeing Rachel released the taut line between his
shoulder blades.

The aromatic smell of marinara sauce drifted through the house and teased his nose. His last meal had come from the food truck that morning and he was suddenly starved. He followed the smell to the kitchen where he caught sight of his office manager hanging up the phone on the wall. She stared at the receiver, unmoving for a moment, her shoulders bowed, then with a deep sigh, she reached for a pile of chopped onions on the cutting board and scraped them into a large, steaming pot.

After this screwy day it was so good to see Jane, more friend, than employee, doing something as normal as cooking. He heard her sniff back a tear as she picked up a large, stainless spoon and stirred the pot. He grinned. "Mom always did say you can tell how good a sauce is by how many tears are on a cook's face."

Jane whirled from her task so fast the stirring spoon splattered bright red sauce across the blue-and-white kitchen tiles. "Patrick!"

"Oops! Sorry!" He raised his hands in self-defense and flashed an apologetic smile at her. "I didn't mean to startle you," he said. "I guess you didn't hear the beep after I disengaged the security system when I came in the front door."

"I-I—" Jane's hand hovered over her heart.

Patrick's smile disappeared when he saw her face blanch. Dammit! He'd scared the woman into an angina attack. He rushed across the room to her side and helped her to a stool at the central island. Taking the dripping spoon from her tight fisted hand, he tossed it onto the countertop. "Where are your pills, Jane?" he asked quietly, his gaze fixed on her face.

"I already took one," she said, bursting into tears.

Stunned—he'd never seen Jane cry except for the day she buried her daughter, Suze's mother—all he could do was fuss over her until he found out what was wrong. There was more going on here than his unexpected arrival. She was antsy as a sparrow perched on an exposed electrical wire.

He patted her shoulder. The tissue box on the counter was empty, so he snagged a paper towel from the marble spindle on the island and tucked it into her restless hand. "Tell me what I can do, Jane," he said helplessly. "Did you get bad news on the phone?"

"Phone?" She stared at the wall, and then glanced quickly away. She waved a hand at him. "No. It was a...wrong number."

Somehow he didn't believe her, but unless she was willing to talk to him, he was at a loss what to do for her. He watched her sniffle into the paper towel. Then she blew her nose indelicately. When she looked him in the eye, her expression disintegrated and she started to cry again. "Sorry," she choked out around the tears. "I haven't been home," hiccup, "in two days and, and, I-I-I'm just tired!"

He felt like a heel. He'd put too much on her shoulders, not thinking about what the extra work might do to her health. She'd been dry for nine years since coming out of rehab and going to work for him, but she'd been so liquored up for most of her adult life, her body had never fully recovered. *This* he could fix. "I'm the one who's sorry," he said, pouring her favorite orange soda over ice and snatching up the stirring spoon. "You just sit there and I'll finish dinner."

Walking over to the stove, he gave the pot a stir before he grabbed more paper towels and cleaned up the sauce splattered on the floor and lower cupboards. When he finished, he looked at Jane. "Where is everyone? John told me you picked up Rachel from the hospital."

"I convinced her to lay down with Amanda and Suze a few hours ago. They're all taking a nap."

He nodded toward Jane. "You should have taken one with them," he said. "After you eat dinner, I want you and Suze to go home. Don't come into work tomorrow. Take the day off. Relax."

The woman stared at him like he'd lost his mind, but he was happy to see she'd stopped crying. She wiped her eyes with a corner of paper towel. "I can't take a day off in the middle of the week. The schedule is overflowing and—"

Patrick frowned at her. "Take the day off, Jane."

"But—"

"Do I have to fire you?"

Jane looked startled. "You're the boss," she said, glancing at the kitchen clock. "Speaking of which, boss, didn't you have a meeting with the Landers at six o'clock?"

Patrick shrugged. "I had to reschedule."

"Something's wrong," Jane said, the statement sounding more like a question. "You disappeared this afternoon and didn't come back."

"I was with Jack at the police station." The muscles between his shoulder blades tightened again. He knew he'd have to address today's events sooner or later, but he'd hoped to wait until after dinner. "We've got a problem."

Her eyes widened. "Let me ex—"

"Jane, please," he interrupted. He knew she was upset by the recent attacks on the sites. She seemed to be taking every hit personally lately. Not that he wasn't doing the same. It *felt* personal. "Just listen. If I have to explain this more than once, I'll go nuts."

Rachel stood frozen in the doorway trying to decide whether to go or stay before someone noticed her. She wasn't in the mood to talk to anyone, let alone the man standing in the middle of the kitchen with Jane. Their problem was Rachel, of course. But she was done with people running her life so it was impossible to turn away and let them decide her fate.

Why did she take the pain pills Sam prescribed before releasing her from the hospital? She'd awakened from her nap feeling nauseous and weak as a kitten. It took her a full ten minutes to pull on panties, a peach-colored tee and jeans. When she reached down to pick up her bra from the floor where it had fallen, she'd almost passed out. It was still lying on the carpet upstairs.

She was not up to fighting strength, and needed to be!

"Come on in, Rachel." Patrick looked straight at her, his left eyebrow quirked like he'd been aware she was hovering there all along. "You should be in on this conversation, too."

Despite the invitation in his voice, his intense stare pinned her in place. Her heart beat too fast, but she chalked that up to her concussion, altitude sickness, and the residual effects of the pain pill. The tremor that fluttered through her bloodstream though? That was pure sexual attraction.

She gave herself a mental shake. It was insanity to think of going there. She hadn't recovered from her last fall from grace.

Pressing her hand protectively over the scars on her abdomen, she walked past Patrick toward the island centered in the middle of the large, sunny room. "Amanda and I won't be a problem much longer." She scooted gratefully onto a high-backed stool Jane pulled out next to her. "The moment Greg's behind bars, we're heading back to Dallas."

Patrick nodded his approval. "You made the right decision to stay, Rachel," he said. "It shouldn't take long now that there's an APB out on Bishop."

"I hope so." She unclipped the baby monitor—bought to listen for trouble during her traumatized daughter's naps—from the waistband of her jeans to reassure herself it was handy, setting it on the marble counter in front of her. "Greg managed to avoid arrest by the FBI for nearly a week. He's nothing, if not resourceful." It was one of the reasons it had taken her so long to escape him. She'd had to find a foolproof way to get Amanda out from under his thumb.

Yeah, look how that turned out. The FBI couldn't hold him.

A shiver raced through her. She was taking a chance by staying in Denver. But, much as she wanted to keep Amanda out of Greg's hands, she was stuck. Rachel had a concussion and couldn't risk becoming completely incapacitated. What would happen to Amanda then? She had no choice but to take a chance the Denver police would arrest him and eliminate the threat quickly.

If they didn't...?

Squelching her apprehension, she missed part of Patrick's reply. "...worry, Rachel," he said. "They'll find him." He took a stool on the other side of the island, tweaking her pulse dangerously. "However," he continued, "we should revisit how we're going to protect you and Amanda."

The grim expression on his face wasn't reassuring. "When we talked at the hospital last night," she said, "Jack said we'd be safe enough here if we stay in the house with the security alarm turned on. I promised not to go outside, and the police are only a phone call away. What more can we do? If we're not protected here, if Jack lied—"

Jane put a hand over Rachel's forearm to stop her words. "You said there was a problem, Patrick," she said quietly, looking at her boss. "You spent the afternoon with Jack at the station. What's going on?

A myriad of emotions swept over his handsome face. Worry. Anger. Weariness.

Dragging a hand over his expression, he closed off whatever he was feeling. "Let me back up a bit for Rachel," he said, looking at her. "About eleven months ago, my construction company, Thorne Enterprises, began experiencing some problems. Equipment breakage. Supplies disappeared. Innocuous things, at first, but it didn't take me long to start wondering about all of the bad luck."

"That wasn't all it was, was it?" She already suspected where this story was headed.

"I didn't think so. The police didn't agree." Patrick shrugged. "Things got worse. A couple of sites were vandalized. I started losing bids I was certain were mine."

Jane, silent until now beside Rachel, gasped. Her fingers fluttered a moment on the counter top before she clasped her hands together. "You found out who's been messing with you?" she asked.

Rachel thought Jane's voice sounded odd, but dismissed it when Patrick stood abruptly. "I wish!" He stalked across the kitchen, picked up a spoon and stirred a pot of spaghetti sauce Rachel had smelled all the way upstairs when she'd awakened earlier. He set the utensil down again before turning to look at her. "The police haven't been able to give my problems much attention because they're bogged down trying to find a serial killer who's been preying on young women in Denver for months."

"You're talking about the Angel Killer, right?" she said. "I saw a newscast about the coed who went missing last week. They think she's his fourth—" she stopped when she saw his expression. She didn't have to finish the news anchor's speculation about the missing woman being one of the victims.

"Yes." Patrick nodded. "We're talking about the Angel Killer."

Jane shifted on her stool. "What does this have to do with our sites?"

He didn't answer her for a long moment, but then he leaned on the kitchen counter by the stove and crossed his arms like he was putting up a wall between the question and the answer. "It's been suggested our saboteur might be the same person who's kidnapping these women."

"What?" Rachel stared at him.

"You're joking," Jane exclaimed at the same time.

He pushed away from the counter. "I wish I was," he said, returning to the island to sit down. He ran his fingers through his thick, dark hair. "They not only think they're one and the same, but they believe I know him."

"That's insane." Jane's forehead furrowed. "Why would they think that?"

He glanced at Rachel, and then answered Jane. "They identified some of the clothes left by the saboteur at Southgate on Monday. They belonged to the missing girl. And, thanks to the way the clothing was displayed, they think he was sending me a message."

"Oh, my god. How awful!" Nausea churned in Rachel's stomach. *And she thought she had trouble.* "What kind of message?"

He snorted with disgust. "I haven't a clue. I was bombarded with questions by Jack and the task force all afternoon, trying to figure out the connection."

Jane, her face pale, asked the question Rachel didn't know how to ask. "T-They don't think you had anything to do with the kidnappings, do they?"

He flashed a crooked smile at his office manager. "Thanks for the vote of confidence, Jane."

"I didn't mean to imply, I'm not saying you—" she stammered to a stop. "Patrick, that's not what I meant."

"I'm in the clear." His laughter lightened the doom-and-gloom feeling permeating the room. "I have at least ten ironclad alibis for the last kidnapping. I was at Jack's bachelor party with all of his cop friends. In fact, I have alibis for all of the kidnappings, even the first one back in November when I was snowed in at the family cabin. Remember, it took them two days to clear the roads so I could get out? "

Jane nodded, and then she suddenly smiled. "Only you could turn a bachelor party into a rock solid alibi, Patrick." Her laugh boomed in Rachel's ear, ratcheting up her headache. "Getting liquored up and taking lap dances until four in the morning is not usually cause for celebration."

"Well, I can't say it was much cause for celebration when I had to sober up and drive to Cheyenne either. Thankfully, I'd switched to soda around midnight when we started playing poker. Mona Johannes still took me for a hundred bucks. I swear that woman cheats."

"Patrick Thorne!" Jane sounded scandalized. "You invited a woman to Jack's bachelor party? What did you do, play strip poker?"

His smile looked so naughty and sexy Rachel's heart went all aflutter. "Mona is Jack's partner, Jane," he said. "She's one of the guys. *She* arranged for the stripper. And if I wanted to play strip poker it wouldn't be with a bunch of cops."

Jane chuckled. "Still—"

"I'm just glad I was with Jack and his brothers in blue last Thursday," he said, sobering, "or my butt would still be sitting in an interrogation room. My alibi also doesn't change the fact a young woman's been kidnapped and she's somehow connected to me."

Rachel's air caught in her throat when he looked directly into her eyes. "Which brings us back to our problem," he said. "We're going to add another layer or two to your protection just in case Bishop isn't the only danger."

She frowned. "You think your saboteur will come after me and Amanda?"

He shook his head. "We're just covering our bases."

She'd conceded so much to Jack and Patrick already. She'd sworn not to let another man gain control over her. Today, she had *two* of them managing her life. But what could she do until she was certain Greg wasn't a threat any longer? Or worse, she wasn't running with Amanda into a more untenable situation without any support? "Just tell me what you want to do."

He leaned back on his stool. "You can't stay here alone. For the next day or two, you won't be out of my sight. Which means you and Amanda will have to come to work with me.

"Jane," he said to his office manager, "I need you in the office, but I'd like to bring Suze to Southgate with us, too. Jack and I believe everyone will be safe enough inside the site trailer, but we don't want Amanda getting bored."

What about me? Rachel wanted to ask. What was she going to do for two or three days confined to a small construction trailer with a four and five-year-old? She'd gotten used to spending her days outdoors or working in Katy's greenhouses. They might as well put her in a jail cell.

"And, until the department can shake an officer loose or they arrest your ex," Patrick said to Rachel, "I'll be sleeping here."

That caught her attention!

When she began to argue with him—she couldn't have this man in the same house with her and her misbehaving hormones—he put up his hand to halt the words. "This is not negotiable. I'm here for the duration. We'd move you to my house if I had a security system installed, but the system in this house is already in place and Jack's hoping to wind this up and get Bishop off the streets before we have to look at other long-term options."

She couldn't get the "I'll be sleeping here" part of his plan out of her head. Just sitting in the kitchen with Patrick was making her pulse do the happy tap dance. The thought of him sleeping anywhere in the house made her crazy. Not that she'd been sleeping in months. Still—

He looked at Jane. "Call Candy and Gus Sanderson first thing in the morning and tell them Joe will be picking up Buck tomorrow afternoon around four o'clock. He can't get down to Colorado Springs until after school gets out. Thankfully, it's an early release day."

"Wait a minute." Things were moving way too fast for Rachel's scattered thoughts to process. She'd met Patrick's foster brother, the high school counselor at breakfast on Sunday but— "Buck? Who's Buck?"

Jane grinned. "Buckwheat. Evelyn and Ross's English mastiff. He's the most adorable thing you'll ever meet."

Patrick nodded. "He's got a great rapport with kids and will be Amanda's shadow. No one will mess with her when he's around."

She didn't want any more men around—she was already surrounded by too much testosterone—but a dog wouldn't be so bad. Except for Amanda's Labrador puppy, Rachel had never owned a dog. Though Boomer was only a puppy, she'd felt safer with him on the isolated ranch where she and Greg had lived in California. He'd yipped at everything and everyone. She wished he hadn't wandered off and gotten savaged by the coyote. Amanda was inconsolable when she and her daddy found him barely a week before their lives fell apart.

"What else?" she asked.

"That's it."

"We're both shadowed every minute of every day." She couldn't quibble about the safety measures—she'd do just about anything to protect Amanda—but she didn't have to like the necessity.

"It's only until Jack rounds up Bishop, Rachel. Once your ex is behind bars, you can go back to weeding Mom's gardens or return to Dallas, whatever you want. The point is you'll both be safe."

Patrick's conciliatory smile softened her objections. It was the way he'd said her name, though, that melted her insides. "Okay. I guess we can make this work that long."

For the next half hour, they discussed the specifics of how they'd implement the new security precautions. With Patrick sleeping on the couch in his parents' living room, they'd all have breakfast together. When Jane arrived with her granddaughter, Rachel, Amanda, Suze, and Patrick would drive to the Southgate site where he was spending most of his time this week. After Joe brought the dog home tomorrow, he'd also accompany them wherever they went. Jack would have a police car stop at the site periodically to check on them.

As Rachel listened to Patrick talk, she suspected these procedures were going to put everyone out, but if they could work around them, she'd just have to find a way to grin and bear it too. It wasn't like she felt up to doing much with her altitude sickness and concussion, and it *would* get her away from the house. Something she hadn't realized she'd been missing until yesterday. If sitting in a hospital bed felt like an outing, she'd been cooped up too long!

Rachel was just thinking about going upstairs to wake the girls for dinner when the doorbell rang. Patrick answered the door, coming back barely a minute later with a mid-sized parcel in his hand.

"Were you expecting a package?" he asked Rachel with a frown.

She smiled, thinking about her conversation with Katy when she checked in with her nightly phone call. After she mentioned her lack of sleep, Katy offered to send her some romance novels Rachel had left unread at the nursery office for those times she'd actually sit down and take a break. Considering how often she'd thought of Patrick's half naked body in the moonlight since she'd first spotted him, she'd almost begged Katy to send an entire library. After Greg, she shouldn't still crave what those books described, yet she did. "Yes. Katy said she was sending a couple of things."

When he handed her the box, she was surprised it wasn't particularly heavy. Not as heavy as it would be with four or five hardback novels. She hesitated. Maybe it wasn't from Katy. She had to have sent it overnight and this didn't look right. In fact, it didn't have a return address. "Did you have to sign for this?" she asked Patrick.

He frowned. "No. Why? Is something wrong?"

"No." She chastised herself for her disquiet. It was a package, for crying out loud. It was probably from Katy and she just forgot to add the return address. Maybe she only sent a few of the paperbacks. The box certainly hadn't come from her mother's estranged family in Dallas. She hadn't bothered to tell them where she was going because they were still upset and fighting what her great-aunt Amanda had done with her estate when she died three months ago. Her lawyers were talking to their lawyers and that's the way it would continue until the case was settled.

The only other person from her old life that knew she was in Denver was Greg...and, that's where these prickles of anxiety were born. He hadn't exactly been in a gift-giving mood yesterday when Patrick chased him off the property.

"Rachel?" Patrick said, his hand holding out scissors to cut through the tape sealing the contents, his gaze searching her face. "Are you sure nothing's wrong?"

"No. I'm good," she replied with a tight smile. She took the scissors from Patrick's hand and slit the tape. Setting the shears down, she gathered the courage to lift the flaps and expose what was inside. For a moment the contents didn't register. Then, her heart hiccupped. Stopped.

From her seat across the kitchen island, Jane peered into the box. "Oh! That's pretty," she said, smiling, unaware Rachel's stomach had begun to roil like a mass of angry rattlesnakes.

"Rachel?"

Patrick's voice seemed to come from far away, and she was incapable of responding. Her fingers trembling, unable to stop herself, she lifted the gorgeous blue silk dress from the box by the shoulders. Her knees grew weak as she remembered where she'd last seen the designer dress. It was the one she'd been wearing the night Greg raped her. The night he'd beaten her senseless.

In the next moment, she spotted the leather horsewhip resting in the bottom of the box where it had been hidden from view beneath the dress. There were rust-colored stains streaked across the top eight inches of the otherwise pristine buff leather that encased the whip.

Blood. Her blood.

The shaking in her hands raced up her arms. She fought to push down the bile climbing her throat. Losing the battle, she dropped the silk dress into a pile on the floor, turned and raced out of the kitchen down the hall to the bathroom. She barely made it. Her knees hit the cold, porcelain tile seconds before she emptied the contents of her stomach into the toilet.

Immobilized by Rachel's sudden disappearance from the kitchen, Patrick stared at the empty doorway she'd run through. "What...?"

The sounds of vomiting coming from down the hall kicked his brain into high gear. Why hadn't he asked for the details of Rachel's "troubles"? Oh, yeah, he'd become a heartless ass and hadn't wanted to know. But, looking down at the horsewhip curled innocently at the bottom of the delivery box, remembering the brutal look in Greg Bishop's icy blue eyes, he did know. He cursed.

Stalking across the kitchen after Rachel, he looked over his shoulder at Jane. "Jane, don't touch anything," he said. "Call the precinct. Tell them to get a car here. Now!"

Leaving his office manager to it, Patrick raced down the hallway toward the bathroom where he could still hear Rachel alternately vomiting and groaning. The sight that met his eyes when he stopped in the doorway made him curse.

Rachel knelt on the floor with both hands braced on the toilet seat and retched into the bowl. She swayed despite her efforts to hold position.

Patrick didn't think before he took action. Kneeling at her back, he did what his mother always did when he was sick as a kid and feeling weak with the flu. He placed his right hand across Rachel's clammy forehead to support her head, his left to the back of her T-shirt where he rubbed upward from the base of her spine to her neck.

At his first touch, she shied away with a startled cry, but another spasm ripped at her stomach and distracted her from what he was doing. She began to settle as he held her in place and continued to rub her back. Up. Down. Up. Down. She leaned into the third upward stroke.

When her T-shirt rode up with her position change, exposing a strip of skin above the waistband of her jeans, he remembered how much better his mother's warm hand felt on his naked back. He dipped his hand under the material to Rachel's silky skin before he realized his mistake.

For a moment, he hesitated, aware of the dangerous territory he'd promised himself he wouldn't breach. He'd acknowledged only this morning that his attraction to Rachel was unreasonable. He was supposed to turn her and little Amanda over to Jack soon, let a police officer take care of them so he could return to his side of the hedge. So he could put his libido back into the deep freeze.

That intent was fading under the heat of her skin burning into his palm, his protective instincts kicking in and pushing everything else aside. Despite the sour smell of vomit that permeated the bathroom, the delicate scent of lilacs rose from Rachel slim curves and curled around his senses to remind him she was a woman. A woman in trouble. His calloused hand, unbearably sensitive on the small of her back above her form-fitting jeans, felt both intrusive and possessive.

What he was doing was helping her though. She stopped vomiting, her stomach emptied, although a dry heave wracked her. Once. Twice. She swayed, clearly weakened.

You're already committed to helping her. You can't stop.

His jaw tight, he slowly inched his fingers up her spine. Two inches. His massage stopped when Rachel's silky smooth skin gave way to a raised line of roughness. Another fraction upward felt smooth. Beyond that, he bumped over another, thicker line. Then another. A sick feeling slammed into his gut when he realized what lay beneath his hand.

Falling back on his heels, he yanked the T-shirt up so he could look at Rachel's back above her jeans. Every place he'd touched rough skin was a raised, puckered scar. There were at least ten of them, some running horizontally across her back, some crisscrossed, some wrapped around her waist and hip to what he suspected were more scars on her belly. They were pink, shiny, not the white color of old scars.

Anger swelled, his suspicions confirmed. Bishop might not have knocked Rachel down the other day, but it looked like she'd been beaten fairly recently. With the horsewhip that sat in the box on the kitchen counter? "I should have killed him when I had the chance," he muttered, barely able to speak around his rage at what her ex had done to her.

Rachel must have heard the anger in his low voice or felt his fingers tighten on her T-shirt because she looked over her shoulder, cried out, and yanked her shirt down. "Don't!" she sputtered, trying to scoot away.

Patrick looked into her wild eyes and cursed his stupidity, but he refused to let her go. He *couldn't*. He lowered the toilet seat and flushed it, gathered her into his arms, stood up and sat back down on the closed lid with her on his lap. "Shh, Rach," he said, pushing his voice into a reassuring calm he did not feel.

With her nestled close, he could feel tremors tear at her slim frame testifying to the fragility of her composure. She was so close to completely unraveling, it was all he could do not to set her down, find Bishop, and rip his head off. Trying to keep his voice low and non-threatening almost took more control than he had. "You're safe, honey. I won't let him hurt you. He can't hurt you again. It's okay."

Rachel looked up at him with stricken, brown eyes. "I-I'm sorry! I can't—oh, dear God, he—" She burst into tears.

A hard knot developed in Patrick's chest right under the spot where her tears soaked his work shirt. He held her closer with each shudder, with each sob, although he told himself he should pull away. He wanted to regain his distance, but his ability to do that crumbled the moment he touched Rachel in his parents' back yard yesterday and stood toe-to-toe with her ex-husband. *Had it only been yesterday?* He hadn't been able to walk away then. He wasn't walking away from her now.

"Rachel," he whispered into her hair, his hand tucked protectively around the back of her neck. "Stop, honey. It'll be okay."

All he had to do was figure out how.

When Rachel woke up in the dark bedroom that she'd been using since her arrival in Denver, she peered at the digital clock sitting on the dresser.

Two o'clock. She'd only meant to sleep until midnight, just long enough to gather her strength before she ran again.

This time, she had to do it alone. Katy could no longer help her. Evelyn and Ross Thorne meant well when they'd offered her a place to hide, but she was no longer hidden. She couldn't jeopardize them or their family any longer. She couldn't bear the thought of Greg taking out his anger on Patrick. It was as unbearable as thinking about her ex-husband getting his hands on Amanda.

She had to break ties with everything and everyone she knew to keep her daughter safe. She couldn't allow anyone to talk her out of bolting like the frightened rabbit she was or she didn't stand a chance of escaping Greg before he followed up on the threat he'd made with the contents of the box delivered before dinner. The police officers that showed up in response to Jane's phone call had removed the box and contents from the house, taking it with them to the station so they could contact the delivery service and the driver in the hope of tracking it back to Greg.

The package removal didn't eradicate the threat from Rachel's mind.

Message received. Loud and clear.

Put on the clothing I picked for you when I dressed you to suit my desires. Relinquish control of yourself and don the persona that serves my desires, or suffer the consequences. "'Til death, darlin'. You'd better get it because, next time, it'll be your precious brat. And, next time...I...won't...stop."

Looking down at the little girl she loved more than life itself, snuggled into her side, Rachel watched her sleep. Amanda's eyelids twitched in a dream. Her face twisted with distress. She whimpered, as she'd often done in the six months since they fled San Francisco and began sleeping together. Rachel swept baby-fine hair off Amanda's face, her fingers tracing lightly over her tender skin from temple to jaw. Over and over. Until Amanda settled into a deeper sleep again with a long sigh.

Rachel continued the caress, as much to soothe her child as herself. She hated feeling so helpless. Amanda used to sleep like the dead, hardly moving, never waking once she curled up in her new, big girl's bed with puppies painted all over the headboard. She'd been a bright-eyed, loving four-year-old whose worst nightmare was a scraped knee.

Until the night Rachel limped out of her bedroom six months ago.

Her little girl's peaceful dreams had been replaced by nightmares. Nightmares she couldn't share with her mama since she'd stopped talking. There was little doubt she'd heard everything her father said and did that night. Rachel wished she knew whether Greg said something to Amanda before leaving them alone in the house in a vain attempt to escape the FBI warrant. She'd never know until the doctors could help Amanda work through her trauma.

They'd barely started before Greg's release from jail. Emotional danger had been replaced with physical danger, and she didn't have a clue how to protect her child from either. Her heart skipped at the thought of what Greg might do to his daughter if Rachel didn't give in to his threats.

She pushed the worries to the back of her mind before they could take hold, and inhaled deeply, imprinting Amanda's scent on her senses, a mix of little girl, the lilac talcum powder she shared with her mother after each bath, and a hint of something new but somehow reassuring.

It was a scent she knew. *Patrick.* Amanda smelled like Patrick.

He'd given the four-year-old one of his T-shirts to sleep in when they'd had a sleepover while Rachel was in the hospital. She didn't realize the child had dragged the shirt home with her until after Amanda took her bath. The T-shirt was over her head and swamping her little body with material before Rachel saw it and her daughter refused to take it off, her head shaking stubbornly when her mama tried to reason with her.

With the trauma of the past twenty-four hours, Rachel decided it wasn't worth fighting over. It wasn't surprising Amanda found comfort in Patrick's scent. Her mama certainly did.

Not that Rachel needed the illusion of comfort now. That's all it was. Illusion. What she needed was strength. Strength to pack the rental car, to hit the road again. Strength to go it alone. She'd become too dependent living with Katy. She'd not been confident enough to walk away from the support Katy and her friends, Evelyn and Ross, had offered her. She'd been too scared to strike out on her own last week. Tonight, she had no choice.

Another glance at the dresser and the red numbers of the clock blurred. Sharp pain traveled from the back of her head in both directions. She was tempted to close her eyes again, give in to the sweet oblivion of sleep, but it would only delay the inevitable. And, as her father used to tell her every time she dug in her heels about something she didn't want to do, it was time to make a decision. *Fish or cut bait, little chickadee. You can't do both.*

With a sigh, she erased her father's unwelcome voice from her mind and gingerly eased off the bed. There were pain pills that would clear her head in her purse downstairs, but putting the city lights of Denver in her rearview mirror was all she could concentrate on. She'd take some pills after they put a couple hundred miles behind them. Maybe.

Assured Amanda was sleeping peacefully Rachel eased the curtains open a few inches to allow moonlight into the bedroom. Picking up the over-sized backpack she'd found in the closet earlier, she began transferring items from their suitcases into the bag. An extra set of clothes for both of them. Socks and underwear. Toothbrushes.

Amanda would miss her doll, but Rachel was not sneaking next door to Patrick's house to get it. It was one reminder of her ex-husband she wouldn't be sorry to see gone forever. She'd buy another one for Amanda. Although the way she clutched Suze's doll in her sleep, maybe that wouldn't be necessary. Their temporary trade could just become permanent. Suze would be happy to keep Becca.

Culling their meager belongings proved difficult because she'd arrived in Denver with only the bare necessities and items she couldn't live without...like her mother's monogrammed silver mirror, brush and comb set. But, Patrick had keyed in the security panel before they'd gone upstairs to bed so she couldn't just throw their suitcases out of one of the bedroom windows without tripping the alarm. A backpack made more sense, especially when she'd also be carrying a sleeping child.

She'd slept in a cotton tee and loose-fitting shorts. So, once she'd tied tennis shoes on her bare feet, she settled the backpack on her back and picked up Amanda in her arms, her fluffy blanket tucked around her. Rachel's head swam, but she waited until the dizziness passed, then left the bedroom. She made her way down the stairs sidestepping the two that squeaked, not stopping until she reached the archway on the right that led into the living room. She peered into the room at the dark lump on the couch that delineated Patrick's body where he slept. As he'd promised he would.

It was that promise, more than exhaustion, that had allowed her to fall asleep earlier. For the first time in years she'd felt able to relinquish her anxiety, if only for a few hours to rest up. Once she hit the road, it might be days before she'd feel safe enough to stop and sleep.

Staring at Patrick's unmoving form, she fought her impulse to go to him and ask him to hold her like he had in the bathroom after Greg's package was delivered. She'd never felt as safe, as secure, as she had in those minutes she'd cried in his arms. Listening to his deep voice promise her that everything would be all right, she'd desperately wanted to believe him. She'd soaked up his words and the feeling of security like she was a parched prairie flower and he was the long-awaited rain.

She should be appalled at how easily he'd walked past defenses she'd bolstered for years. She hardly knew the man!

The reminder she'd met Patrick less than forty-eight hours ago kicked her self-protective instincts into high gear and forced her to turn her back to the living room. Walking across the entry, she silently passed through the swinging door into the unlit kitchen. Just inside, she paused to pick out the outlines of the central island and bar stools that bisected the large room between her and the breakfast alcove on the other side. A sliver of moonlight lit the table through the drawn curtains revealing her purse right where she remembered leaving it.

Afraid the lights would hurt her eyes and make her headache worse, not to mention awaken Patrick in the other room, she didn't bother to turn them on. She grabbed her purse off the table and walked toward the kitchen door, where she paused to listen to the Victorian house creak and groan, settling sounds she'd grown used to the past few days. Nothing stirred.

Still, her hand didn't reach for the glowing security keypad. Once she punched in the sequence of numbers Patrick taught her to turn off the system, once she walked out the door, she would be vulnerable. But, more than that, she'd be alone again.

She was so tired of being alone! *Which is how you got into the current mess you're in, little chickadee.*

Her father's voice in her head hurt her heart worse than anything Greg ever did to her. She would have thought ten years would have allowed the painful memories to fade. They'd only gained intensity over time. She'd been thinking about her dad a lot lately. She longed to hear his gruff voice tickling her ear as she laid her head on his strong chest. She still dreamed of feeling his arms close around her shoulders, squeezing until she laughingly protested.

She'd felt loved back then. Childhood memories. Why didn't she re-member the arguments they'd had when she was in high school? His angry, dismissive words when they'd argued that awful day her senior year when he walked out of her life forever?

Why are you standing here wasting time wandering down memory lane when you need to get out of Dodge?

The thought forced her to key in the numbers with trembling fingers. The beep that told her the security system had disengaged sounded too loud in the nighttime quiet. Praying the sound hadn't reached the living room, she opened the door, turned the lock on the knob to keep Patrick safe, and hurried out into the night with Amanda.

11

Patrick woke to the beep from the kitchen alarm, his Glock already grasped in his right hand. His adrenaline pumped him to full alert. He was off the couch like a shot and halfway across the entry before he heard the snick of the door closing. Had someone come in, or gone out?

His eyes already adjusted to the darkness, he eased to the kitchen entrance. Frowning at the closed swinging door, he pushed it open just enough to peek his head around it, low and tight. He scanned the room. No one. A moment later, a bulky shadow backlit by moonlight passed across the kitchen window heading toward the back of the house.

Grateful he'd fallen asleep in his jeans and boots, he didn't hesitate to cross the room to the door. Looking down on the knob locked from the inside, he cursed. Burglars and felonious exes didn't lock up behind themselves. And—he sniffed the air—they didn't smell like lilacs. Rachel had bolted. Jack warned him she might. Why hadn't he listened?

Gun in hand, he left the house on Rachel's heels, keyed in the security system so no one could sneak in while he went after her. It was considerably brighter outside with the full moon overhead so he traversed the length of the side yard toward the back of the property quickly. He stuck to the shadows until he entered the dark maw between his garage and his mom's hulking greenhouse behind which he knew Rachel had hidden her rental car.

Thanks to the recent heat wave in Denver, a couple of upper windows had been left open to vent the greenhouse so a myriad of luscious scents drifted on the night air from the plants his mom cultivated to create the floral arrangements she donated to local hospitals and senior centers. But Patrick still caught another whiff of lilacs and knew Rachel—and Amanda, since he knew Rachel would never leave without her—had passed through here.

He hoped he hadn't missed them completely, that Rachel hadn't already driven off where he couldn't find her. He'd never forgive himself if she or Amanda were hurt!

Rounding the corner of the greenhouse he came to a dead stop. His gun hand fell to rest at his side. *He'd found them.* Amanda was sound asleep in her mother's embrace. Rachel stood, fully exposed in the moonlight, in front of her rental car.

Just before he lambasted her for her foolishness, he registered the tarp tossed to the ground, the open hood. Pieces of the engine scattered all over the fenders and grass. The passenger side mirror partially ripped off. Rachel didn't move as she stared at a screwdriver sticking through the front of the radiator. A piece of hose, sliced more than once, jammed into the hole usually covered by a radiator cap.

Someone had violently trashed her only means of escape. *Bishop!*

Thousands of needles of awareness raised the tiny hairs on the back of Patrick's neck. Was Rachel's ex still in the shadows watching her?

Patrick lifted his gun hand, scanned the area. There! A large silhouette of a man darted to the right through a break in the natural wall of evergreen trees his mother had planted along the alley. Patrick raced to the gutted car to get between Rachel and the danger.

Rachel must have heard the noise of the retreating figure because she gasped, pivoted on her heel, and ran in the opposite direction, straight into Patrick's arms.

Thankfully, she hit him sidewise or he'd have crushed Amanda between them. Rachel's shoulder still hit his torso hard enough to knock the air out of him. "Oomph!"

Squealing, she tried to escape his arms as they came around her and Amanda. He didn't have time for this. "Rachel!" he said tersely. "It's me."

She froze long enough, he was able to wrap his free hand in one of her backpack straps and pull her out of the swath of moonlight toward the protective gloom between the buildings. When they were deep enough in the shadows, he whispered into her ear. "I'm going to let you go," he said. "When I do, drop to the ground next to the garage and stay put until I come back for you."

"B-b—"

"There's someone there. I have to go," he said, stroking the back of his knuckles over her cheek.

She was gasping for air like a beached bass and, reminded of her altitude sickness, he gently eased her to the ground. "Just be quiet...and breathe."

"Greg—"

The terror in her voice tore at his insides. "He won't hurt you. I won't let him. Remember?"

He watched for her nod of acceptance. Then, seeing Amanda's big brown eyes open and fixed on him, he smiled at her. "Take care of mommy. I'll be right back," he said to reassure her. Then, for reasons he didn't want to analyze, he leaned down to kiss Rachel's trembling lips.

Before he could think about deepening the gentle caress, he straightened and raced back the way they'd come. He'd probably missed his chance to capture Bishop while he secured Rachel and Amanda but maybe he'd catch a lucky break.

In full stalking mode, Patrick skirted the moonlight surrounding Rachel's sabotaged car and pushed his way into a gap between two evergreens several yards north of where he'd seen the figure go through. It was a small space, branches and pine needles tore at his torso, making him regret his impulse to take off his shirt before he dozed off, but he was hoping to retain an element of surprise when he came out into the alley in a different spot.

Stepping into the alley, he spotted his prey less than ten feet away, fumbling around on the ground next to a dark sedan, like he was looking for lost car keys. He was in luck tonight!

Patrick raised his weapon and sighted in on the man's broad back. "Freeze!" he ordered. "Hold it right there."

The man stiffened.

With Rachel's ex-husband in his sights, Patrick could feel his anger rise. He wanted to beat the man senseless, make him feel the agony he'd forced Rachel to endure. "Stand up and turn around, Bishop. Slowly!"

"I'm not—"

"Do it or I'll shoot your cowardly carcass right there."

The figure rose and turned slowly until his face was clearly illuminated in the moonlight. "I'm not Greg Bishop," he said, raising his hands in surrender.

Patrick looked at the stranger, for the first time wondering if he'd captured his saboteur. If Jack and the task force team were right, though, he knew the Angel Killer. He'd never seen this man before. His fingers tightened around his gun grip. "Who are you? And what are you doing, sneaking around in the bushes?"

"Larson Cook." His right hand dropped to the inside of his charcoal-colored jacket.

"Don't even think about it." Patrick motioned with his Glock. "Get that hand up where I can see it."

The man sighed. "I'm private security," he said. "My I.D. is in my wallet."

Private security? Patrick frowned. "If this is a trick, I'll shoot you where you stand."

"Understood." Slowly reaching inside the jacket, he withdrew a brown leather wallet and tossed it to the ground at Patrick's feet.

His gun, and gaze, fixed on the man Patrick squatted and picked up the wallet. When he flipped it open, he skimmed the man's credentials. Larson M. Cook. Consultant. NIC Security. Concealed carry license number. Patrick's gaze sharpened on the man. "You have a gun on you?"

Cook nodded. "Right jacket pocket."

"You're a lefty?

Another hesitant nod.

Patrick wasn't proceeding until Cook was disarmed. "With your right hand, take the gun out of your jacket and toss it to the ground."

A frustrated snort greeted his demand. "This is ridiculous, Thorne," he said. "We're both on the same side."

He knew Patrick's name. "Explain."

"You're trying to protect the James woman and her child." Cook lowered his arms to his side like he wasn't concerned he could be shot at any moment. "So am I."

Rachel leaned against the garage wall where Patrick had deposited her and did as he'd instructed. She breathed. She murmured quiet reassurances into Amanda's long blond curls. She prayed.

Patrick had gone after Greg. She hoped he caught him. Then, this horror would be over and she could find some semblance of normalcy again. But, did she really want Patrick to confront Greg? She knew what her ex-husband was capable of, the lengths he'd go to get her and Amanda back. She hadn't thought he was capable of killing to get what he wanted...despite his brutal attack on her their last night together. Yet he'd been sitting in a Federal prison for the past six months, his anger building, and the first thing he did was attack Simon? If Patrick's brother was correct and Simon didn't come out of his coma, Greg had already crossed that line to murder.

The memory of her rental car sitting only yards away, torn to shreds, gave her worries strength. Anything, anyone that stood in Greg's way was ripped apart. She couldn't bear it if that *anyone* was Patrick.

Where was he? He'd been gone, what, five minutes? Ten? It was difficult to tell without pulling her cell phone out of her pocket and she didn't want to illuminate their position.

Had Patrick found Greg? Had they struggled? Was Patrick injured? She'd seen the gun in his hand, felt certain he knew how to use it by the comfortable way he held it, but Greg could have knocked him out. Was her ex-husband sneaking back to drag her and Amanda off to their doom?

Screw this! She couldn't just sit here like a lamb left for slaughter. If nothing else, she needed to get Amanda back to the protection of the house.

Her decision made, she scrambled awkwardly to her feet with her little girl cradled in her arms. *Too late!*

Shuffling noises, footsteps made her peer at the shifting shadows to her right, the direction Patrick had gone. Was it him? Or was someone else approaching? She pulled Amanda closer until the little girl squirmed in protest. Rachel loosened her grip, her heart pounding too loud in her ears.

The silhouette of a man broke out of the darker shadows. Tall, like Patrick. But bigger, wider. The gait was all wrong. She quickly catalogued his features. Rugged face. Crooked nose, probably broken. Brown hair. A stranger. The man Greg hired to track her?

She looked into his eyes. They were cool, assessing, and fixed on her and Amanda. *Run!*

Before she could make her limbs function, another silhouette walked into view behind the stranger. She called a warning. "Patrick! Don't—"

"I've got this, Rachel," he said. Only then did she see Patrick's gun pointed at the stranger's back. "Stop," he ordered.

Rachel watched the man stop six, seven feet away, thankfully out of reach.

"Rachel," Patrick said. "Take Amanda back to the house. When you get to the kitchen door, disengage the security system. It's been reset."

She looked at the stranger, hesitant to turn her back on him.

Patrick must have read her mind. "We'll wait. Go. Get Amanda inside."

Turning on her heel, she hurried toward the house. When she arrived at the kitchen door, she punched in the security code, entered the house, and turned on the overhead lights. She could hear Patrick and the stranger walk across the wooden porch outside, behind her, and rushed in the other direction. She didn't stop until she reached the swinging door on the other side of the kitchen.

When she saw the two men enter the room, she searched Patrick's unyielding expression. He looked...upset.

His words belied that impression. "Go tuck Amanda into my bed on the couch," he said. He smiled at her daughter. "You can warm it up for me. That okay with you?"

Amanda nodded.

His smile disappeared when he looked again at Rachel. "After you get her settled, come back. We have to talk."

Tucking Amanda into Patrick's makeshift bed, Rachel realized why he hadn't suggested taking Amanda back up to her bedroom. Snuggling into his pillow, Amanda promptly sighed and closed her eyes. Rachel would have given anything to join her daughter, to close out the world and the two men who waited for her in the kitchen. She suddenly didn't want to confront Patrick. Or the stranger.

When Rachel walked back into the brightly lit kitchen, Patrick could barely restrain himself from pulling her into his arms and chewing her out for trying to run out on him. He frowned. No, not *him*. The situation. She'd snuck out without any thought to the dangers. If the man sitting in a chair across the room had been Bishop, she and Amanda might be—

He cut off the thought and took a step toward her. "Give me the backpack," he said, holding out his hand.

She hesitated, but then shrugged it off and handed it over.

He registered that the pack was his—an older one he'd tucked into his bedroom closet when he enlisted in the army after high school—before he tossed it onto the counter. Out of Rachel's reach. "Sit down," he ordered.

She stiffened. "I'll stand," she said, glaring back at him.

"Suit yourself." He was glad the distress in her angel-soft brown eyes was eradicated by her anger with his high-handed manner, but he was still pissed at her for taking such a stupid chance, jeopardizing her and Amanda's safety. He wanted to lock them up. Tie Rachel to the bed upstairs. Make sure she stayed there if it meant making love to her over and o—

Stop right there, Thorne. You're not jumping that fence.

He'd been sucked in too deep already. The moment the cops had Bishop behind bars, he had to extricate himself, walk away. He couldn't do that if he took Rachel James to bed. The way his heart hurt when he saw the way her arms covered her waist, where her scars were still healing, he knew it might already be too late.

Patrick glanced at Cook, watching them from across the room, a knowing look in his eyes. The man saw too much. Patrick turned his irritation to the situation at hand. He pulled the security specialist's wallet out of his pocket and handed it to Rachel without looking at her. He knew when she opened it because she drew in a sharp gasp.

"Okay, Cook," he said, pulling the man's gun from his waistband at the base of his spine where he'd tucked it after unloading it. He set it on the counter, leaving the bullets he'd ejected in his jeans pocket. "Tell us who you are and don't stop until you get to the part about what you're doing here."

The man reiterated what was laid out on his I.D. card. Patrick believed he was who he said he was, but he intended to have Jack run a background check on him all the same. "And you were skulking around the bushes why?"

"I already told you, Thorne. I was hired to protect the woman and child."

"Me and Amanda," Rachel said, dropping into a chair at the center island, the man's wallet dangling from her fingertips.

He nodded. "Yes."

"So," she scowled, "you're saying you're not the one who trashed my car."

"No! I mean, yes. I'm telling you I'm not the one who trashed your car." Cook shook his head. "I discovered it in that condition just before you showed up."

"You just found it." Patrick's disbelief was clear.

"Yes. I was checking the perimeter of the property when I found the car, just before the woman—"

"For God's sake, 'the woman' has a name," Rachel spat out. "Stop talking about me like I'm not sitting right here."

Hiding his smile at her display of spunk, Patrick fixed on one specific detail of Cook's explanation. "How long before? Did you see anyone else?"

"No."

"You must have heard something, Cook. You can't cause that kind of damage in complete silence."

"You didn't hear anything either," he pointed out.

A valid point. However, Patrick noticed the security man was avoiding eye contact. "What aren't you telling us?"

Cook took his time responding, evidently trying to determine how much he would reveal. Then, he sighed. "I came on duty and relieved the day guard."

"Day guard?" Rachel interrupted. "You mean you've been watching me day and night? That's, that's—"

When she looked up at Patrick and shook her head, shock in her eyes, he put a reassuring hand on her arm. He glared at the security consultant. "Finish your story."

"The first thing I did when I came on duty was check the perimeter. I didn't see anything then." The man frowned. "I didn't notice the tarp over the car had been messed with until half an hour ago. When I took the tarp off, I saw the condition of the car. That was minutes before the wo—"

He glanced at Rachel before he finished. "Then Ms. James showed up and you appeared."

"You took off the tarp."

"Yeah," he said. "I screwed up not catching it earlier, but I can tell you that car wasn't trashed tonight. It couldn't have been done recently. As you said, one of us would have heard it. But our detail didn't start until this morning, when," he nodded at Rachel, "Ms. James was released from the hospital."

"So you think the damage was caused last night?"

"That's my thought." He nodded. "No one around to hear. And the perp took the trouble to cover it back up with the tarp. He didn't want it to be found...unless someone tried to use it."

"Greg." Rachel's voice was low, resigned.

Cook looked at her. "I'm sorry I scared you, Ms. James."

For some reason, Patrick didn't like the way the man was looking at her, like it really mattered to him that she accept his apology. "Sorry doesn't cut it, Cook." He stepped into the man's line of sight. "If everything you say is true, and don't think I'm not having the police check you out, it doesn't explain what you're doing here in the first place. Who hired you to guard Rachel and Amanda?"

He hesitated, glancing at Rachel. "Dixon Grey."

Her gasp behind him made Patrick turn. "You know him?" he asked.

Rachel nodded. Her eyes filled, but the tears didn't fall. By the expression on her face, Patrick couldn't tell if the strong emotional response was caused by sadness or anger.

Her flat voice didn't give him a clue either. "Dixon Grey's my father." She rose stiffly from her chair and left the room without another word.

12

"We should talk about your father." Patrick looked over his coffee cup at Rachel as she walked back into the kitchen at the crack of dawn the next day. "Sooner, rather than later."

Glancing at the lightening sky reflected in the window beyond the breakfast nook, she walked to the coffee pot and poured herself a cup of coffee, bypassing her usual creamer and sugar. She took a fortifying sip of the strong, bitter brew without speaking and examined Patrick's freshly showered hair and clean work clothes, his broad, gloriously naked chest of hours earlier completely covered. The shirt he wore didn't affect her physical response to the man one iota, beyond her urge to take the offensive thing off.

She turned away from the impulse and went to the refrigerator to pour creamer into her coffee. She stirred in a teaspoon of sugar. She wasn't ready for this! She'd dreaded this moment since she'd walked away from Cook's announcement that her father had hired him to watch her. She'd been unable to close her eyes after she'd gathered up Amanda from Patrick's makeshift bed in the living room, taken her upstairs and tucked her into their bed, never waking her. She'd felt nothing for the longest time, just watched her little girl sleep.

Listening to the murmur of men's voices when Patrick escorted Cook to the door around three a.m., she'd heard the door close, the beep of the security system when it was secured. She was aware Patrick walked up the stairs to stand outside her unlocked bedroom door, called her name. All she could do was sit perched on the edge of the bed, stroking Amanda's hair, feeling dead inside.

Her shock didn't wear off until long after Patrick gave up and went away. Then the feelings, the emotions, the pain slashed through her. Ten years without a word from her father! Ten years she'd torn herself up wondering where he was, how it had all gone so wrong between them, that he could walk away without looking back. Ten years to convince herself she could live without a father who didn't love her.

"You okay?"

"No," she admitted before she could stop the revelation.

"You want to talk about it?"

"No." She wished for the dead feeling to return. It was preferable to the pain that had rushed in and lodged in her heart. She went to the breakfast table and sat down. "You have a right to some answers, though," she said, her gaze on Patrick.

"How long has it been since you saw him?"

Who is your father? Why didn't you tell us you had somewhere to run? When can I dump you on him so I can go back to hammering nails and be done with your murderous ex-husband? Those were the questions she'd expected. Not this quiet, thoughtful question, like he cared. "Ten years last month. April twenty-fourth."

Silence met her flat tone. Patrick took his assessing gaze off her face, reached across the table, picked up a piece of toast from a stack, and slathered it with his mom's homemade strawberry jam. He surprised her when he set it on a small plate in front of her and picked up another slice for himself. "I gather it wasn't a good break," he said conversationally.

She fingered her toast, smearing jam on her thumb. She licked it off, the sweet burst of fruit flavor on her tongue, reminding her she hadn't eaten much at dinner the previous night after throwing up everything. Suddenly starving, she didn't stop until she'd eaten two pieces of toast with jam, a section of juicy melon Patrick put in front of her, and two cups of coffee. It was more breakfast than she'd eaten in months, usually opting for coffee and a toaster pastry before running off to wrestle Kolthern Nurseries back into the black after Greg had nearly bankrupted Katy's livelihood.

"Feel better?" Patrick lounged back in his chair with his coffee.

Guilt washed over her. "I'm sorry I ran out on you last night. I-I—"

"You were in shock," he said, his gaze fixed on her.

She shook her head. "No, I meant when I left the house. I didn't think—"

"You didn't think I could protect you and Amanda."

"No! It wasn't like that. I just, I-I was scared," she said. "I didn't want to put you in any more danger. I couldn't bear it if you were hurt," she winced mentally at the revealing admission, and then added quickly, "or Jane or Suze or anyone."

Patrick leaned forward and put his hand over hers, effectively stopping her ramble. "It's my choice to keep you and Amanda safe until the police can assign someone or they put your ex in jail. I'm trained. I can take care of myself. But you can't run away every time you get scared. I can't protect you if I don't know where you are, what's going on. Last night could have ended a lot differently if I hadn't caught up with you or if it had been your ex-husband in the alley, instead of Cook."

Rachel swallowed. As much as she might want to put her troubles behind her, sitting in the darkness between the greenhouse and garage last night worrying about this man's safety, she'd realized she couldn't leave Denver until this was over. She was too worried Greg would take his rage out on Patrick before he came after her again. It was already too late to run and, despite her instincts telling her not to place her life in another man's hands, she did trust Patrick. "I'll stay put. For now."

"Good." His big hand gently squeezed hers.

His warmth and strength seeped into the sensitive skin over the back of her hand and she didn't want to break their connection, but becoming aware of other places she was becoming warm, she pulled away. Flustered, she licked a bit of sticky jam off her lower lip. She was surprised to see an answering heat flare in Patrick's eyes. She did it again without thinking. Same response.

She looked away and picked up her napkin to wipe her mouth clean. What was wrong with her? She might trust Patrick to keep her and Amanda safe, but she didn't want *that* kind of attention from him. She was never going to give a man that much control of her life again, no matter how sexy he was or how love-starved she—

"Rachel?"

The question in Patrick's voice made Rachel wonder what he might be reading in her expression. She lifted her chin. "I'm sorry. I was thinking about what I can do to help."

Patrick's head tilted as he studied her. "You could help by telling me about your dad, and why he's suddenly come out of nowhere and hired protection for you. I can't keep you safe if there are secrets between us."

Her heart sank. So much for her hope he'd forget about the first man to break her heart. "Okay," she said tightly. "You want to talk about Dad." She dropped her napkin over the toast crumbs on her plate, the words building behind the dam in her throat until they overflowed. "The last time I saw my father I was seventeen, in the senior year of my fourth high school, and he walked away from the motel room we were living in to chase after his next "Big Time" dream.

"My dad was, is still for all I know, a bull rider. A roper. He filled in occasionally as a rodeo clown one year. He dragged me and Mom through one rodeo circuit after another. Did that stop when Mom got sick and died when I was twelve?"

Standing abruptly, her chair scraped the blue-and-white tile floor. Unable to stop moving, she crossed the kitchen to pour herself another cup of coffee. "It didn't slow dear old dad," she said with a frown at the empty pot. "He spent every dime he made in prize money to travel to the next rodeo, pay for one more ride."

She stood, stiff, rushing to get it all out before her taut nerves could shatter. "I went to fifteen different schools in the five years after my mom died, if I went to school at all, and he just kept dragging me all over the country." By the time she paused, she was panting like she'd run a marathon.

"And when you were seventeen?"

The gentle question somehow eased the pain of the memory, pulled her far enough away from her anger so that she could respond. "When Dad wasn't riding or roping, he spent his spare time hanging with the cowboys and ranchers, his ear to the ground for every pie-in-the-sky scheme they threw his direction." She snorted. "I don't think I heard what had him all excited that last time. I just knew he was moving us. Again.

"He couldn't wait until I graduated in three weeks. I wanted to stay in Dallas, go to a community college. Get a degree. I wanted a home that had a front door without a number on it!

"I refused to go. He left."

"A minor." Patrick scowled. "Alone in a motel room."

Rachel shrugged. "I celebrated my eighteenth birthday the day I graduated. But, by then, I wasn't alone anyway. My Great-Aunt Amanda showed up out of the blue and packed me off to her place outside Dallas." She paused and looked down at the empty mug in her hand. Then she set it on the counter and went back to the breakfast table to sit down. "It's funny," she said. "If Dad had only stuck around a few more hours, he wouldn't have had to chase after another one of his pipe dreams. He would have been set up for life."

"What do you mean?"

"My mother's estranged family is into cattle and oil. When Great-Amanda died in February," she paused, "she was worth over eight hundred million."

"Whoa."

Her laugh didn't hold any humor. "Yeah, whoa. Mom's entire family disowned her when she ran off with my dad. My great-aunt had a soft spot for Mama, though, so when she heard about the rodeo Dad was riding in she decided it was time to mend some fences. When she found me alone, she promptly took me in, made sure I graduated, and got me into Stanford." Rachel's dream college.

That dream turned into a nightmare after she met and married Greg. Although, if she'd known then what she knew now, she'd still have married him if only to get her sweet Amanda. Many believed she'd named her child after her great-aunt, but the truth was she picked the name because it meant "worthy of love." By the time her baby arrived in this world, Greg had made it clear he only wanted a baby to make "the childless old bat" happy. It was the only reason he'd agreed to the *in vitro* procedure that gave her Amanda when Rachel proved infertile.

"So, Great-Aunt Amanda is dead. Who's her beneficiary?"

"Me."

"You're joking."

Rachel shook her head. She couldn't help but watch Patrick's expression, looking for something beneath his surprise. His eyes didn't glaze over at the thought of what she stood to inherit. No avarice. No sly look of anticipation. He simply looked shocked. And it wasn't the shock the remaining James men, her three uncles, showed when her great-aunt's will was read and they discovered their aunt gave all of her money to "that bastard, born of the bastard who ruined our baby sister."

"You think your dad wants the money."

"What else can it be? It's been ten years."

"It's what your ex wants, too, isn't it?" Patrick waited for her nod before he leveled her with his next question. "What is he holding over you that would make him think he can get it by threatening you?"

Her breakfast climbed her throat at the thought of the whip lying in the bottom of the box sitting at the police station. Patrick was stepping a little too close to her most precious secret, a secret she'd guarded with her life since the day Amanda was put inside her. *You tell anyone the brat isn't yours, ruin my access to the James broad's coffers, and I'll take the brat away from you and make her pay.*

Rachel may have broken down and told her great-aunt the truth when she learned she was changing her will just before she died—Greg would never get his hands on the James fortune through Amanda now—but Rachel knew he could still get to *her*. The truth was she'd carried Amanda but, in the eyes of law, she wasn't her real mother, her blood. Greg would have the stronger claim in a court of law. Having all the money in the world wouldn't make a bit of difference. And he *would* make Amanda pay if his hand was forced. Of that, Rachel had little doubt.

"Rachel?" Patrick prompted. "What's he holding over you?"

"Nothing," she said, unable to look him straight in the eye. "He's just like my father, motivated by money, and he'll do whatever it takes to get his hands on it."

He wasn't convinced she was telling the truth, she could tell by the questioning lift of his eyebrow. "Seems to me your father is only trying to protect you, and he's not sparing any expense. I already spoke with Jack this morning. The security firm your dad hired is top notch and expensive. In fact, Jack thought it might be a good idea to use—"

"If you're going to suggest I let my father's hired thugs watch me, forget it. I'm not the golden goose for everyone to salivate over." She leapt from her chair, furious at Patrick for being so obtuse—he'd heard nothing she'd said—she couldn't stay in the same room with him. "I'm going to get Amanda out of bed. Let's get this day over with. If I'm lucky, Jack will find Greg by sundown and I can go back to Dallas, where I belong." With that parting salvo, she stomped out of the kitchen.

By the time she returned downstairs with Amanda, her ire had cooled. But she still wasn't ready to talk to Patrick. Thankfully, he said nothing while she fed Amanda her favorite marshmallow cereal, just watched her until she thought she'd scream with frustration. Ten minutes later, Jane arrived with Suze, and she and the girls followed him to his work truck parked in front of his house.

The moment she saw the two new car seats buckled into the back seat of his crew cab truck, she felt like a royal bitch. Patrick didn't deserve her anger. In fact, he'd done nothing but help her and Amanda, kept them safe. "I'm sorry," she said, stopping him with her hand on his arm when he opened the back door for the kids to clamber inside. "You've done so much for me, for us. I-I—"

"Forget it," he interrupted her apology, leaning past her to buckle Amanda and Suze into their seats. He smiled at the girls before turning his cool gaze on Rachel.

Her heart twinged at his obvious rebuff. She climbed into the passenger seat, buckled herself in, and watched Patrick walk around the front of the truck to open his door. Only then did she see the piece of paper folded in the middle of his seat. He frowned, picked it up. When he opened it and read it, his jaw tightened.

"Is something wrong?" she asked.

Patrick's gaze fell on her and she caught a fleeting expression of, what, uneasiness? Worry? "No." He shook his head and jammed the note into his shirt pocket. "Just business."

She didn't believe him. But he clearly wasn't willing to talk about it and they were soon on their way to the Southgate site.

Another surprise awaited them when they walked into the site trailer twenty minutes later. Patrick had been busy after she left him in the kitchen last night. He'd had someone set up a play area in one of the small rooms down the hall from the main office, filling it with toys brought from Suze's dormer playroom above his home office. The girls were soon happily building skyscrapers with a box of Legos.

One of the two desks that faced each other in the main office was cleared with the exception of a stack of children's books with several paperback novels someone—Jane, perhaps—had generously thrown on top, leaving room on the desk for the laptop Rachel had brought with her to keep busy. The other desk was piled high with blueprints and files, which concerned her a bit since she suspected it was Patrick's and she was afraid she'd have to watch him all day *not* talking to her. But, once he got her situated and showed her how to work the radio he had for her to keep in touch, he instructed her to leave the door locked at all times since both he and his assistant had keys. Then he left them alone.

The day proceeded more quickly than Rachel could have hoped. Although initially irritated to be dropped out of sight in the trailer like someone's dirty laundry, she opened her laptop to a landscaping design she'd been working on for Katy before she'd fled Dallas and lost herself in the joy of creativity. She suspected Katy had suggested expanding her nursery offerings to landscaping to make Rachel happy, and Rachel had no idea what she'd do if she could never return to Dallas, but she had to finish the designs for the four new commissions Kolthern Nurseries had acquired before she left.

She read books to the girls, and they shared lunch with Patrick's accommodating assistant, Skip Davis, who brought them a picnic lunch from a local delicatessen. She was startled to discover the self-effacing man with the shy smile was Patrick's brother-in-law. It was news to her that Patrick had been married, although she wasn't quite sure why it surprised her. The man was sinfully attractive and the women in Denver couldn't be completely oblivious.

Skip hadn't told her how his sister died, only that it's been almost two years ago. There'd been such a devastated look in his dark eyes when he spoke of her, she didn't have the heart to pursue the topic. She couldn't help but wonder if Patrick's eyes held the same desolation when he thought about his dead wife.

Skip left her and the girls to finish their dessert of ice cream sandwiches and, before she knew it, it was three o'clock and she was listening on the radio to the crew checking in for second shift. Patrick called her, too, and told her he was coming for them soon so she packed up her laptop and readied the girls. More tired than she expected—the altitude in Denver was kicking her butt—she was ready to go home.

Wait. She'd made her home in Dallas with Katy. She couldn't start thinking of the Thorne house as her own. She was a temporary tenant, a house sitter. Actually, she was a squatter no longer in hiding. And, pretty as the Rocky Mountains were outside her bedroom window each morning, she should bolt back to the wide open vistas of Texas prairie grass where she could see the danger coming for miles.

No one wanted her here, least of all, Patrick. He'd avoided the trailer, avoided *her*, the entire day. Much as she didn't want to admit it, his rejection bothered her. There was a hard knot in her middle that grew as each hour passed without a word from him. She'd heard him talking over the radio to his employees several times, but he'd never come to his office, not even for lunch.

She was a problem thrust upon him, and she couldn't forget that. The all-too-masculine contractor was another kind of danger to her, one she hadn't seen coming until it was too late. Somehow, in the span of only a few short days, he'd tapped into her scarred heart and given her a glimpse of what she'd longed for her entire life...a man who could care about her. Not her family connections. Not the money she stood to inherit. *Her.*

Patrick had gotten too close. He was a bigger threat to her heart than any man who'd come before him. She had to get away from him as soon as possible. Too bad she'd promised—only this morning—to stay put until Greg was behind bars.

13

Patrick walked between the two main condo buildings toward the Southgate site trailer where he'd left Rachel and the children this morning, his emotions jumping back and forth between anticipation and dread with each step. He'd managed to avoid going into the site office all day, shamelessly using Skip to run to the trailer to locate blueprints, grab keys off the rack, and other tasks he'd normally have done himself. He'd asked Skip to buy lunch for Rachel and the kids and eat with them because he, cool, single-minded ex-Ranger, was too intimidated to be in close proximity of a brown-eyed woman who was turning his brain into putty.

That didn't stop him from lingering within eyesight of the trailer all day. If he was drawn away by a problem elsewhere, he was quick to finish and return. On the one hand, he wanted to push Rachel away. The woman got under his skin too easily. On the other hand, he longed to pull her closer and take up the battle against her demons.

Her demons were proving to be particularly nasty. He thought of the note he'd handed over to his brother this morning, the one he'd found on his truck seat when he took Rachel and the kids to work. The words were pieced together from magazines or newspapers and pasted into place like a ransom note, which was disturbing enough. But it was the message itself that made his blood run cold, just as it had when he read it before stuffing it into his shirt pocket so Rachel wouldn't see it.

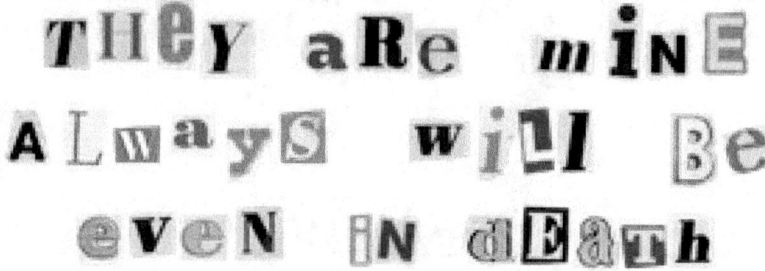

He knew the threat was aimed at him, that Bishop was staking his claim warning him away from Rachel and Amanda. What concerned him, though, was what the man might do once he realized Patrick wasn't going to turn tail and run. That he would protect them no matter what Bishop threatened.

It was the last line of the note that disturbed Patrick most. The way it was phrased he believed Bishop was saying he was prepared to kill Rachel, if he couldn't have her, then no one else would either. It was a common threat for abusers and, God knows, Rachel's ex-husband was vicious enough to take things to the next level. Patrick only had to think of Rachel's scars to remember the man was capable of unconscionable brutality.

The thought pushed him more quickly toward the trailer, his longing to see Rachel and assure himself that she was safe gaining a stranglehold on his emotions. Every time he was stopped by a contractor, a crew member, or supervisor to answer a question or give an order his irritation grew. Why were so many of his employees wandering around the site instead of doing their jobs?

Second shift, boss man. In addition to his regular crew working fourteen hour days to get everything done on the schedule, he'd added another shift of part timers. He smiled at the second shift supervisor as he walked past, feeling foolish for his erratic behavior. Jack had *really* better find Bishop before Patrick went completely nuts.

When he was within half a dozen feet of the trailer, as if his thoughts had drawn her there, the door opened and Rachel walked down the metal stairs toward him, a bright smile on her face, her halo of honey blond hair shining bright in the late afternoon sun. She was safe and within his sight, and he was damned if the day's tension didn't unwind between his shoulder blades.

Thorne, you've got it bad.

"We're ready," she said, coming within arm's reach.

So was he.

A vision played with his mind. Rachel lying in the sunlight wearing nothing but this same welcoming smile. His hands buried in her tousled curls as he made slow, sweet love to her. The glow of her climax blossoming across her cheeks. "Give me a minute," Patrick cleared his throat, "to pick up some files and blueprints, and we can go home."

Home. He hadn't lived in his parents' house since he left for the army at eighteen, but it had begun to feel more like home than his own house on the other side of the cranberry hedge. And it was all because of this woman...who was looking past him with a horrified expression on her face.

Turning on his heel, he looked directly into the bloodshot, green eyes of a middle-aged, balding man with a golfer's tan and a .22 in his hand. A .22 that was pointed dead center at Patrick.

"You killed her!" The gun shook. "Y-you killed my baby!" The gun shook so hard it looked like it might go off at any second, even without the index finger tightening and loosening over the trigger.

Patrick eyed the man, his training kicking in as he quickly assessed the situation. Unhinged man in front of him. Rachel behind him over his left shoulder. More than a dozen workers and supervisors, frozen in a gauntlet of shock on both sides of them. Maybe more he couldn't see. There were too many innocent bystanders. No matter how he proceeded, this was bound to get nasty if he couldn't gain control of the situation. Fast.

"I didn't kill anyone," he said, his voice calm for the crazy man. "Why don't you put that gun down? We'll go into," his gaze bounced off the trailer several feet away where Amanda and Suze were safely tucked away, "somewhere and talk."

"Liar! I saw! What you did—" Huge tears ran down the man's lined cheeks, a river of anguish. "You, you, oh, dear God, you—"

The gun lifted and Patrick found himself looking directly down the barrel. A pull on the trigger, at this range, and Patrick was a dead man.

"Mister. You don't want to do this." The husky, Southern voice to his left warned Patrick that Rachel was moving into danger closer to him. *What was she doing?*

The gun waved in her direction, and Patrick knew real terror for the first time in his life. His heart pounded. Sweat popped out on the back of his neck. He reached out a hand to stop her, to push her behind him again. But she was just out of reach.

She didn't stop moving until she stood slightly between him and the gunman. "Whatever you think Patrick's done," she said, still in that same soothing tone that melted Patrick's insides, "this isn't the way to deal with it, Mister...what's your name?"

"M-Manning." The gun dropped a fraction. "Bill."

Patrick was surprised he'd answered, but more stunned when he recognized the name. William Manning was a lawyer, a councilman...and the father of the coed who'd gone missing last week. *Jesus!* "Manning—"

"No!" The .22 swiveled back in his direction. The man's trigger finger twitched.

"Mr. Manning! Bill," Rachel drew him off again. "Please, don't do this. You have to know this is wrong. Let's sit down and talk."

Sirens sounded in the distance. Patrick prayed the police hurried. This could go south any second, and he or, worse, Rachel would be lying in the dirt with a bullet in their chest.

The councilman stiffened, his head cocked as he listened to the noise of approaching rescue. The .22 stopped shaking as it settled back on target.

The man stared into Patrick's eyes, and he knew. He was going to die. He watched, unable to do anything to stop him, as Manning's finger pulled the trigger. Crack! Crack! Two sharp reports rent the air, followed by shouts and screaming.

A searing pain ripped into Patrick's side where one of the bullets grazed his ribs on his right side. He didn't feel the second shot. He looked down expecting to find a bloom of red growing in the middle of his chest. Nothing. For long seconds, he couldn't process why he wasn't dead. Then he glanced back up, in time to see his brother-in-law in free-fall, Skip's arms wrapped around the councilman as he tackled him. They hit the ground together. The gun flew out of Manning's hand into a circle of workmen before it hit Patrick that the second bullet had missed him.

Skip had Manning in a deadlock and several of the crew rushed in to help, but the councilman wasn't fighting them. He lay in the dirt crying, great heaving sobs of a broken man with nothing left to lose. In the next instant, a phalanx of police cars showed up in a blare of sirens and the squeal of brakes. Patrick frantically searched the confusion, terrified he'd find the second bullet had found another target—found Rachel—but he didn't see anyone with an injury. Then he spotted Rachel rushing toward him.

"Are you okay?" she said, her hand spread wide over his heart.

He drank up the sight of her, long legs encased in blue jeans, an ultra-soft, button down shirt the color of the summer Colorado sky hugging her curves. He scanned her frame to make sure she was truly okay, his seized heart only then releasing blood into his veins in a rush. He sucked oxygen into his lungs, the hot summer mountain air tinged with the scent of lilacs and Rachel.

His hands shook with adrenaline now that the danger was over. He reached one up to cover her hand. His fingers curled around hers. He pulled them away, breaking the connection, shock giving way to anger. "Are you out of your mind? You could have been killed. He had a gun, for God's sake!"

She stepped back and put her fists on her hips. "I know he had a gun!" She glared at him. "I had to do something to stop him from shooting you. It was working, too—"

"Until he pulled the trigger!" he shouted back. His fear for her couldn't drain fast enough.

She might have died and all he could do was watch it happen. It was his fault...just like it was his fault Karly died.

Rachel looked down, like she was searching for a retort, but then her expression changed to one of alarm. "Oh, my God, you're bleeding!" She drew close again and her fingertips probed the tear in his work shirt where the bullet had grazed him.

He flinched at her touch. His side stung like the devil, but her concern washed over him like a balm. "I'll live," he said.

When she looked away from the wound to his face, he expected to see tears. Remorse. "Of course, you'll live!" She pushed away from him, like she couldn't get away from him fast enough. "God protects drunks and fools, and men who think they can't be gored by a bull or ripped apart by a bullet or...whatever. No! You just jump right in and don't consider the people you leave behind, and, and... it's not, it's not okay! Okay?"

He recognized the aftermath of fear and adrenaline loosening its grip on her, but there was something else reflected in her stricken eyes. An emotion he dare not begin to interpret. He just knew it tore at his heart. "I'm a trained professional," he said reasonably. "I had it all under control."

She snorted. "Like hell, you did."

He almost smiled at the fierceness in her voice, but he couldn't forget how terrified he'd been at the thought of her being killed. He wanted to shake her. Touch her. Kiss her senseless. He forced himself to stop at sliding his hand around her neck to pull her closer so that they were not quite touching. "Maybe not," he said quietly, searching her gorgeous brown eyes. "But did you consider what would happen to Amanda if you got yourself killed?" *What it would do to me to lose you?*

She gasped. "I-I—" Her expression darkened with bewilderment.

Guilt ripped through him as he saw her confusion replaced by horror at what she'd done. She couldn't have had Amanda in her thoughts when she stepped into danger. It looked like he wasn't the only one fighting strong feelings here, and that both elated and scared him witless.

He didn't do relationships. He didn't get involved with damaged women. Not since the one he married took her own life rather than bear his child.

"Excuse me." The voice over Patrick's right shoulder sounded harsh in his ear.

"What?" he murmured, lost in Rachel's gaze and his tumultuous feelings.

"Patrick," Jack said, walking into view. He didn't finish whatever he meant to say and scowled at the blood on his shirt. "I should have you locked up." Motioning over his shoulder to a paramedic, he clipped out orders. He shook his head at Rachel when she began to say something. "Not another word from you either, Rachel, unless it pertains to the situation. Go with Detective Johannes. She'll take your statement."

Rachel glanced at Patrick but then she turned on her heel and walked away with Jack's partner, hips swaying like a red cape to a bull. Patrick watched every step she took until she disappeared up the stairs into the site trailer.

"If you can please give me your complete attention," Jack said dryly, "I'd appreciate it. We do have a city councilman sitting in the back of a cop car and that's just the tip of the mess we're dealing with at the moment."

With Rachel out of sight, Patrick was able to release his hold on the pain burrowing into his side. "If you don't mind, Jack," he growled, "can we talk over a paramedic?" He sagged into his brother.

Jack cursed, grabbed him under one arm, and helped him across the open area to a nearby truck where they were intercepted by two paramedics. "You idiot, you're supposed to dodge the bullets," he muttered to Patrick easing him down onto the open tailgate. He winced when the first responder cut his work shirt away from the wound. "The good news is it looks like the bullet only furrowed your sorry ass."

When the man flattened a sterile pad over his burning ribs, Patrick flinched. "And the bad news?" he asked his brother.

"It'll probably need stitches." Jack's grin was crooked, relieved.

Patrick smiled back, already feeling better just sitting there. At least the world had stopped spinning. He shifted on his butt and listened to the second responder radio in his vital signs. He looked over the shoulder of the man working on his side to the councilman sitting in the police car twenty feet away. "You found her," he murmured, working through the events of the last few minutes.

His brother didn't ask who he meant. "Yeah, we found her." He scowled at Manning, hunched over his knees, the heave of his shoulders his only movement as he continued to sob. "He identified her remains less than an hour ago."

Patrick cursed. He knew how heartbreaking it was to go to the morgue to identify someone you cared about. He'd had to do it when Karly died. But, he'd never seen the kind of desolation that darkened Manning's eyes before he shot Patrick. "It was *him*, wasn't it? It was bad." He knew he didn't dare identify the man, not when the paramedics could hear everything they said, but his brother knew he was talking about the Angel Killer.

Frustration and anger flashed in Jack's green eyes. "Worse than bad."

He looked down at the red blotch seeping through the white bandage on his side and forced images out of his head. He knew the basics of how past Angel Killer victims were found. No father should have to see their daughter that way. It was no wonder Manning had gone insane with grief and lashed out. "He thinks I did it. Why?"

Jack considered him for several moments as if unable to decide whether to respond. "The mayor's office is kept apprised of our investigations. The councilman must have learned we'd asked you to come in after your vandalism, assumed you were a suspect, and we just weren't telling him." His lips tightened briefly before he continued. "Patrick, I'm not saying I think what he did was right, but you didn't see—"

He paused and shrugged, like he too had to shake off the image burned into his brain. "I should have done something though. I should have made sure Manning was escorted home."

Patrick shook his head. "You can't have known how he'd react."

"I know how *I'd* react."

Seeing the stark rage in his brother's eyes, he knew exactly what Jack would have done to the animal that hurt someone he loved. Patrick couldn't hold that against him. He might do the same given the right circumstances, if he loved someone that much.

Two faces, both with haunted brown eyes, jumped to the forefront of his mind. *Rachel. Amanda.* The thought of either of them brutalized, lying dead in some sterile morgue was more painful than the bullet wound to his side. *Whoa. Are you so far gone on that you'd kill for them?*

He sat a little straighter on the truck bed when the answer immediately slammed into his brain. He was already prepared to go the distance for them, to keep them safe from Bishop. "I'm not pressing charges, Jack," he said with a nod toward the police car.

His brother nodded his understanding. "Manning's still facing charges, but with your unwillingness to pursue it and the extenuating circumstances, he'll have an easier time of it."

"Just make sure he's solid on my innocence before you release him from custody again, okay?"

Jack grinned. "You've got it." He sobered, glancing at the white trailer sheltering Rachel and the children from view. "You have enough on your plate."

The paramedics finished up their work with him and started packing up their gear. "Yeah, I do," Patrick said, looking to Jack for assistance. "Too much to be sidelined by a trip to the hospital."

"Patrick, you should get checked out."

"I need to be with Rachel and Amanda twenty-four, seven, remember? You saw that note," he reminded him. "Can you spare anyone to protect them?"

"You know we don't have the manpower."

Patrick didn't say anything. He let his brother work through his options, which he knew were limited, especially with the discovery of a new Angel Killer victim. "I'm patched up for now. Sam can come to the house to stitch me if it becomes necessary." It wouldn't be the first time their doctor brother stitched one of them at home and Jack knew it. Patrick figured he had just enough energy to speak to Skip—his brother-in-law *did* save the day when he tackled Manning and he owed him a huge thank you, at the very least—before he could take Rachel, and the little girls, home.

He watched his brother talk to the paramedics for a few minutes. There were a lot of frowns and shaking heads, but a few minutes later with a sidelong glance at Patrick, they picked up their gear and left without him.

Flexing his torso, Patrick cringed at the sting of pain that immediately raced up his side. He schooled his expression when Jack returned to the truck bed where he sat. "Are we done here?" he asked. "Can we go?"

Jack raised an eyebrow. "You're going to have to work on your 'He-Man' routine before you let Rachel see you. If I can see the amount of pain you're in, she will, too. If we want her to stay safely put in the house tonight, you need to convince her you're good to go. She's already in enough danger. We need to lock her down tight."

Patrick frowned. "Then, I was right. The note I gave you was a direct threat. Bishop will kill her if he can't have her?"

"Our resident shrink believes it's a real possibility. With enough anger, anyone is capable of murder. When we told him about Rachel's doctor friend in a coma, he said anyone standing in Bishop's way, real or imagined, could become his next target." He ran his fingers through his hair. "Patrick, we need you behind a wall of security as much as we need Rachel and Amanda there. This could get ugly if we don't find Bishop soon, and we still haven't figured out how you're tied to the Angel Killer."

Patrick's shoulders tensed at the reminder of how the task force had torn his life and business apart. They knew more about him than even his parents, but not one name popped up as a potential serial killer. With over fifty employees and the number of clients he had and competitors and...well, it was the task force's job to sort it all out.

Concentrate on the threats you can see. "I can look after myself, although after today, I'm going to start carrying my gun for extra insurance," he said.

"You've kept your conceal carry up-to-date?"

He nodded. "I'm not taking any more chances with Rachel or Amanda. I'm going to call Rachel's dad, too, and ask him to put the security outfit he hired back on duty."

"Rachel will never forgive you," Jack said.

He shrugged with a negligence he didn't feel. "She has to be alive to not forgive me and that's all that matters to me at this juncture. Bishop will think twice if he has to get through two walls of security to get to them." And after what he'd heard this morning about Rachel's father, it was about time her old man did something to protect his daughter and granddaughter.

Three Weeks....
Two Days....
Three Hours....
...'Til death.

"We have to kill Skip." The monster's growl reverberated up from the depths of Robby's pounding skull as he watched the emergency rig and ambulance drive away from the Southgate construction site.

Standing on the sidelines listening to a couple of the crew discussing the shooting, he shook his head. *We need him.*

"You do. I don't!"

He agreed with a slight nod. *I need him right where he is. Close to Thorne.*

"Lot of good that will do you if the goody-two-shoes keeps saving the son-of-a-bitch."

When it matters, Skip won't be an obstacle. He'll die with Thorne.

"When?"

The plan is in place.

"Death doesn't need a plan."

You'll get your chance. Robby pushed the monstrous voice away. *We have other things to do.*

"This one will disappoint you, too, you know. Just like the others." An awful chuckle slithered through Robby's mind. "Then, I get her."

You're wrong. Robby headed for his truck with the dispersing work crew. Thinking of his Angel, of how soon they'd be together again—thank God he'd driven past that Auraria campus bus stop yesterday after he'd cleaned up what the monster had done to his last plaything—he couldn't help but smile. He wouldn't allow past mistakes to stop him from doing what he must. *It's her. When I get everything in place and bring her home, you'll see.*

The monster chuckled again, but he slunk back into the darkness prepared to wait. "We'll both see."

By the time Patrick parked at the curb in front of the elder Thorne home more than an hour later, Rachel was ready to scream to break the silence between them. She longed to talk to him about the incident with the councilman, about the news the man's daughter had been added to the growing list of the Angel Killer's victims. She wanted to ask about the bullet wound in Patrick's side. She couldn't see any blood on the fresh work shirt he'd changed into before he came to get her and the children from the trailer, but she longed to beg him to hold her, just for a moment, so she could assure herself he really was okay.

She could do none of those things because then she'd be forced to confront the stupidity of her actions. Why had she jumped between Patrick and the gunman when she had a little girl who was depending on her?

Amanda was her life, her reason for everything she'd done these past five years. Yet, in that one moment, her only thought was to save Patrick.

Unprepared to go down that path of self-discovery, she remained silent and stared blindly out the passenger window. Even the precocious Suze hadn't spoken a word since they'd left Southgate. The moment Patrick turned off the truck Rachel opened her door and climbed out into the late afternoon sun. Then, she helped the girls out of their seats. They each picked up a travel bag filled with toys and books, while she carried her laptop, leaving Patrick to trail behind them toward the front porch on the house.

They had to wait for him to unlock the door, but they were soon inside the foyer. She would have dashed up the stairs with the children, put some distance between her and Patrick, but he forestalled her. "Girls," he said quietly. "There are chocolate graham crackers in the cookie jar on the kitchen counter for a snack. We'll be there in a minute to pour your milk."

Rachel glanced at him, saw his taut expression, and took a step toward the kitchen. "I'll help them."

Patrick shook his head. "Go ahead, girls," he said.

His highhanded order irritated Rachel but she smiled at Amanda, watching them with her too serious brown eyes. "Go ahead, baby," she said. "I'll be along just as soon as I take everything upstairs." Once in the bedroom that she shared with Amanda she would take a few moments to pull herself together, away from Patrick's scent, his searching gaze, and the uneasy questions he'd raised in her head.

She had to get away from it all, if only for a few minutes. She'd call Jack. She hadn't had the opportunity to ask him if they had a line on Greg's whereabouts. Deep down, she knew if her ex-husband was behind bars, Jack would have told her. But that didn't stop her from hoping he'd tell her otherwise. Then she could pack up Amanda and be back on the road to Dallas. Tonight.

The children shot off toward the kitchen in a flurry of sneakered feet, leaving her standing in the foyer with Patrick. Rachel heard the lid come off the cookie jar before she turned toward the stairs. "I'll be back in a minute."

"Wait, Rach," he said.

Suddenly exhausted by everything that had taken place in the last three days, she sighed. "Not now, Patrick. Please?"

He studied her expression. Then, he frowned. Before he could say anything the front door opened behind him, and a monster walked in.

She gasped at the sight of the biggest dog she'd ever seen lumbering across the door's threshold into the foyer. Easily two hundred pounds, the English Mastiff's massive head would have butted her in her chest if he hadn't been pulled up short on the leash held in Patrick's foster brother, Joe's hand.

He smiled as he followed the dog into the house. "Hi, Rachel," he said. "It's good to see you again."

"Again?" Patrick raised an eyebrow in question.

Rachel smiled. "Joe and I met Sunday at breakfast, before your parents left for the Virgin Islands." Of all of the foster brothers that she'd met then—every last one handsome enough to make any woman's heart stutter—she'd felt most at ease with the high school counselor. She had a feeling he saw a lot more than he let on, yet he didn't judge. She eyed the fawn-colored dog. "I gather this is Buck," she said. "He's so...."

"Huge?" Patrick's brother grinned, laughter in his blue-green eyes. "We should have thought about bringing him home earlier. No one wants to mess with a two-hundred thirty pound dog that looks like he eats burglars for breakfast. He'll be the best protection for you and Amanda."

Patrick's scowl made it clear to her that he didn't like being left out of the conversation. Or was it because Joe's comment implied the dog was better able to protect them? "Thanks for going to Colorado Springs to get him," he said.

Joe looked surprised at his sharp tone. "No problem. Even though he does like to go back to play with his sire when Mom and Dad go on vacations, Buckwheat was more than happy to come home." He ruffled the dog's fur. "Weren't you, boy?"

Rachel eyed the humongous dog. "I don't know how Amanda will react to such a big animal. The only experience she's had with a dog is the Lab puppy we had before we left California." She'd only had the pup a month before it was killed the week before they'd fled Greg. They might have lived on a ranch, but Amanda had had little exposure to animals because their home was more of a showplace Greg used to display his success than a working ranch. "I see why Buckwheat might be a good protector, but I'm worried he'll scare her."

"Bucky!"

Suze's squeal behind Rachel startled her, alerted her that the adults were no longer alone. She turned in time to see Suze grab Amanda's hand and drag her toward the dog.

"Suze—"

Patrick uttered one sharp word. The Mastiff promptly sat back on his haunches and, with a tilted head, calmly watched the girls approach. Patrick's hand on Rachel's forearm kept her from dashing between her daughter and the dog. "Wait," he murmured. "Let them sort this out themselves. Buck loves kids, but he won't move until I release him."

Amanda dug her heels in about two feet shy of the animal. Rachel frowned when she saw how tiny the four-year-old looked standing in front of the dog. Not a dog...a horse! The top of Amanda's blond head barely came to the middle of the mastiff's shoulders. The animal looked down at her. She looked up at him.

They stared at each other for several long moments. Then, Amanda pulled her hand out of Suze's, walked straight at the dog, wrapped her arms around him as far as she could reach, and expelled a long, audible sigh of contentment. The dog huffed and lowered his head to rest gently on top of her head.

Rachel's heart ached when she saw the lone tear that trailed down her daughter's cheek as she nuzzled the dog like he was a long lost friend she'd just found. Did she think she was looking at a grown up version of her puppy, Boomer? Although they did have similar coloring, the two dogs were different breeds. Buckwheat was so much larger than Boomer would have grown. But, Amanda was so traumatized by Boomer's death, maybe it wasn't so far fetched she'd connect with Buckwheat, especially since one of her favorite shows was Clifford, the Big Red Dog.

A full minute passed before Amanda stepped away from Buckwheat and stood there petting his fur like she couldn't stop touching him. She smiled at Suze.

Her friend looked over her shoulder at Patrick. "Can me and 'manda feed Bucky?"

"Sure. It's time for his supper," he said. "His dish is in the pantry." He gave another sharp command to Buckwheat. The dog stood.

Joe released the leash from the dog's leather collar and Suze turned toward the kitchen, Amanda's hand caught in hers. "Come on, Bucky. Chow time!"

The dog aimed his nose toward the kitchen door. The sight of the two little girls leading the lumbering animal like they had an invisible leash was almost comical. Rachel watched them disappear into the kitchen before she turned back to Patrick and his brother. Finding herself being studied by two pairs of discerning male eyes, she stammered nervously. "I-I'll just take all of our stuff upstairs. I'll be right back."

Without waiting for either of them to stop her, she left the brothers standing in the foyer and raced up the stairs to the bedroom she and Amanda had been sharing since their arrival. She walked into a disaster.

Her gaze darted around the room. It looked like a tornado had swept through it, hitting this section, missing the next, only to touch down in another spot. The closet door that was filled to the brim with stored Thorne childhood memories gaped open, its contents yanked out and rifled through. Her empty suitcase and Amanda's were lying on the tossed bed covers, their contents strewn across the floor among the feathers from her shredded pillow. Amanda's special tooth fairy pillow hadn't escaped destruction either.

Greg! Dear God, while she and Amanda were tucked away at Southgate, he was here digging through their belongings? Bile crawled up Rachel's throat when she saw gaping wounds in several of her shirts where he'd ripped into the material.

Then, she saw the message on the dresser mirror, printed with permanent marker in large black letters.

HE CAN'T SAVE YOU BITCH! GIVE ME BACK WHAT'S MINE!

For an instant, she flashed back six months, heard the swishing sound of Greg's horsewhip in the air above her. She felt the first searing pain across her belly. Vicious words crashed through her senses, threatening words against her. Against Amanda.

"No!" The cry barely left her lips before she whirled on her heel and ran for the door. She slipped on a pile of pillow feathers and fell to her hands and knees. Quickly clamoring to her feet, she stumbled toward the hall.

Amanda!

Patrick stood at the bottom of the stairs, catching his brother up on recent events when he heard Rachel cry out. "Stay with the kids!" he ordered, taking the stairs two at a time in the other direction. He ignored a searing flash of pain from his side when he rounded the balustrade at the top.

He ran into his old bedroom, and directly into Rachel. She hit him so hard, he grunted. His arms automatically came up around her back. His left shoulder slammed the door jamb when they lost balance. The impact zinged pain in a straight line down to his ribs, loosened his grip.

Rachel squealed and beat at him with her fists. "Let go!" she sobbed. "Let go!"

Looking into her wild eyes, Patrick realized she wasn't aware of her surroundings. She was in full flight mode. One glance over her shoulder into the trashed bedroom and he knew why.

Was the intruder still here?

Stiffening at the possibility danger remained, his hands closed over Rachel's upper arms. He gave her a little shake. "Rach," he said, forcing her to see *him*, not the demon she was fleeing.

Her eyes cleared. "Greg! He was here!"

He nodded to the room behind her. "Did you see him when you came in?"

"No." Her head shook back and forth slowly. Then, she gasped. "You think he's still here, in the house?"

"No," Patrick replied, kicking himself for not setting the security alarm when they left for the site this morning. He'd been too concerned about the site security. "But I have to make sure. Stay here."

"But, Amanda—"

"Joe's got her." He urged her back into the room and sat her down on the only empty spot on the bed. He hated to dump her in the middle of the destruction, but until he cleared the house, it was the best place to leave her. "*This* room is safe, too. Everything's exposed and there's nowhere to hide. Hang tight here for a few minutes."

Leaving the room, Patrick went to the top of the stairs and called down to Joe. "Stay with the kids in the kitchen. Set the security alarm. Then send Buckwheat on patrol."

His brother didn't ask for an explanation, but Patrick heard the alarm beep that told him the house was secure. In the next instant, Buckwheat's huge head poked out the kitchen door as he began his usual rounds, quietly moving from one room to the next as Patrick's father had taught him when he was a pup. It had been his nightly ritual the past five years.

Aware it would take the dog several minutes to finish his patrol downstairs, Patrick checked the upstairs himself. He efficiently searched four of the remaining five bedrooms before Buckwheat appeared at his side and touched Patrick's hand with his muzzle. They finished their sweep together.

Only then did the pair of them return to his old bedroom. He wasn't surprised when Buckwheat stuck his head through the door and growled low in his throat. The dog might not see the intruder, but he could definitely smell him.

Patrick placed his hand on the dog's collar and uttered a command to sit before walking around the animal and entering the room. The sight that greeted him made his jaw tighten. Greg had been thorough when he tore everything apart, but that destruction didn't compare to the devastation marring Rachel's expression as she looked up at him from her position on the bed. Her hands were curled around something metallic, the item pressed to her breasts. Blood trickled through the back of her fingers.

With a curse, he stepped over the debris to hunker down in front of her. He gently pulled her fingers away from the shattered hand mirror gouging her tender flesh. She gave one tug of resistance, but released her grip. Fresh blood seeped from the pads of three fingers, and he could see a chunk of glass imbedded in the middle of her palm.

Scooping her into his arms, he strode from the room out of sight of the wreckage. He carried her past the mastiff guarding the hallway and down the passage to his parent's bedroom. He didn't stop moving until he sat on the king-sized, four poster bed with her in his lap. "Rachel?" he said. "Sweetheart, talk to me."

Brown eyes met his, dark and bruised with pain. "H-he, m-mama's—"

Patrick didn't need to hear the loss shadowing her voice to know the mirror had a special meaning for her. "It's okay, honey," he said, stroking her satiny cheek. "We can fix it. Let's deal with your cuts, first, okay?"

"I'm fine," she said quietly.

Patrick hated to let her go because he wasn't convinced she *was* fine, but he had to check in with Joe, have his brother call in the cavalry. *At the rate things are going, you should keep the police station on speed dial.* "I'm going to get the first aid kit," he said. "Will you be alright here for a few more minutes?"

She nodded, wrapping her arms around her waist protectively.

His jaw clenched. "I'll be right back."

Downstairs, he quietly told his brother about the trashed room so the kids weren't alarmed. They looked perfectly happy drowning their graham crackers in glasses of milk. "Keep them distracted?" he asked. "Let me make a couple of calls and take care of Rachel's hand."

"You might take a look at your side, too. Unless that's Rachel's, you're bleeding."

Looking down, he saw his brother was right. He'd reopened his wound running up the stairs, when he collided with Rachel, or when he carried her to his parents' bedroom. Blood was seeping into his work shirt. Not much, but enough to be a pain in his ass. "I don't have time for this," he said, pulling the material away from his ribs.

He lifted an eyebrow at Joe. "Call Sam? Tell him I need stitches. I can't go to the hospital so he'll have to come here as soon as he can leave the ER."

When he agreed, Patrick left the kitchen. Pulling his cell phone from his jeans pocket as he located the first aid kit in a cupboard in the downstairs bathroom, he called the precinct and talked to Jack, who promised to swing by the house first chance he got. In the meantime, a patrol car was on its way. Then, squaring his shoulders, Patrick made the call he dreaded most.

It was easy to tell Jack he could live with his decision to pull Rachel's father back into her protection—thanks to the security consultant, Larson Cook, he had the man's phone number—but actually taking that irretrievable step was more difficult than he expected. Rachel was not going to be happy.

After introducing himself to Dixon Grey and telling him what he wanted him to do—Grey didn't quibble, just tersely asked if Rachel and Amanda were okay and protected until he could get the security detail back on track—Patrick carried the first aid kit upstairs to his parents' bedroom. He considered telling Rachel her father had asked to see them, his voice tentative, unsure, but one look at her face told him to wait. With the way Rachel feels about her old man, he didn't think she'd be receptive.

He walked into the room and sat on the bed next to her. "Amanda's fine," he said before Rachel could ask. "She's spoiling her dinner with Suze chowing down on chocolate graham crackers."

Rachel's flashed a relieved smile. "Thanks for checking on her. I probably shouldn't worry, but she's all I have."

"You have every right to be protective, Rach. You're her mother," he said. "But, I'm here now. I'm going to help you through this, if you'll let me."

Her gaze locked on his, she didn't say anything for a long moment. He wondered what she saw when she looked at him. Did she see a man she could trust? Considering her history with men, would she truly trust any man again? He wanted, on some visceral level, for her to trust him.

When she nodded, he smiled and drew Rachel's injured hand to him. "Tell me about the mirror," he murmured to distract her while he pulled mirror slivers from her skin. "You said it was your mom's?"

She didn't make a sound when he pulled the larger piece from her palm. "It's part of a brush and comb set," she said, her voice too quiet. "It was all I had left of her."

Patrick glanced up, caught by her sad acceptance that her last connection to her mother was lost forever. "When did you lose her?"

"I was twelve."

"I'm sorry. That had to be tough for you and your dad," he commented.

"It was tough for *me*," she murmured. "I lost two parents the day mom died."

"What do you mean? This morning, you said you didn't break with your father until you were almost eighteen."

Rachel pulled away. "Dear old dad was gone from my life long before he left me in that hotel room." She started to stand.

His hand wrapped around her wrist so that he could pull her hand back into his lap. "I'm not finished," he said, holding her still until she subsided.

In silence, he wiped a sterile gauze pad, laced with Betadine solution, over her fingertips to clean them. Blood welled up on her ring finger. He applied pressure on it for a full minute to stem the flow before wrapping the tip with a bandage. He worked quickly on the other two sliced fingers and then turned to the slash on her palm before asking his next question. "How did she die?"

Rachel gasped. Because he'd hurt her hand or he'd crossed into territory he had no right to tread? He watched a myriad of expressions cross her face.

For the longest time, she said nothing. Then, she spoke. "Her appendix burst. She said it was the flu. Most of the symptoms were flu-like. She didn't tell us how bad the pain was until, well, the infection killed her. If dad hadn't gone off to another rodeo in a nearby town, if she'd gotten care in time, she wouldn't have died."

Patrick put the last piece of tape on the gauze he'd wrapped around her hand. "You blame your father for her death," he observed, suddenly more wary about the phone call he'd made fifteen minutes ago.

"It *was* his fault!" She stood and walked away from the bed, then back. She stopped a foot away and looked down at him. "Dad didn't make it to the hospital until two hours after she'd died."

Her arms wrapped around her middle in that familiar way he was beginning to hate because it threw a wall between him, with him on the other side with all of the other men who'd hurt her. He snagged her around the waist and pulled her into his lap. When she tried to wriggle free, he wrapped his arms around her so she couldn't escape without a struggle. He knew she wasn't running from him, but from his questions. "He wasn't there. How does that make him responsible?"

"He was *never* there," she said. "He knew she was sick and he didn't love us, love *her* enough to put off one freakin' ride."

Patrick knew he'd pushed as far as he dared. Still, he thought she was too close to the problem to see that a twelve-year-old's perceptions might not be right on target. "I don't see how the man couldn't love you," he murmured before leaning down to kiss the corner of her mouth.

He knew it was a mistake before he did it, but it didn't matter. His lips touched hers, and his brain short-circuited. His touch was gentle at first, but too soon it wasn't enough. His tongue traced the seam of her mouth until she opened to him with a sigh. Their tongues met, retreated, and then pushed deeper. He crushed her lips beneath his, his next kiss neither tender nor tentative. He feasted on her taste, her moan of acceptance. He wanted more. Too much more.

Beneath Rachel's curved bottom, he grew hard. When she wiggled in his lap, he thought he'd burst from his jeans. *Slow down.* Too difficult. He didn't want slow. He wanted to take her hard and fast, and more than once. For days, this woman had been driving him out of his mind. He longed to lay her down on the bed and caress her from head to toe. He wanted to see if all of her skin smelled like lilacs or just the sensitive zones at the base of her neck and wrists and, if he was lucky, behind her knees.

His fingers twitched with the urge to strip off her clothing, one piece at a time until she was naked and writhing beneath him. He would—

Through a blur of lust, Patrick heard a man clear his throat. "I didn't know kissing was on the regularly prescribed list of treatments for bullet wounds."

Patrick tore away from Rachel and looked over her head at his brother, Sam, standing in the open doorway, six-foot-three inches of weary doctor still wearing scrubs and a wild haired look that spoke of a tough day in the ER.

"Of course," Sam drawled, "I'm so far behind on my medical journal reading, I could have missed that one." He studied the woman in Patrick's arms. "Hi, Rachel."

His acknowledgement must have broken her immobility because she cried out and scrambled off Patrick's lap, leaving his hardened condition exposed to his brother's observant gaze. Patrick ignored his raised eyebrow to examine Rachel's flaming cheeks, to the arms that wrapped around her waist. "Your timing is impeccable, Sam," he said tightly.

Sam shrugged. "Joe said you need stitches. I'm just off a thirty-six hour shift, so here I am. I can come back, but it might be ten hours before I surface again."

"No!" Rachel walked toward the doorway. "You don't have to leave. I'm going." She bolted from the room.

Patrick listened to her footsteps pause outside her trashed bedroom where she said something to Buckwheat, but she didn't linger. The next thing he heard was her running down the stairs, then the sound of voices that told him she'd joined the others in the kitchen.

"You should work on your technique, Patrick. I think you scared her off."

The humor in Sam's voice pissed Patrick off. "Screw you, Sam." He shot a pointed look at the medical bag in his brother's hand. "Do me a favor. Give me some anesthetic before your next quip."

His brother grinned. "I only brought enough for the stitches so you'll just have to bite your tongue."

He entered the room and ordered Patrick to take off his shirt. His smile disappeared when he saw the bloody bandage the paramedics had applied to his wound at Southgate. He peeled it off, none too gently. "Jack was right," he muttered, bending to his task. "I should just put you in a medically induced coma so you'll stop doing stupid things that can get you killed."

He had a feeling his brothers were talking about more than his gunshot wound. Getting involved with Rachel James was proving just as dangerous. "I love you, too, bro," Patrick gritted out before he bit his tongue against the sting of the local.

The next three days passed in a sort of haze for Rachel. Objectively, in the back of her mind, she recognized the weird disassociation between herself and the real world. Early in her marriage to Greg, whenever she became overwhelmed by his control, his demands, by the very fact that her "perfect" marriage was a suffocating sham she had to maintain to protect Amanda, she'd found a way to push it all away. She moved. She talked. Her life went on as normal. Anything that threatened her equanimity was shunted aside. She relaxed her guard only when she was alone with Amanda.

She knew the anxiety and trauma of this past week was at fault for her ennui. Add in an irresistible craving for a man she shouldn't trust and the loss of her last connection with her dead mother, and she'd fallen back into that protective bubble she hated.

Greg had never noticed, or maybe he was simply happier with her living as an automaton. Patrick, however, did notice. She'd caught his frowning gaze on her time and again this morning as they ate breakfast before going to Southgate. It might have been Sunday, but the site was bustling as everyone worked to meet deadlines. Patrick came by the trailer almost hourly on one excuse or another, finally asking if everything was all right when he brought lunch for her and the girls. Her turkey-and-avocado sandwich settled like cement in her stomach, but she assured him everything was fine.

Everything wasn't fine though. She felt colder, more disconnected, as the day progressed. A feat considering the outside temperature reached into the triple digits by noon. The moment they got home from Southgate and ate dinner, she threw herself into Amanda's bedtime schedule. She read several books to her, gave her a long bath and tucked her into bed. When she went downstairs to take Amanda's empty milk cup to the kitchen, she'd put off Patrick's request "to talk" and ran upstairs into her own shower.

She closed her eyes, allowing the sting of hot water to pour over her head. She wanted to crawl into bed and sleep for twelve hours straight. She hadn't done anything more strenuous than sit in the trailer finalizing the schematics on the first landscaping job she'd emailed to Katy this afternoon. Her sleepless nights were catching up with her.

With a sigh, she leaned on the shower wall. She'd been running flat out on nerves and adrenaline since learning Greg's release from jail was imminent. Forced to abandon Katy and the new life she was building for Amanda, she'd run away to Denver, only to be found again. She'd discovered her dad, missing for more than ten years, was not only alive, but inserting himself into her life for reasons she didn't want to guess. She'd been shot at, her rental car and belongings destroyed, and she was falling for a man she had no business wanting.

It was the last thought that had niggled at her most since she confronted the gunman on Patrick's behalf on Friday. He'd been right to accuse her of not thinking about Amanda. Rachel hadn't done anything that stupid since she was thirteen and jumped into the arena between her dad and a raging bull bearing down on him after he'd been thrown. Her only thought then was to save her dad. She hadn't thought twice about saving Patrick either.

No. She wasn't falling for the man. She'd fallen. Hard. It was the only explanation for her actions.

Her response to Patrick's kiss was the clearest evidence of her fall from grace. She not only hadn't pushed him away, she'd thrown herself into the experience. The trauma of the day escaped her mind when his lips descended over hers. Demanding a response. Coaxing her to open to him. Tasting her as she'd longed for in her darkened room at night ever since she'd first spotted him in the moonlight.

If Sam hadn't arrived...her eyes snapped open and stopped the erotic images before they could form in her mind. She grabbed the washcloth and scrubbed soap all over her body. When the action didn't eradicate the longing zipping through her bloodstream, she reached out and turned down the water temperature until goose bumps raced across her skin.

The truth is she'd had little experience with the kind of sexual attraction she felt for Patrick. Besides Greg, her only sexual encounters were with the boy—that was the only thing to call him since he was barely nineteen, too, at the time—she'd lost her virginity to their freshman year in college. Their relationship was a fumbling two week affair that quickly lost its luster. When all was said and done, she didn't understand what all the fuss was about sex.

It was two years before she'd bothered to look at another man. When Greg came along, a junior with confidence to spare, she'd been ripe for the picking. Looking back, she'd been more attracted to Greg's self-assurance than his lovemaking. After a year of marriage, she'd started to believe she was as frigid as Greg accused her of being, that what she'd read in novels was pure fantasy.

What she felt for Patrick was new, and a little frightening. She became another woman in his arms. Her instincts told her to trust him, for once take something for herself, but could she take one night and then walk away without losing control of her life to another man? She hadn't completely escaped the one she'd married!

Her hand grazed the scars on her stomach. Greg had set his stamp of possession on her the night he whipped her. He didn't respect the divorce decree she'd tucked in her bag before leaving Dallas. She couldn't misinterpret the message he'd sent when he'd scrawled on the mirror and ripped into her belongings. If he had his way, she'd never be free of him so how could she consider a relationship—even a fleeting one—with Patrick?

She blew off her agitation and turned off the shower. It was time to stop this nonsense, take control of her chaotic feelings. A towel draped around her traitorous body, she wiped the steam off the bathroom mirror and glared at her expression. "You're leaving Denver the moment Greg's behind bars," she reminded her mirror image sternly. "You have no business starting anything with Patrick."

No matter how "un-frigid" he makes you feel.

Toweling dry, she readied herself for bed. She patted her favorite lilac talc all over her skin and put on the football jersey Patrick found for her to replace the nightshirt Greg had shredded. She tugged on the hem in a vain attempt to make it longer, but knew it was no use. The moment she raised her arms, she felt the material creep up her behind. Her *naked* behind.

She made a face at her damp panties hung on the towel rack where she'd put them after rinsing them. Damn Greg for leaving her only the one pair she'd been wearing. She had to ask Jane to pick up a few things for her tomorrow. She couldn't ask Patrick to take her shopping. He'd already done so much. He dealt with the police, cleaned up the disaster Greg made of her bedroom, and sorted their belongings so she didn't have to face the mess again. Thankfully, most of Amanda's clothes had escaped unscathed. Only Rachel was left practically naked.

Giving the shirt hem another jerk, she left the bathroom. She traversed the long hallway toward the bedroom at the front of the house, grateful when she didn't run into Patrick. She could hear the ten o'clock news on the television downstairs, the anchor reporting the horrible news that another coed had disappeared during the night. Rachel sympathized with the poor girl's parents. She'd die if she knew that monster, the Angel Killer, had her little girl!

Though she could hear Amanda breathing on the baby monitor she carried, she pushed faster toward her destination. Thanks to Greg's destruction, she and Amanda were forced to change rooms. Amanda picked a small room attached to the Thorne's master bedroom. It was decorated for a young child, with a fluffy, leaf green bedspread and kittens gamboling after butterflies on the walls. Rachel had to admit the room felt cozy and safe—it could only be accessed through the master—so she'd tucked her little girl into the double bed soon after her bath.

Walking through the main bedroom, she looked in on Amanda. She frowned when she saw the baby doll, Becca, stare back at her from the jumble of covers like some evil toy from a horror movie. She hadn't noticed the girls traded dolls again until she tucked Amanda into bed. She wished the vile thing would just disappear forever.

It was ridiculous to be so unnerved by a toy, but Greg gave it to his daughter and the doll had a knowing look glittering in her blue eyes, a self-satisfied smirk on her porcelain mouth, like she was Greg's partner in crime and carried secrets that could harm Amanda. Too bad the children hadn't traded back a day earlier so Greg could have trashed it along with the rest of their belongings.

Maybe it would still get crushed beneath the weight of the two-hundred thirty pound dog stretched the full length of the bed alongside Amanda, the spot Buckwheat had commandeered his first night home before Rachel could stop him. He shifted so the doll's head disappeared under his massive torso. "Good dog," Rachel whispered.

Buckwheat lifted his head to stare at her. He huffed when Amanda whimpered in her sleep, then put his head down and nuzzled her hand until she buried her fingers in the folds of his furry neck and settled back to sleep with a gentle sigh.

"I'm sorry," Patrick said in a low voice behind Rachel. "I confined him to the kitchen when I took out the trash. But he'd nosed the swinging door open and disappeared by the time I got back."

"He's certainly claimed his spot," she said, too aware of Patrick's proximity, the wisp of air that warmed the curve of her ear when he spoke.

His chuckle ran pleasantly up and down her spine. "Actually, it is his spot. This is the room Mom and Dad set aside for the little ones they still occasionally take on while they're waiting for permanent foster care. Buckwheat seems to understand when kids are hurting."

Rachel wanted to tell him to remove the animal, but after the way Amanda just responded to him, she knew she wouldn't. If Buckwheat would help her little girl, the dog stayed. The truth was she hated the idea of sleeping alone in the master bed another night. "I'm still close by when Amanda has a nightmare." She held up the baby monitor. "This thing picks up everything. I got it so I can get things done while she sleeps."

"Does she have nightmares often?"

The question startled her into facing Patrick. A mistake. He was too close. He wore a plain black T-shirt and well-worn jeans, but he might as well have been naked the way her libido perked up. A damp lock of hair fell over his forehead and, suddenly, she could visualize him in the downstairs shower, buck naked, steamy water running over his muscular body as he rubbed soapy hands all over his skin. Inhaling his clean, masculine scent, her eyelids lowered to capture more of the imagery running rampant in her head.

"Rachel?" Her name was almost a growl.

Her eyes widened. Abruptly changing direction, she walked away from him toward the king-sized bed. *Good grief! Not that direction either!* She stopped in the middle of the room, turned her back on the four-poster, and wrapped her arms around her middle. "Yes," she said, responding to Patrick's question. "She has dreams almost nightly since," she paused, unable to discuss her last night with Greg, "for months."

"Did Bishop beat her, too?" Patrick asked sharply, putting two and two together without her help.

"No, thank God," she said with a violent shake of her head. "But that's the night she stopped talking." She hadn't left Greg fast enough to protect her little girl, and guilt was a constant pang in her heart. "I was taking her to a doctor who specialized in traumatized children, but we had to leave Dallas before she made any real progress with her."

Patrick scowled at the doorway into the smaller bedroom. "She needs help."

She nodded. "I'm stuck until we can put this mess with Greg behind us. As soon as we return to Dallas, I can get her back into therapy."

"I'll talk to Joe. He was a counseling psychologist in Chicago before he returned home two years ago, although," he shook his head, "he stopped taking on patients after he started working at the high school. Sam might have someone at the hospital who can work with Amanda if she prefers a woman doctor. If it's been months, maybe a new approach will help."

Rachel stared. At every turn, this man did wonderful things for her and Amanda. "Thank you," she said.

"No problem."

"Why are you doing all this?" The question escaped before she knew it had been bothering her for days. What kind of man took on the kind of trouble she'd dragged to his door, without hesitation, without expecting anything in return?

For a moment, she wasn't sure he'd respond. His dark eyes were fixed on her and, inexplicably, she remembered she only wore a light dusting of powder beneath his football jersey. He wasn't looking at her in an inappropriate way but a zing of awareness skimmed through her bloodstream. "Patrick?"

Her whisper of his name broke his gaze. "No child should be traumatized by those who are supposed to love her," he said. "I want to help her."

"No, I meant," she waved her arm to encompass the house, "*all this.* You're protecting us from Greg, throwing your life into disarray."

He shrugged. "Anyone would do the same."

No, they wouldn't. Touched by his inability to acknowledge the caring, protective man she knew him to be, Rachel's insides melted. "I appreciate everything you've done for us," she said.

"You're welcome."

He stared at her so long she could feel the pull of sexual tension between them. Or maybe that was just her hormones taking notice. She wondered what he'd do if she walked over and kissed him.

"I'll go call my brothers. G'night." Then, he was gone, the bedroom door shut tight behind him.

Working to calm her ratcheting pulse, she crawled onto the four poster bed. Aware she wouldn't fall asleep any time soon, despite the fact it was after ten o'clock, she propped her back on the carved headboard and reached for the romance novel Jane gave her this morning. Running her index finger over the figure on the cover, the hero's broad chest gleaming above his tartan, she compared the character's physique to Patrick's. The contractor might not carry a sword like one of her favorite warriors, but he was a sexy rescuer nevertheless. He could carry her into his keep and claim her like some beleaguered princess any time!

"Oh, for goodness sake," she exclaimed, tossing the book aside. A romance was the last thing she should read tonight, not when the masculine fantasy she craved was elsewhere in the house making phone calls. Maybe there was something else to read in Ross Thorne's office behind the stairs. She'd spotted a couple of espionage thrillers on his shelves a couple of days ago.

She glanced into the other room and checked on Buckwheat lying alongside Amanda. It looked like he was sound asleep, but then he opened his eyes and stared at her. He exhaled a huff of air that assured her that he was on guard duty; she could dash downstairs for a different book. If she hurried, she could get back to her room without running into Patrick again.

Decision made, she picked up the shawl Evelyn Thorne had thrown over the end of the bed and enveloped her body like a sarong, adding another six inches of material below Patrick's football jersey. Feeling less exposed, she grabbed the baby monitor and walked toward the bedroom door. She was passing the huge antique dresser when she spotted a bubble-wrapped package centered in the middle of the mahogany surface.

Greg had returned and left another threat?

Alarm swept through her senses. Then, she saw a flash of silver peeking from one end and recognized the delicate engraving. She crossed to the dresser, picked up the bulky package, and began to unwind the bubble wrap. When the wrapping fell to the floor, she cradled her mother's hand mirror.

She stared with disbelief at her unbroken reflection. Her fingers trembled as she slowly traced the swirl design hammered into the silver frame. A couple of tiny scratches remained but the worst of the damage had been smoothed, repaired. Turning the mirror over, she examined the mono-grammed letters on the surface.

LMJ. Laura Margaret James.

"Oh, Patrick," she murmured, holding the precious memento to her breast. She hadn't questioned his appearance in her bedroom tonight, but he must have been delivering this package. Overwhelmed by his thoughtful gesture, several moments passed. Then she left the master bedroom and went to look for Patrick. She found him coming up the stairs.

He smiled and stopped a couple of steps below her so they were at eye level. "I spoke with Sam about Amanda. He has a friend who—" He frowned. "What's wrong?"

"I-I—" She held out the mirror. "You fixed it."

"Sorry I don't have the brush and comb yet, but the silversmith said it would take more time to repair the other pieces. He was able to hammer out the dents and replace the mirror though." He flashed a crooked smile. "I hope it helps to have this piece while you wait for the others."

How did she explain that he'd just handed her mother back to her? "You fixed it," she repeated.

He gave a negligent shrug, like it was no big deal. "It means a lot to you."

Without thinking, she leaned over the edge of the top step and kissed him. It was a chaste, grateful caress...at first. Then, it transformed into something else. Something hot and voracious. Needy.

That quickly, Rachel couldn't get close enough. The desire she'd been fighting in the shower flamed higher and burned through any thoughts of self-preservation. "Patrick," she whispered. "Kiss me back. Please?"

She wasn't sure he'd heard her, but then he groaned and his big hands circled her upper arms. "Rachel." Her name sounded more like a plea than a warning to stop so she was startled when he set her away from him. "If I kiss you back," he growled, his fingers warm on her skin, "I'll forget I'm supposed to be protecting you. Even from me."

The desire blazing in his eyes was too tempting to ignore. "What if I don't want that kind of protection from you?"

His gaze sharpened. "You don't know what you're saying."

She might never have experienced real passion, but she instinctively knew making love with Patrick would be different. Just once, she longed to be with a man who made her feel truly desired. A man who set her on fire with one look. "You don't want me?"

"Since that first night in the moonlight."

Her blood heated at his rough admission. She hadn't realized he saw her sitting on the porch that night, watched her visually caress him, sure of her anonymity in the shadows. She'd built so many fantasies in her head since then. Fantasies where she could revel in the way he looked at her, the glittering edge of passion in his dark eyes showing a man on the verge of losing control, a man who'd carry her with him.

Like he was looking at her now.

Before she could worry that she wasn't ready for Patrick in the flesh, his large hand wrapped around the back of her neck. He pulled her into another kiss. It wasn't hard, or demanding, but the caress of her dreams.

He worshiped her lips. He sipped. He nibbled. He captured the sound of her moan on his tongue.

When she swayed, they almost lost their balance on the stairs. "Whoa," Patrick murmured. His hands on her hips, he pushed her back on the landing. "This isn't such a good idea," he said.

"But—"

The sweet appeal in Rachel's Southern whiskey voice rammed through Patrick's defenses more effectively than if she'd tackled him with another of her soul stealing kisses. The look of confusion and, God help him, passion in her luscious brown eyes called to him. His pulse pounded in his ears.

"Shh," he said, taking the last two steps to the landing. He walked her backward until she bumped into the solid wall between the two bedrooms that anchored the top of the stairs, her breasts warm, yielding against him. "Now," he said, "we won't fall down the stairs."

He took the mirror from her hand and placed it carefully on the hall table to his left before his head dipped again. He nuzzled her flushed cheek, her fragrant hair, the corner of her mouth, teasing, never quite allowing himself to settle into a proper kiss.

A sane voice in his head ordered him to take his hands off her, push her away, but the voice went silent when he tangled one hand in her silky blond hair. He angled her head to give him access to the tender area beneath her jaw. Making his way to her pulse, he took his time over that sweet spot before moving to the other side. "You taste as delectable as you smell," he murmured, his free hand capturing her breast.

She cried out and thrust more fully into his hand.

Gently pinching her nipple through two layers of cloth, he was rewarded with another demanding cry. Anchoring Rachel between his aching body and the wall, his left hand flat beside her head, he trailed his free hand down her sweet curves to the bottom of the shawl she was wearing over his old football jersey. He slowly gathered the material upward until he uncovered bare skin.

He froze. "You're not wearing panties." The words scraped like gravel in his throat.

"Is that a problem?"

"Only if I had a chance in hell of sending you back to your room without taking you right here, up against this wall."

Talking to her in his parents' bedroom fifteen minutes ago was difficult enough when he saw how feminine and sexy she looked wearing his old jersey. It had taken everything he had to force his libidinous carcass out of the room. Once he realized she'd gone commando beneath all of that innocence—

"No chance," Rachel said, her sultry smile cutting him off at the knees.

He cursed when she pulled his T-shirt from his waistband and the back of her knuckles seared his bare stomach. "Not here," he ground out. He took her hand and dragged her through the nearest doorway. With the light from the hallway guiding him across his brother, Ben's old bedroom, he led Rachel to the queen-sized, brass bed. He tossed the coverlet aside and eased her onto the cool sheets.

When he started to follow her down, she stopped him. "Shut the door?"

"Let me see you, Rachel."

"Please? No lights?" She stared up at him and shrugged. "I-I don't want you to see my scars."

Patrick's insides twisted. He wanted to tell her the scars didn't make him want her any less, but he didn't think she was ready to hear how close to the edge he was. He walked to the door and closed it, shutting off the glow of light from the hall lamp. With the heavy drapes drawn on this side of the house, it was difficult to see much. But he knew every square foot of his family home so he walked back to the bed, pulling his T-shirt over his head on the way. He tossed it in the general direction of the chair before joining Rachel on the bed.

"Wait. Could you put the baby monitor somewhere?"

He hadn't noticed she was carrying anything besides the mirror. Hesitating, he remembered why Rachel had come to Denver...and it wasn't to satisfy his demanding libido. Whatever she'd said in the hallway, she wasn't ready for this. She couldn't be. "Amanda needs you."

Rachel tucked the monitor in his palm. "It picks up a whisper, remember?" she said. "Buckwheat's with her, too. Just put it on the nightstand."

The dog would guard Amanda with his life, Patrick knew, but—" Are you sure?"

"Please," Rachel said.

The urgency he heard in her Southern drawl convinced him, so he did as she asked. Then, lying on his side, he brought her flush with his rigid length, straining his zipper. She sighed. Her hands drifted over him, cool flutters over his scorching skin. Every touch made his muscles contract, each caress building on the next, until he ached for release.

When she flicked his nipple with a fingernail, a punch of lust ripped a ragged path to his balls. They tightened unbearably inside his jeans, the heavy material the only thing that kept him from plunging into Rachel like a randy teenager. He sucked in air when her hand grazed the bandage covering the nine stitches Sam stapled into his side on Thursday.

"Does it hurt?" she asked.

"Not as much as it will if you stop touching me," he admitted with a small laugh. "You'll just have to be gentle with me."

Aching to have her naked—and soon—he fumbled with the knot between her breasts and released the shawl. Unwrapping her like a present, he tossed the material over the side of the bed to the floor. His football jersey quickly followed. Rachel finally naked in his arms, he forced himself to slow down. He'd been dreaming of this woman forever. He was going to take his time.

He nuzzled her fragrant skin over her collar bone, the tops of each breast, around her nipples never quite touching them. He played with her until she arched closer in demand. Only then did he draw her into his mouth. He suckled one nipple, wrapped his tongue around it and tugged until the tip grew hard and distended.

"Oh!" She quickly released the top button on his jeans, the rasp of the zipper loud in the dark room. Her hand dipped behind the waistband of his briefs and cupped him. She whispered his name. "Patrick."

The air around him was laced with the scent of desire, lilacs, and Rachel. He wanted to see her, but somehow the darkness that surrounded them forced him to use his other senses which made each sensation stronger. More intense. With each stroke of her fingers, he lost another piece of his mind.

Her skin grazing his, the slender curve of her butt firm in his hand felt as good, no, *better,* than he'd imagined. He'd dreamt of making love to Rachel for days. He longed to make all of his fantasies a reality, kiss her from head to toe and back again. Explore her secret places. Find her sweet spot. Make her scream with her climax.

He wanted to look into her angel-soft, brown eyes and watch her come apart. Then, he'd finally, *finally* push inside her and put out the fire that had only flamed higher each day he was around her.

The image of Rachel sheathed tight around him, crying out as she reached for her orgasm, pulled a frustrated growl from his throat. The woman made him crazy stupid. He didn't have a condom!

There might still be one hidden in a corner of his old dresser down the hall, but if he found it, did he dare trust Rachel's protection to fourteen-year-old latex? She rocked her heat against him, his dilemma becoming more urgent by the second.

A voice whispered in his head. *Shuck your jeans and just claim her. Hard. Fast. Damn the consequences.*

"Rachel, stop," he said loud enough to smack down his libido. He caught her shoulders and gently pushed her away. "I can't do this."

She froze. "I-I—" A heartbeat passed before she whispered. "You don't want me. It's the scars, isn't it? Even in the dark...oh, God!"

When she tried to scramble off the bed, he pulled her back. A mistake. The position made it difficult to think coherently. "It's not the scars, sweetheart. I don't have a condom."

"Oh."

He felt her relax. "There are other ways," he said, unable to let her go.

"It's okay," she said at the same time.

"What?" Patrick wished the moon shone through the drawn curtains so he could see her expression. "Honey, I have to protect you."

"I'm clean. So, unless you have a disease," she stopped to lick a sensitive spot below his ear, "we're good." She traced an erotic path to the hollow at the base of his throat. Her tongue dipped into the indentation there.

His throat tightened. Trying to talk a woman out of making love to him was a new experience for him. It would help if his dick wasn't still waiting impatiently for him to get on with the program. *She's good. You're good. What's the hold up?*

Swallowing a curse, his heart raced. He wanted to accept Rachel's assurance at face value. If he couldn't see her, he wanted to feel her. *Really* feel her without anything between them. But, that way lay stupidity and he just couldn't—

"I can't...get pregnant," she said, nipping his skin.

"We can't depend on the time of the month, Rachel. And I sure don't think I'll have the willpower to pull out once I'm inside you, not that *that* method is foolproof either."

She stilled, drew back. "You don't understand. I can't get pregnant. At all. Ever." She paused. "I'm infertile."

How could this vibrant woman be infertile? Had something happened after Amanda was born? Patrick knew he should feel relief at the news it was safe to give in to his base impulses. Moments ago, he'd been dying to be buried deep inside her, protection or not. But now, all he could think about was how beautiful she'd look growing huge with a child. His child.

He was taking too long to respond, but the notion of Rachel carrying his baby stunned him. It was one thing to want her in his bed. It was something else when he thought about making her a permanent fixture in his life. He'd made a vow—

"It's safe. Can't we leave it at that and take this moment?"

He wanted to, desperately, but— "Tell me again that you want this."

"Oh, I want this," she said, "more than you know."

Out of arguments, he gave in to what they both wanted. "Come here, then," he said, kissing her until they both struggled for air.

Rachel's mouth caressed a searing path over the too tight skin right above his heart, his ribs and lower. His muscles jumped. He could barely think. Only breathe. And feel. Until he knew he had to quench this scorching desire in this woman soon or die. "Rachel!"

She pushed his jeans and briefs down together, and he sprang free. He groaned when she gave the tip of his shaft a lingering caress.

He kicked his jeans over the side of the bed and rolled Rachel beneath him. Their tongues tangled, mated. Rachel's legs wrapped around his hips, and he groaned with pleasure, riding the edge of his control.

"Honey, slow down. There's no hurry." Capturing her wrists, he carried them over her head.

With a gasp, she went completely rigid beneath him. It took a moment for the blood to return to his brain. Realizing what he'd done—this first time had to be about her pleasure, not his—he released her wrists. "I won't hurt you, Rach," he murmured. "Just tell me what you want. Show me what you need."

"I-I'm no good at this."

He heard her insecurity, felt it deep inside his gut. It took everything in him not to leave the bed and go track down Rachel's ex-husband. He wanted to hurt him for crushing the sensual creature he knew was inside her. The woman brought Patrick to his knees without trying, and she seemed completely unaware of her power over him.

"Just do what feels good." He rolled onto his back and pulled her on top of him. Her long, slim legs straddled his hips, bringing them together in too many ways that tested his control. But he raised his hands to the pillow above his head. "I won't touch you unless you ask me," he said. "Take what you want, whatever gives you pleasure."

For an eternity, Rachel couldn't think. She was too aware of the way she fit atop Patrick, like she'd been made just for him, for this moment. The heat building at her core burned away the anxiety that had rushed inside her when he'd held down her wrists. She knew making love with Patrick would be different—she'd counted on it—but she hadn't expected the exquisite fire between them. It was exhilarating...and a little scary.

It wasn't until that moment she realized Patrick could hurt her so much worse than Greg ever had. And those scars wouldn't be visible on her body. They'd be imbedded in her soul. She'd fallen for Patrick and that made him much more dangerous.

What was more frightening? She didn't care. She wanted him anyway. If it hurt her later to leave him behind, she'd still have this one night.

"Rachel?" His chest rumbled under her palms where she leaned over him.

"I'm okay," she said. Her sensitized breasts skimmed the hair on his chest as she bent down to kiss him.

She might not know what to do or ask for, but she loved kissing this man. She took her time stroking his mouth with hers, pressing her tongue to the seam of his lips, and silently begged him to let her in. When he didn't respond, she moaned her frustration. "Kiss me back."

He didn't hesitate. His head lifted off the pillow as he seduced her mouth. He sipped. He nipped her lower lip. Their tongues tangled for several glorious moments...until it wasn't enough.

"Touch me," she demanded.

"Where?"

Patrick's question rasped through the darkness and, for the first time, she wished the lights were on so she could see his face, witness the passion lining his masculine features. She could hear it in his voice, feel it in the way he hardened beneath her. "Anywhere," she whispered. "Everywhere."

Without light, she didn't see his hands. It made his touch that much more intense. The fire inside her blazed higher with each touch of his hands on her waist, over her belly, upward to her breasts. He caressed slowly, exploring her like he was memorizing it by touch alone. By the time he reached her breasts and held them in his palms, she couldn't stifle a whimper. His thumbs scraped back and forth over the tips of her breasts. "More!"

He tweaked her nipples and she felt the tug between her thighs where he was cradled. Her legs squeezed his hips. She rocked up and down his shaft seeking satisfaction she knew only he could give her.

"You're killing me, Rach."

The harsh tone of his voice stole her air and tightened her desire. His heartbeat a thundering tattoo under her hand, he took nothing more than what she was ready for. No man before Patrick had considered her feelings like this, been willing to give her pleasure at the expense of his own. She wasn't afraid of him losing control with her, maybe never had been. This was Patrick. The man who stood between her and Greg, who protected her and Amanda without expecting anything in return. She felt like a whole woman in his arms. Wanted. Desired.

Unable to wait any longer, she leaned down and nipped his chin, her fingers moving down to clasp him. He bucked into her hand and groaned. "Then, come with me. We'll die together, Patrick," she said. "Love me. Now!"

She expected him to turn her beneath him and plunge into her. But he must have realized she wasn't ready for that, not this time. Instead, he pulled her earlobe into his mouth and suckled it. His fingers traced over the scars on her back. Distracted by what his tongue was doing, she didn't even flinch at the touch.

Then, she was at his tip. His hands on her hips, he guided her into place. Too soon. Too much. Too late to slow things down. He pulled her down, one slow, agonizing inch at a time, until he was buried inside her.

"You feel...so good. So hot."

So good! She knew it would feel this way with Patrick. Warm. Wet. Hardened steel, wrapped in velvet. No discomfort. No aversion. She wanted him to stay buried inside her forever. A frisson of desire spiked through her. "I, oh please—"

She didn't say the words, yet he knew what she wanted. He circled her waist with his hands and guided her. Up. Down. Slowly. Then, more quickly.

Her hands spread on his shoulders, she rode him. She cried out with each thrust. "Yes!" she said when he picked up the pace. "Oh! Oh, please!"

Reaching for the pleasure she'd always craved, she was aware of nothing but her rhythmic movement above Patrick, the scent of their lovemaking weaving through her senses. When her climax crashed over her, she cried out his name. Moments later, he exploded inside her, and she could have sworn she saw stars in the blackness of the room around them.

16

It was an eternity later before Rachel became aware again. She held herself in place above Patrick on arms that trembled. Her inner walls still spasmed around him. Her air came in bursts, and her ears were ringing. "That was—" She couldn't find her voice, let alone the word that fit what she'd experienced in his arms.

"Incredible," he finished for her.

"Incredible," she agreed. *Unexpected. Immensely satisfying.*

"Are you all right?"

Rachel was amazed at how wonderful she felt. "I'm perfect."

He suddenly grew still beneath her. "No, you aren't," he said harshly. Not releasing her, he rolled with her to his right, reached over her shoulder and flipped on the bedside lamp. "You're crying!"

In the bright light, she blinked at his scowl. She swiped at her cheek and looked at her fingertips with surprise. "I'm crying." She gave him a tremulous smile. "I've never done that," she stammered to a halt before she continued, "never felt anything like that before."

"You've never climaxed?" Patrick grinned, clearly pleased with himself.

She shook her head. "I thought there was something wrong with me."

Patrick's grin disappeared. "There's absolutely nothing wrong with you."

"Yes, there is. I'm, well," she hesitated before she finished, "I'm frigid."

"Who told you tha...? His scowl deepened. "Never mind, I know. Listen. You are not frigid." A burst of laughter rumbled from his throat. "For god's sake, woman, you can fry the brains right out of a man. Do you think I wanted this," he thrust against her, reminding her of their intimate position, "to happen?"

"Great," she muttered, jerking away to stare up at the ceiling. "I make men do things they don't want to do." Just because she'd just had the best sex in her life didn't mean Patrick was similarly affected.

"That's not what I meant." Patrick tugged her back into his arms so she couldn't escape his gaze. "Honey, whatever your ex told you, I'm certain the problem isn't yours." He pushed a tendril of hair off her temple. "If you weren't so incredibly hot and sexy, you wouldn't make me so nuts. I could spend the next three weeks in this bed with you and it wouldn't be enough."

Rachel couldn't dismiss the sincerity in his eyes. "I'm still not exactly whole," she admitted without thinking.

"What does that mean?"

It meant she was speaking with her heart and not her head. She might trust this man with her body, even her heart since she'd already lost it to him. Did she dare tell him her deepest, darkest secret? Once the words were spoken, they could never be taken back.

Somehow, though, staring into Patrick's warm brown eyes, she knew her last secret would be safe with him. He would protect Amanda no matter what. "I thought I couldn't," her eyelids dropped briefly, "well, you know. I thought there was something wrong with me, that my inability to have children is the reason I didn't enjoy sex."

"But you have Amanda, and we've just proved you're anything but frigid." He flashed a smug smile. "The problem isn't yours."

"You proved me wrong about my ability to achieve an orgasm," she conceded with a small smile. "I still can't have children."

"Did that asshole tell you that?" His gaze sharpened. "We didn't use protection, Rachel. Is it possible you're wrong about that, too?"

He didn't move, but she felt his withdrawal. "No. I'm not wrong about that, Patrick." She laughed without humor. "Don't worry. You're safe."

"That's not—"

"It's okay," she said. Suddenly feeling the need to cover up, she scooted away from him and pulled the sheet up under her arms, her back to the hard brass behind her. *Fish or cut bait, little chickadee.*

Her father's favorite saying wasn't welcome, especially under these circumstances, but it did push away the last of her doubts. She tucked a pillow behind her shoulders before she dared to look at Patrick, lying on his side facing her. Nervous under his watchful gaze, she ran a hand through her tumbled hair. "Do you remember Simon?"

"The doctor in a coma?"

"Yes." She blinked away the reminder her friend might still die. "Simon helped me and Amanda run away from Greg six months ago," she whispered painfully. "I think, well, it's my fault he attacked Simon."

"Your ex might not be responsible." Patrick picked up her hand and frowned at the fading bruises on the underside of her wrist where Greg grabbed her the day he'd found her. She tried to pull away, but Patrick held on. He lifted her wrist and pressed his mouth over the tenderness. "I know it's what it looks like," he said, looking at her, "but you can't take responsibility. It was Simon's decision to help a friend."

"I still feel guilty." She sighed. "Anyway, I'm trying to tell you why we don't have to worry about...what we did."

"Make love, you mean." He grinned at her.

Rachel found herself grinning back, until she had to come back to her point. "Simon's more than a friend. He is, *was* my fertility doctor. Greg and I knew him in college and we went to him when I didn't get pregnant."

She rushed on. "Tests showed there was nothing wrong with Greg." She fiddled with the sheet beneath her fingertips, unable to look at Patrick for the next part. "There *is* something wrong with me. M-My eggs aren't viable." Her throat closed up on the revelation. She was as distraught now telling Patrick she was less than a woman, as she was that fateful morning she sat in Simon's office when he broke the news to her.

"Ah, Rach." Patrick sat up and wrapped her in his arms. "I'm sorry. I know how much you love children. You should have half a dozen. I've seen you with Amanda and you—

"Wait. That's what he meant when he said she was his," Patrick said, his voice low.

"Who?"

"Bishop. The day we met he said, 'I'm here now and you can't have my daughter. She's mine.' She's his blood."

Dear God, how could she have expected Patrick to understand?

"She's mine in every way that matters," she said fiercely. "I may not be her biological mother, but I carried her for nine months. I delivered her.

She's my daughter, and no one's going to take her away from me!" The urge to run was almost overwhelming.

"No one will take Amanda from you." Patrick eased them both down flat on the bed and jockeyed her into position above him until her breasts covered his chest and they were eye-to-eye. He thrust his hands into her hair and pulled her down for a mind-blowing kiss.

And, that quickly, Rachel no longer felt the urge to run. Patrick's kiss, his touch, enticed her to stay right where she was, in this bed. In his protective arms.

"This is what your ex is holding over you."

It took a moment for her brains to unscramble. "What?"

"Your ex. He wants your inheritance and he's holding Amanda's paternity over your head to get it."

The conversation touched on some uncomfortable truths, but she couldn't run away from them anymore. Separating from Patrick's distracting heat, she lay on the bed and faced him. "Yes, he needs Amanda to get his hands on it."

"You said you're the—"

"Beneficiary. Yes, I am. He thinks it's going to Amanda, but I told my great-aunt the truth. I asked her to change her will. Between us, we earmarked a huge portion of the estate for charities and trusts that can't be accessed easily or at all, but there's still enough left to entice Greg." She could see Patrick working through the information. "And no, it won't matter if I tell him the truth. All he has to do is take my little girl away. He knows I'll do anything to keep her, even if it means giving him every last penny of what I can access."

"But that's not all." Patrick's eyebrows lowered. "The message he left in the bedroom, he wasn't talking about the inheritance, was he? If he can take Amanda back any time, he has all the power. So what else does he want?"

"Me," she whispered. "To his mind, he owns me." Bile rose in Rachel's throat as she remembered the words he'd left on the dresser mirror. *GIVE ME BACK WHAT'S MINE!* The possibility she'd have to turn herself over to him to keep her daughter safe, to live the rest of her life under his control, made her insides churn.

Her fingers touched her scars. "Patrick. I'm worried the police won't find him. That I'll live the rest of my life running. Hiding."

"Sweetheart, listen to me. He doesn't own you." Patrick traced the back of his knuckles over her scars. "These don't mean he owns you either. All they mean is that he's a brutal son-of-a-bitch who deserves a jail cell."

"But—"

"No buts. Bishop will have to go through me to get you or Amanda. Trust me. Trust Jack and the police. When we tell them what he's really after—"

"You can't tell them anything!" He was asking too much, to relinquish complete control over her life. Over her precious Amanda. "I trust the police to follow the letter of the law," she said tightly. "If they learn Amanda isn't mine and Greg demands her back, they'll have no choice but to turn her over. Promise me you'll never tell anyone."

"Rach, be sensible. The man won't go to those lengths. He's wanted for attempted murder, arson, and a host of other charges. They won't give an innocent child to a man like that."

"You don't know him like I do. He'll find a way to escape prosecution. If he is sent to jail, he'll make sure I don't get her just to punish me." She scrambled off the bed. Grabbing the football jersey Patrick had tossed to the floor before making love to her, she covered herself before looking at him. "You have to promise to keep my secret, Patrick or, so help me, I'll take Amanda on the first flight out of Denver."

He scowled. "I can't protect you if you—"

"Promise or I'm gone." Much as it would hurt to leave Patrick behind, especially after the way he'd made love to her, considering her feelings for the man, she had to ensure Amanda never fell into her brutal father's hands. "Please, Patrick," she pleaded.

He searched her face for several long moments. "I promise," he said. "Despite what you think, I want to keep Amanda away from her father as much as you do."

Rachel felt better with his promise, but now she became aware that she was standing in the middle of the room wearing nothing but an oversized shirt looking down at the man she'd just had sex...no, made love with. She could smell Patrick on her skin, feel him inside her. She longed to crawl back into the bed and recapture the wonder he'd shown her, but was unsure where they went from here. "I should go."

Patrick tossed aside the sheet that covered him, stood up, and walked toward her completely comfortable with his nakedness. Rachel felt a thrill of excitement go through her, a zing of anticipation when he stopped directly in front of her. "No more running, Rachel." His hand around the back of her neck, he pulled her close. "Don't regret what we just did."

"I don't." She bit her lip. "I just...."

What? Gave all of herself to a man for the first time in her life? Fell in love? Put her daughter in his hands in the hope he wouldn't ultimately betray them both as every other man in her life had done?

He smiled crookedly. "This thing between us is scary, I know. I should never have let it happen."

There it was! "No problem," she said, her hurt clear in her tone. "It won't happen again. I'll—"

He cut her off with a hot, drugging kiss that went on and on. She moaned as he picked her up and carried her back to the bed. When he climbed in after her, he yanked her beneath him. "I should never have made love to you," he said, his voice rough, "because I knew once wouldn't be enough. When I'm around you, I'm distracted. I can't keep you and Amanda safe."

Relieved she wasn't the only one affected, Rachel wriggled with pleasure. "Then, why are we here again?"

Patrick growled. "I told you, dammit. Once isn't enough!" He reached for the lamp on the bedside table and turned it off, plunging them into darkness.

Then he kissed her, his skillful hands building the fire inside her once more. And she was lost in sensation with the man she loved despite all of her good sense.

When Rachel woke up, she was still nestled in Patrick's arms. She didn't know what startled her awake, but hearing her daughter's breathing over the monitor on the bedside table, she knew Amanda was okay. She listened to the sounds of the old Victorian settling and decided she'd awakened because she wasn't used to sleeping with anyone. Amanda didn't take up as much of the bed as Patrick.

She was tempted to turn on the light so she could watch him sleep, yet she didn't dare wake him if she ever expected to climb out of bed before dawn. He'd made love to her twice more so she was a little sore, but it was her worry Amanda would wake up to find her mother gone that made it imperative that she leave the sensual world Patrick had carved out for them the past few hours. It was time to rejoin the real world.

Rachel eased out of his embrace and left the bed. After being surrounded by his warmth, her skin broke out into a rash of goose bumps in the air conditioned room. She searched the floor for the shawl, but couldn't find it in the dark. Locating Patrick's football jersey, she pulled it over her nakedness. Warmer, she picked up the baby monitor and left the room, shutting the door most of the way so the hall light didn't shine directly on the bed.

After checking on Amanda and Buckwheat, who gazed up at Rachel with what she was sure was an accusing look for her desertion, she reclosed the master bedroom door and padded downstairs to the kitchen. A glass of milk might help her get back to sleep...in her own bed.

The kitchen door swung shut behind her before she turned on the overhead lights and glanced at the clock over the stove. Three o'clock. Ugh. She'd have to be up again in a couple of hours to get herself and Amanda ready to accompany Patrick to Southgate. What she wouldn't give for a sleep-in this morning!

Opening the refrigerator, she reached into the back for the milk carton. Her head buried, she heard the distinctive beep of someone disabling the security alarm ten feet away. She crouched behind the negotiable protection of the eggs, butter, mustard and ketchup bottles lining the refrigerator door, and peeked around it in time to see the exterior doorknob turn. The next thing she saw were strong male fingers curling around the edge of the door as it opened.

Horror seized her heart at the thought of Patrick and Amanda upstairs asleep, unaware of the danger breaking into the house. Rachel grabbed a large bottle of soy sauce in one hand and a half-full, pint jar of almond butter in the other. She didn't stand a chance of catching the intruder unaware, not with the lights blazing overhead, but maybe she could lob her weapons fast enough to throw him off guard so she could escape the kitchen and run up the stairs. A head start. That's all she needed.

She straightened slowly, squeezing her glass missiles tightly in both hands. She leaped out into the open—the soy sauce raised over her head—and looked into dark startled eyes very much like Patrick's.

"Whoa, Rachel!" Ross Thorne raised a hand in surrender. "Don't shoot. It's us."

Patrick's mother, Evelyn, poked her head around her husband's shoulder. "Oh, dear! We did scare her, Ross. I told you we should get a motel until morning."

Rachel lowered her weapon and worked to subdue the rush of blood in her head. "I-It's okay. I'm fine," she said, noticing the crutch tucked under Ross's right arm. His knee on that side was bandaged, in a brace, and everything around it was an ugly, swollen mass of black and blue. It probably hurt like the devil. "Besides, it looks like you should be in your own bed tonight."

Evelyn shut the door behind her. "It seems like we've been traveling for a week trying to get home. We had to fly into Colorado Springs and rent a car for the last leg." She went to the breakfast nook to pull out a chair at the table for her husband. "Ross, sit before you fall down."

"Evie, will you stop—"

The swinging kitchen door slammed open and Patrick ran into the room. "Don't move, you bas—" he said, his arms outstretched in a shooter's stance, a Glock steady on the intruders.

"Good to see you're carrying protection, son," Ross quipped. His gaze ran from the gun down Patrick's naked body and back up again.

Patrick's arms dropped to his sides. "Mom. Dad. What are you doing here?"

His mother snorted. "I think the same question could be put to you, Patrick." She grabbed a dish towel from the rack and handed it to him, then glanced at Rachel while he tried to cover himself with the miniscule cloth.

Rachel's face heated with embarrassment under Evelyn and Ross's appraisal. She wasn't wearing any underwear and Patrick's football jersey covered her but she noticed, tugging at the hem, she'd put the shirt on inside out in the dark. With her bed-tossed hair, his parents would have to be blind to not know what she and their son were doing earlier tonight.

Just let me crawl into the pantry now!

Evidently, Patrick didn't feel the same embarrassment. He walked behind the center island so that he was only visible from the waist up, and then tossed the towel onto the counter in front of him. "Dad, how did you get in here?"

Ross raised an eyebrow in a manner that reminded Rachel of his son. "We live here, Patrick. We have a house key and the security code."

Patrick scowled. "No, I mean, how did you get past the security guard outside? He wouldn't have let you in without calling me first."

Evelyn shook her head. "We didn't see anyone."

Wait. "Security guard?" Rachel stared at Patrick. "You brought Dad's goons back without telling me?"

"Not now, Rachel." He stalked around the island toward his father. "Dad, give me your shirt. There's supposed to be a guard out there. I've got to find him."

Jockeying his crutch under his arm, Ross began to rise from the chair. "I'll go with you," he said in what Rachel suspected was his "cop" voice. "Back you up."

"You can barely stand, Dad. Just give me your shirt," he said. When Ross handed him the multicolored tropical shirt, he tugged it on and aimed for the exterior door. "I'll be back in—"

Rachel's gaze fixed on his muscular buttocks below the shirt hem, she didn't realize the door was opening until Larson Cook, the security consultant who'd found Rachel's trashed car, rushed in, his gun in his left hand. "Thorne," he said with a downward glance. His gaze shot back up and fixed on Patrick's parents. "There's a problem?"

"You might say that," Patrick said tersely. "The problem is that my parents caught you with your pants down and somehow walked right past you. Where were you?"

Cook raised an eyebrow, but he didn't say the obvious, or look below Patrick's chin again. "I thought I heard something in the alley and went to investigate. Turned out it was a couple of cats f—," he paused to glance at Evelyn and Rachel before he said, "fighting."

If Rachel weren't so ticked Patrick had brought her father's guards back, she might have laughed at the man's discomfort. "Well, you can go home. You're fired."

The man straightened. "Beg your pardon, Ms. James, but you can't fire me. Your father is my employer so he's the only one who can. The Thornes can throw me off their property. I'll still do my job, from the public sidewalk and alley, if necessary."

"You were re-hired on my say so, Cook," Patrick said. "But screw up again and you're out of here, no matter who hired you. Understood?"

"Understood," he said. He tucked his gun into a shoulder holster beneath his jacket, and acknowledged Evelyn and Ross with a nod. "Welcome back, Mr. and Mrs. Thorne. I'll just do another sweep of the perimeter. Excuse me." Then he walked out the way he'd come in.

The door barely closed behind the man when Rachel confronted Patrick. "How could you let dad's hired thugs come back here? You know how I feel. I thought you were on my side."

"Of course, I'm on your side." Patrick straightened. "But, I won't take a chance on you or Amanda getting hurt because you can't deal with your father or what he did."

"Patrick," his mother said, quietly. "Maybe we should postpone this dis—"

"This has nothing to do with what he did," Rachel said, her fists on her hips, "but what he wants. I refuse to give him another chance to throw me and Amanda away."

"He wants what I want, your safety, dammit!" He glared at her. "You'd know that if you'd talk to him like a grownup, instead of ignoring him like a hurting twelve-year-old."

She jerked back like he'd slapped her.

"Patrick Michael Thorne! Stop yelling at Rachel this minute!" In the silence that followed Evelyn's order, she glared at her son. "Now, if you would be so kind as to go put on some pants, we can talk like civilized human beings. Or, better yet, go home. We've been traveling for three days and your dad is injured, in case it's escaped your notice. He should be in bed."

Lowering his head, Patrick sighed heavily. He looked calmer when his gaze skimmed over Rachel to his mother. "Sorry, Mom." He frowned at his dad's knee brace, and the two men exchanged a look Rachel couldn't interpret.

Ross nodded to his son without saying a word, and then stood and grabbed his wife's hand. "We'll all sleep better with Patrick parked on the living room couch, Evie."

"But—"

"Enough, woman. He stays." After he got his crutch situated under his arm, he hobbled across the kitchen toward the hallway with Evelyn fussing around him.

As they passed Rachel, Evelyn turned to Patrick with a stern eye. "*Couch*, son."

Color filled Patrick's face. "Yes, ma'am."

17

Dressed in a bright pink sundress, Amanda stood on the bench seat in front of the vanity mirror, her gaze fixed on her mother's reflection. Rachel finished braiding her fine, blond hair into one pigtail down to her shoulder blades. Then, Amanda sat on the seat while Rachel tied her sparkly pink tennis shoes. "So what should we have for breakfast?" Rachel asked with a smile. "Cereal or muffins? Miss Jane left banana muffins."

Her daughter shrugged, not looking particularly excited by either option.

Rachel would happily sign over her great-aunt's estate to have her little girl respond the way a normal child would. A demanding whine for marshmallow cereal without the cereal would have been welcome this morning. She'd never had a chance to ask Patrick last night about his phone call to Sam. They'd gotten a little sidetracked making love.

Had Sam suggested a doctor for Amanda? She would have to ask Patrick, if she ever went downstairs again. She wanted to see him, yet she didn't. After last night, she was feeling particularly vulnerable this morning.

She also dreaded facing his parents after the awkwardness of their arrival, but knew she couldn't put it off forever. How could she deny that, yes, what they suspect happened between her and their son *did* happen?

The evidence stood right in front of them under the glaring kitchen lights, her wearing practically nothing, her hair a tumbled mess from Patrick's roaming fingers. Her face and neck burned with more whisker burn than embarrassment. She'd looked well and truly loved when they walked in. And, Patrick? He'd run into the room naked!

The memory of the man racing to her aid when he thought she was in danger, not stopping long enough to put on pants, made her heart flutter. He'd crashed into the kitchen like one of the sexy, protective warriors from her books. With the bandage over his ribs, he'd even carried a battle scar. She hoped his parents interpreted her quick flush of color as embarrassment, and not her overwhelming desire to drag him back up the stairs to give him his reward.

Heat washed through her. Patrick was right. One night wasn't nearly enough. He made her feel so much, showed her a side of herself she'd thought was missing.

How could she still want him, though after the way he'd roared at her in front of his parents? And what about the bodyguards? On the logical hand, she knew she should be grateful for the extra protection. The police hadn't been able to put Greg behind bars yet, and Patrick couldn't be with her and Amanda every second of every day. On the other, more emotional hand, she wanted to smack Patrick for being just one more man controlling her life.

Worse, he'd talked to her father without discussing it with her first. If he'd told her what he wanted to do, she would have forbidden him to make the call. It was not his decision to make.

She didn't want—or need—her dad's help. He wasn't coming back into her life just so he could get his hands on Great-Aunt Amanda's money. Much as she'd like to believe there was an acceptable reason for him to show up after all of this time, she just couldn't. It would break her heart to watch him walk away from her a second time. And she refused to allow him to hurt Amanda once.

Rachel knew what she had to do with the money her great-aunt left her, and it wasn't to hand it all over to the men in her life. She'd decided last night after everyone went to bed, when she was stuck wide awake trying not to relive every second of Patrick's lovemaking, it was time to call her lawyer and have him set her proposal in front of her uncles. It might not be enough to get them to withdraw their challenge to the will, but it was worth a try to start a dialogue with them. She didn't want all that money for herself—God knows, money couldn't buy happiness—but she had to keep her promise to her great-aunt.

Flashing a smile at Amanda, she helped her off the vanity stool. Her little girl's hand clutched in hers, she escorted her downstairs to the kitchen.

"Good morning, Rachel," Evelyn called out merrily from the stove. The tall, spare woman looked fresh as a daisy in Bermuda shorts and a sleeveless cotton shirt, an apron with decorative spills all over it that said in bold letters, "It takes real talent to get food into the pot." Evelyn eased pancakes onto two plates on the counter and handed one to Amanda. "Do you like blueberry pancakes, sweetie?"

Amanda nodded with more animation than she'd shown the muffins her mother suggested earlier.

Evelyn motioned toward the table. "Then, find a seat and dig in." She glanced at her husband. "Ross, please stop reading that newspaper and pour some syrup on Amanda's pancakes."

Patrick's dad winked at the little girl, folded his paper, and reached for the bottle. He'd poured a sticky lake over her single pancake by the time Rachel walked around Buckwheat, planted at his master's feet, and sat at the table with her own breakfast.

Grateful Patrick wasn't there—she wasn't ready to deal with him yet—she bit her bottom lip and waded in. "I'm sorry you couldn't sleep in your own bed last night, Mr. Thorne," she said, pouring creamer into her coffee. "Amanda and I will move out of the master suite this morning."

It was a great excuse to avoid going to Southgate with Patrick. She'd strip and remake the bed in the room at the top of the stairs, too. It was bad enough the Thornes suspected she and Patrick slept together without providing incontrovertible proof.

"It's Ross, and that's really not necessary," he said. "Amanda's safe in the adjoining room with Buckwheat, and she needs her mother nearby." He frowned down at the brace on his right leg. "Besides, it's easier to get in and out of the twin bed in the boys' old sick room next to my office. I can't say I was looking forward to negotiating the stairs on crutches."

"I'm happy enough in the other twin, too," Evelyn said from her position by the stove, wiping a hand on her apron. "In forty years of marriage, the only time I've slept alone was when Ross worked graveyards. Now he's retired, I'm catching up."

"Sprain or not, I'm still able to outrun you, woman." Ross grinned at his wife, a naughty glint in his dark brown eyes.

Wow. Rachel suddenly knew where Patrick got that look that melted her bones. "I meant to ask last night. What did you do to your leg?"

Patrick chose that moment to walk into the kitchen from outside, dressed for a day at work, his hair still damp from a shower he must have taken at his house. "I want to hear this one, too, Dad." His intense gaze tangled with Rachel's before he looked away. "You and Mom weren't supposed to be home from the Virgin Islands until Jack's wedding in three weeks."

Ross shook his head at his son and mouthed, "Don't mention—"

Handing a cup of black coffee to Patrick, Evelyn caught the silent warning. She frowned. "For goodness sake, Ross, I won't fly off the handle because I'm not the least bit involved in my son's wedding arrangements. I respect Jack's reasons for not upsetting Maggie's family."

"But you said you were going on vacation," Patrick said, "precisely because you couldn't stand being left out of everything."

"I'll admit it was bothering me a bit, but that's not the real reason why I agreed to go. I just didn't want Jack to stress, worrying that I was stressing. Your brother's going to have enough on his plate once he marries that family." She shrugged. "I have five more chances to plan a wedding."

Despite her conciliatory tone, it sounded to Rachel like Evelyn had reservations about her son's future in-laws.

"Jack's not marrying Maggie's family, Mom."

"Want to bet? Just because you didn't have to deal with Karly's dysfunctional parents...oh, fiddle." Making a face that made it clear she hadn't intended to reveal so much, she walked back to the stove and flipped three large pancakes onto an empty plate. "The point is a man and a woman brings more than themselves into a marriage." She returned to the table and set the plate in front of Patrick. "More relationships are destroyed by a spouse's family than you can imagine."

"In-laws can be hard on a marriage at the best of times," Ross agreed, handing the syrup bottle across the table to Patrick. "Mom and I didn't have to deal with any of that because neither of us had any family to make things difficult. But, to be honest, I don't think your mom's father would have been happy with her decision to marry a man on a lowly cop's salary."

"Like he'd have anything to say about it." Evelyn bent down to kiss Ross. "I chose you. If he loved me, he'd have accepted my decision. Eventually."

"With any luck, Maggie's family will settle down once they're married," he said, a crease over his brow. "If nothing else, the baby will distract them. They're really excited about their first grandchild."

Evelyn shrugged. "Let's hope Jack won't have to wait that long."

The older Thornes shared a look before Patrick pointedly reminded them of his question. "So it was your knee that brought you home early. How did you hurt it?"

Evelyn snorted. "Your father caught a downdraft parasailing."

Ross snorted, and shifted in his chair. "The island doc said it's just a sprain. We could have stayed, spent the rest of our vacation lying in a hammock on the beach, but your mom insisted we come home."

"You might have been killed, Ross," Evelyn said, irritation and worry in her voice. "You're sixty-four years old and shouldn't have—"

"Ah, Evie." Ross pulled the woman down onto his good knee. "You're just ticked I went first and you didn't get your turn. I agreed to see our doctor when we got home, so stop nagging on me."

"Fine. But, if I'm right and the doctor says your ACL is torn, you owe me a prime rib dinner at The Timber Wolf." Evelyn placed both hands on his jaw and kissed him. "And next time, Mr. Hotshot, I get to go first."

"I'm sure I speak for all of my brothers when I say I'd be more comfortable if you'd both keep your feet on the ground," Patrick said dryly, taking a bite of blueberry pancakes.

His parents grinned. Then, Patrick's brother-in-law, Skip, walked in from outside.

Rachel hadn't seen him up close since the incident with the councilman. He was wearing his usual jeans over his lanky frame. Today, they looked new and he sported a white button-down shirt beneath a dark blue suit coat. Add a striped tie, his dark brown hair slicked back with some sort of gel, and it looked like he was going on a date. "Good morning, Skip," she said. "You look very nice today."

"I'm visiting my sister's grave." He shuffled his feet. "It's her birthday."

"Oh." Seeing Patrick's stony expression across the table, Rachel's heart sank. He'd never mentioned his dead wife and she'd been too afraid to wade into what she suspected were deep waters. Did he still love his wife? Rachel had no illusions he had strong feelings beyond lust for her, which caused a pang in her heart.

When she looked at Evelyn, she found her watching Patrick, too. "Your flowers are ready inside the greenhouse door, Skip," she said, rising from Ross's knee. "Leave them in the water bucket until you get up to the cabin or they'll wilt."

"Did you want me to take yours with me, Patrick?" he asked.

Patrick blinked. "I didn't—"

Evelyn interrupted. "That would be nice, Skip," she said. "I put both bouquets in the bucket." She gestured to the food on the table. "Before you go, would you like some blueberry pancakes?"

"No thanks, Evelyn. I grabbed a breakfast sandwich on the way over." He smiled at Rachel. "I'm happy to see you're none the worse after Thursday."

"I'm not the one who saved the day," she said, remembering the horror she'd felt when she realized Patrick might be killed right in front of her. "I haven't had a chance to tell you, but thanks for what you did."

"I had to protect Patrick." He looked at him with hero worship. "Karly may be gone, but he's still family. He gave me a job and a home when I came back from the army after Karly...um, he gave me purpose again."

Patrick sat stiffly in his seat, clearly uncomfortable with his brother-in-law's praise. Or was it the second mention of Karly's death that was causing the trouble? "Still a heroic thing to do, Skip," he agreed, "and we're all grateful for your quick thinking. You saved our lives. I meant what I said last night. Don't hurry back to work today. It'll take at least four hours to get up to the cabin and back, so stay the night and return in the morning. You know where to find the key."

Skip shook his head. "Can't. We've got trouble at Southgate. It's why I'm here...besides the flowers, I mean. Seems the landscaper we contracted ran off to Mexico with his office girl. He left his wife and crew high and dry."

Patrick cursed, and then glanced at Amanda, who stared at him across the kitchen table with wide eyes. He gave her a reassuring smile before he spoke to Skip again in a calmer voice. "They've barely started landscaping the first building. There's at least two weeks of work, maybe three. Please tell me he left someone in charge of the project."

"I wish. According to the employee I talked to, boss man was too cheap to pay a crew lead. He was running the show," Skip said. "His guys want to work. They just have no one to give them direction. Or pay them. He cleaned out his business accounts, along with his personal ones."

Pushing his plate of uneaten pancakes into the center of the table, a muscle ticked in Patrick's jaw. "The grand opening of the first two buildings is already scheduled. There has to be someone who can take over."

"I've made a few phone calls." Skip shrugged. "All of the available landscapers either have full schedules for the summer or don't have the resources to handle a project of this size in the time we have left."

Evelyn spoke up. "Rachel can do it, Patrick. She's has a degree in landscape design and she's going to be Katy's partner when she returns to Dallas. She can take over the project, and you can pay the crew yourself."

"I can't—" Rachel started to say when she processed what Evelyn said. *Katy was offering her a partnership?* She'd mentioned the possibility of training her to take over once, years ago when she'd first worked for Katy the summer before she went off to college and met Greg, but they hadn't discussed it again. If asked a couple of weeks ago, she'd have been thrilled. She wasn't planning to give up her landscaping dreams after her great-aunt's estate was settled. But, she glanced at Patrick, so much had changed.

"She can't," he said firmly. "She may have the skills, but I can't guarantee her safety if she's running all over the site."

His gaze bounced off Rachel and she wondered if this was his way of distancing himself after last night. He'd made it clear, then, he hadn't wanted to get involved, but he had and now he couldn't look at her?

Suddenly furious with the man, her own gullibility, she straightened her shoulders. "You insisted on bringing back my dad's bodyguards, Patrick, so let them guard. I'd rather be connected at the hip with them doing something useful than sitting in the trailer twiddling my thumbs." She rushed on before he could shoot her down. "You have the blueprints for the job, right?"

Their gazes locked and, for a moment, she lost herself in the heat of his eyes. His next words washed over her like a bucket of ice water. "Of course, I have blueprints. But what about Amanda and Suze?" he asked. "Are you planning to traipse them all over the site, too? The idea is to keep them safe and that means keeping them hidden."

Her anger dissipated under his argument. She dare not expose the children. Greg would jump on any chance to get his hands on Amanda.

"Maybe I can help from the safety of the trailer," she conceded. "I don't have to be hands on. I could give the landscapers direction and someone on your crew can monitor things for me."

"I don't think—"

"The girls can stay here under lock and key with me and your dad, Patrick," Evelyn interjected. She smiled at Amanda. "Would you like to spend the day with me and Suze baking cookies, sweetie?"

Amanda's head bounced up and down excitedly. Then she glanced at her mother.

It broke Rachel's heart to see her little girl's eyes dim. Of course, Amanda would jump at the chance to bake cookies. It was her favorite thing to do with her mother before their life fell apart. Once they reached Dallas, Rachel was so busy trying to save Katy and her nurseries that baking had fallen by the wayside.

Maybe the normal activity was just what her daughter needed. Between a security system, Buckwheat, and Patrick's policeman father, she'd be safe enough here at the house. The question was could she let her daughter out of her sight? They'd never been further than a room or two apart since they fled the west coast. "Do you want to stay here all day with Miss Evelyn and Suze if Mama's not here?"

Her little girl nodded vigorously, her eyes pleading.

Was Rachel the only one having separation anxiety? "What about your doctor's appointment?" she asked Ross.

"I doubt we'll get one today," he said, "but if we do, we'll take Amanda with us. I may not be able to do a 50-yard sprint, but I'm perfectly able to guard her."

Evelyn nodded. "And Ross taught me self-defense. We'll protect Amanda like our own."

Rachel looked at Patrick, who was following the discussion with a closed expression. "Looks like you all have it planned out," he said quietly.

Too quietly. "If you don't want me to work for you, if you don't think I can do the job, just say so, Patrick. You won't hurt my feelings." Her feelings *would* be hurt, but she was a big girl.

"I've seen your blueprints for Katy. I have no doubts you can do the job. My concern is your safety."

She understood—she'd be exposing herself—but she felt more confident knowing a guard, not to mention an entire work crew, would be with her every second. As long as Amanda was happy and secure, she really wanted to do this. Getting her hands dirty was what she loved about landscaping, and she owed Patrick so much. "If you find it's not working, you can lock us back up in the trailer and I'll do what I can from there."

"It's settled then," Evelyn said briskly, reaching out to touch Amanda's cheek. "We're going to make oodles and oodles of cookies, sweetie. Maybe we can do something crafty. Suze loves to make noodle pictures. Do you like them, too?"

Amanda nodded happily.

Patrick pushed his chair away from the table and stood. "I have things to do before we can go," he told his mother, who glanced at his uneaten pancakes. "Thanks for breakfast, Mom. Sorry I can't stay to finish." He looked in Rachel's direction without actually meeting her gaze. "Be ready to go in half an hour."

He nodded to Skip. "Let's talk to Jane about rearranging a couple of things on the schedule before you take off for the day."

Rachel watched the kitchen door close behind the two men. She'd wondered what would change between her and Patrick after their lovemaking. Now, she knew. Patrick hadn't done or said anything to suggest he was as aware of her as she was of him. Add business and the reminder a dead wife also lay between them—one she suspected Patrick still loved—and her hope he might actually care about her was crushed.

Hurt ran over her, quickly swallowed by the protective armor of anger. The man showed her heaven, and then snatched it away? *Fine.* Cool and professional was what Patrick wanted? That's what he'd get.

Two Weeks....
Four Days....
Five Hours....
...'Til death.

"Still waiting to kill Thorne?"

Robby didn't appreciate the monster's snide tone because it reverberated through his aching skull like a jackhammer, drowning out the sound of the backhoe digging a trench behind him. Bad things kept happening to Patrick Thorne—some of *his* design, some just good fortune smiling down on him—yet the contractor kept coming up smelling like roses.

He'd been excited when he heard the landscaper ran off with his mistress, leaving Thorne without a way to finish the Southgate project in time for the grand opening next month—Robby couldn't have planned a better blow to Thorne Enterprises—but barely twenty-four hours had passed and the problem was already solved. Not a hiccup in Thorne's precious schedule.

And, this time, Robby didn't have Skip to blame.

His stomach cramped as he watched the James woman point where trees should be planted on a berm at the edge of the project fifty yards away. She laughed at something one of the men said, shook her head, and then they examined one of the trees together. The woman obviously knew what she was doing. The huge man that hovered at her back, never more than four feet away, kept an eagle eye on their surroundings and marked him as the bodyguard Thorne had hired. *I'm beginning to see your point.*

"Kill! Kill! Kill!"

The churning darkness in Robby's brain began to grow until it blurred his eyesight from the outside corners, creeping inward. A frisson of fear swept through him, but he battled the maelstrom back. Yet, it wasn't easy to regain control. The monster was becoming stronger each day. Soon, he wouldn't be contained, and Robby would lose himself forever to the blackness. For that reason alone, he might have to change his timetable for Thorne.

But, not yet. His Angel hadn't said the words. If he gave her more time, she would make the right decision. He knew it. The date of Thorne's death wouldn't matter once she made the right choice. Maybe tonight when he took her the present he'd bought her. *We wait.*

The darkness howled.

18

Patrick stared in shock at the man who'd tracked him down to the unfinished third floor of the final Southgate building. Grant Colbert had been a thorn in Patrick's side since he won the contract late last fall to build the real estate mogul's luxury home in the countryside north of Denver. He'd scrambled to get the dirt work done, the house closed up before winter settled in, but Grant had demanded so many changes through the following months, the interior wasn't signed off until last week.

"You fired the landscaper? For god's sake, why?" He knew the moment he saw Colbert's expression tighten that he could have phrased his question more diplomatically. It wasn't as if he'd lost money on the contract because Colbert insisted on paying for all of the changes, but he was tired of the man's manipulations. Patrick had finished two fifty-unit Southgate apartment buildings in the time it had taken him to build this man's twelve-thousand square foot house.

"I can make him fix whatever he did wrong," he said. "Finding another landscaper at this late date will be next to impossible and you want the job finished in plenty of time for your Fourth of July party."

Normally an even-tempered man, despite his demanding pickiness, Colbert blew up. "That asshole's not stepping foot on my property again. It was bad enough his workers put a tree through my office window and he refused to repair the damage. But then, he had the audacity to tell me I have to pay for another tree to replace the one they put through the window!"

Patrick wasn't thrilled he'd have to tear crew off one of his other jobs to replace the window and chase down the landscaper for payment. But those weren't his biggest problems at this moment. "I'd be upset, too, Grant," he said in a conciliatory tone. "Finding a replacement landscaper now is going to be tricky. All the good ones are book—"

One of Colbert's trademark have-I-got-a-deal-for-you smiles crossed his face. "Already covered. I spoke to the woman doing your landscaping here. She's giving me a bid. Looking out my window at *that* all day, she can charge me the moon. I'll pay it.

"She's coming out to my house to get the lay of the land, but I doubt there's any question we can work something out. I already called in a glazier to fix the window. The landscaper responsible for the breakage will foot the bill if he wants to continue working in this town.

"So we're back on track, Rick, and everyone's happy. Just tracked you down to fill you in." He shook Patrick's hand, turned, and walked through the stud wall toward the temporary elevator that had brought him to the third floor. He lifted the crossbar blocking the open shaft, stepped inside the cage, replaced the bar and started his descent with a push of a button.

Watching the man's hundred dollar haircut disappear from view, Patrick cursed. Not at Colbert's persistent use of an abbreviated version of his name or because the man managed to get on-site without a hard hat, but because the landscaper the man evidently hired was Rachel. Patrick should be happy the man had solved his own problem for a change. He didn't have room for another schedule delay.

In the past twenty-four hours, Rachel had proven she could do the job. The missing landscaper's crew was working happily and efficiently under her direction, and she'd made more progress with the project than he'd expected. He didn't, however, want her to work for Grant Colbert.

He tried to tell himself it was because he didn't want her sidetracked from the Southgate project. But, the truth is it was Colbert setting his personal sights on Rachel that bothered Patrick most. The real estate agent was rich, powerful and, according to Jane, "Sin, walking on two legs." His office manager practically drooled every time the man called.

Jealousy reared its ugly head, and he didn't like it. Making love to Rachel was a monumental mistake...and inevitable. Her gorgeous brown eyes had sucked him in the first day they met. Her sultry, Southern voice and scent had woven through his senses for days, her smiles become as crucial to him as the blood in his veins. And the woman had walked away from their one heat-filled night together without a backward glance. Since breakfast yesterday, it appeared Southgate was the only connection left between them.

His hand tight around his radio, he ordered Rachel to come to him. She tried to explain she was in the middle of something. He simply turned off his radio. Ten minutes later, she stomped off the elevator across the bare floorboards to his side, her daytime bodyguard, Carl Sprang, trailing behind her. "You called," she said in a calm voice that belied the fire in her doe brown eyes.

Sorry for allowing his jealousy to dig a deeper chasm between them, he forced a casual tone into his voice. "Just had a visit from Grant Colbert. He said you're going out to his place to check on his landscaping requirements. I thought you'd planned to be here this week to facilitate this project."

Taking off her hard hat to wipe sweat off her brow before putting it back on absently, she frowned. "I told him I was too busy to accommodate his time frame, but that I'd take a look at his property to see what it would entail...when I got the chance. I didn't make any promises."

"Good." Patrick was more relieved she wasn't set on working with the man than he was about ensuring Southgate met the launch deadline next month. *Not good.* "You'll want to get on top of the job here so you can leave once they get your ex behind bars."

Her lips pursed. "In a hurry to get rid of me?"

"Of course not. I only meant—"

Aware the bodyguard was watching their exchange with too much interest, Patrick nodded toward the elevator. "Wait downstairs, Sprang. Rachel's safe with me here and this conversation is private. I'll escort her down when we're finished."

The man looked questioningly at Rachel, not moving toward the elevator until she nodded, which cranked up Patrick's tension another notch.

Once Sprang was gone, he caught Rachel's hand and pulled her around the closest finished wall. Then, he confronted the one topic that had been gnawing on him since he woke up to find Rachel gone from his bed. "Rach," he said in a low voice. "We have to talk about the night the folks came home."

For a long moment, he saw a different kind of fire build in her eyes. She licked her lips, like she could still feel him there, nibbling on her mouth, feasting on her. Her pulse quickened under his fingers. The memory of her taste, the heat radiating off her lilac scented skin, so close, yet so far, made him want to take her again. Right here.

With a gasp for whatever she could see on his face, she tugged her hand away and bumped into the drywall behind her. "There's nothing to say."

He could think of a thing or two. *"Come back to my bed,"* for starters. Followed by, *"Don't go back to Dallas. Let me take care of you and Amanda.* "That's it? I know I made a mistake when I made love to you but—"

"What do you want from me, Patrick?" she interrupted, pain in her eyes. "I-I can't work with you, if, if...I'm leaving as soon as Amanda's safe from her father," she finished in a rush. "Please don't make this any harder for me."

He reminded himself he hadn't wanted to get involved with Rachel from the start; he didn't do broken women any more. Looking into her eyes, that vow sounded hollow. He wanted Rachel, baggage and all. He wanted to protect her from Greg, from everything that hurt her or Amanda.

Like you wanted to protect Karly? Your baby? "I need you at Southgate, Rachel. That's all." The lie almost choked him.

"Patrick, I can't get into the—" His lead HVAC man came to a dead stop as Patrick glared at him. "Excuse me. I'll just—"

"What, Knowles?" Patrick said before the crewman could turn on his heel and walk back around the wall.

The man grimaced. "I'm not sure how it happened, but I got locked out of the maintenance room at the other end of the building. If I can get back in there, I'll finish up this floor today."

"I'll let you get back to work, Patrick." Rachel tried to walk around him.

He frowned. He wasn't sure what there was left to say but he wasn't finished with this conversation. "Wait here," he ordered. "I'll go unlock the door and—"

She flashed a quick smile at his crewman. "I can come back later."

Patrick refused to step aside so she was forced to acknowledge his presence. "Rach, I sent Sprang downstairs, remember? I'll take you back to him. Wait here. Or wait by the elevator. Don't go anywhere by yourself."

Her lips firmed over what he suspected was another argument, but then she nodded. "Fine."

Assured she wasn't going to bolt the moment his back was turned, Patrick walked off with his crew member.

Two Weeks....
Three Days....
Eight Hours....
...'Til death.

Leaning into a two-by-four stud in the shadow of a wall where the arguing couple couldn't see him watch their exchange, Robby almost laughed out loud. The irritation on the James woman's face when she turned her back on Thorne was gratifying. Robby was too far away to hear what they were talking about before the crewman interrupted them. Whatever it was, Patrick's tension, his sexual frustration when this woman was within range, was almost palpable.

It was the first thing about this disastrous morning that gave him any real pleasure. If *he* couldn't tear another strip from the contractor's hide, at least someone else could. Too much was going Patrick's way. Robby wanted him destroyed, emotionally and physically, before he killed the man...which is why Rachel James had risen to the top of his list of ways-and-means to that destruction. He just hadn't figured out how to use her to hurt Patrick most.

His own plans had ground to a standstill. He'd been trying since his arrival this morning to set up his next punishment, yet he either ran into a super-vigilant crew member or the wandering security guard was interrogating him. Security was only supposed to be on site after the crews left. Since the James woman was running all over Southgate saving Patrick's ass, an extra guard had been added to the day shift, too.

These security measures were killing him. But they were nothing to what his Angel had put him through these past four days since he'd snatched her from the life she'd made for herself away from him. At the thought of her hidden away in their secret place waiting for his return, he grew lightheaded. A mixture of elation, frustration...rage...tore through him.

She was the one—despite what the monster whispered in his ear—so why did she continue to deny him? All she had to do was admit her love for him. He'd give her the world, as he'd always done.

He'd known since he was thirteen years old Heaven was a place he'd never enter. Not after the things the monster had done. *Things he'd done for her. Always for her.* He'd been battling the darkness forever for his Angel. Every time the monster won, he lost himself so deep in the bowels of his own personal Hell he barely escaped. He was afraid he couldn't do it again. He'd grown weaker with each descent, while the darkness grew stronger. He had to win this time. Win, or die.

"Last chance. Last chance. Last cha—"

He winced. Since leaving his Angel behind last night, his anxiety had become a living thing feeding on his insides. Eating at his control. Threatening to expose his blackened soul for everyone to see.

"Last chance."

Robby kicked the wall base plate with his right foot hard enough to silence the taunting monster. Waiting for the exquisite pain to ease, he cocked his head to listen to a couple of the crew exchange a crude joke as they hung drywall over the naked studs down the hall, the sound of screws tightening into wood studs, a radio announcer promising the next caller a pair of Red Rocks concert tickets.

The DJ followed up with a news report. "The police are still looking for the young coed taken...."

Last chance.

The myriad of construction noises drifting up and down the floor faded from his consciousness. He'd lost his window of opportunity to attack Patrick's precious business today. There were too many workmen crawling all over the five story building and someone was bound to question why he was hanging around here when he was supposed to be elsewhere.

The encroaching darkness wouldn't let him leave though. He had to hurt Thorne. Now. It was an ever-present knot burning a hole inside him that demanded results, and the clock was ticking. He looked down at the folded paper clutched in his gloved hand, then stared at the wall the James woman had gone around a minute earlier.

The killer inside him smiled. *Ohhhh, even better. This will be fun!*

Listening to the rat-tat-tat of hammers and nail guns through the half empty shell of the apartment building, Rachel paced the floor in front of the elevator shaft while she waited for Patrick. She was so angry with the man all she wanted to do was run back outside into the fresh air. She needed sunshine, to dig in the dirt alongside her crew, to push the pain of Patrick's rejection away.

It hurt that he only wanted her to finish up her job at Southgate and get out of his life. Oh, he didn't say it quite that way, but she knew it was what he'd meant. The man might still want her in his bed—there was too much heat and intensity in his eyes for him to deny he was attracted to her—just not enough to ask her to stick around any longer than necessary. She was still a problem in his life, one he hadn't wanted. She'd dragged him into her mess when she claimed him as her boyfriend in front of Greg. It was her own fault she was hurting.

She should be happy she'd had one night with Patrick, that she'd experienced true passion, without relinquishing herself to yet another man. Yet, she wanted more.

Heat raced through her at the memory of his big, calloused hands molding her curves, the feel of his skin brushing over hers, his hard length slipping inside her softness. She'd felt both swept away and protected by his willingness to let her take control, to find the passion she'd buried deep inside her, to explore her desire over and over.

Realizing she was panting, as much by the lust-filled memories as the furious speed she was pacing the floor, she stopped. "This is nuts," she whispered. "Stop longing for a man you can't have. It's over!"

After a quick look around to make sure no one heard her talking to herself, she frowned. Where was everyone? She could hear the noise of the crew and subcontractors working this half-finished floor of apartments, but she suddenly felt very much alone standing in front of the elevator shaft.

How long had she been tearing her heart out while she waited for Patrick to escort her down three floors? She understood why he didn't want her to go anywhere by herself, but this was ridiculous. With the security he had in place, Greg couldn't get this deep into the site without being challenged by someone.

She had things to do, and they didn't include agonizing over her stupidity in falling for Patrick Thorne. She'd left her crew unloading the nursery delivery truck without supervision when Patrick ordered her presence like she was some sort of...employee. Which, she grimaced, is what she was to him. An employee.

It was time to get back to work. Peering down the open shaft, she could see the top of the elevator cage resting one floor below her. Her bodyguard was waiting on the first floor below that. It wasn't necessary for Patrick to escort her into the elevator, just to pass her on to Carl when it got to the bottom. The only thing that stopped her from pushing the call button was her promise to wait for Patri—

The hard punch between her shoulder blades caught her by surprise. One second, she was craning over the security bar. The next, her middle crashed into it and she flew head first into empty space.

Her screech of terror filled the shaft. For a precious moment, her arms flailed. Desperately, she reached for one of the metal support braces that crisscrossed the opposite wall. The fingernails on her right hand scraped over one slim ledge, slid off. She screamed again when her left hand managed to catch on another metal piece and she slammed into the wall.

Pain ripped through her fingers, arm and shoulder, loosened her grip. She scraped down the angled brace until her hand caught in the vee at the bottom. With a grunt, she threw her right hand around the opposite ledge, the sharp angles biting into her palm. Her feet dangling eight feet above the elevator cage, she screamed again. "Patrick! Help!"

"What the—" a deep male voice shouted. "Hang on, Rachel!"

Unable to look over her shoulder to identify the crewman behind her, Rachel prayed for strength. Her fingers cramped, yet she didn't dare reposition her hands. The muscles in her shoulders burned like a thousand fire ants burrowed under her skin.

"Rachel!"

The harsh voice behind her added to her rising panic. "Patrick! I'm," she swallowed, "slipping!"

Patrick's heart stopped when Rachel's fingers shifted on one of the angle iron cross braces that had stopped her fall down the shaft. If she lost her grip and fell to the metal cage below her, she would be badly injured, if not outright killed. He watched with horror as her hard hat fell off her head and crashed to the cage below. "Hang on, sweetheart!"

Ramming the security bar up out of the way, he lay down on his stomach. Then, he leaned out over the edge of the shaft and tried to snag her by the back of her jeans. She dangled two feet beyond his fingertips.

"Push the elevator button," a crewman suggested.

"No! Don't touch it," he shot over his shoulder. "If you call the elevator, she'll end up above us, if she doesn't get crushed between the cage and the wall as it rises."

Rachel groaned. A shudder wracked her slender frame, her knuckles white around her precarious hold. They were running out of time.

Think, damn it, think. "Don't let go!"

"H-hurry." Her voice shook with strain.

Adrenaline kicked Patrick's brain into high gear. He barked orders to the crew around him. "John, grab three of those four-by-fours," he pointed his foreman to a pallet of wood eight feet away. "Cope, Martinez, find rope or something to tie around my waist."

It seemed to take forever, but he soon had an extension cord wrapped around his middle. The instant John secured the four-by-fours across the shaft, the ends jammed into cross braces above Rachel's head, Patrick crawled on his hands and knees across the makeshift bridge. The cord around his waist tightened once when the two crewmen holding the other end didn't let it out fast enough.

Then, he looked down into terrified, brown eyes. "I'm here, Rachel," he said firmly to quell her distress as much as his own. Jockeying himself into position above her, he straddled the boards and reached down to wrap his hand around her right forearm just below her elbow. "You can let go now."

"I-I can't!"

"Yes, you can," he said. "One hand at a time." He gently squeezed her arm. "This one first. I'll catch you."

"I—"

"Trust me, Rachel. I won't let you fall."

Her eyes wide, she jerked a nod. It seemed to take an eternity before her grip loosened on the angle iron. Patrick took her weight with a grunt. He knew he was bruising her forearm, but he tightened his grip and lifted her toward him until her left hand came off the ledge, too. She dangled below him on one arm and he thought he might lose his grip when his bullet wound twinged a reminder he wasn't yet healed. But then, she swung her free hand up, grabbed his other hand and he hefted her into his arms with one massive jerk to the collective gasps of his crewmen.

His heart raced as he held her. With Rachel out of immediate danger, all he wanted to do was hold her tight and never let go. "You're safe. You're safe," he whispered repeatedly into her hair. He looked into her eyes and, still shaken, quipped, "You couldn't wait for me five minutes?"

She smiled crookedly and dove back into his arms. "I'm sorry," she said into the crook of his neck.

When a tear rolled over his skin, he closed his eyes and cuddled her. Then he glanced over her shoulder at his foreman, bracing one of his massive legs on the four-by-four bridge with another large crewman at his back. "Ready?" John mouthed.

Patrick nodded before he reluctantly lifted Rachel away. "Honey, we're not out of the woods yet." He began to remove the cord at his waist to wrap it around her. "Let's get you out of this elevator shaft."

She paled when she realized what she had to do, but her lips firmed. "Okay."

"I'm going to help you get to your hands and knees on the boards. Then I want you to crawl to John." Patrick smiled his encouragement. "You can do this, Rach. Just take it slow. I'm right behind you."

Letting her go was tough but once he got her to the boards, her removal from the shaft was accomplished with efficiency. John lifted her to the solid flooring, with Patrick right behind her. He didn't relax until the makeshift bridge was removed and the security bar fell back across the opening.

"How the devil did she fall into the shaft, Patrick?" John said in a low voice as they both watched Rachel, perched on the stack of four-by-fours sipping water from a bottle one of the crew handed her. "The bar was still in place."

"That's what I want to know," Patrick muttered. He crossed the floor toward Rachel. With each step, his anxiety for her was replaced with more questions...and anger. He'd almost lost her, and it was his fault. She should be locked up somewhere safe, not traipsing around a dangerous work site.

Her lips curved into a smile as he drew near. "Patrick, I—"

"Do you realize how close you came to killing yourself?"

Her smile disappeared. "You think I threw myself into that shaft on purpose? I was pushed!"

"No. I mean—" He paused, not sure what he meant.

The memory stole through his head. Brutal. Breath stealing. Karly, lying on the slab in the morgue. His identification. The report that witnesses said she jumped in front of the bus that ran her over. The relentless belief she'd taken her own life because of their argument over her pregnancy, her worry of family history being passed on to their innocent child.

He blinked at the woman in front of him. Not Karly. Rachel, the woman who gave her heart, body and soul to protect a child that wasn't hers. "Tell me how you ended up in the elevator shaft."

"I already told you." Her eyes narrowed. "Someone snuck up behind me and punched me in the back." Bristling, she stood up and began to pull at the buttons on her work shirt. "Want to see the bruise? It might be difficult to delineate it among all the other bruises, but hey, I'm happy to reassure you that I'm not imagining things."

"I believe you." Patrick caught her fingers before the third button was pushed through the hole. "You just scared the crap out of me," he said, soothing as he buttoned her back up. "I want to find whoever did this to you so they can't do it again."

"Oh."

The confusion, anger, and hurt in her eyes prompted him to pull her into his arms. He kissed her temple. His heart rate settled the longer he held her. When he remembered he was standing in the middle of an unfinished floor at Southgate with a dozen of crewmen watching, he set her back. Not that he cared that every last one knew Rachel was his to protect.

God help the bastard who tried to push her to her death. When Patrick found him—

His foreman nodded when their eyes met. "Can I talk to you a minute, Patrick?"

"Whatever it is can wait, John." All he wanted to do was take Rachel home and check her injuries, assure himself that she was alright, but he still had no idea how she'd ended up hanging for her life in the elevator shaft. He had to call the polic—

"This can't wait." John waved something in his hand.

About to put him off, an odd-looking letter on the creased paper caught Patrick's eye. Was that another...?

"Rach," he guided her back to the pallet of four-by-fours, "sit here a minute. Let me take care of this and then we'll talk."

When she nodded, he dragged the back of his knuckles over her cheek. "I'll be right back."

Moving several feet away with John, he reached for the note. "Where did you find it?"

John kept his voice as low as Patrick's. He nodded toward the elevator shaft. "Over there, about three feet beyond the opening. It must have gotten kicked aside when we all came running."

Reading the note, put together with letters cut from newspaper and magazine headlines, Patrick had little doubt this threat was the companion to the one he'd found in his truck almost a week ago.

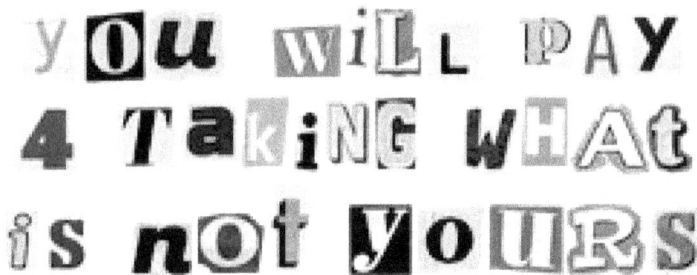

Anger ripped through him again, only this time, he had a target. Bishop. Patrick wondered how Rachel's ex-husband had found a way onto the site without anyone seeing him. If he did manage to get on site, unseen, how did he get to this floor with the note, shove Rachel into the shaft, and escape without getting caught?

He didn't. It's wasn't Rachel's ex-husband.

Patrick's stomach churned as his brain worked around the dangerous thought. Rachel would have seen Bishop come up the elevator. She was standing right there. Maybe he was already in place when Patrick summoned her, but the man couldn't have known she'd be there at that specific moment. God knows, Bishop was capable of murder if the attack on Rachel's doctor friend was any indication. But, despite his threats, it was unlikely he'd kill his only access to the James fortune.

Giving himself a mental shake, Patrick re-examined the note. It was the same as the first one. If both were the same and Bishop couldn't have gotten on the site, then someone else left both notes and pushed Rachel into the shaft.

He frowned at his foreman, suspicion raising its ugly head. Had John found the note on the floor or did he pull it from his pocket to make sure Patrick got the message? He had missed seeing it. But then, he was so focused on Rachel's precarious position, he wasn't looking at the floor. For all he knew, the note was right where John said he'd found it.

Jack's task force was convinced Patrick knew his saboteur, was almost as certain the saboteur and the Angel Killer were one and the same. John had been Patrick's foreman for most of the nine years he'd been building Thorne Enterprises. It was hard to believe John was his saboteur, let alone the Angel Killer. The man fit the gentle giant persona to a "T".

Ted Bundy fooled the people who knew him for years as he killed countless women.

A shiver raced under Patrick's skin as he scanned the open floor, examined the faces of the workmen standing around watching the proceedings with avid interest. Maybe it was one of them. John and at least three crewmen reached the elevator shaft before Patrick arrived. A dozen crew had collected by the time he crawled out of the shaft with Rachel. For all he knew, whoever pushed her might not have stuck around to admire his handiwork.

"What does it mean?" John asked, motioning toward the note.

Patrick smothered his uneasiness. "It means no one leaves the building until the police get here." So Jack can take names and sweep the entire floor for fingerprints, evidence...whatever. So Patrick didn't have to look into the eyes of his crew and wonder which one of them hated him enough to destroy everyone and everything he held dear.

19

Rachel ached from head to toe thanks to the wrench she took in the elevator shaft yesterday. She'd ignored Patrick's insistence she get checked out at the hospital—nothing was broken and she was so sick of hospitals—but she'd been forced to depend on her landscaping crew to do the heavy lifting this morning. Simply scraping wood chips around newly planted trees was proving a challenge.

She rested both gloved hands on the rake handle and rotated her shoulders to ease the ache there, grateful Patrick hadn't pulled her off the job altogether yesterday. She refused to be locked back up in the trailer. Short of firing her, he'd had little choice but to let her have her way. He'd not been happy about it though. If Jack hadn't shown up and put an end to their argument, pointing out she was safer out in the open under the eyes of her watchful crew and bodyguard, she had a feeling she wouldn't be standing in the sunshine today.

She understood Patrick's concern. Especially after she learned about the threatening notes. She wanted to be angry at the man for keeping the first one from her—she could have told him it wasn't from Greg, it wasn't his style—but Patrick was so upset about the attack on her, she let it go.

It was a lot harder to ignore the fact she'd made it onto the Angel Killer's radar. As a slim blond, she wasn't his physical type—he seemed to prefer women with dark brown hair and curves—which is why Jack was more convinced Patrick's saboteur and the Angel Killer were one and the same, that her attack was meant to punish Patrick for some reason. The message on the note backed up his logic, which is why the police vetted everyone in the building before they let anyone go home.

She knew Jack's task force would dig deeper into the history of each, maybe request DNA tests from anyone they red flagged. The size of Patrick's crew had prevented them from identifying specific suspects before. The one good thing that had come out of the incident was the police could investigate further into the lives of the thirteen crew and subcontractors who showed up for her rescue.

The biggest revelation to Rachel came after the last of the crew left, when Patrick lost his temper with Jack. He'd accused the police department of dragging their feet in not capturing Greg or the serial killer, endangering everyone. Jack didn't say anything for several minutes, letting his brother rant, until he finally said something to him that ended with, "This isn't helping, Patrick. Go to the trailer with Mona and shut down the rest of the site for the day. I'll bring Rachel down in a few minutes, after the techs finish up, and you can take her home."

Patrick glanced at her, opened his mouth to say something, but his brother stepped between them and he stalked off.

Jack watched him get into the elevator with his partner and disappear. Then he walked to where she sat on the wood pile. "I hope you realize he doesn't usually lose control like that," he said. "Your fall scared him. It's brought up memories of Karly—" He stopped, scowled.

Rachel couldn't let the reference pass. "Everyone hushes up every time Karly is mentioned, Jack. Why?"

"She died."

"Don't be obtuse," she said. "*How* did she die?"

His head tilted, he studied her. "Patrick will probably kill me, but I think you should know what you're up against so you'll give him time to wrap his head around his feelings for you. He's under so much pressure to keep you safe he's not thinking clearly."

"Patrick doesn't—"

Jack scoffed. "You think he hugs and kisses all his employees when they get hurt?"

When she didn't respond, not sure what to say, he smiled. "I got an earful from several of the crew. Take my word for it. Patrick cares about his people, but you've kicked his protective instincts into high gear and his feelings are controlling his actions."

"I don't mean to—"

"Don't get me wrong. I'm happy you've pulled him out of the emotional hole he's been in the last two years. He deserves happiness after everything he's been through."

"Does he still love her?" It wasn't what she'd intended to ask, but it was out there, so she waited for his response.

"That's a complicated question, one you should ask Patrick." Jack sat down next to her and watched two technicians pack up their crime scene bags.

"Karly was—" He stopped, and then started again. "Mom met Karly at the homeless shelter where she volunteers. She brought her home one night, about two and a half years ago.

"Dad dragged all of us boys home, one after another, when he pulled us off the streets and set us on the straight and narrow. It wasn't Mom's usual M.O. though. There'd been a fire at the shelter, and they were looking for temporary housing for their guests." He shrugged. "Karly never returned to the shelter."

"Patrick married her."

He nodded. "Karly was both a woman and a child. She was sweet, but tortured by her past. Things I don't think she shared with Patrick. She didn't stay long in any one place until she found a haven with Mom and Dad, and then Patrick."

Jack's comment sounded almost like a criticism and she was quick to defend Patrick. "It's in your brother's nature to take care of the people around him. Look at everything he's done for me."

"Well, Karly certainly triggered his protective instincts big time," Jack agreed. "They married in just weeks. Six months later, Karly was dead." He looked at Rachel. "He's avoided getting involved with any woman since. You've shaken him out of his comfort zone."

She triggered his protective instincts. Like Rachel did? As much as she didn't want to compare herself to Patrick's dead wife, Rachel's story was too similar to dismiss. Evelyn had allowed her, a troubled woman, into their home. Everything Patrick had done since the day they met was aimed at protecting her. Was Jack saying she was just another of his mother's charity cases, one Patrick couldn't resist?

A knot lodged in her throat at the thought of the way she'd practically seduced Patrick the other night. He'd done nothing but protect her and Amanda, and Rachel had thrown herself at him. No wonder he'd distanced himself after their one night together. Yes, he'd hugged her yesterday, kissed her as Jack pointed out, but she wondered if Patrick's actions were simply an unconscious response to the danger they'd escaped.

She took a breath—at least, she tried—and was rewarded with a twinge in her ribs. Slamming into the shaft wall when she stopped her fall had given her more than a few new bruises.

One of her crew called out to another and yanked her from her self-pity. Reminded she was supposed to be working, not torturing herself over a man she couldn't have, she checked on the rest of the crew scattered along the berm. There were three two-man teams planting trees and bushes, while two more repaired an incorrectly installed sprinkler line.

She appreciated how quickly the team had rallied behind her. They were happy to keep their paychecks coming, but she got the impression they hadn't been too thrilled with their previous boss's management style. Evidently, that's all he did...manage. He didn't get his hands dirty and his crew liked that she worked alongside them. As a result, they were making better progress on the project than she and Patrick had hope—

Rachel's phone vibrated in her jeans pocket, startling her. Her heart raced. Only four people—Katy, one of the managers Rachel put in place at the Kolthern Nurseries, Patrick and Jack—were given the number since she'd activated the phone six months ago. She called Katy nightly so they could discuss Kolthern nursery business and check up on each other, but the cell hadn't actually rung since her arrival in Denver.

She glanced at the caller ID, and pushed her hard hat back. "Hi, Katy. I sent the Silver's blueprints this morning. Sorry I didn't get it to you last night."

"You had enough to worry about. How you feeling today?"

"More stiff and sore than when we spoke last night," she admitted. It could have been worse. It didn't hit her until after she'd gone to bed that she could have died. Sleep was a long time coming after that. "It's better than the alternative."

"Yes, it is."

Her friend's voice was too quiet. "What's wrong?"

Silence greeted her question. Then Katy sniffed, cleared her throat.

Was she crying? "You're scaring me. What's wrong? Tell me you aren't in the hospital again!" She'd only found out a couple of days ago the older woman wasn't in Austin with her brother at his dude ranch. Rachel should never have left the stubborn woman behind in Dallas.

"Of course not. I'm fit as a fiddle," she replied firmly. There was another pause. "I do need to tell you something though."

Alarm squeezed off Rachel's air. Her friend didn't prevaricate like this unless she had bad news. "Just spit it out, Katy."

"Your dad's in the hospital."

Her heart stuttered. "What?"

"Your dad. He went into ICU a couple of weeks ago. Pneumonia. But then he fell and broke his hip and—"

Intensive Care Unit? Two weeks? Rachel's knees buckled. She sat down hard in the pile of wood chips at her feet. When Carl Sprang headed toward her, she waved him off. "Are you saying he's," she hesitated, "dying?"

"I-I don't know. He wouldn't let me tell you before." Katy sniffed. "I know how you feel about what he did, but he's asked to see you and Amanda. Please don't miss this chance to mend your fences."

It was a struggle to get the words past the lump lodged in her throat. "Where?" She swallowed. "Where is he, Katy?"

"Denver Central."

"He's here?" When he'd hired guards to protect her and Amanda, it had never occurred to her he was this close. She also hadn't questioned how he knew where she was or that she was in trouble. Just hearing his name had lit her anger and shut down her brain.

Her pulse galloped. With dismay. Anxiety. Eagerness. Confusion. Rachel knew Katy and her mother were friends in college. Katy had never mentioned her father. Did Katy know where he was when she sent Rachel and Amanda here? Of course, she did. He'd been in the hospital for two weeks! What else hadn't Katy told her? The questions swirled through Rachel's head, each one leading to yet another.

"Rachel?" Katy's voice broke through her bewilderment. "I'll never ask anything again, but you have to do this. Go see him, if only for me? Please? Don't let him...I can't stand it if you two don't make up before...just go, girl."

For several long moments, she couldn't speak. "I-I'll call you." Clicking the off button, she tried to stuff the phone back into her pocket but couldn't quite get the device secured while sitting on the ground.

A strong, masculine hand came out of nowhere and Patrick helped her to her feet. He eased the phone from her nerveless fingers and tucked it into his shirt pocket. When she swayed, he pulled her into his arms. "Tell me what I can do," he said his voice gentle.

Getting lost in his dark eyes, she didn't question why he was there at the exact moment she needed him. "I—"

Her forehead fell down to his sun warmed work shirt as she fought for composure. She filled her lungs with Patrick's scent, the mix of sweat, sawdust and man that made her pulse race. Then settle. Drawing on his strength, she lifted her head and told him what she had to do.

The smell of antiseptic easily overpowered the aroma of half-eaten patient lunches stacked on a rolling rack several feet away, ready for removal, but did little to subdue the air of illness that had saturated the hospital walls over time. Of course, Rachel knew that notion was all in her imagination. The Pulmonary ICU at Denver Central was modern and clean, and one of the best chances a patient had of beating the odds. And, from the sounds of it, her father required the best.

Was she finally to see her dad after all of these years only to lose him? After spending the past fifteen minutes with his doctors, that possibility felt all too real. If they were dealing only with the pneumonia that had put him in the hospital, it was one thing. But, thanks to the degenerative disease that was a byproduct of her father's rodeo career and his fall that broke his hip the day after his admission, his doctors hadn't been able to agree on the best treatment.

His orthopedist wanted to replace his fractured hip, saying it would be harder to fix the longer they waited. The anesthesiologist was concerned he might not survive the surgery because of the risk of intubation with a pneumonia patient. The pulmonologist didn't want to risk affecting his respiration so pain meds for the hip were out of the question while he battled pneumonia. He could O.D. on narcotics and stop breathing altogether.

The pneumonia had finally responded to treatment so the doctors decided it was time to address his hip fracture. Her dad's surgery was scheduled first thing in the morning, which is why he wanted to see her and Amanda.

She could refuse—she wasn't sure she was ready to put all of the pain behind her, not under these conditions—but could she live with herself if she ignored his request and he didn't come out of surgery? Memories of sitting in the hospital with her mother, watching her die one small piece at a time, swept over her.

Her step faltered.

"You don't have to do this, Rach." The rumble of Patrick's words steadied her as much as the warm knuckle that traced down her cheek.

She looked down at Amanda, her small hands enveloped by Patrick's on one side and her own on the other. The way they stood together, they were almost a closed circle and that calmed her further. She glanced down the hall toward the waiting room where they'd left the bodyguard her father hired to protect her. "Yes, I do," she whispered. "I can't run anymore."

Patrick gave her a reassuring smile. "I'm right here if you need me."

That's why she'd be okay. The man hadn't left her side since he suddenly appeared on the heels of Katy's phone call. She'd warned him she was calling Rachel about her father before actually doing it, and he'd dropped everything to protect her. As he'd done since the day they met. No matter what took place once she walked into Room 5, she knew she could trust Patrick to be there to pick up the pieces.

God, don't let there be too many pieces!

She gently squeezed Amanda's hand and wondered if she was making a mistake exposing her child to the man her mama knew.

She smiled tremulously. "Let's go meet your grandpa, baby," she said and started walking again until she reached his room. Without pause, her back straight, she opened the door and crossed the threshold.

The overhead lights were turned low and what seeped into the room around the closed blinds on the window were dim thanks to the dark storm clouds racing across the Colorado skies. Rachel hesitated. Was her father really expecting her? *Maybe Katy was simply meddling, and he hadn't really asked to see her.* Her friend knew how Rachel felt about their break...and didn't approve. She'd said as much more than once. Was this her way of forcing the issue?

Her free hand clammy on her skirt, she peered at the figure lying on the bed. "Dad?"

"Get in here, chickadee. I'm decent." Her father chuckled, the sonorous sound from his twice broken nose so familiar it hurt. "At least, I'm covered up. I haven't been decent since, um, well, you know me and dates and figures. Guess St. Peter's going to have that date when it comes down to it."

If he hadn't spoken, called her by that ridiculous nickname she'd hated growing up, she would have turned right around thinking she'd entered a stranger's room. Rachel didn't want to think too much about her father facing St. Peter either, so she walked into the unit. The closer she got to the bed, the more shaken she became by her father's condition.

From what the doctors told her about the infection he'd been fighting, she'd been prepared for the tubes and equipment, his pallor. But the affable teddy bear of a man who'd dragged her all over the country and made her life positively miserable—her words in one of her journals—had been reduced to a shadowy figure of a man she barely recognized.

A lifetime of anger and hurt simply melted away. She leaned down to kiss him on the cheek. "Hi, Daddy."

The brightness of his dark chocolate eyes hadn't dimmed, yet the last ten years hadn't been kind. Deep lines, caused by pain and too many years in the sun, bracketed his mouth. She remembered her mother saying, with all of the bones he'd broken riding the rodeo circuit, he was likely to be in a world of hurt as an old man. It was clear the price had come due.

He ran a hand over his graying hair and grinned at her like they'd never been separated by angry words and ten years of bitter silence. "Had hoped to gussy myself up a bit before you arrived, but guess I fell asleep."

"You're still the handsomest man in the room."

"Not anymore, chickadee," he said, looking over her shoulder where Patrick hung back.

He lifted a tremulous hand. "Dixon Grey," he said. "We talked on the phone. It's good to finally meet you, Patrick. Thanks for taking care of my girls for me."

Patrick leaned in past Rachel, their shoulders touching, and shook her father's hand. "Mom and Dad have talked about you over the years, Mr. Grey. Glad to meet you, too."

"Dixon," he said, his gaze watchful. "Mr. Grey is too formal if you're planning to marry my girl. I know your people are Catholic, so that's one thing in your favor. Though a practicing Catholic man doesn't play around with his woman without a couple of wedding rings between them."

"Dad!" Rachel flushed as she thought about Patrick's lovemaking. Where had her father learned such intimate details? Cook? Sprang? Or was her dad just fishing?

"What?" He raised a hand covered with tubes. "It's not like I have a whole lot of time to dilly-dally around playing twenty questions, chickadee. Either the man's intentions are good ones or they ain't. My time may be short. It may not. But I'm making sure you don't mess up with this one." He fixed a stern eye on Patrick. "So answer the questions, son."

Rachel was startled when Patrick responded. "I have nothing but good intentions, Dixon. Yes, I'm a practicing Catholic. And I'll only marry Rachel when she's good and ready."

"That's all I wanted to know." Her father grinned. "Can't blame a man for making sure our girls are taken care of properly when I'm gone. You can take care of them, right? You putting your troubles behind you at that construction firm of yours? "

"Yes, sir," Patrick said. "We're working on that problem."

Her father knew an awful lot about what was going on outside his hospital room, Rachel decided. Memories rose up from when she was younger, the number of times he managed to dig out secrets she didn't want him to know, like when she was fifteen and fell in love with a nineteen-year-old drover named Carson. She'd followed that blue-eyed cowboy everywhere, until her dad caught her and warned him off. It's when she started to buck his control over her life.

She didn't like that he believed she was going to marry the good Catholic boy he'd made her promise to find after the incident with Carson—maybe, if she'd listened, she wouldn't have messed up her first marriage so badly—but the old man suddenly had color in his cheeks. She didn't have the heart to naysay any of it and watch it all drain away.

Patrick had played into her father's hands, but she had a feeling it was because he was trying not to upset him either. He'd been seated next to her when the doctors explained the necessity of keeping her father calm before he went into surgery. Thankfully, the way Patrick phrased his response, he hadn't really lied about anything. He wasn't going to marry anyone again, certainly not Rachel. She might have "kicked in his protective instincts" as Jack claimed, but that didn't mean the man loved her.

Her father turned to Amanda, who was peeking at him from behind Rachel's left hip. "Seems to me your mama's lost her manners altogether, pumpkin. I'm your grandpa." He held out his hand, but he was obviously already tiring because it fell to the bed an instant later.

Rachel was astounded to see Amanda step closer to the bed. The little girl covered his motionless hand with hers, right over his IV. "No, baby! You can't touch—"

"The hell she can't," her father croaked. He rearranged the tubes a bit, rolled to his side, and enveloped her hand in his palm. "Let me look at you, sweet pea."

Amanda silently gazed up at her grandpa and he stared down at her like she was the Seventh Wonder of the World. "You're the spitting image of your mama and grandma. All moonstruck hair and baby-doe eyes," he said, a tear trailing down his pain-lined face. "Wish you could have met your grandma. She would have loved you."

Rachel's eyes filled at the love she saw in his eyes. Her heart ached at the thought that love might disappear if he knew Amanda wasn't really her own. Remembering how much it hurt when he'd walked away when she was seventeen, she stiffened and took a protective step nearer her daughter's back.

"Amanda, honey," Patrick spoke up beside them, "why don't we find your grandpa some fresh water to drink, maybe have an apple juice ourselves?"

Her gaze moved from adult to adult. Then, she nodded and pulled out of her grandfather's grasp.

Taking the little girl's hand, Patrick smiled at Rachel. "We may be gone a bit. We're heading to the cafeteria to grab a snack."

Rachel knew what he was trying to do, but she suddenly wasn't ready to be alone with her dad. How did one recapture ten lost years? There was so much anger between them. "You don't have to go all the way—"

"Take your time, Rach." He wrapped his hand around the back of her neck and pulled her close to settle his mouth over hers, like it was the most natural thing in the world for him to kiss her in front of her father. "We'll be back," he murmured.

Then, with a big smile for Amanda, he walked her toward the door. "Maybe they'll have cookies, too. Would you like that?" Rachel watched her daughter nod, and then they were gone.

"That's a good man you've got there," her father said behind her.

Patrick was a good man, but she didn't have him. She turned her back on that depressing thought and faced her father. "Yes, he is. He's been there when I needed him." She couldn't think about the time when he wouldn't be there anymore.

"Unlike me, you mean." Her dad's observation sounded sad and questioning at the same time.

"I didn't say that."

"You didn't have to, chickadee." He shifted on the bed so that he was lying propped on the pillows. He fumbled with the oxygen tubes in his nose before he spoke again. "You're angry and have every right to be. I can't take back what I did, wouldn't want to, even now, knowing how things turned out. Don't think I don't have regrets, all the same."

"Why do you keep calling me that?" she asked, unwilling to deal with the past yet.

He grimaced. "Sorry. You hate that name." He shrugged. "You've just always been my little chickadee. Hard habit to break. I'll try to stop."

"Chickadees are boring little birds." Nothing special. Certainly not missed when they flew away.

"They're cute as a button and so were you. And, just like the chickadee, you were curious about everything and everyone around you." A ghost of a smile twitched on his lips. "No matter where we went, it took you less than ten minutes to investigate your surroundings, make friends. Cowboys. Rodeo clowns. Ranchers. You were always surrounded by a flock of people, all wanting to make you smile, bring you treats, and give you rides."

"Oh." Thought of that way, the nickname didn't sound half bad. Almost tender. Emotions welled inside her alongside the memories. "Remember the time that old geezer put me on the back of that red bull when I was seven?"

Her father snorted with disgust. "Bull's name was Killer Mayhem. He never broke out the gate the same way twice. Killed four riders in his career. You shouldn't have been within ten feet of that animal, let alone set on his back. Seeing you there near gave me a heart attack."

"The way you yelled, I thought for sure I'd get paddled like some of the kids on the circuit."

"I loved you too much to raise a hand to you, girl."

Rachel listened to the hiss of oxygen from the tubes inserted in his nose. "What changed?" she asked, her voice strangling in her throat. "W-Why did you stop?"

"Loving you? Darlin' girl. Never stopped." He grimaced, as if in pain, before he began again, noticeably weaker. "That's why you're here. So much to say before I die...."

She reared back. "You're not dying!"

"That's in God's and the surgeon's hands." He stopped again, longer this time.

Concerned, Rachel was about to call the nurse for assistance when he smiled crookedly. "Stupid pills. Make me groggy. Still must...make peace. Tell you what I did. Just in case."

Just in case? Her knees wobbled. Leaning on the bed, she took his hand. "We don't have to—"

"Get the papers," he said, waving to the other side of the room. "Top drawer."

When she did as he asked, she found a folder with her name on it. Her new name. Her parents had named her Rachel Felicia Grey. Greg had insisted on calling her Felicia because it "sounds more upper crust." When the divorce attorney asked her if she wanted to take her name back, she'd been re-born plain old Rachel James, eradicating Felicia and taking her mama's maiden name.

She carried the folder back to the bed, afraid to guess what was inside. "What is this?" She held it out to him.

"My Last Will and Testament," he said, refusing to accept the folder. "That's your copy."

"Dad! You're not going to die!" She wouldn't allow the idea to settle into her brain. She might not have seen him in ten years, but she'd been aware he was out there. Somewhere. She couldn't think about a world without her dad in it.

"Not planning on dying, girl. Have every reason to live now you're here," he said with a small smile. "But I learned a thing or two about how things get done. I've learned to plan, with a small amount of success."

He nodded at the folder clutched in her hand. "Open it."

She did as he instructed and stared at the squiggly words on the page, her eyes suddenly awash in a blur of tears. She made a pretense of reading, but then a number jumped out at her. *Ten million*...her gaze shot to her father. "What...how...?"

He chuckled, but ended up choking on the laughter. When he stopped coughing, he shrugged. "Your great-aunt took good care of you, and what I have is just spit compared to her estate. But I want you to have something for Amanda if the James family doesn't accept her into the fold. Something of her own."

The air froze in Rachel's lungs. Dear God, he knew her secret. "Why wouldn't they?" she prevaricated.

"You told your great-aunt the little one wasn't your blood."

"Amanda's my daughter whether she's my blood or not!" The argument was out before she was able to pull it back. If he didn't know her secret for sure before, he did now.

"Damned straight, she is which is why we took action to protect you both from the James family, as well as Amanda's daddy." His dark gaze grew tender. "I don't mean to ruffle your feathers, girl. I already love her like my own. I've got half a dozen pictures of her on my desk. That animal you married doesn't deserve to claim her."

"Wait." She frowned. "You have pictures of Amanda?"

"Have a roomful of you both." He fiddled with his oxygen mask. "For ten years, I kept my promise to your Great-Aunt Amanda to stay away. But she's dead and that promise is broken."

Rachel was beginning to feel like she'd wandered into a cattle chute backward. She knew danger was coming, but she couldn't see it. "What are you talking about?"

Her father took her hand. His fingers trembled, but his grip firmed, like he didn't dare let her go until he'd finished. "I made a deal with your great-aunt. I leave you with your mama's family and, as long as I get regular reports and photos, I stay away."

"The day you left—"she stared at him in consternation. "You sold me? Like a ratchety old horse you didn't want any more?"

"Sell you?" He snorted. "You think I took money from the snooty James family?"

"Then why did you leave me?"

He squeezed her hand. "Ah, little chickadee, you wanted so much more than I could give you. You'd set your sights on college. You wanted *roots*, a home of your own." He let go of her hand and looked away at the closed window blinds, lost in his memories. "Your great-aunt wanted to give you those things, too. She had as many regrets as I did about how the family treated your mama when she ran off and married me." He looked at her. "You were so angry all the time I figured you'd be happier with your mama's family."

Rachel tried to remember exactly what was said that day. Her dad had his final ride that afternoon, and she knew they were hitting the road to the next town. Again. She remembered her anger building before he came back to their motel room. She'd been researching local colleges on the internet, something she did in every town they visited her senior year, though she knew enrollment was out of the question. Their credit was nonexistent, and they'd never stayed anywhere long enough for a guidance counselor to help her find grants and scholarships. All she could see of her future was a succession of motel rooms trailing from one rodeo to the next with her father.

Then, he'd walked into the room and started spouting off something about yet another new job and she'd lost her temper. She didn't remember much else but screaming at him until he turned around and left. "You were excited about some new enterprise someone convinced you would make tons of money. If it wasn't Great-aunt Amanda, who was it? Or was that just a trick?"

A smile flickered across his lips at some memory. "I was excited all right. Ran into an old rancher I'd worked for years before I met and married your mama. He had a proposition for me. Wanted to expand his ranch operations in Montana and breed bulls for the rodeo. He had no family left, so he offered me a partnership if I'd run it for him."

"That's quite a proposition." She was impressed. Her dad had always been respected on the circuit, both for his riding acumen and his animal husbandry. He'd been raised on a ranch before his father lost the property to bad management practices and back taxes when he was seventeen.

"I worked for the man near eight years. When he saw my heart was on the circuit, he let me go with his blessing. He was more a father to me than my own, and we occasionally ran into each other over the years." He shrugged. "I knew you didn't like being tossed all over the country while I tried to find work that would pay enough to get me off the circuit. I was tired of getting tossed off bulls, too. I was ready to rope all of your objections and drag you with me, but then your mama's aunt came to me and offered to take you in, give you the things you wanted."

He stopped and took several deep pulls on his oxygen. "I knew the job could tank like so many times before, so I decided it was time to let you go. Find your way to what would make you happy. It about broke my heart to leave you behind."

"I was so stupid, Dad," she whispered. "I thought—"

"It's not stupid to want a better life," he said around a wide yawn. "You were so much smarter than I ever was, just like your mama. She would have wanted you to go to college to make something of yourself." He gave her a small smile. "Can't say I'd do it the same way again. I should have talked to you about it, instead of just leavin'." He shrugged. "Water under the—"

"Bridge," she finished for him. It was another of his favorite sayings she'd forgotten. She waved the folder at him. "There's a lot of water here. I gather your partnership was successful."

He yawned again. "Bought the breeding operation from the old man six years ago." His eyelids began to droop but he forced them open. "He died five months later, leaving me the whole ranch. No kids, remember? Told me to pass it on to mine," he trailed off, "if you ever talked to me again."

Her heart ached. "We have a lot to catch up on, Dad, so you're not passing on anything for a long while yet, okay?" She leaned over the bed and kissed his leathery cheek. "It's time for you to get some rest."

"Love you, little chickadee," he whispered, his eyes closing. "Don't fly away."

"I love you, too, Daddy," she said, tears running freely now that he couldn't see them. "I'll be here when you wake up."

Patrick glared out his office window the following Monday. The ominous thunderheads building overhead fit his current mood. The last thing he wanted was another schedule delay when he'd already dug deep into overtime. He dragged his free hand over the back of his neck while the other hand strangled the phone receiver as he listened to his potential client become his *ex*-potential client.

"Their bid was how much lower?" Customers seldom revealed why he didn't get a project so he couldn't afford to ignore information freely given. Especially when the situation stank like last week's sewage line break.

This wasn't the first time in the past few months his rival, Chet Standish Ltd. undercut one of his bids. Once was a coincidence. Twice might be serendipity. But the last four times they'd bid the same job?

His customer ran down with an apology, which forced Patrick to scramble for something to say. "No problem. I understand." He ended the call with a pleasant "thanks for considering my firm" spiel that threatened to choke him.

The moment the client hung up, Patrick picked up his aluminum pencil holder and flung it across the room. His missile flew through the open doorway connecting his office with the file room, striking a cabinet on the far wall with a satisfying metallic bang.

A pencil rolled across the oak floor back into his office. Jane rushed into the room behind it, wielding a fistful of folders like a weapon. "What's wrong?"

He cursed. He'd forgotten she was filing in the next room. "I—" he searched for an explanation that wouldn't make him sound like a complete ass.

He knew he wasted his time when, over Jane's shoulder, he spotted Rachel. He wasn't proud of a lot of his actions lately, not where she was concerned. He'd avoided discussing the night his parents' returned home. Unable to deal with his unreasonable desire for her, he'd put distance between them by treating her like an employee. He'd further strained their relationship when she was pushed into the elevator shaft. He blamed himself for putting her in danger and not protecting her, but he'd taken it out on her instead. He'd meant to talk to her the next day, but he'd gotten the call from Katy about Dixon and the opportunity was lost.

Except for brief appearances at Southgate to instruct her landscaping crew, she'd been at the hospital with her father since his hip surgery. Patrick still slept on his parents' living room couch. The operative word was "slept". Except for breakfast, he'd been too busy taking care of Thorne Enterprise projects to join the family for meals, simply falling into his makeshift bed each night like a dead man. The bodyguards had seen more of Rachel than Patrick these past three days, which is why he soaked up the sight of her like a parched man.

Instead of her usual jeans and button-down, cotton shirt, today she wore a blue blouse that looked like silk. He longed to unbutton it and uncover the more satiny texture of her skin beneath. Her multi-colored skirt skimmed her curves like a lover's hand from the wide black belt at her waist to the swirling hem around her calves. Rachel looked sexy and incredibly touchable and it took everything he had to resist the temptation to cross the threshold into the other room, back her into one of the file cabinets, and touch her everywhere.

Their gazes locked for several heartbeats—long enough for his jeans to strangle his brain cells—before Rachel turned away and walked out of sight. He pushed his hormones down, not sure how much longer he could keep his distance. He knew a relationship with Rachel was temporary—she repeatedly reminded him she was leaving—but he hadn't wanted the break to be so abrupt. Or so soon.

That Rachel seemed fine with the status quo bothered him, especially since he'd declared his intention to marry her to Dixon. He'd said it to placate the man, but the more he thought about it....

Jane stepped in front of him, breaking his eye contact with the other room. "Patrick? The phone call?" she prompted. "We lost another contract, didn't we?"

Patrick shook off his distraction to look at his office manager. Each missed contract bothered Jane lately, so he gave a negligent shrug like they hadn't just lost the multi-million dollar project that would have funded formal offices for Thorne Enterprises. "It's no big deal, Jane. We don't have time and manpower for the Schubert complex anyway."

"Bullshit. You don't bid projects you can't complete."

He smiled wryly. The woman might look like a society matron who took High Tea at the ladies' club every afternoon, but she tended to speak more like a rough-edged crewman. Her language had toned down in the years since she'd dried out and come to work for him, yet she still didn't pull her punches. She was honest and outspoken, which is why he trusted her like he trusted his own mother.

"Who got the job, Patrick?"

The sound of a file drawer closing in the other room ratcheted the tension between his shoulder blades another notch. Forcing his gaze back to the woman in front of him, he leaned back in his chair. "Standish got this one," he said. "He's either found a way to severely cut corners or he's so determined to make sure we go under he'll take losses until we hang up our tool belts."

Folders fell from Jane's fingers and scattered across the clutter on his desk. She dropped into the chair in front of him. "Patrick." Her voice cracked on his name. She pushed her salt-and-pepper hair back from her face with a hand that visibly shook. "I-I, um, oh God, I have...to tell you something."

Patrick frowned at the way the older woman's facial expression twisted. He knew her angina escalated quickly when she was under stress. "Whatever it is can wait," he said. "Where's your nitroglycerin, Jane?"

"I'm not having a heart attack, just an attack of conscience," she retorted. Then, she burst into tears.

Rachel rushed into the room, took one look at the crying woman, and glared at him. Shocked, he rose from his chair. But Rachel's scowl stopped him from walking around the desk to Jane's side. Not that he knew what to do in these situations. Give him a cracked roof brace, a broken water main, anything but a woman in full meltdown.

On her knees at Jane's feet, Rachel murmured something in a low voice. "Could you give us a few minutes, maybe fix a cup of green tea for Jane?"

At first, the words didn't register with Patrick. Then, he started. He could do tea! He bolted from the room. Standing in his kitchen minutes later, he listened to the microwave hum and analyzed Jane's emotional collapse. In all the years she'd worked for him he'd never seen her fall apart like this, not even straight out of rehab. What the hell was going on? Jane had had two bad cases of the waterworks in the past week and, whatever was going on, Rachel seemed to be in the middle of it.

That became more evident when he walked back toward his office and overheard Rachel. "Are you sure you're ready to do this, Jane?"

"I can't take it anymore," the other woman replied. "I have to tell him."

Walking into the room, he set Jane's tea on the desk where she could reach it. Rachel's expression closed off when their shoulders touched as he rounded his desk where he felt most comfortable. More in control, which was an obvious illusion with Rachel close enough to sabotage his senses.

She'd planted herself against the wall on his left where she blocked his access back around his desk. To provide a buffer between him and Jane?

He studied the older woman's face. Evidence of her tearful outburst made her appear older than her fifty-two years. "Okay, Jane," he prompted. "You've got my attention. What do you have to tell me?"

"I-I—"

Tears welled in her eyes, but she ignored them and blurted, "You're losing business because I sold information about Thorne Enterprises!"

The air in his lungs seized. "What are you talking about?"

Shrinking back in her seat, Jane didn't shield her eyes from his accusatory glare. "I'll tell you everything, but you have to promise not to let them have Suze when I'm sent to prison. She'll die in that house. She's better off with complete strangers than those people!"

The non sequitur threw him so he latched onto the part that made sense. "Suze's in danger? Where is she?"

"She's upstairs," Rachel said, "playing with Amanda."

Reassured the child was okay, Patrick waited for Jane to clarify her outrageous statement. Another tear started a trail down her cheek. He crushed renewed stirrings of sympathy, slowly accepting that her admission might not be a joke.

"Please promise me," she said. "No matter what I tell you, you'll protect Suze."

Patrick thought of the precocious little girl he'd welcomed into his home the past five years. Suze's playpen and mobile had a corner in Jane's office at the front of the house when she was barely two weeks old. Her tricycle had marred an erratic line in the wood finish along the narrow hallway between her grandmother's front office and his in the back parlor. There was a large playroom upstairs that he and a number of his crew kept littered with toys. Suze's constant chatter and laughter had filled his huge, empty house six days a week her entire short life.

He'd been unable to save his wife or unborn son. "I won't let anything happen to Suze," he said roughly.

Jane nodded. "Thank you, Patrick."

"I'll do it for Suze," he said, unable to get past the woman's betrayal. "Tell me who I'm protecting her from before we get into why you're trying to destroy my company."

"Suze's uncle is out to destroy you. Not me."

Uncle? "You said her mother never revealed the biological father's name."

"She didn't," Jane cried out. "His older brother came to me four months ago with a letter Susan wrote telling him about little Suze. Toward the end before she died, Susan was desperate for money. She must have thought he'd pay her to disappear."

Ice sank deep into Patrick's gut. "Who is Suze's father?"

Jane hesitated too long, as if she didn't dare speak the name. After a moment, she appealed to Rachel. "Please? I just...can't!"

Patrick stared at Rachel. "*You* know?"

She placed a hand flat over her stomach in that protective manner that told him to back off, but he couldn't give her the space she needed. "Well?"

"Suze's father is Donald Standish."

"Chet Standish's younger brother?"

As much as he wanted to reject the confirmation of his worst fears, Rachel's nod wouldn't allow it. "Chet Standish blackmailed Jane."

Unable to look at either woman as he came to grips with what their revelations meant he swiveled in his chair and glared out the window at the lowering Colorado sky. Jack had checked out Patrick's competitors months ago after his first vandalism report. Everything came back clean, even for dear old Chet. It was no secret he'd been tapping into his wife's trust fund hard lately to keep little brother off the courthouse dockets for all of his DUI and drug charges, but the authorities weren't able to connect him to Patrick's recent troubles.

What had they missed?

Jane grimaced when he turned back to face her. "Patrick, I'm sorry. I should have told you—"

"What did Standish pay you to sell me out?"

"Nothing! I swear I'd never take a dime to—"

Somehow, not taking money made his sense of betrayal worse. Not that he believed her. "What did he promise you, Jane?"

She scooted forward in her seat and slapped her hand on the desktop so hard tea splashed out of her cup on one of the file folders she'd dropped there. "He promised to take Suze from me." Her voice rose with each word. "He promised to turn her into a drug addict and whore like his brother made my Susan. He said he'd take great pleasure in handing her over to a man he knew who specialized in little girls to make sure it was done properly. That's what he promised me."

She glared at him. "So fire me. Throw me in jail. Do whatever you feel you have to. Just keep your promise so Suze doesn't end up living with those animals!"

Rage seared through him under Jane's attack. He was wrong. If a portion of what she claimed were true, his wrath had nowhere to go. "What," he forced calm into his voice, "did Standish ask for in return?"

"Your bidding formula."

Every contractor had his own personal system for figuring manpower, supplies, discounts and schedules. "You handed him the power to destroy me."

"Yes. But I've been fixing it." She collapsed back into her seat, her blast of defiance exhausted. "I *thought* I'd fixed it. I've been working with your subcontractors to cut costs. I didn't tell Standish about the two part-time crews and, between Skip and I, you have a list of new suppliers giving you the deeper discounts you've been using to calculate your last few bids."

"Skip's in on this plot, too?"

"No! All I told him is that you wanted to cut costs, find alternative supply sources."

Patrick believed her. Considering Skip's eagerness to please it wouldn't have taken much for Jane to convince him to cover her tracks. "If you sabotaged the information you gave Standish, how is he still undercutting our bids?"

"I wish I knew!" She reached out a hand to him across the desk in supplication, but drew it back quickly. "I'm sorry, Patrick. I wanted to tell you. This secret's been killing me for months. I didn't know what else to do."

You could have confided in me. You might have trusted me to help you to protect Suze.

For that matter, why hadn't Rachel told him what was going on? She knew how worried he was about his bottom line, what it meant to his employees if Thorne Enterprises went out of business because of these insidious attacks. He looked into her gorgeous brown eyes, wondering how many more secrets lay hidden there. "How long have you known this and didn't tell me?"

"Please don't blame Rachel," Jane blurted out. "I just told her."

"Just now," he looked at Rachel, "when she was questioning your decision to tell me." He knew he was being unfair but he was done with half-truths and lies. Even lies of omission.

Rachel did nothing to defend herself. Like the unattainable fairy queen she sometimes reminded him of, she simply stood there, pale and silent as she stared back at him. Then, as if he'd proven himself beneath her notice, she looked away and frowned. "Jane? Are you all right?"

Patrick glanced at Jane and saw the distress lining her eyes, the twist of pain around her mouth. No. The woman was not all right. "Where are your pills, Jane?"

"I'm fine." She shook her head, grimaced again, and then reached into her slacks pocket for her pillbox. "It feels good to have this off my chest."

His concern grew as he watched her slip a tiny pill under her tongue.

"You know what really hurts? It's knowing you'll never forgive me for what I've done. You're family and I-I—"

Tears ran down her cheeks. "Do you think you can have me hauled off to jail before Suze comes down for her snack? I don't want her to see me in handcuffs."

What the woman needed most was an escort home to bed before she ended up in the emergency room. "I don't think—" he began before he noticed they had company.

"Don't take my Grandma to jail!" wailed Suze from the hall doorway.

"You can't do this, Patrick," Rachel argued at the same time.

Amanda, standing next to Suze, said nothing but her big brown eyes shouted her distress louder than words.

"Quiet!" He waited until everyone's gaze rested on him. Then he crooked an index finger at Suze, drawing her into the room. When she came to a stop in front of him and he saw the devastation shadowing her face, the way her lower lip quivered, his heart squeezed.

Suze tilted her head and considered him in that too grown up way he knew so well, as if she could see truth lodged deep in his soul if she looked long and hard enough. "What's a whore, Mr. Patrick?"

The unexpected question sideswiped him. Disturbed by how much Suze overheard, he picked her up and set her on his lap. "That's one of those words you can forget, Suze."

"Like the bad words in the naughty jar?"

Thanks to exposure to her mother's drugged out friends before Susan died last year, the child understood entirely too much for a five-year-old. He refused to add to her education so he'd created the naughty jar to teach his crews to watch their profanity in the office. At ten bucks a pop, it hadn't taken long for the men to learn. These days, the jar tended to fill up on its own and Patrick banked it in a college fund for Suze. "Yeah," he said, "like those."

She didn't say anything for a while. Patrick could practically hear the gears turning in her head. He'd learned from experience to brace himself when the little girl got that look in her eye.

"If Grandma says she's sorry, do I gots to live with the animals at the zoo?" She gave a half-hearted shrug. "Monkeys are fun, I guess. But lions are real mean. Can't I be your Suze-Q no more?"

A band tightening around his throat, he hugged the little girl close. "You'll always be my Suze-Q, munchkin," he said. "No matter what." She snuggled into his shirt, which alternately made him feel ten feet tall and terribly inadequate. After a few moments, he cleared his throat. "Don't you worry about this grown up stuff. Grandma's not going anywhere but home with you."

He glanced across the desk at Jane, who nodded her acceptance to postpone their discussion. "She's not feeling very well. Do you think you can take care of her?"

Everything right with her world again, Suze nodded vigorously. "I can make scaphetti in a can if I climb on a chair. I watched Grandma lots of times."

He shook his head. "No climbing and no cooking. You can tuck Grandma into bed and give her the remote. How about if I come with you and cook some of those dinosaur pasta things you like so much?"

"Dinosaurs are yucky." She made a face and jumped off his lap. "I like space ships and stars."

"Patrick," Jane said, slowly rising to her feet. "An escort isn't necessary. I promise we won't go anywhere but home so you know where to find me."

"That's not why I'm offering, Jane. You might need," he paused and downplayed his concern about her health for the little girls listening to him, "something."

"I'm already feeling better," Jane assured him. "I'll take it easy for the rest of the day." She smiled wanly and shrugged. "I-I'll call Jack when I get home."

He didn't think she could handle much more stress. "You're sure?"

"I'm sure. Don't worry, Patrick. I'll make it right."

The funny thing is, despite her confession, he trusted she *would* make it right.

Suze tugged on his hand. "Can 'Manda come, too? We forgot our cookies."

Rachel scowled at Patrick so he had no illusions she'd been distracted from the real reason Jane was going home before the children had their afternoon snack. "Grandma can use your help, sweetie," she said. "How about I put your cookies in a plastic bag so you can take them with you? Amanda can share with you another time."

Problem solved, Suze nodded. "'kay."

Ten minutes later, Jane and Suze headed home, which left Patrick alone in the house with Rachel and Amanda. He was grateful to see the little girl return to the playroom upstairs while Rachel took over Jane's office and the crews radioing in for the second shift. He took the time alone to wrap his thoughts around the day's revelations, figure out what he was going to do to recover from this latest assault on his carefully constructed world.

Sitting in his office chair with his elbows on the desk, he rested his forehead in his palms. He closed his eyes. He was a drowning man. One more descent below the surface and he might never come up again.

He'd lost a project that would have secured his bottom line. His office manager sold him out. A competitor was out to destroy him, and he felt betrayed, shocked, and angry. The weird part was he wasn't as upset about the loss of the Schubert contract or Jane's part in its loss as he was by the fact that Rachel had questioned Jane's decision to tell him what she'd done.

What was wrong with him?

Sure, the week since his parents' return from the Virgin Islands had been challenging. When he'd told Rachel their lovemaking was a mistake, he'd wanted to reclaim some distance between them. But then, he'd turned right around and made love to her again. He hadn't thought about anything but the feel of her skin, her scent and taste filling his senses, the pleasure of making love to every inch of her.

When his parents walked through the kitchen door into the house that night, it could have been her ex-husband. If it had been an hour earlier, Bishop would have been up the stairs at the bedroom door and it wouldn't have impinged on Patrick's lust soaked brain in time.

Worse, after a discussion with Jack about the note found after Rachel was pushed into the elevator shaft, he was no longer certain the first threatening note he'd found in his truck was from her ex-husband. If they were right, Rachel had become his saboteur's new weapon against him. The thought of the Angel Killer setting his sights on Rachel terrified him more than Bishop or losing his business.

He didn't dare let his guard drop again.

How was he supposed to keep that resolve, though, if his first thought when he spotted Rachel standing in the file room wasn't about what stood between them? No. His first impulse was to march into the next room, strip her naked, and bury himself deep inside her. No words. No preliminaries. Pure desire demanding release. Just thinking about it made his hands sweat and his balls ache.

The woman drove him crazy. He couldn't sleep, his dreams haunted by the feel of her beneath him, her sighs whispering across his skin. Since learning she'd never climaxed until that night, there was nothing he wanted to do more than make her cry out her own satisfaction, over and over. He woke each morning with a raging hard on and a voracious hunger to claim all of her searing caresses and lush kisses for himself.

It was worse in broad daylight when he was forced to watch her interact with his crew at the job site. He was tempted to post a "Keep Off" sign on her. Wherever she went the crewmen, single and married, gay and straight, became grinning Lotharios. They carried her tools around, bought her meals off the roving food truck, and generally tripped over their work boots to accommodate her...while he was left with her watchful silence. The only time they spoke to each other these past few days was when she was forced to confer with him about the Southgate landscaping project before she headed to the hospital to be with her father.

He tried to remind himself he'd locked down his desire for a reason. But then she'd smile at his parents over the breakfast table like she had this morning. He'd get a whiff of her lilac scent on the air. They'd accidentally touch hands reaching for a piece of toast or salt shaker, and he'd spring into a state of aching readiness. He longed for her touch. If he thought he could simply drag her off to bed for one more night and get her out of his system, he'd do it. But he was afraid it was too little, too late. He craved...everything.

He wanted to talk to her, and bounce new ideas off her quick mind so he could see the spark of excitement lighten her eyes. He missed her smiles. He missed her arguing with him. Somehow, she'd burrowed under his skin and become an itch he might never scratch out.

"The second shift supervisors have checked in so I'm leaving."

Rachel's curt announcement from the open doorway caused an unexpected surge of alarm in Patrick's chest. He pushed it down and lifted his head. "With Jane gone," he said, "I need you here to cover—"

"I don't care what you need," she said, marching into his office. She stopped in front of his desk and glared at him, clearly waiting for him to say something. When he said nothing, she snorted with obvious disdain. "If you throw that poor woman in jail, Patrick Thorne, I'll never speak to you again."

Her confrontational tone set his back up and his response was layered with too much of his frustration. "Then, before you stop talking to me altogether," he said, sitting back in his chair, "explain why you were encouraging Jane not to tell me Standish was blackmailing her."

Rachel snorted indelicately. "I wasn't encouraging or discouraging her. She was upset, and I didn't want her to do or say anything rash until she'd had time to calm down."

"Were you planning to keep her secret, if she'd asked you?"

"What do you want me to say? She'd just told me. I didn't have time to process anything before you came back with her tea."

"Well, sweetheart, let me process it for you." He leaned forward over the desk. "Blackmail isn't a secret you keep to yourself. It's a criminal offense, and you can go to jail, too, for aiding and abetting. What were you thinking?"

"I told you. I didn't have time to think. *Then.*" She glared at him. "Want to guess what I'm thinking now?"

Patrick didn't have to guess. Her anger with him was clear in her expression, in her stiff stance. He also knew the answer to his question. She'd have kept Jane's secret. Aware of what Rachel had done, what she'd endured living with Bishop in order to protect her own daughter, she'd sympathize with the other woman. He understood the urge to protect the children, which took the heat out of his anger. It didn't make her lack of trust in *him* any easier to take.

When he didn't say anything, she crossed her arms in challenge. "What are you going to do about Jane?"

"I haven't decided," he said, irritated as much by Rachel's persistence as his desire to kiss the scowl off her face. He already knew he wouldn't have Jane arrested, not for selling him out at least. Jack might have other ideas. If Standish turned out to be Patrick's saboteur, and Jane had kept it secret knowing they'd connected him to the Angel Killer, well, Patrick didn't see a way for Jane to walk away unscathed.

Whether he'd fire his office manager was still up for grabs, too. He might understand why she'd betrayed him. It didn't mean he could trust his business with her again. Yet, if he fired her, what would happen to her? To Suze? Dammit! When did everything get so screwed up?

Standing abruptly, he went to the plan rack in the corner behind him and chose a blueprint at random. Returning to his desk, he set Jane's cup of untouched tea aside to the credenza so he could spread the blueprint on the file-strewn surface. Silence filled the room while he studied the diagram without actually seeing it.

He lifted his gaze. "I won't discuss this with you, Rachel. It's none of your business how I handle my employees."

He didn't remind her she was one of those employees, but saw she received the message by the way her eyes widened. "So fire me, too, because I'm speaking my mind," she said with a lift of her chin. "Jane confessed her secret. What she did was wrong, but there were extenuating circumstances. She fixed it."

"Try telling that to the rest of my employees with families to support." He allowed the blueprint to roll up with a snap. "How do you propose I pay them if there's no work? For all I know, Jane's actions are related to all of the problems we're having on-site."

Rachel stared at him like he was one screwdriver short of a toolbox. "She's not dragging Suze around after hours poking holes in your precious walls, and she sure didn't kidnap and kill that coed. This has nothing to do with your saboteur."

The reminder about the display of clothing nailed to his project walls turned his stomach. "Jane's confession doesn't address everything that's gone wrong in recent months, but she knew Jack believes the saboteur is his serial killer. Even if Chet Standish isn't the Angel Killer, I can't ignore the fact she jeopardized the livelihoods of my crew."

When it looked like she was about to argue, he cut her off. "I understand you sympathize with Jane's troubles," he said. "It doesn't, however, excuse her behavior."

With a gasp, she reared back like he'd slapped her. "I sympathize with...?" She stiffened. "Fine. Her situation isn't that much different than my own. Do you think there's no excuse for my behavior, too? Is that what you really think?"

"No! It's not what I think." He ran his hands through his hair. Unable to stand the hurt he saw in her eyes, he rounded the desk and approached her, until he was close enough to smell the delicate lilac scent that was becoming as crucial to him as the air in his lungs. "Rach, I'm sorry. This has nothing to do with you. It's no excuse, but Jane's news hit too close to home and I-I—"

He paused, suddenly unsure what to say or do to fix things between them. "To hell with it," he whispered, cutting off his apology with a kiss. Closing his arms around Rachel, he showed her exactly how sorry he was for everything. His ill-considered comments. The way he'd pushed her away after his parents' return. The strain that had grown between them since that night. He wanted to love her. Touch her. Convince her to stay so he could explore this demanding desire that haunted his nights and left him aching.

With a groan, he deepened the caress. Claimed more of her scent. Their breath mingling, hard, fast, he ran his hands up and down her arms. Stroking. Soothing. Reaching behind her with one arm, he swept everything off his desk. The noise of falling debris barely subsided before he laid Rachel back on the bare surface, without breaking the seal of their lips, and settled between her legs where he longed to be, where he belonged.

The scorching assault on his senses went on and on until he felt something warm and wet drop onto the back of his hand cradling her face. Lifting his head, he looked down at Rachel lying frozen and still beneath him, her blouse unbuttoned to expose the lacy bra she wore, her skirt pushed up her thighs to accommodate his hips. He saw where his five o'clock shadow had chafed the tender skin over her jaw, the bruised fullness of her mouth. Another tear dripped onto his hand. He pulled away quickly. "Rachel! Oh, God, I'm so sorry! I-I didn't mean, I can't believe I—"

A deep voice behind them cut him off. "Is everything all right in here?" Larsen Cook, who protected Rachel at night, stood in the doorway.

Patrick caught the time on the wall clock. Four-forty. Cook and Sprang usually changed shifts at the house after six o'clock, so they must have switched early for some reason. Stifling a groan, he blocked Rachel's nakedness with his own, and looked over his shoulder at Cook. "Everything's fine."

The security consultant's flinty gaze sharpened on the debris at their feet. "I have to hear that from Ms. James," he said.

"E-Everything's fine." Rachel's tremulous voice didn't sound too convincing.

When Patrick turned back and tried to help her to sit up, she batted his hand away. "I've got it." Blinking back tears she stumbled off the desk, her skirt falling down to hide her legs. She buttoned her blouse up to her neck with fingers that fumbled. "I have work to do," she muttered, walking around him. "Come on, Cook." She snatched Patrick's truck keys off the wall rack and fled his office with Cook in tow.

Patrick listened to Rachel run up the wooden stairs and, a minute later, back down again with Amanda. They clattered past his office. The last thing he heard was a clap of thunder so loud it almost buried the sound of the front door slamming behind mother, daughter, and bodyguard. As the storm broke over Patrick's head, he sat back on the front edge of his bare desk like a marionette with its strings cut.

What had he done?

21

Time passed while he sat there beating himself up over Rachel's anger and pain, his own idiocy, but he eventually became aware of the violence of the weather outside. The storm had broken with a vengeance, what his father called a "gully washer". It was the kind of storm that caused six-inch thick tree branches to snap and crash through roofs like they were made out of paper-mâché. The wind drove the rain almost vertical so it slammed into his office window in sheets. With the sheer volume of water these infrequent storms dumped, it didn't take long for the streets to overflow with water the predominately clay soil couldn't soak up.

Rachel and Amanda are driving through those streets completely unaware of the dangers.

Larsen Cook was with them. He'd know what to do in this storm. If Rachel would take his advice. She'd accepted the bodyguard's renewed presence in her life but, when she felt threatened, she took risks. Like the night she ran away after she received the threatening package from her ex-husband.

The memory yanked Patrick from his inertia. Rummaging through the debris scattered on the floor, he tried not to think about how it all got down there. He located his radio beneath a file folder kicked under one corner of the desk and tried to raise Rachel on it. Nothing. Several of the crew responded to his call promising to watch for her so he knew the radio worked, but he didn't find the knowledge reassuring.

Rachel might deliberately ignore his radio calls if she were upset enough. He tried Cook's cell number, but he didn't pick up either. That ratcheted up his alarm.

Don't panic. If they aren't at the site, they probably just went home next door.

He dialed his parents' house. "Have you seen Rachel and Amanda?" he asked his mother when she picked up.

"Not since I dropped them off at your place after our hospital visit with Dixon. Rachel said she had to pick up something," she said. "Aren't they there?"

"If they were, do you think I'd call?" he snapped. Pacing the floor from one end of his house to the other, he moderated his voice. "I'm sorry, Mom. I'm just worried. They went out again almost an hour ago and I can't find them."

It was his fault they were out there in the storm. When he should have been reassuring Rachel he'd make everything right with Jane, he'd goaded her into an argument instead. Then he'd practically ravaged her on the desk without considering her feelings. He wasn't any better than her brutal ex-husband. It would be a miracle if she ever forgave him.

"You two are quarreling, aren't you?" his mother said into his ear. "That's why Rachel's not sleeping. I thought it was worry about Dixon's recovery, but she told me today she was happy with his progress."

Patrick looked through the leaded glass in his back door in time to see lightning strike a couple of miles away. He jumped when the thunder crashed through the house seconds later. "How do you know she's not sleeping?"

His mother snorted. "She's been creeping down the stairs in the middle of the night to work at the table in the breakfast nook. Two of the stairs squeak, you know."

He did know. His dad caught him sneaking out of the house a couple of times as a teenager before he accepted he'd never pull one over on his policeman father and decided to fly right.

Before she re-connected with her father at the hospital, Rachel had been working at the site trailer on the landscape designs for Katy. But then, she'd taken over the Southgate job so it wasn't surprising she felt it necessary to work in the middle of the night to finish Katy's projects. But was that the only reason she wasn't sleeping?

Was she as restless as Patrick? He wanted to believe she was missing him as much as he did her, but he had no illusions. She was devastated by what he'd just done. He'd seen the bleak look in her eyes before she ran away.

"Yes," he admitted to his mother, turning his back on the storm outside to resume his pacing. "We had a disagreement." A weak word to describe his stupidity.

"Are you sure that's all it is because she's not eating either. It's not like her to—"

His mother's words stopped registering as his gaze fixed on Rachel's radio sitting on one corner of Jane's desk. She'd left without it? Rachel wasn't upset enough to leave Denver in the middle of a storm, was she?

Memories of the day he and Karly argued, the way his wife ran away after their argument, the horrible events that led to her death, reared their ugly heads. "I've got to go, Mom," he said abruptly. "Call my cell if they show up."

"Patri—"

He hung up and rolled his shoulders to ease the fear threatening to paralyze him. Rachel wasn't Karly. She wasn't suicidal. Greg Bishop was still out there somewhere. She wouldn't leave Denver until Amanda was safe from him. Staying presented another problem, though. Rachel had become a target for Patrick's saboteur as well. That meant danger was coming at Rachel and Amanda from two different directions. Could it have become too much?

Dammit, where were they? Why hadn't Cook guard responded to Patrick's call?

His gut twisted. He'd allowed his dick to endanger the very people he wanted to protect. He had to find them.

He snagged his radio off his desk, and then picked up Rachel's so he wouldn't get caught without a functioning battery. Digging out his wet weather gear stored in the hall closet, he also grabbed a couple of flashlights and his emergency pack, still packed from his last hiking trip into the mountains to Lost Lake. He didn't know how long it would take to find the missing trio. He wanted to be prepared for anything.

With no idea where they'd gone, he could only hope Rachel had the good sense to pull the truck to the side of the road somewhere until the storm passed or he tracked her down. She'd said she had work to do, so he'd start with the one project he knew she was working on.

Using the base radio on the credenza behind Jane's desk, Patrick checked in with his crew at Southgate again. None of them claimed to have seen her. That didn't mean she wasn't there. The way they all catered to her, if she'd told them she didn't want to talk to him, they'd cover for her. He understood. He could live with that. They could lie through their teeth as long as she and Amanda were safe.

With a growl of frustration, he decided to check Southgate himself. If she'd actually gone somewhere else, well, he'd cross that bridge when, *if* he came to it. Climbing into his dad's half ton pickup, the one he'd been using so Rachel could use his larger crew cab, the sense of impending disaster that had built all day suddenly took form. He'd never felt so helpless.

And for the first time since he'd buried his wife and unborn son nearly two years earlier, he prayed.

A vicious gust of wind smacked the three-quarter ton pickup broadside, wrenching at the steering wheel beneath Rachel's hands. It had been stupid to let her pain and anger drive her from the safety of Patrick's office out into this storm with her daughter. To compound her foolishness, she'd only stopped at Southgate long enough to pick up the directions the real estate mogul, Grant Colbert, had given her the day he proposed she submit a bid. He'd waited five days while she sat with her father at the hospital. She could have waited another day to make this trek out to the property. But, when Larsen Cook suggested they wait out the storm, she'd still been too upset with men in general, and Patrick in particular, to listen.

Living all over the country growing up, she was used to severe weather conditions so she didn't think Cook's concern was necessary. It didn't help Patrick tried to call the bodyguard either. That, more than anything, drove her out to the empty county roads northeast of Denver's airport where ten-acre country estates were springing up like exotic wildflowers.

Every mile she traveled, however, the storm worsened and she regretted forbidding Cook from taking Patrick's call. She'd mentioned where they were going to his foreman, John Branson, but the man had been loading his truck to go home for the day. Who knew if he would miss them if they didn't come back?

Her bravado weakening, she glanced at the man sitting in the passenger seat. Somehow, Cook's calm demeanor and the fact he hadn't fastened his seat belt—to keep his mobility in an emergency situation, he'd explained the first time she mentioned it—eased some of the tension from her shoulders. "Keep your eyes peeled for the abandoned barn with *Stirling Stables* painted on it," she said. "We should be able to spot four-foot letters across the front of it, despite the rain."

Peering through the rain-washed windshield, she tried to spot the building which would pinpoint how far they were from the next turn. Between the deceptive sameness of the open prairie roads, the dark pall of the storm, and their distance from city lights that might cut the gloom, it was difficult to spot the various landmarks in Colbert's directions. She should have called the man, told him she wasn't taking the job, not traipsed out here to scope it out!

Why had she thought to take on another project after Southgate was finished? Maybe it was because Colbert was so complimentary when he'd asked her to draw up a design for him, and Patrick had taken exception to the man's manner. She shouldn't have allowed her conflicting emotions to provoke her into accepting the challenge. The police were closing in on Greg. Jack had reported only yesterday that they'd found the motel where he was staying, although he'd checked out by the time they got there. Soon she'd be free to go about her life again and she would take Amanda back to Dallas where they belonged.

Rachel had every reason to return to Texas with Katy's proposal to make her a partner on the table. After months of backbreaking work to save her older friend's livelihood after Greg destroyed it, she had a personal stake in seeing its continued prosperity.

But, with Katy's health no longer keeping her from running her own affairs, and the managers Rachel had trained for all three nurseries, she didn't really need Rachel any longer. The truth was Rachel needed Katy. Rachel had originally planned to get her friend back on her feet, then leave. However, she'd also found a hole to crawl into, a place to lick the emotional and physical wounds she'd sustained during her disastrous marriage. And, for the first time in years, she'd found peace and some facsimile of contentment.

Katy recovered. The question was, had Rachel? Her dream was always to have a landscaping business of her own, but was this the way she wanted to get it? Once Great-aunt Amanda's estate was settled and she paid off the last of debts threatening Katy's homestead, Rachel could buy her own nursery. A whole franchise of nurseries. For that matter, she could quit working altogether and fill her life with luncheons and cocktail parties as her mother's brothers expected of her.

It wasn't the life she wanted for herself or for Amanda. So the question came down to one thing. Would she return to Texas because she wanted a stake in Kolthern Nurseries, or was she simply looking for a familiar bolt-hole to dive into so she could lick fresh emotional wounds? The ache buried deep in her heart since she left Patrick's office suggested the latter.

If she didn't get away from the man—and soon—she'd do something she'd really regret. Like beg him to love her back. Patrick didn't want her that way. He'd made that abundantly clear after his parents' return. Pain lanced through her breast at how easily he'd pushed her from his bed, out of his life. How long would it take her to do the same?

When he took her in his arms in his office, laid her down on the desk and kissed her like he was desperate to have her again, as he had the night he'd shown her what lovemaking could be like between a man and a woman, she'd almost caved. One second longer under his sensual demand and her twitching fingers would have taken a life of their own. She would have grabbed him and never let go. She'd been *that* close to settling. For his desire. For whatever scraps he reluctantly gave her. It took every ounce of willpower she had to walk out of his office.

She hadn't felt this much desolation about losing someone since her father left her behind in that motel room. For ten years, she'd believed her father never really loved her. She knew differently now, but the painful loss she'd felt then was still a sharp memory.

It was a good thing she'd come to her senses and never admitted her love to Patrick. He'd never know he had the power to hurt her. She might leave a large portion of her heart behind in Denver, but she could still slink back to Texas with her pride intact. Anger and pride. They'd sustained her more than once in the past. The only thing that mattered was the love she had for her daughter.

She glanced into the rear view mirror at Amanda sitting in her car seat, a teddy bear she'd found stuffed in a door pocket clutched in her arms to replace her doll left behind in Suze's playroom. Lightning flashed through the stormy darkness and gilded Amanda's honey blond hair. The loud boom of thunder that immediately followed made her little girl jerk in her seat. Her brown eyes widened with fright as she stared back at her mama.

Rachel didn't have time to reassure her because, just then, a full sheet of plywood came out of nowhere and smashed into their left front fender.

She gasped. Her heart thundered as she watched it flip over the hood into the field beyond.

Something her father once said jumped into her mind. *Distractions are a killer in the arena, little chickadee. Give that ol' bull a chance to get into your head and he'll run you straight through.*

Evidently, Cook agreed. "That was close," he said. "You might think about pulling over until the worst passes."

"Easier said than done," she muttered. Driving rain made it difficult to gauge where the shoulder began or ended. There was a four-foot drop into a drainage ditch on both sides of this stretch of road. The last thing she wanted to do was to misjudge the distance and drive off the edge.

Suddenly, it began to hail. Hard. Visibility ahead of the truck's front bumper shrank from a quarter mile down to ten or twelve feet. A deluge of ice pounded the metal hood and roof, the noise in the cab a relentless din in her ears. A golf-ball-sized chunk of ice struck the upper right hand corner of the windshield launching a spidery series of cracks. One raced from the impact point across the top of the windshield just above her line of sight.

Her nerves bounced with each impact. "What kind of tornado activity do you have here?" she asked Cook.

"We've been known to have them," he said, his gaze darting back and forth across the road, like he was searching for a funnel. "Especially out here on the plains."

A small gasp from the back seat made her look in the rearview mirror again. "It's okay, honey," she said, her voice shakier than she liked. "We're almost there."

They could be five minutes away or completely turned around. Rachel knew they weren't okay. Hail blanketed the road like snow, at least an inch thick, and it didn't show signs of easing. She'd lived all over the country and never experienced a storm like this!

Slowing until her speedometer hovered below ten miles per hour, she checked the headlights reflected in her rearview mirror the last fifteen minutes. Thank God, they weren't completely alone on this stretch of open prairie. The lights drew closer as if the other driver, too, felt less intimidated by the storm with her taillights guiding his way. In the next instant, they disappeared.

She didn't have time to do more than decide the other vehicle must have turned into a driveway she'd missed before she spotted *Stirling Stables*. Slowing further, she prepared to pull off the road. "We're less than a mile away from the turn into the Colbert estate," she said, "but we can wait out the storm here."

"Good i—" Bright lights abruptly filled the truck cab, cutting Cook off.

Startled, she risked a glance over her shoulder and saw a large vehicle close in with terrifying speed. High beams flashed, blinding her before the driver lost traction on the slick road and his headlights slid to the open prairie on her left. She registered a quick impression of a dark truck, the silhouette of one occupant in the cab, before he straightened and she was again pinned under the glare of his headlights.

Greg! His truck was a smoky gray color, wasn't it?

Alarmed, she automatically pushed her foot harder on the accelerator. But, it was too little, too late.

Cook shouted a warning. "Hang on! He's right on our tail!" His voice was obliterated by the sound of metal grinding metal when the other truck struck.

Her head snapped forward. The steering wheel shuddered beneath her hands. Fishtailing on the carpet of hail covering the road, the truck skated sidewise for an unbearable few seconds. Rachel held on for dear life. Throat tight with stress, she somehow regained control.

Her gaze immediately shot to Amanda's reflection in the mirror. She seemed okay in her car seat, if Rachel discounted her small fingers pinched so deep in the teddy's head they almost touched in the middle. She looked like Rachel felt. Unhinged. Terrified. Did she know it was her father trying to kill them?

Greg came in for another attack. Rachel applied more pressure to the gas pedal.

"Don't speed up," Cook instructed tersely, pulling his gun from the holster beneath his jacket as he began to turn in his seat.

Clamping down on her urge to run, Rachel eased her foot off the pedal. But, before Cook could take aim, Greg smashed into them again. Harder than before.

Hit from an angle this time, Cook was knocked off balance, directly into Rachel. His momentum slammed her sideways. Her head smacked the driver's side window with a sickening crunch. Pain exploded in her left temple and cheek. Her fingers slipped on the wheel. The pickup lost traction. Headlights tracking her path, she watched in horror as the edge of the road rushed toward them at breakneck speed.

In that moment, she knew they were going to die. "Patrick!" she cried his name as they went over the edge.

The truck dropped sideways into the drainage ditch. Without thinking, she turned the wheel and the truck rolled. Her body slammed into her seat belt, and then hit the door frame. Agony ripped through her shoulder. Her left hip. Her head snapped forward when Cook's shoulder clipped her before he catapulted through the windshield. Eyes squeezed tight, the squeal of twisting metal and the breaking of glass assaulted her ears. Dozens of knives jabbed her face and hands. Pain. Terror. More wrenching pain. The truck was still rolling when Rachel heard Amanda scream.

"Mamaaaaaaaaaaaaa!"

"I'm going to kill her," Patrick muttered, his fingers white-knuckled on the steering wheel as he struggled to keep the truck and his temper under control. When he'd left the office to chase after Rachel he'd been worried about her. Now he wanted to strangle her when he found her.

What was she thinking driving all the way out here in the "worst storm in twenty years" according to the gleeful weatherman on the radio? She hadn't bothered to stop long enough at Southgate to call ahead to see if her client was home, as he'd done when one of her landscapers told him where she'd gone.

No. The bull-headed woman just pointed her sexy backside toward an empty house in the middle of nowhere in a hailstorm. He'd wring her neck. Then he'd tie her to his bedposts so he could sleep at night. That way he could fire Larsen Cook, who obviously couldn't protect the woman from herself.

He increased his speed. He was pushing his luck considering the road conditions, but he couldn't dispel the worry that lay beneath his anger. "You'd better be sitting on Colbert's doorstep," he muttered half threatening, half praying.

The hail quit as abruptly as it started, which improved visibility considerably. A few minutes later, he spotted the first set of skid tracks in the two-inch mat of hail and ice. His heart stopped, and then started again when he traced the skid back into a straight line. His hands tightened on the steering wheel when he saw another series of erratic tracks thirty feet further. These disappeared off the shoulder and included a reddish trail of transmission fluid that looked too much like blood staining the stark white blanket of ice.

Skidding to a standstill in the middle of the road, he threw his truck into Park, pushed his door open, and ran toward the point where the tracks disappeared. He faltered when he spotted his crew cab pickup, a twisted heap of scrap metal resting upright at the bottom of the ditch fifty yards away. *No! No! No!* "Rachel! Amanda!"

Patrick scrambled down the icy incline to the center of the ditch, dodging bits and pieces of his truck. Skirting his cross-bed toolbox ripped from its moorings, he ran to the left side of the truck where the cab roof had caved in. He tried to yank the driver's door open. It was jammed. All he could see of the unmoving figure slumped over the steering wheel was a head of honey blond curls matted with blood and glass. "Rachel! Rachel, honey...oh, God!"

He clambered onto the battered hood of the truck, reached through the missing windshield, and searched for a pulse on her exposed neck. He let out a ragged groan when he found a slow, steady, rhythm. Peering beyond Rachel into the back seat, he checked on Amanda. Like her mother, the little girl was covered with hail, glass, and blood. Unlike her mother, she was wide awake and staring back at him with big brown eyes. Then, like she'd only been waiting for him to appear and take over her watch, a tear ran down her cheek and her eyes fluttered closed.

Croaking her name, Patrick scrambled through the gaping windshield over the dash into the cab. Kneeling on the bench seat, he leaned over it and called Amanda's name again. When she didn't respond, he cursed and took her pulse. Weak. Thready. His first impulse was to pull her from her car seat. He didn't dare. She might have internal injuries. Both Amanda and Rachel had to get help...fast.

Where was Cook? The thought had barely formed when he looked out the passenger window and saw a massive, dark form lying in the hail twenty feet away, unmoving.

Kicking the passenger door open, Patrick jumped from the truck and ran toward the bodyguard, all the while dialing 911 on his cell. He reached Cook before he connected with the police dispatcher. "Cook," he said, kneeling at the man's side, "how bad are you hurt?"

The man didn't respond.

Staring into his open eyes, Patrick could see that he was dead. But he checked his pulse anyway. When he didn't find one, he pushed the man's jacket aside so he could administer CPR. That's when he saw the large piece of jagged metal imbedded in the middle of his chest, right through his heart. Cook was beyond anyone's help.

"Please state your emergency," the police dispatcher connected forcing Patrick to pull himself together. After giving the woman the general location of the accident and telling her Cook was dead, he described Rachel's and Amanda's injuries.

Leaving the phone line open, he jammed the cell phone in his jacket pocket and rushed back to his truck still idling in the middle of the road. Moving the vehicle closer to the scene, he turned off the engine and pushed the emergency flasher button so first responders could find the accident more easily. Grabbing all of his emergency gear, he ran back down into the ditch to triage Rachel and Amanda until paramedics arrived.

When he reached the truck, he re-entered the cab through the open passenger door. Scraping as much hail and glass off Amanda as he dared, he draped a couple of warm blankets around her and her car seat. Her skin had developed a grayish pallor that terrified him. "Hang on, baby," he whispered brokenly. With a gentle touch of his hand, he tucked a wisp of baby fine hair under the hood he'd created over her head with the blanket.

Then, he slid across the front seat toward Rachel and leaned down to examine the way she was pinned beneath the buckled dash and steering wheel. He couldn't see much of her legs below the dash, but he wouldn't allow himself to think they might be as twisted as the wreckage of his truck. It was bad enough to see how hard the steering wheel cut into her thighs, holding her in place. It was going to be a bitch to extricate her even if, by some miracle, she didn't have any broken bones he couldn't see.

He tucked the last two blankets around her the best he could before he pulled the cell phone from his pocket and updated the dispatcher. The ice melting into his jeans made him shiver. "We have to get them out of here," he said to the woman. "Where's that ambulance?"

Rachel groaned and he dropped the phone on the seat without responding to the dispatcher's assurances help was on its way. He placed his warm hand over Rachel's cheek. Rach," he called gently, then louder. "Rachel! Honey, can you hear me?"

With another groan, she opened her eyes. They were glazed, unfocused, and he was never so glad to see anything in his life.

"G-Greg?" she stammered.

He frowned. The knot on Rachel's forehead told him it was likely she had another concussion and was confused. "Patrick," he said gently. "It's Patrick, honey."

"No. Where is—" She shuddered. Her eyelids closed half way.

For a moment, he was afraid she'd passed out again. But then, she rallied. "Greg," she murmured. "Ran us...off road."

Bishop did this? He searched the immediate area but they were too low in the ditch for him to see far, and he couldn't see the road at all from this position. He hadn't seen another vehicle when he arrived. He was so fixed on locating Rachel and Amanda he might have missed it. He pulled the Glock he'd been carrying since the incident with the councilman from his shoulder holster. "I'll be right back, Rach."

Her right hand clutched his arm. "No. 'Manda," she said weakly. "D-Don't let Gre...." Her eyelids fluttered closed. Her voice grew faint, her last words a whisper. "Save m'baby." She lost consciousness again.

Suddenly afraid he might lose her before help arrived, he kissed her cold cheek. "Don't leave me, sweetheart," he choked out. As he gazed at her, then at Amanda sitting in her car seat, both unmoving, too pale, his heart pinched. They were injured, maybe dying because of him. Not Greg. *Him.* He'd dared to get too close, to fall for the little girl and her mother, to try to help them. He'd failed them in every way that mattered. He hadn't protected them from Greg at all.

"That ends now," he muttered. No matter how angry Rachel was with him, no matter how much she might want to leave Denver with Amanda, Patrick wouldn't let them out of his sight again until he was certain they were safe. He wouldn't fail them again, even if it meant getting closer, knowing he loved them both and would have to let them go when it was all over.

Patrick jumped out of the truck into the mush of melting hail, and re-scanned the ditch in both directions. No one was in sight, but he did spot Cook's gun sticking up in a clump of nearby weeds. He strode over to it and tucked it into his jacket pocket. Then, Patrick climbed the ditch wall to the road and waited for the emergency vehicles he could hear in the distance.

The next forty minutes passed in a blur for Patrick. It took the firefighters and paramedics that long to pry Rachel's unconscious form from the cab of the truck and get her to the hospital. They'd been quicker with Amanda's removal. Five minutes after their arrival she was loaded in the ambulance and Patrick was faced with the worst decision of his life.

A police officer tried to take his statement, though he was too distracted by what the emergency personnel were doing with the woman and child who'd become so important to him. He watched the medics load Amanda onto a gurney and cover her, so tiny and helpless on the gurney. "You coming?" one of the paramedics asked as his partner and a couple of firefighters prepared to carry Amanda up the ditch toward the awaiting ambulance. "You are the father, right?"

Patrick's air froze in his lungs when he realized he wanted to be. He looked over at Rachel's slumped form not wanting to leave her, but then her voice whispered through his mind. *"Save m'baby."* There wasn't anything more he could do for Rachel here, and Amanda needed him.

"I'm coming," he told the paramedic. He looked at the police officer and handed over his keys. "My truck is in the middle of the road above us with the flashers on. Call my brother, Detective Jack Montgomery. Tell him to meet me at the hospital."

The officer straightened when he identified his brother. "Is this related to the Angel Killer case?"

He began to shake his head, but hesitated. All he knew was what Rachel said before she passed out. Had she really seen her ex-husband or had Patrick's saboteur taken another shot at her? "Just tell him this wasn't an accident."

The officer nodded and the two of them walked out of the ditch together, splitting in opposite directions at the top.

Once the ambulance arrived at the hospital, the medical team took over Amanda's care. Refusing to leave her side, Patrick listened to the paramedics give their report on her vital statistics. He watched the nurses cut off her clothes. He signed a form giving them permission to run tests. Once, Amanda woke up. Her eyes scanned the room until she saw him. She reached out a hand to him but the doctors and nurses surrounding her didn't allow him to do more than smile encouragingly before her eyes closed again.

It seemed to take forever before the doctor turned to give him a preliminary assessment of her injuries. "Your daughter's car seat saved her from the worst of the flying debris that caused the cuts on her face and arms. There is one deep laceration on the top of her head where something clipped her. A few stitches should take care of it, but we'll keep an eye on it in case there's swelling."

"If it's not that bad, why does she keep losing consciousness?" Patrick said, watching a nurse clean blood from a cut on Amanda's forehead.

"I don't think she has a concussion," the doctor replied, "but we'll watch her. I'm more concerned about internal injuries. It looks like something solid smacked into her middle. There's bruising over her spleen. There might be more we can't see yet. When she regains consciousness again we can ask her what specifically hurts.

"In the meantime, I'm sending her to Imaging for a CAT scan to get a clearer picture of what's going on inside her head and abdomen. I want you to go with her. Stick close and, next time she wakes up, I want you to talk to her. Get her to tell you—"

"She doesn't talk," Patrick interrupted, "so you won't get anything from her."

"She's what, four? She should be talking."

"Yes. She's four, and she used to," Patrick shook his head, "but she stopped about six months ago. PTSD."

The doctor scowled at him, like he was a bug he wanted to squash. "I was told this was a car accident, Mr. Thorne. If you or your wife has hurt this child, I have to report it."

Stung, Patrick reared back. "I wouldn't hurt a hair on Amanda's head! They were run off the road by someone who does want to hurt them though. You can get the details from my brother, Detective Jackson Montgomery, when he gets here." He ran his hand through his hair. "As for why Amanda doesn't talk, it has nothing to do with the accident. You can confirm that with Jack, too."

"I'm only trying to help your little girl," he said writing something down on the chart in his hand. "I'm required by law to report incidents of child abuse."

Patrick nodded, and considered telling the man that he wasn't Amanda's real father...for about two seconds. He soothed his twinge of conscience over the omission by reminding himself he hadn't actually said he was her father, and there was no one else to make sure she received the necessary care. "I understand. I want you to do everything in your power to help her, so we're both on the same page."

The doctor searched his face, probably trying to determine whether he believed Patrick's sincerity. He nodded and returned to his report. "If Amanda doesn't talk, it's going to be harder to determine her faculties when she wakes up again. It will help to have you nearby though. I don't want her to wake up again surrounded by strangers."

"I can do that."

"Someone will be down in a minute or two to take Amanda to Imaging." The man made another note on the medical chart in his hand and gave it to the hovering nurse. He put his hand on Patrick's forearm, his voice serious. "Stay calm and steady. We don't want to add to her trauma when she wakes up. She needs to see that her daddy isn't worried."

"Should I be?" Patrick's heart ached as if he really was her dad, and he *was* worried.

The man gave him a reassuring smile. "Try to relax, Mr. Thorne. Amanda's in good hands. I'll know more when the test results come back. We'll talk again then."

All Patrick could do was nod. He longed to do something, anything, to make Amanda better. He was out of his element here. He wished Rachel could make these decisions for her little girl. Biting back a curse, he glanced at the large clock on the wall. Had it only been thirty minutes since he left the woman he loved pinned behind the steering wheel of his truck?

Where was that ambulance?

His brother, Jack, pushed his way into the ER bay despite the protesting nurse. He flashed his badge in her direction. His gaze fixed on Patrick. "What happened?"

"He tried to kill them," Patrick said grimly. "Bishop, the Angel Killer, I don't know, *someone* ran their truck off the road. Cook's dead. The first responders were using the 'jaws of life' to get Rachel out but she's still not here. And Amanda is...is—" He had to stop speaking because he could see her lying there, unconscious, and the sick knot in his gut tightened. "I didn't protect them, Jack. I've killed them," he whispered. "Just like Karly."

"You didn't kill anyone." His brother placed both hands on his shoulders and squeezed hard enough to make him wince. "Someone did this and we'll get him, you hear me? But you've got to get a grip on your emotions. You're no good to Rachel and Amanda if you lose it."

Patrick took in a shaky breath. Blew it out. The second one was stronger, more settled. By the third, his head was clearer and the orderly arrived to take Amanda upstairs for her tests. Following the gurney with his brother, he succinctly told Jack everything he knew about the accident and the events leading up to it. He told him about his argument with Rachel, the reason for it, although he did skim over the part about kissing her.

Jack was scowling by the time he finished. "None of this makes sense. Jane's blackmailer points these attacks in one direction. Your saboteur another. The Angel Killer yet another. Add in Rachel's ex-husband and we've got a freakin' mess." He pinned Patrick under his fierce gaze. "Rachel saw Bishop?"

"She said he ran them off the road. I don't know if she actually saw him or assumed it was him. With Cook dead and unable to confirm anything, there's no way to be certain." Patrick shook his head. "Despite everything, my gut says it wasn't Bishop. He wants Rachel and Amanda back. They're no good to him dead. They're the key to the money and—"

"What money?"

Damn. Rachel hadn't wanted him to bring up the inheritance or Amanda's parentage, but he realized the information was the reason he didn't believe this attack came from Rachel's ex-husband. Watching the technicians run the Amanda through their imaging, he told his brother everything Rachel shared with him the night they'd made love.

"What a cluster." Jack heaved a sigh. "Rachel is right about one thing. If Bishop went to the courts and demanded his daughter back, I'm not sure what we could do to legally stop him. Child custody suits can be a bitch under normal circumstances. Add in a mother not biologically tied to the child, and the outcome can be iffy."

He paced the corridor as he processed his thoughts. "Bishop's wanted for questioning in California for attacking the doctor and blowing up his fertility clinic. But, technically, that doesn't make him a criminal in the eyes of the court unless he's formally charged and found guilty.

"Like you, I can't see him killing the golden goose. He gets the kid, he holds the cards." He paused in front of Patrick. "There's still something's missing in this equation. What else does he want?"

"Rachel."

"I get that. She's the one holding the money." Jack shook his head. "No. I'm thinking about the day Bishop trashed her bedroom at the folk's house. He got mean and vicious when he started ripping things up and there was no doubt the message on the mirror was a threat, but I got the distinct feeling from the photos the responding officers took of the scene that he was searching for something. Something he didn't find, and that set off his destructive rampage."

"If he wants something else, I have no idea what it might be." The medical technician waved to let him know they were finishing up the tests. Patrick could see Amanda's eyes were still closed so he turned back to his brother. "The point is I'm not certain Rachel actually saw Bishop in the truck that hit her, which leads us back to who was driving the other truck.

"We have to figure out who I've pissed off, Jack. This saboteur has been taking potshots at my business for months, but the last two times he's targeted Rachel. He pushed her into an elevator shaft. Now this? Who hates me enough to kill the people I care about?"

His head tilted, Jack studied him. "I know we've been through every-thing over and over, but we need to tear your personal and business lives apart again. If your saboteur and the Angel Killer are the same person, *and* he's gunning for Rachel to get at you, there has to be a connection we're missing. There are a couple of leads the task force is following up on so I'll goose them and see what comes back."

"What leads?"

"I don't want to speculate until we've got something solid." He pinned Patrick under his gaze. "I want you to close down all of your projects and stay away from work for a few days."

One look at his brother's face, and Patrick didn't question the necessity. "Done."

Jack nodded his approval. "It's time to circle the wagons. I'm ordering a police detail on Rachel and Amanda here at the hospital. I can get someone here in less than an hour. No one goes in or out without clearance from me. That means you, me, Mom, Dad and the medical staff. Another officer will be with you and the folks when you're not here."

"I'm not leaving the hospital until Rachel and Amanda are released," Patrick said.

"I'll rest easier knowing where to find you."

"Thanks, Jack." Patrick straightened as the orderly wheeled Amanda out of the Imaging room. He smiled down at the little girl, who was awake and staring back at him. "Hi, baby," he said. "I'm glad to see you're awake."

Amanda's lips twisted into a little smile. It disappeared quickly when it pulled at a split in her lip. She whimpered.

Patrick caught her hand in his big one. "I know it hurts to smile. How about we go see some doctors about fixing that right up? That work for you?"

She squeezed his fingers and nodded.

With a last goodbye to his brother, Patrick walked alongside the gurney back to the ER room, still holding her hand. When they got there, the doctor came in and Patrick asked Amanda questions and had her point to places that hurt. By the time they finished, the nurse came in with the CAT scan.

The doctor asked to speak to Patrick outside the room. Before he left, he leaned down to kiss Amanda's forehead and told her he'd be right outside the door where she could see him. He could feel her gaze on him as the doctor quietly explained the images showed that, yes, she had a bruised spleen. But, thankfully, they could find no evidence of other internal injuries.

Just when Patrick began to relax, the doctor continued. "I don't think we should concern ourselves about surgery at this time, but we want to keep an eye on her spleen for the next day or two so I'm admitting her. It's going to take a little while to get her a bed on the pediatric floor, so we'll keep her here until they're ready to take her up."

"Surgery on her spleen? That's pretty serious, isn't it?"

"It can have some long term health effects if we have to operate, but I'm hopeful it won't come to that."

An ambulance pulled up to the ER entrance and several doctors and nurses hurried to the doors to escort paramedics and their patient into the hospital. It took less than two seconds for Patrick to recognize Rachel's gorgeous blond curls. "Rachel," he whispered, ready to rush to her side. But then, he glanced into Amanda's room and saw that she was still watching him.

He walked to her bed and smiled. "Your mama's here, Amanda."

"Mama?"

She said the one word so softly Patrick wasn't sure he hadn't imagined it. He stroked her hair off her forehead with fingers that shook. "What did you say, baby?"

Her eyelids drooped tiredly. "Mama," she whispered, drifting off into sleep.

Patrick stared down at the precious little girl who looked so much like her mother. His throat closed. Amanda spoke! That her first word was to him and not her mother broke his heart, but she'd said something. Had the trauma of the accident broken through her silence? "Sweetheart," he whispered, "your mama's going to be so excited to hear you talk."

He wanted to shout the news, run to Rachel, hug her and tell her everything was going to be okay with her little girl. Amanda talked! And her mama was lying down the hall in another ER bay. He motioned one of the nurses into the room. "Please watch Amanda while I check on her mother?" he asked. "If she wakes up again, tell her where I am, that I'll be right back."

"No problem," the man said. "Take your time."

Relieved, Patrick stalked down the corridor to the room where the doctors worked on the woman he loved. The ER staff knew Rachel was being brought in, and they believed he was Amanda's daddy, so they didn't question his right to enter the room. He listened to the paramedics report on her condition after her removal from the truck. He winced when they said she might have a broken ankle. He was grateful it wasn't worse. Her legs could have been a twisted mess behind the console that had trapped her.

That she kept drifting in and out of consciousness was a bigger concern. He told them about her previous concussion, her altitude sickness, and gave them Sam's cell number so they could request her medical records from his hospital.

When they wheeled her to Imaging, Patrick checked on Amanda. She was still asleep, a natural sleep, according to the nurse, so he decided to take the time to arrange for the shutdown of Thorne Enterprises as Jack requested. Another ambulance arrived in a flurry of noise and screaming relatives, forcing him to find a seat in a much quieter waiting room to make his calls.

Patrick called his mom first. Some of the tension rolled off his shoulders when she informed him that Jack had already been in touch, she and Dad were on their way to the hospital. He promised to update them when they arrived.

Next up was Jane. He told her to stay home, briefly explaining what took place after she'd gone home with Suze this afternoon. "This is all my fault," she said, starting to cry again. "If I hadn't—"

"Stop, Jane," he said. "The accident wasn't your fault. We'll get to the bottom of everything. Just stay home with Suze and take care of yourself.

"Skip will make all of the necessary calls notifying everyone I'm closing down until—"

"You can't shut down Thorne Enterprises!"

"It's done," he said shortly. "With any luck it will only be a few days, but don't worry, you'll get your paycheck."

Jane snorted in his ear. "I don't care about that, Patrick. It's just that this business means everything to you, and I-I never thought I'd hear you say such a thing. I really am sorry for my part in this mess."

Patrick slumped in the waiting room chair, suddenly exhausted. It had been a traumatic day and was far from over. He ran a restive hand over his face to pull himself together. "Nothing means as much to me as Rachel and Amanda, or the safety of my crew," he said. "I don't want anyone else getting hurt."

He then contacted Skip to tell him what to do. "I'll call you back in an hour or so to help you with phone calls, but I can't leave the hospital for a while."

"I get it, Patrick," Skip replied. "Family comes first. You were there when I needed you after Karly—" He paused a long moment, and a muffled conversation took place in the background before he came back. "We know what to do, Patrick, so don't worry about Thorne Enterprises. We've got it covered." Then, he hung up.

Relieved Skip was taking care of his business, Patrick walked back toward the ER bay where Rachel slept. He nodded to the nurse recording her vitals, and turned to see if Amanda had awakened. One of the little girl's nursing team approached him from the hall before he could leave Rachel's cubicle. "Mr. Thorne?"

"Yes?"

"The doctor on Amanda's case has ordered a bed for her. We're hoping surgery won't become necessary, but we like to be prepared for all contingencies." She glanced at her clipboard. "Amanda has a rare blood type. We do have blood available. It would be better if we had a family member with the same blood type available." She glanced up at him. "Are you AB negative?"

"I can't help there." He shook his head, the new worry making him reveal too much. "I'm not Amanda's real father."

"Oh." She frowned. "It would be ideal to have her real father's blood, if it's the same type, so we were really hoping to talk to you, I mean, her father." She stammered to a stop.

"He's unavailable." A good thing, too. If Patrick were in the same room with Bishop, he'd likely kill him. It didn't matter he didn't think Rachel's ex-husband was responsible for running her off the road. There were other issues to settle between them. Like making it clear Bishop wasn't getting Rachel and Amanda back. Ever. They weren't his any longer. They were Patrick's now...to protect, at least. He didn't dare think beyond this moment. When Bishop was no longer a threat was soon enough to deal with his deeper feelings for the two females who'd crashed into his life.

"It would be easiest to have her mother's blood, but since she's not available either—" The nurse glanced at the clipboard again, like it would give her an easy way out of the conversation.

Patrick felt sorry for her discomfort. "Look, Nurse, even if she were conscious and healthy, Rachel isn't likely to be able to give Amanda blood either. She isn't her biological mother."

"She's not? But I thought—" The nurse only looked more bewildered, but she straightened quickly. "I'll just note you're not the right blood type then. Excuse me."

Patrick watched her scurry away.

Rachel's Southern whiskey voice cut into his back. "H-How could you?"

Grateful to hear her speak, Patrick turned with a smile that quickly disappeared when he saw the angry flush in her face. "What?"

"You promised to keep my secret, keep Amanda safe. I should have known better than trust you!"

"I was just—"

He'd screwed up. Badly. "I'm sorry, Rach. I'm just trying to make sure Amanda gets proper medical care." The hospital staff, he realized, were the least of his worries. The only real threat to Rachel's custody of her daughter was the authorities. She'd go ballistic if she knew everything he'd revealed to Jack.

"Get out."

Patrick stiffened. "You can't be serious. I—"

"Get out, and don't come near me or my daughter again." She pointed to the door. "Get out!"

"But—" Her angry glare stopped him.

She searched through the folds of her blanket until she found her call button. When the nurse arrived, Rachel pointed at him. "Get him out of here."

The nurse's gaze went back and forth between them. "But your husband—"

"He's not my husband," she said. "And he's not Amanda's father, either."

The petite woman stiffened and confronted Patrick. "Sir, I have to ask you to leave," she said firmly.

"Rachel, don't—"

She looked away and the nurse spoke again. "Mr. Thorne? Please don't force me to call security."

Angry with himself for the trust he'd thrown away with a few careless words, he stalked out of the room. He almost ran over his parents in his haste. "Mom! Dad, when did you get here?"

"A few minutes ago." His dad's sympathetic expression told Patrick they'd heard Rachel throw him out.

His mother leveled him with "the look", the one he and his brothers grew up dreading because it meant someone was in big trouble. "I'll go check on Rachel," she said quietly. "You talk to your father." With that, she walked into Rachel's room and firmly shut the door behind her.

"You're in deep crap now," his father said dryly. "One pissed woman is bad enough. You have two about to gang up on you." He jockeyed his crutch under his arm and led the way toward the waiting room. "What did you do?"

"Where do I start?" He was more than ready to talk to the one man who'd helped him navigate down every rocky road he'd ever faced. He spent the next twenty minutes telling his father everything.

"Geez, son, and you still had time to fall in love?" His father shook his head in wonder. "I'm impressed. I thought my month-long courtship of your mother was fast."

"I'm not—" Patrick couldn't finish the denial. If he'd learned nothing else today, it was that he did care about Rachel and Amanda. He couldn't imagine being without them. He knew his life would never be the same once they went back to Dallas. That seemed more likely than ever now that Rachel was so upset with him. "What do I do?"

"Apologize every day, four, ten times a day, until she changes her mind and takes you back. It's what I had to do when I screwed up with your mother."

"Telling Mom you can't be with her because you're a cop and she's a blue blood is one thing, Dad," he said. "I revealed Rachel's most precious secret, one that jeopardizes her custody of the child she loves."

"You love Amanda, too, son. You were looking out for her best interest." He put his hand over Patrick's right hand, fisted on his thigh. "When Rachel calms down, she'll realize that. Give her time."

"She's still going back to Dallas, Dad. I can't, I'm not ready—" Patrick couldn't finish. "I do care, but I can't give them what they deserve. After Karly—"

"Don't let Karly kill your life, too, Patrick." He squeezed his hand. "I've held my tongue because your mother's convinced you'll work through your guilt on your own. But you have to accept the fact that none of what Karly did was your fault. She was clinically depressed. Sometimes, no matter what you do or how much you care for someone, bad things happen. It's not like you pushed her in front of that bus." He leaned back in his chair. "I haven't spent more than a few days in Rachel's company, but I can tell you she's nothing like Karly."

No. Rachel was nothing like Karly. Rachel was strong, independent. She wasn't afraid to take on a brutal ex-husband, to make personal sacrifices to protect the child she loved with a true mother's fierceness. It didn't mean Patrick hadn't screwed up their lives. He'd destroyed Rachel's trust and jeopardized Amanda's safety. "I have to go," he said, standing abruptly.

His father frowned up at him. "Where are you going?"

He should be running for the emergency exit, but he knew he wasn't leaving until he knew Rachel and Amanda were okay. When they were out of danger, well, he'd cross that bridge when he came to it. "I want to peek in on Amanda, if I can get near her. Then, I'm getting coffee. You want one?"

"Sure. I'll wait here until your mother comes out."

"You have every right to be angry with my son, Rachel, but you know Patrick loves you, don't you?" Evelyn snagged a chair from one corner of the room, dragged it bedside, and sat down.

Rachel sniffed back tears she'd refused to release until Patrick left the room. She took the tissue his mother handed her and wiped her eyes. "He wouldn't have revealed my secret if he cared about me." Would she always love men who ultimately caused her pain?

"Men do and say stupid things when they're out of their comfort zone." Evelyn snorted. "Believe me, I know. I raised six boys. Even Ross isn't immune. They all like to think they have control of everything. When it comes to matters of the heart, though, they lose control and that confuses them."

"You don't understand. What he did—" Rachel shook her head when she felt her anger weakening. "If I lose Amanda, I-I, how can I forgive him?" Not that it mattered because she knew Evelyn had it wrong. Men made love to women all the time without having feelings for them.

"It's difficult to see beyond your hurt," she said, patting her hand. "But, it will work out."

Unable to deny her feelings and lacking confidence that anything would ever work out between them—she didn't have the heart to hurt Evelyn, who'd given her so much—she said nothing. She was almost grateful when a physician entered room and ended the conversation.

"Ms.," the man glanced at the clipboard in his hand, and frowned, "James. Ms. James, I'm the doctor assigned to Amanda's case. Could we talk for a few minutes?"

Rachel reached out to Evelyn when the older woman began to rise. She took her hand, very comfortable with the woman who reminded her so much of her own mother. "Whatever you have to say can be said in front of Evelyn."

The doctor nodded. "The nurse told me the man who's been posing as your husband is, in fact, *not* your husband." His scowl deepened. "I was informed you're not Amanda's mother either. Only someone with legal custody can sign admittance forms for her."

"I have legal custody, Doctor," Rachel said with confidence. It would take a court of law to deny her rights, dammit! "Amanda *is* my daughter."

"I knew there had to be some confusion," he said with a genuine smile. "For Amanda to have your rare blood type, she had to be your daughter."

"But—" When she was artificially inseminated, Simon told her he would try to match the appearance of the donor mother to her as closely as possible, but down to the same blood type? Was that kind of accuracy even possible?

The doctor handed her the clipboard and asked her to sign the admission forms, forcing away her confusion. He explained Amanda's injuries. "We want to keep a close eye on her for the next couple of days, which is why we're admitting her."

"Thank you, Doctor. I feel so much better knowing she's not in immediate danger."

"We'll take good care of her." He smiled. "This brings me to my next point. We do have a blood bank available, but we prefer to have a family member with Amanda's blood type on call in case surgery becomes necessary. You may have the same blood type but you can't be a donor. We wouldn't put your baby at risk. Is there another family member we can talk to?"

She froze. "What did you say?"

"We'd like another family member—"

"No." *Baby?* "What baby?"

23

"You're pregnant."

Rachel stared at the physician like he'd inexplicably grown two heads. "That's not possible."

He nodded. "When you came in, one of the first things we did was cross match your blood type and check for pregnancy. We can identify the presence of hormones in the bloodstream only a few days after conception now." He consulted his clipboard. "We can conduct another test to verify the results, but according to your blood work, you are pregnant."

"I-I—" Rachel glanced at Evelyn, counting back to the night Patrick had made love to her. It had been eight days since she'd learned lovemaking could be as spectacular and satisfying with the right man as she'd read in books, so the time frame was possible. But what about the battery of tests Simon had done when she and Greg were trying to get pregnant?

Simon told her the problem was hers, that she wasn't fertile. Was it all just a monumental mistake or...oh, God, had Simon lied? Why would he do such a horrible thing? He knew how empty she'd felt, how devastated she was when he broke the news to her. She'd cried so hard it had taken Greg forever to calm her dow—

Greg. Her con artist, ex-husband. This was his doing. She knew it!

Evelyn picked up her limp hand. "Rachel, sweetie, are you okay?"

No. She wasn't okay. If she was right, Greg had perpetrated a con on *her*, his own wife! From the day they'd met, when he "accidently" ran into her on the Stanford campus her junior year? From the beginning of their marriage?

Rachel was pregnant before she discovered what kind of man she'd married, and then it was too late. She quickly learned Greg would con his own mother if there was a profit in it for him. He'd been prepared to do whatever it took to get at the James family coffers, even lie about her not being Amanda's mother.

Her pulse hitched. If she was truly Amanda's mother, that meant Greg was the infertile one. Simon had lied and helped Greg use Rachel's belief in her infertility to control and manipulate her. Is that why Simon helped her to escape California six months ago, given her money to get help for Amanda? He'd felt guilty for his part in the con? All those years, everything she'd endured to keep Greg happy to shield Amanda from her father...the memories raced through her head, made her insides turn cold. She placed her hand protectively over her stomach.

"Ms. James? Are you feeling dizzy? Nauseous?" The doctor approached the side of the bed and took her wrist in his hand.

Staring at Patrick's mother—her baby's grandmother—a whole new array of thoughts flashed into her head. She'd promised Patrick it was safe to make love without protection. *She was carrying his baby.* She was returning to Dallas. *Would he let her go if he knew?* How could she tell him? *He didn't love her.*

She blinked. "I-I'm fine," she said. "I'm just surprised." She summoned a smile for the doctor. "To answer your question, no, there is no one else with Amanda's blood type available. When can I see my daughter? "

Her daughter! Eager to see Amanda, she tossed off the sheet and tried to swing her legs over the side of the bed. Searing pain ripped through her left ankle, reminding her it was badly sprained, about the same time the doctor tried to stop her. "Whoa! You're not going anywhere until we get a secure bandage around that ankle. Then, we'll see about wheeling you in to see Amanda. Okay?"

Reluctantly, Rachel nodded and watched the doctor depart, her thoughts flying in a hundred different directions at once.

She was pregnant.

Amanda was hers.

Greg couldn't take her little girl away. Ever.

No wonder he hadn't followed up on his threats over the years.

She was so gullible.

She was having Patrick's b-

Suddenly registering the silence in the room, she caught Evelyn staring at her middle. The woman looked up into Rachel's eyes. "When will you tell Patrick?"

"Tell him what?" she prevaricated.

Evelyn's left eyebrow rose. "You're not going to tell me the baby belongs to someone else, are you? The night Ross and I came home, well, I wasn't born yesterday, young lady. I can put two and two together, and I don't think you're the type to sleep around."

You're a slut, but a selective slut. Is that what she was saying?

315

Rachel forced down an inappropriate urge to laugh and settled back into her pillow. She fiddled with the sheet beneath her fingertips. "I'm sorry," she said to the woman her own mother had called friend, the same woman who'd provided Rachel with a bolt hole to escape Greg. "I don't know what to say, Evelyn. I-I didn't mean for it to happen."

"You think I'm upset that it did?" Evelyn shook her head. "I'm not. It's about time someone special came along and made my stubborn son feel again. I'm glad it's you he fell in love with."

She did laugh then, but without humor. "Patrick doesn't have those kinds of feelings for me."

"He may not have said it, but he loves both you and Amanda. It's so obvious Ross commented on his surly behavior this morning at breakfast. Said Patrick had better hurry up and resolve whatever was wrong between you two before he had to knock both of your heads together." She nodded at Rachel's surprise. "And that man has to be hit over the head with a two-by-four before 'girly emotions' impinge on *his* manly senses."

Certain Evelyn was only trying to cheer her up, Rachel gave her a wan smile.

"So, tell me I'm going to be a grandma," Evelyn said with a broad grin. "Say it out loud once and it will be easier to tell Patrick."

"You're going to be a grandma." She wasn't sure if she wanted to laugh or cry. If Patrick did have feelings for her...no, she couldn't think about "what ifs". "Please don't tell Patrick. Not yet. I'll tell him when the time is right."

Evelyn's smile faded. "I don't like keeping secrets, honey. They always seem to come out at the worst time and bite you in the fanny." She sighed as if at a troublesome memory. "If Patrick finds out on his own, well, I don't want to see either of you hurt."

"It will only be for a few days," Rachel said. "I have to, oh, please, forgive me, but I have to wrap my head around this news myself. I promise, I'll tell him when the time is right."

When that might be was negotiable because Rachel knew the revelation wouldn't make a difference to her plans. She loved Patrick too much to trap him into a one-sided relationship. She'd be devastated if he demanded she stay because of the baby, and not because he loved her. He was too honorable to demand she get rid of the baby and, God help her, she could never give up the precious gift she carried inside her.

No. Despite what she'd just promised her baby's grandmother, she was afraid there would be no "right" time to tear her heart to shreds.

Patrick paused outside the closed door where he knew Rachel and his mother were talking. It took every bit of his self-control not to march in and order his mother to leave so he could take Rachel in his arms. He longed to kiss her angry mouth until she forgave him. He needed to assure himself that she was okay. He wanted to tell her that Amanda spoke!

He could do none of those things. The petite woman that had thrown him out of Rachel's room glanced over the nurse's station computer at him, and he walked on. Slowly. Beyond the nurses' station, he could see the door to Amanda's room was ajar so, if he took his time, he could peek in on her. It might be only a glimpse, but he had to take a chance. He'd promised her he'd come back. If she was alone in the room, he would try to slip insi—

His air seized in his lungs. The room was empty. Amanda wasn't lying in the bed where he'd left her.

You miscounted the rooms. Convinced he'd made a mistake, he retraced his steps. No. This was Amanda's room.

Pushing the door wide, he scanned every inch of the small space. No little girl. The male nurse he'd left her with was missing. He turned around to find the nurse hurrying from the nurse's station in his direction. "Where's Amanda?" he demanded before she reached him.

The woman stared up at him, her expression stern. "Sir, you're not supposed to—"

Unable to shake the feeling something was desperately wrong, Patrick cut her off. "Where's Amanda? I left her with one of you people," he said. "Did she take a turn for the worse? Did they take her up to surgery? I don't care if you think I have no rights, you have to tell me."

"She's right there, Mr.—" she hesitated when she glanced into the room behind him. Her forehead creased in perplexity. "They must have taken her up to Pediatrics," she said slowly. "I didn't see. I was talking to the father of the teenager brought in after your wife, I mean, Ms. James came in."

"Check!"

He stalked behind her to the nurse's station. He wasn't encouraged when she pulled a chart from the stack—presumably Amanda's—examined it, and muttered something before she picked up the phone. He listened to her side of several conversations as she tried to locate Amanda. With each call, his gut grew colder. He knew the little girl wasn't in the hospital before the nurse hung up the phone and looked at him.

"Call security," he ordered before he pulled his cell from his pocket.

He jammed it back in his pocket when he saw his brother and a uniformed police officer walk through the exterior ER doors. He met them and his father, who joined them from the waiting room. "You're too late, Jack," he said tersely. He wanted to tear into his brother. Jack had returned with his promised security in under an hour, but that didn't matter. "Amanda's gone, and her nurse is missing."

Jack spat a virulent curse that prompted a gasp of shock from a woman in the nearby waiting room.

"Jackson!" Using his crutch, their father shepherded the group into a corner, away from listening ears. "Get a hold on yourself, Patrick," he said, his free hand steady on his shoulder. "We'll find them."

His dad nodded toward the uniformed officer, peered at his badge. "Officer Glenn, go find out what you can from hospital security. Have them organize a search for Amanda and the missing nurse. They're here. We just have to look." He glared at the back of the departing officer.

Patrick didn't often see his father rattled. *He didn't believe Amanda was still in the building any more than he did.* "Rachel," he said. "Someone has to tell Rachel." She'll be devastated when she realized how badly he'd screwed up. Again.

"She knows," his mother said from his right. "Her ex-husband just called her cell phone with his demands. She's getting dressed. I tried to stop her, but—"

Patrick spent the next fourteen hours arguing with Rachel, his brother, Jack, his parents, and the cadre of FBI agents who'd descended upon the hospital within thirty minutes of Greg Bishop's phone call. Patrick's objections were ignored by everyone. The only reason he was standing in his parents' living room watching Rachel get outfitted with a listening device was because Jack ran interference for him with the FBI. The big surprise was that Rachel, after a brief conversation with his mother, agreed to let him stay.

Running out of time to stop the plan Rachel had set in motion, he glared across his parents' living room at the FBI tech clipping a mic to her lacy bra, as if the two women were alone in the room and not within viewing range of half a dozen male agents. Patrick's fingers twitched to pull the edges of Rachel's blouse together, so they couldn't ogle his woman.

Get a grip. No one's looking, but you and the female agent...and Rachel isn't yours. You threw away that opportunity when you revealed her secret and broke her trust.

He straightened away from his position leaning against his dad's easy chair as the agent fiddled with the microphone one last time and walked to the end table where her equipment case rested. With her out of the way, he approached the one woman who'd turned his world upside down and made him crazy in a couple of short weeks.

Rachel's shuttered expression stopped him, but he was close enough his lungs filled with the luscious scent of lilacs and warm woman. Ignoring the "hands off" message in her eyes, he reached out and gently traced his thumb over one of the dark circles that testified to her sleepless night, a bruise from the accident stark marring her pale cheek.

His gaze traced the wide black and blue line that started at the top of her left shoulder, ran over her collarbone across her chest to disappear behind her blouse over her ribs, where the truck seatbelt had caught her in the rollover. He examined her arms below the short sleeves, the bruises and scratches from her attempts to save herself when she was pushed into the empty elevator shaft at Southgate.

She looked so fragile after the trauma of these past few days, he was afraid a puff of air would break her into a million pieces. He'd learned she was stronger than she looked. That didn't mean he wanted her to confront her brutal ex-husband like this. It was insanity.

When she swayed without her crutch to support her, he put his hands on her arms to steady her. "You can't do this, Rachel," he said, his voice low, insistent. "There has to be another way."

"Greg's instructions were specific. I show up at the zoo or I'll never see Amanda again," she said, straightening her spine. "I don't care what I have to do. I'm getting her back."

That's what concerned him. Her ex-husband wanted both Amanda and Rachel, so what was to stop him from forcing her to go with him when he had them together? "Honey," he said, aiming for a more measured tone. "Think about it. He has no reason to return Amanda. She's his ticket to your great-aunt's estate, and his one bargaining chip to control you. You can't just hand yourself over to him."

"Do you think I haven't thought of everything that can go wrong? It's all I've thought about every waking moment since he kidnapped my baby from the hospital," she cried, her voice cracking. "I have to do this if we're ever to be free of him. Don't you see that? I trust the FBI and Jack," she laid a slim hand flat over his heart, "and you to keep us safe."

Despite yesterday, she still trusted him?

Something loosened inside Patrick. He couldn't stop what he did next if his life depended on it. He pulled Rachel into his arms and kissed her like they were alone in the room. He poured everything into the caress, his regret for what he'd done to hurt her, the feelings for her he could no longer deny, and his desire to claim her as his own.

When Rachel moaned in response and her tongue darted into his mouth, the tenor of their kiss changed. It became carnal, passionate. Their tongues met, retreated, promising seductive delights he didn't dare explore without a bedroom door between them and the world. It had been too long since he had her beneath him crying out his name as she...a cough behind him reminded him the world wouldn't wait.

He reluctantly lifted his head. "We'll pick this up later," he promised as he dug deep for control. He tugged her gaping blouse closed over her breasts and began to button it.

The simple action helped him to focus on the task at hand. If Rachel was going to do this he had to treat this like a mission, put away his reservations, and show his confidence that everything would turn out. "Stick to the plan, Rach," he said, his voice rough as he tucked her blouse into the waistband of her flower-covered skirt. "Concentrate on getting Amanda away from Bishop as fast as you can." He glanced over her shoulder at the agents watching them. "I don't care what the FBI wants you to do beyond that."

"They only want what I want, Patrick. My freedom. Amanda's freedom. She comes first." She jockeyed her single crutch under her left arm before she reached up to drag her fingers over his taut jaw. "I promise, the moment I get what we need or it looks like I can't do it, I'll grab Amanda and run in the opposite direction."

Patrick crushed the mental image of the two of them running for their lives before it could threaten his self-control. He fell back on repeating the points she already knew. "I'll be in the FBI van in the parking lot," he said, "but, if you get into trouble, yell bloody murder. The zoo's been open half an hour, so undercover agents are already in place around the rhino enclosure."

He hated that he couldn't personally keep Rachel under surveillance within the zoo grounds. Jack convinced him that they couldn't take the chance. Bishop might recognize him. So, he was stuck in the van listening to everything go down. He was sure to go out of his mind until he had Rachel and Amanda back in sight again.

"It's going to be fine," Rachel said in a low voice he knew only he could hear. "I, we, there's something I have to tell—"

She shook her head. An odd expression flickered across her face. "We'll talk when this is all over. Okay?"

He nodded to reassure her. His hand cradling the back of her neck, he pulled her in for another soul-destroying kiss.

"Patrick?" Jack called over his shoulder. "It's time to go."

Releasing Rachel's mouth, he watched her lick her lips, sigh, and then bend down to pick up Amanda's doll—the only thing her ex-husband demanded Rachel bring with her—from the sofa cushion. As she stuffed the doll into Patrick's old backpack, he hoped Bishop didn't notice the fresh stitching in the fabric around the porcelain neck, wrists, and feet where the FBI had repaired the doll after discovering what the con man had hidden inside.

When Rachel straightened, she gave everyone in the room a brave smile that made Patrick's lips thin. He knew by the tremble of the free hand she placed over her stomach that she was terrified, rightly so considering the man she was confronting.

It was all Patrick could do not to put his fist through the nearest wall as he followed Rachel and the roomful of agents out the front door.

Rachel sat in the back seat of the cab—Patrick's backpack clutched in both hands—and swallowed the gorge rising in her throat. She glanced at the undercover agent driving her to her destination and wished she dared tell him to turn around. The only reason she didn't run straight back into Patrick's arms where she felt safest was because the two people she loved were in front of her.

She watched the dark SUV Patrick, Jack, and two FBI agents rode in turn the next corner as they sped to get into place in the surveillance van already parked in the zoo lot. She would arrive at the front entrance by taxi. If everything went according to plan, she would have Amanda in sight within the next ten minutes.

Her pulse raced as she thought of the events of the last twenty-four hours, the roller coaster ride of emotions that had torn at her since Jane revealed her secret in Patrick's office. Rachel's anger with him. Their kiss. The attack on the road that killed Cook, and put her and Amanda in the hospital. Discovering she was pregnant with Patrick's child. His revelation of her secret. Amanda's kidnapping.

Her nerves jumped as she remembered Greg's call on her cell at the hospital. "I've got the brat," he'd spat in her ear. "If you ever want to see her again, you'll do exactly what I say. *Exactly*. And I'd better not see any cops or that asshole boyfriend of yours, either. If I do, Amanda pays. You hear me, bitch?"

She'd heard him all right. She heard the brutality, no longer masked in his voice. The edge of desperation underlying his frustration and anger at being denied what he desired. Listening to his instructions, she knew she wouldn't walk away from him with her daughter unless she obliterated his threat from their lives once and for all.

The moment her ex-husband hung up, she called Jason Sommerfield, the FBI agent that she'd dealt with in California, the man she'd given the evidence they used to arrest Greg the first time. Once she explained what she wanted to do, Sommerfield coordinated with agents in the Denver office to set up this morning's sting. He'd flown in to assist and was in the SUV with Patrick and Jack.

She'd never questioned her decision to use the FBI to rescue Amanda...until now. So much could go wrong. She didn't know what kind of shape Amanda was in. Had Greg hurt her? Was her spleen injury aggravated when he kidnapped her from the hospital? Security tapes showed him entering her emergency room like he belonged there; he wore the missing nurse's uniform after knocking the poor man out and stashing him in a closet. Greg might have been stopped if he'd tried to take Amanda out the ER entrance, but he'd used a wheelchair to take her deeper into the hospital, like he was moving her to her room. Instead, he simply wheeled her out a main entrance unchallenged.

The man seemed to have a plan for everything. It was one of the reasons it had taken so long to figure out a way to escape him the first time. They'd succeeded temporarily, but at what cost? Her traumatized little girl had crawled into a silent hole where no one could reach her. And Greg? Greg had found them again.

How would she get her daughter away from him this time? What was she going to have to do to get him to spill his guts so that the FBI could put him away forever? So they'd be free of him? Her mind swam with questions she couldn't answer.

Concentrate on the prize, little chickadee, her father's voice whispered in her head. His words smothered the anxiety chewing on her composure. Amanda was all that was important. Amanda.

After fourteen hours of worry, fear, and worst case scenarios running through her head, she was going to see her little girl again. *Her* little girl. She was confident the DNA tests she'd requested before leaving the hospital would reveal the truth, a truth she knew in her heart. Whatever else happened after she confronted Greg, she'd make sure he couldn't take Amanda away from her in a court of law. Greg wouldn't walk out of the zoo today. The FBI, Jack and Patrick would see to that.

Heavens, but she wished Patrick was holding her again, making her believe this was all going to work out. Telling her he wanted her to stay when it was finished.

"You ready, Ms. James?" The agent driving the cab looked at her in the rearview mirror as he pulled up to the curb at the main entrance to the Denver Zoo.

"I'm ready," she said with a decisive nod.

Unbuckling her seatbelt, she eased Patrick's pack over her bruised back and shoulders. Hands freed, she opened the cab door, got out, and tucked her crutch under her left arm. Her muscles screamed in protest despite the three over-the-counter pain pills she'd taken an hour ago.

She resisted the impulse to scan the parking lot behind her and locate the van where she knew Agent Sommerfield, Jack, and Patrick were hidden. Just knowing that they watched and listened helped her to take the first step toward the line of people handing over their entry passes and tickets. Despite the fact the zoo had been open less than an hour, she could see the grounds beyond the gates had already filled with a number of summer visitors.

It promised to be another scorcher of a day. There were pockets of kids in similarly marked summer camp T-shirts dashing around parents and their families, all out for a full day of fun and animal viewing. Jack suggested that Greg picked this public place knowing he wouldn't look out of place with a four-year-old at his side. Greg most likely believed the number of people would allow him to get lost in the crowd should it become necessary for him to disappear. She preferred to believe numbers worked more in her favor, allowing the undercover agents to hang closer without being spotted.

When she got to the employee at the gate, she reached into the breast pocket of her cotton blouse—a bright neon-green to make her more visible—and presented the member pass the FBI had provided. The man smiled, glanced at the crutch and walking cast the doctor gave her to better support her sprained ankle, and invited her to go through the swinging gate meant for those with wheelchairs and carriages.

Show time.

Aware Greg could be watching, she followed his instructions and aimed right along the main walkway she'd seen on the zoo map the FBI pulled up on the internet. With the aid of her crutch, she made her way past a group of snack shops, skirted the enclosures that made up Predator Ridge, and passed the Wild Encounters Amphitheatre. She tried to spot the undercover agents she knew were tracking her. There were so many people wandering the grounds she couldn't pick out specific individuals.

She gave up that pointless exercise when she approached the pachyderm enclosures and her gaze zeroed in on Greg and Amanda. Her pulse leapt when she saw them standing at a bar fence in front of a pair of rhinos. Greg dressed deceptively casual in jeans and a polo shirt while Amanda wore a sundress, lace-trimmed socks and shiny dress shoes. It matched Greg's standard photo shoot look of the perfect family on an outing.

The picture, however, was marred when Rachel got close enough to see her little girl wince as Greg pinched her tender arm in his big paw. Infuriated by his cruelty, Rachel's gaze skimmed over Amanda looking for injuries. Her poor baby had obviously been crying awhile, her eyes red and swollen. She looked so pale in the sunlight, so shell-shocked, Rachel believed she'd fall over if Greg let go of her arm. Who knew what was going on inside her small frame? Her spleen was already bruised.

"Let her go," she said harshly, stopping directly in front of Greg.

"I don't think so, darlin'." He sneered. "She's my insurance policy." He scanned the walkway over her shoulder.

Rachel was grateful she'd been unable to identify any agents because that meant he couldn't spot them either. "I wasn't followed."

"You'd say that even if you were." He yanked Amanda closer to his side. Amanda cried out.

"For God's sake, Greg, can't you see she's going to fall over? Let go!" Not thinking about it first, she punched him hard in the solar plexus with the heel of her open right hand.

Rachel wasn't sure if Greg was shocked by the punch itself or her temerity, but he grunted, released Amanda's arm, and staggered back a step.

She snatched her little girl out of his reach. *She had Amanda!* Holding her close, she was tempted to run in the opposite direction and call it a day. But, she wasn't moving particularly well on her crutch and she suspected Amanda wasn't in any condition to run either. Besides—Rachel's gaze tangled with a steely-eyed woman's as she settled on an empty bench next to a baby carriage five feet away—this would never be over until the FBI had something concrete to put Greg away permanently.

Praying her instincts were right and the woman was FBI, she turned to Greg who'd recovered his wits. "Amanda can sit over there," she said before he could act on any retaliatory impulses he was considering, "while we talk."

His lips thinned with displeasure. "Don't bother. We're leaving."

No way was she going anywhere with him, especially now that Amanda was no longer in his clutches. "If you want my cooperation, Greg, we have to talk first."

His icy blue eyes blazed in his too handsome face for several long moments. Rachel began to think he'd flat out refuse, but then with a snort of disgust and another scan of the area, he made a sharp motion toward the bench. "I won't have to listen to her sniveling if she's over there."

Rachel didn't give him a chance to change his mind. "Come on, baby," she said to Amanda, who looked up at her with trusting brown eyes.

Disturbingly aware Greg watched her, she escorted Amanda to the shaded alcove. She lifted her onto the bench next to the woman, farthest from danger. "Is it all right if my daughter sits here with you?" she asked loud enough for Greg to hear. "She's tired and I have to talk to...her daddy."

"Of course," the brunette said with a nod and smile. The woman patted the pile of empty blankets in the carriage. "My little one's sleeping, so I'm going to sit here in the shade awhile. I have some cookies if your daughter's hungry."

Rachel smiled at Amanda. "Baby, this nice lady will keep you safe until mama comes back. I'll be right over there where you can see me," she said with a nod in Greg's direction. She lowered her voice. "When I'm done we're going home with Mr. Patrick, okay?"

Her heart cracked a little when she saw the way Amanda's eyes lit up at Patrick's name. She'd fallen for the man as hard as her mama had. Rachel didn't want to think about how difficult it was going to be for them both to walk away from him when this was over. Just knowing he was in the zoo parking lot listening to everything made the time they had left with him feel too short. Once Greg was in custody, her reason for staying in Denver was gone. Baby or no baby.

Crushing the painful thought, she caressed tears off Amanda's face. "Stay here," she said. "You can have two cookies while I'm gone. Be good for this nice lady, okay?"

Her daughter nodded, as did the FBI agent. "We'll be fine," she said in a quiet voice. "Take your time."

Relieved Amanda was secure, she forced herself to walk back to her ex-husband where he stood next to the rhino enclosure. With any luck, he hadn't seen anything that would alert him to the fact that he'd just lost his only bargaining chip.

"Okay, the brat's sitting," he said, a curl in his lip. "Talk. We have an appointment in," he glanced at his watch, "an hour, and we have to get across town."

"Appointment with whom?"

His face tightened, as it always did when she'd questioned him during their marriage, so she backpedaled quickly. "You said you have a plan, but you haven't shared it with me. Where you're taking us."

"I don't have to tell you anything." When she simply stared at him with a carefully blank expression, he snapped. "We're updating our passports. We're getting new photos." He stared with disgust at the bruise she carried on her face from the truck accident. "We'll pick up makeup."

Dear God, he planned to drag them out of the country? "Where are we going?"

"Dubai."

"Why?"

He frowned. "What's with the twenty questions?"

She didn't want to alert him to her real motives, but she had to tell him something to deflect his suspicions. "I may have rolled over for your demands when we were married, but I sure don't intend to live in the dark anymore."

His right hand fisted, but he didn't strike her. "That's the second thing we have to fix today."

A frisson of anxiety ran through her at his calm conversational tone. "What?"

"A judge is marrying us at five o'clock."

Over her dead body! She'd marry the man she loved in a heartbeat...if he asked her. Well, maybe not even then. No way would she trap Patrick in marriage to provide her baby with a father. "Sounds like you have it all planned out," she said. "So we're going to Dubai for a honeymoon...with a four-year-old."

Greg looked at her like she was completely witless. "If you must know, I'm picking up some things."

Bingo. That's where he'd hidden the money he'd conned. The FBI techs had discovered a plastic bag with a piece of paper with several account numbers and two safety deposit keys inside the doll cavities when they'd carefully ripped the porcelain doll apart last night. But there was nothing to indicate where the accounts might be located. She was betting the FBI would find them in Dubai.

"Did you bring the doll like I told you?"

Biting her lip over a surge of insecurity, Rachel struggled to peel the backpack off her sweaty back without jogging the wire under her shirt. She unzipped it and pulled the doll into the sunlight. "I'll go give Becca to Amanda." She didn't want him to look too closely at it. "She's probably miss—"

He snatched the toy from her hand. "You're an idiot, Felicia," he said sharply. "The brat's smarter than you." He began to pull the porcelain head off the cloth torso.

Stop him!

"My name's not Felicia anymore, Greg," she said. "And, I'm not going to stand here and take your abuse."

Distracted, the hand holding the doll dropped to his side. "You'll take whatever I say you'll take," he said. He yanked her several feet down the paddock fence where he backed her into a huge flowering bush.

With nowhere to retreat, her ankle on fire from several missteps, she was suddenly back at their ranch in California, staring into the cruel blue eyes of the monster she'd married. The zoo crowd over his shoulder disappeared from her senses as the smell of his cologne drowned her in a sea of bad memories that ended with their last brutal night together.

A flicker of movement over his left shoulder drew her gaze to the FBI agent protecting Amanda. She'd stood and was staring at them. Her hand motioned quickly toward what Rachel suspected was another agent for assistance.

Swallowing her flash of alarm—Greg couldn't hurt her...much...with FBI agents this close—she shook her head slightly at the female agent. Rachel hadn't accomplished everything she'd set out to do yet.

The agent held up her hand in a halting motion to her fellow agent, and then slowly reclaimed her seat beside Amanda, never taking her eyes off Rachel.

Reassured she'd regained control of the situation, Rachel belligerently confronted Greg. "Or else what? You'll attack me like you did Simon?"

Greg took the bait. "Your knight in shining armor double-crossed me. He got the fiery death that he deserved." His smile was nasty.

Simon might never come out of his coma and she felt compelled to wipe the gloating smile off Greg's face. "It's a good thing he didn't die, then," she retorted, "because no one deserves to die that way."

He snorted with derision. "He's dead," he said. "I made sure of that when I blew up his clinic. No one fucks with me and gets away with it. You should remember what I'm capable of."

He'd admitted it out loud. He had tried to kill Simon, blown up the clinic. *One more item ticked off the FBI's "want" list. She could stop right now and they'd have enough to put him away where he couldn't touch her or Amanda again.* Her hand on her stomach, she took courage from the tiny life resting beneath her scars. "I remember everything."

"Few people know me like you do," he said. "But even you don't know everything."

Revulsion ripped through her at his expression of superiority. "I get that," she said in a conciliatory voice. "The FBI must have been really surprised when they had to let you go."

It still stung that they hadn't warned her of his release. She suspected they'd used her as bait, and that she'd been left in the dark because they knew Greg would make a beeline straight to her. She knew how desperate they were to find the money he'd conned, especially after their evidence disappeared.

Greg smirked. "Those morons couldn't find their ass with both hands."

The ever-stoic Agent Sommerfield, from the San Francisco office, must be cursing Greg in the parking lot. However, she also knew the agent was aware someone in his office was responsible for the loss of the evidence they had against Greg. "How did you 'disappear' their evidence?"

"Why do you care?" He paused. "Son-of-a-bitch! You really didn't come alone, did you?" He scowled and searched the walkways around them. "Where are they, your rescuers?"

"I followed your instructions," she assured him, sweat trickling between her breasts at the lie. "No one followed me. I'm not—"

"Don't bother." He grabbed her wrist in a painful grip. "I should have known you'd stab me in the back, you bitch," he gritted out. "We're out of here." He dragged her down the pachyderm fence toward Amanda's bench.

The female agent rose and Rachel waved her off again. She didn't want her to leave Amanda's side. "No!" She tore out of Greg's hold so he was forced to stop and face her. "You can't have Amanda and you can't have me."

"You're my wife. I'll do whatever the hell I want with you. The brat, too," he said, his expression thunderous. "I'm not letting either of you go, and if that means beating you again, beating the brat—"

His unfinished threat would have made a difference six months ago when she believed he was Amanda's biological father and she had to take whatever he dished out to protect her innocent daughter. Not now. Anger ripped through her. "You aren't touching either of us ever again," she said.

"You can't stop me." He sneered. "You won't walk away without the kid, and she's mine. Do I have to remind you of my promise our last night together?"

"I remember every last word you beat into me," she said, fighting down nausea. "It doesn't matter. I know your secret."

An odd expression crossed his face. "What secret?"

"You lied. I don't know what you had on Simon to force him to help you with your con, but I know Amanda's mine. Not yours."

"You're out of your mind," he said, less confidently. "You can't have childr—"

"I'm pregnant, Greg," she said, thrilled to say it out loud. *She was having Patrick's baby!* "Tell me again that I can't have children, you pathetic liar. Even if it were true, I told Great-Aunt Amanda to change her will before she died. You can't access any of her estate through Amanda because she's not getting a dime. So, we're finished here."

Greg blanched. Then, his face suffused with rage. "You bitch! That money is mine. Mi—"

He wrapped his large hands around her neck before she could react. She felt his hot, angry breath wash her face, the spit of raging words she couldn't hear through the sudden rush of blood in her ears. The sunlight around her dimmed as she scraped at his grip with her right hand. His fingers tightened further and black spots winked in front of her eyes.

Her lungs burned. She felt herself fall toward a black abyss. A wild thought tumbled through her mind. *I was wrong. He can kill me before help comes.*

"Mamaaaaaaa!"

Somewhere, in a distant part of her brain, Rachel heard her daughter yell her name. *That can't be right. Amanda doesn't talk.*

Time passed in a blur. Something smacked hard into Rachel's shoulder, knocking her and Greg off balance. His grip loosened and she gasped for life-saving air. Her left hand squeezed around her crutch in an effort to stay upright.

Blinking furiously against dizziness, she saw a strange man wrestle Greg away from her. Greg punched the guy and turned back to Rachel.

Amanda ran in front of him, screaming. "No! Daddy!"

Dear God, where did she come from? Rachel stared in horror as Greg bore down on her daughter.

"You little bitch, I'm going to kill you like I did your mongrel dog," he ground out in rage, lunging toward Amanda.

"Don't you touch her!" Rachel rushed into the fray and smashed her metal crutch upward between Greg's legs crushing his testicles.

He howled and dropped to the ground, writhing.

The female agent took a belligerent stance over Greg, her gun pointed at his chest. "You're under arrest, Bishop," she yelled.

Half a dozen more agents converged on Greg. They yanked him onto his stomach—still contorting on the pavement, an agonized keen ripping from his throat - and handcuffed him.

Rachel swung around to find her little girl glaring at her "daddy", her fists opening and closing with agitation. "You. Hurt. My. Mama," she said between huge, gulping sobs. "You pwomised." Her lips twisted with the powerful emotion she didn't hold in anymore. She looked completely unraveled and so beautiful in her rage.

Rachel dropped her crutch and fell to her knees. She cried out at the sharp jab of pain in her ankle. She ignored it, fell back on the hot pavement, and gathered Amanda into her lap. She rocked back and forth for several minutes, the terror of watching her little girl launch herself into danger slow to release her.

She pushed Amanda back and searched her face. "Are you okay?" she croaked, her throat raw from Greg's abuse. She caressed her little girl's damp cheek, looked into big, brown eyes so like her own, and grinned. "You talked! Oh, baby, you talked!" Rachel had thought her daughter's voice had been a figment of her imagination in the truck accident.

Amanda nodded, burst into tears, and threw her arms around her mother's neck. She squeezed so hard it was difficult to breathe, but Rachel didn't care. She just let her little girl crawl into her embrace and cry like a dam had burst inside her. Big noisy, cleansing sobs.

"You're okay, baby." Rachel hugged her, murmured into her fine hair. "Mama's here. Mama's here." She looked up to the sky and thanked her lucky stars that her daughter wasn't injured, and stared straight up into familiar green eyes.

"Jack," she whispered brokenly. "Did I get enough? Is it finished?"

"It's all there on the recording." He smiled at her with admiration. "You were amazing. Sommerfield is ecstatic. Bishop's going to prison for the rest of his life." He hunkered down to examine her burning neck, winced at what she was sure were new bruises. "You two okay?"

She nodded. A hot tear trickled down her face, his sympathy overwhelmed her. The only thing that would make her more okay was being held in his brother's arms. "Where's Patrick?" she asked.

He looked away...and didn't answer her question.

One moment she was sitting on the hot pavement with Amanda on her lap. The next, Jack reached down, plucked Amanda out of her arms and handed her off to the agent with the cookies. "Ms. Diana's going to take you over to the bench so we can check you over," he reassured Amanda. "I'm right behind you with mama, okay?" Before the little girl could do more than nod, he reached down and scooped Rachel into his arms.

Jack sat Rachel on the bench in the shade next to her daughter. "Okay, munchkin, let's take a look at you," he said to the little girl, still avoiding Rachel's eyes. He busied himself with his examination as "Ms. Diana" walked away to join her counterparts.

Rachel searched the nearby grounds, the path in the direction Patrick would have come. There were dozens of people, some clearly FBI and law officers, the others gawkers stopping to soak up all of the unusual excitement. "Jack?" She waited until he looked directly at her. "Where's Patrick?"

She didn't think he was going to answer her. But then, Jack sighed and sat back on the bench. "Gone."

"Gone where?"

"I don't know."

Rachel wasn't prepared to play twenty questions with the man. "Tell me what you don't want to tell me, Jack, and get it over with."

"Ah, hell, Rachel," he said, wringing the back of his neck in obvious frustration. "He just left. We were sitting in the van listening to everything that was happening here. When one of the agents radioed that Bishop had attacked you and was in custody, that you were secure, we all jumped out of the van and raced for the entrance."

He frowned. "Sommerfield and I did anyway. I didn't know Patrick wasn't behind me until after we got past the gate. When I looked back, he was gone."

A hole opened in her heart. *He'd walked away.* "He heard about the baby."

"We heard."

She'd been afraid to tell Patrick, afraid his protective instincts would demand she marry him to provide the baby with a father. She didn't want him that way, but how could she have been so wrong? She was such an idiot, holding onto the hope he'd come to love her the way she loved him. He didn't want her. Why would he want their baby?

"You didn't tell him you had someone waiting for you in Dallas, did you?"

Numb, she stared. "What?"

"The baby's father."

Realization dawned slowly. "You think, oh, my God, he thinks it's not his?"

"Is it?"

"Of course, it is!" She was getting angry now, but at least it washed away some of the pain inside her. Patrick's actions made a lot more sense if he thought the baby wasn't his. Would it make any difference if he did know?

"I must tell him," Rachel said.

Jack's eyebrow rose. "You love him that much?"

This wasn't a time for prevarication. "Yes. I love him that much."

He grinned crookedly. "Good. You should tell him."

Hope sprang to life in Rachel's heart. "Where do I find him?"

There was no time for him to answer because two paramedics, dragging a stretcher covered with medical bags, showed up. "Ma'am," one of the medics said, "we're here to take you and the little girl to the hospital."

Jack stood. "Go with them, Rachel."

"But I, we—"

"You have a little girl and a baby counting on you to take care of them," he said. "I'll find Patrick."

"Do you know where to look?"

"I have an idea." He smiled at Amanda. "You take care of your mama, okay?"

"Okay."

Rachel gasped at the whispered word. It was still such a shock to hear her daughter speak.

"You keep doing that, munchkin. Talking, I mean." Jack leaned down to chuck her under the chin. "Your mama needs to hear it. All the time."

Amanda nodded.

"Good girl." With that, he was gone.

Rachel prayed he found his brother soon. She wouldn't allow herself to think about the possibility Patrick really didn't care enough to come back to her.

25

What was he doing here? Patrick stared out his dusty truck windshield at the Thorne family cabin hidden thirty miles deep in the mountains northwest of Denver. He debated whether to turn off the engine or turn around and drive back to the city.

"I'm pregnant, Greg. Tell me again that I can't have children, you pathetic liar."

Patrick crushed the sound of Rachel's luscious voice in his head. "Yeah, right," he muttered, his frustration palpable. "Like there's anything in Denver for you to go back to."

His construction sites were shut down. He couldn't go to Southgate to salvage his teetering business thanks to a saboteur and serial killer still on the loose. With Bishop's arrest, his babysitting duties were no longer necessary. His brother would already have secured Rachel and Amanda at the hospital under police protection, just in case. Jack certainly didn't need Patrick's help. He couldn't return to his home office because he was avoiding his parents. If he had to dissect everything he'd done wrong since he jumped the cranberry fence between their properties to rescue Rachel, he'd go out of his mind.

"I'm pregnant."

The words had haunted him these past two hours as he drove to the cabin. Had she'd known when she made love to him? Of course, she did. It was yet another of Rachel's secrets. But why would she tell him she couldn't get pregnant? *Because you weren't going to make love to her without protection.*

For a moment, after hearing her tell Bishop she was pregnant, he'd reveled in the idea the child might be his. But then, he realized it wasn't possible. It had only been a week since the night he'd given in to temptation and made love to Rachel over and over like an insatiable teenager.

Patrick smacked his fist on the steering wheel, the sting in his hand reminding him it didn't matter why she'd done it. She was pregnant and Patrick had no choice but to watch her run back to Dallas. The loss was eating him from the inside out. Rachel. Amanda. A baby.

Which was the real reason he'd bolted like his pants were on fire because he loved Rachel enough to want her whether the baby was his or not.

Patrick was glad he hadn't revealed his feelings to Rachel. *You're here to remind yourself why you vowed not get involved with yet another broken woman, why her leaving is best for everyone. Clearly, you learned nothing the day Karly died.*

The memory of that day pounded through his head as he turned off the engine and climbed out of the truck. He took a fortifying breath of the pine-scented mountain air. Then, he walked across the open meadow behind the old homestead to the family cemetery where seven generations of Thorne's—eight generations counting his unborn son—were laid to rest.

Karly's suicide prevented him from burying them in the Catholic graveyard in Denver, where the more recent Thornes had a family plot. But she had loved coming here. It seemed right that she would rest where she had been happiest during their brief, six month marriage. His innocent son deserved to be laid to rest with the Thornes, too. The decision to bring them both here had been so easy.

Coming back was the hard part. After spending most of his free time here every summer, even as an adult hiking these mountains, he'd returned only once after burying his family. The first anniversary of their death had almost torn him in two. All he could think about was never seeing his son born, teaching him to build things, never going camping or fishing together.

Jack had found Patrick lying on their grave, drunk and incoherent, crying over the injustice of what Karly had done. His brother spent the next few days scraping his sorry ass back together. He hadn't been back to the cabin since.

Until today.

He'd grown up thinking he'd be like his parents someday with a Victorian full of happy kids, some his, some fostered, all raised in a household with two loving parents. The loss of his wife and son cured him of that dream. When he'd left the mountainside with Jack last year, he'd made his decision. No more women, especially broken women with trouble in their wake. His rescuing days were over.

It was almost poetic he was returning to bury his heart here, so close to the second anniversary of Karly's death. *You're right back where you started*.

He shoved at the rusted iron cemetery gate, not yet prepared to think about Rachel and Amanda leaving him, the ache in his heart too fresh. The

345

gate squealed open when he threw his hip into it, and he made a mental note to oil the hinges before he went back to Denver.

When he stood over his wife and son's grave, he stopped. He looked at the bouquet drooping over the side of the urn attached to their headstone. These must be the flowers Skip left when he visited on Karly's birthday, their color and freshness now faded. The second bouquet his mother sent with Skip lay on the ground ripped into pieces and ground into a patch of Kinnikinnick. He smiled sadly at the thought of deer munching the forest ground cover and discovering the hothouse flowers only to turn to the more savory summer blossoms popping up around the headstone.

A profusion of mule's ear, skunk flower, and Colorado Blue Columbine covered the grave. Karly would have loved these much better than the hothouse blooms anyway. They were only married a month the first time he'd brought her here. One of her favorite pastimes on the weekends that followed, whenever he could break away from business, was to sketch the wildflowers.

She'd carried a diary with her, always writing something in it if she wasn't sketching. It was something she'd learned to do, she'd told him, after she'd had a breakdown when she was twenty. She'd told him her own sad story then, about her college boyfriend. He'd been killed by a mountain lion during a camping trip with her brother, Skip. She'd fought depression her entire life, growing up with an alcoholic mother and abusive father. But she hadn't found a way to deal with it until that one life changing event had pushed her over the edge.

Her poor brother, Skip returned from the Army just days after her death. He'd been as devastated as Patrick that he hadn't arrived in time to save her. Patrick was often surprised at how well balanced Karly's brother seemed after growing up in the same environment. It was odd how one child could persevere and blossom, while another disintegrated under similar circumstances. Maybe it was because Skip was eight years older and didn't suffer the same kind of abuse from his father that Karly had.

Patrick had believed she had her depression under control. Or maybe he'd just been too busy building Thorne Enterprises to notice the signs. He hadn't known she was upset about the baby until they argued that fateful day. Would she have taken her life if he hadn't been blindsided and lost his temper? Would she still be here if he'd gone after her, if he'd fought harder for her and their child?

Karly often withdrew from him when she was upset. He'd learned early in their marriage to give her the space she needed. She always came to him when she was ready, and they'd discuss whatever was bothering her, resolve the problem. Not that day.

He waited for the pain of regret and guilt to burn through him. It came, but it was tempered by the knowledge he would never know what she was thinking when she walked out on him. She was gone.

Her secrets aren't gone.

The thought gave him pause. Karly had never shared her diaries, saying they were her "safety zone", the one place she could share her worst nightmares, and then return to the real world without them. The day he'd buried her at the edge of the meadow, he'd boxed her belongings and jammed it all in the darkest corner of the cabin eaves. As far as he knew, they were still there.

Last year, he wouldn't have considered prying into Karly's diaries. It was too painful. But now? Maybe the diaries would shed some light on her actions that last day, and give him some peace. "Forgive me, Karly," Patrick murmured, "but I have to know."

Determined to lay his questions to rest, he left the cemetery and walked back to the two story cabin. As he came around the front, Jack pulled up in his Jeep.

"What are you doing here, Jack?" Patrick said as his brother climbed out of the vehicle.

Tossing his sunglasses on the driver's seat, he closed the door. "Came to find you. Bring you home."

"You found me." He turned his back and located the front door key in one of the rustic flower pots on the porch. "But I'm not going home." He hefted the key in his palm.

Jack squared his shoulders, a sign he was on a mission and Patrick was about to get his ass kicked if he didn't cooperate. "Then we talk here."

Whatever his brother was there to do, Patrick wasn't interested. Without a word, he opened the cabin door and entered the stuffy main room of the original homestead. Skip must not have stayed overnight when he was here last week, as Patrick suggested, because the place didn't smell like it had been aired yet this season. Tossing the key on the barn door kitchen table, he walked around the downstairs opening the windows.

Once fresh air billowed all of the curtains, he stopped in the middle of the kitchen and glared at his brother. Jack watched him from the open doorway. Patrick tensed as he asked the one question he knew he shouldn't. "Are Rachel and Amanda okay?"

"No."

"Bishop was secure," he said tightly. "They were safe when I left. What happened?"

"You left."

"What are you talking about? Are they okay or not?" He realized he was shouting.

Jack closed the door and walked to the kitchen area in one corner of the room. He turned a chair and straddled it like the back rungs would serve as a buffer between them. "Do you love Rachel?

"What?"

"It's a simple question. Do you love her?"

Patrick dropped into a chair on the other side of the table. The question threatened to make him lose what little control he'd regained on the way up here. Of course, he loved Rachel. That didn't mean he could have her. Or that he could watch her walk into another man's arms.

"I thought so." Jack looked like he wanted to punch Patrick in the nose. "The baby's yours."

Patrick stared. He hadn't realized how much he wanted it to be true...was afraid it was true.

Standing abruptly, he walked to the sink. He ran the water until it cleared, filled a tea kettle, and set it over a flame on the gas stove. Then, he pulled out two mugs and a jar of instant coffee. When there was nothing else for him to do, he stared out the kitchen window at the forest line beyond the meadow. Where Karly was buried. Where his baby boy was buried.

"Talk to me, Patrick." Jack's voice was quiet. "What are you afraid of?"

"Failing them. Losing them. Take your pick." The words were out before he could stop them. He turned. "I messed up so badly with Karly. It would kill me to lose Rachel and Amanda." And the baby...even if it wasn't his.

"I knew this was going to come back to Karly." Jack pinned him under a hard look. "You have to let her go. You can't know what was in her head. And bro, just for the record, Rachel isn't Karly."

"Don't you think I don't know that?" The women were polar opposites. Rachel was soft and inviting and giving. She'd sacrifice herself to protect her child. She was strong and independent, and he'd fallen in love with her despite his resolution to stay away. Karly had been weak. Fragile, both emotionally and physically. Karly....

"Well, I don't have time to sit up here and watch you drink yourself into another stupor."

He picked up the whistling tea kettle and waved it at his brother. "Does it look like I'm drinking?"

"Not yet." Jack tilted his head, his no-bullshit expression firmly in place. "Karly's gone. It's time you put her to rest."

Patrick banged the teakettle down on the butcher block and took a moment to control his irritation. Finally, after a count of ten, he nodded. "I know. The truth is, before you drove up, I was on my way upstairs to find Karly's things. She kept some diaries. I was hoping that if I knew what she was thinking, I'd understand why she did what she did."

Jack studied him for a full minute. "Want some help?"

"Yeah. I think I do," he said, the weight on his shoulders lifting. Of all his brothers, Jack was the closest in temperament and understanding. It was one of the reasons he'd tracked him to the cabin last year. Jack had somehow known Patrick needed someone to pull him back to the land of the living.

"Lead the way, runt." Jack's descent into the familiar childhood taunt grounded Patrick.

His brother at his back, he took the staircase to the second floor that his dad had built on to the cabin. A hallway bisected the cabin, with two bedrooms on either side. Bypassing the four small rooms, they went to the end of the hall. He didn't hesitate until he stood outside the door that led to the storage space under the eaves.

"Are you ready?" Jack stood at his back. Jack always had his back.

Was he ready? Did he truly want to know what Karly was thinking in the days and weeks before her death? They'd been married less than six months and, God knows, they hadn't been all lightness and love. She'd fought depression for years and it didn't magically disappear on their wedding day. He'd often felt helpless when she withdrew into herself. She'd cry for hours and there was nothing he could do for her. She'd sent him off to work, saying he had a business to run. He'd accepted the easy way out. He should have been more understanding, spent more time with her when she was having a bad day. He hadn't been there when she needed him most.

He'd never be ready. "Let's do it." His jaw firmed, he opened the door and climbed the stairs into the low storage room under the eaves. Ducking his head, he made his way across the cluttered space to the four medium-sized boxes stacked in one corner. He handed two to Jack, and followed him with the other two down to the kitchen table.

Looking down at what little remained of his wife's life, he felt the regret swell inside him. He cleared his throat.

Jack looked at him. "You sure you want to do this?"

"It's just," he paused, "it's disconcerting to see how little Karly added to her personal belongings in our time together. It's almost like she knew she was moving on and had to keep her bags lightly packed. She told me once she didn't dare stay in one place too long because she was afraid her past would catch up with her."

"You can't take responsibility for the life she had before you."

"I know." Guilt still banged around inside him, but it forced him to push a couple of boxes across the table to Jack. "Take a look inside those," he said. "We're looking for her diaries."

Patrick opened the box in front of him. It was filled with clothes, some pictures from their courthouse wedding, a pair of shoes, and a book with the first wildflowers she'd pressed between the pages. Jack found more of the same in the box he opened. No journals with Karly's distinctive scrawl.

"Here's something," Jack said. He reached into his second box and pulled out several journals. He handed a couple to Patrick.

They took turns reading whenever they found something of interest. But generally, the books were filled with sketches of places and people Patrick didn't know. One of the entries mentioned her psychiatrist's suggestion she put her thoughts and feelings into pictures and tuck them away where they couldn't hurt her.

Jack read an entry that revealed she'd had suicidal thoughts before Patrick met her. He was suddenly grateful for his brother's presence. He might not have continued this probe into Karly's secrets alone.

For several minutes, the only sound in the room was of pages being turned. "Whoa," Jack said. He held up several sketches he'd found folded between the pages. "Some of these are pretty dark and menacing." He frowned. "It's hard to believe this is the same woman you married."

Patrick nodded. "I knew she fought depression, but I had no clue she carried this much pain and despair. It must have been frightening." Karly also had the sweetest smile and a gentle nature that called out to him. It made him want to curl himself around her to shield her from the harsh realities of the world. That was, if he was honest with himself, the reason he'd married her. He'd wanted to rescue her from the darkness.

How could he have failed so abysmally?

At the bottom of the final box, Patrick uncovered two more diaries. A quick skim told him the first one held entries from the months before their mother invited Karly home with her. He set it on the table with the others, unread, and picked up the last journal. It began the day of their marriage.

I got married today. His name is Patrick and he's wonderful and beautiful, inside and out. He's gentle and kind. He never screams at me, like mama did. He doesn't frighten me like...no, that time is behind me now. That's why I'm starting this new book. A new name. New life. A new book to keep my good memories.

Her words struck him so hard he had to escape them. Abandoning the diary on the table, he stood and walked away to look out the window. Pages rustled behind Patrick telling him that Jack had pulled the journal to him, but he did nothing to stop his brother from reading about his life with Karly.

Watching the night settle over the meadow, he knew he hadn't been successful at keeping the darkness from creeping back into Karly's life. He knew her father abused her until she was nine, when he disappeared from her life. She'd told him the day he didn't come home from his factory job was the best day in her life. Only when her drunkard mother fell down their apartment stairs a year later, and Karly was removed to foster care, did she begin to heal. It couldn't have been easy being separated from her brother—Skip was of legal age then—but she said he wasn't able to provide her the care social services could give her. Then, to lose her college boyfriend?

"Who's Robby?"

Startled, Patrick turned back to Jack. "She mentions a Robby?"

"Yeah," he waved the diary. "About a month before she died."

"I got a letter from Robby today."

"I don't know anyone by that name. Maybe an old friend from college?"

"Maybe."

"I don't know how he found me here. It's been three years since I saw him in Memphis. He doesn't know I'm married now. I'm afraid to tell him about the baby."

Patrick had been careful not to let his family know about the pregnancy, but his brother didn't seem surprised when he caught his eye. "You told me last year when you were drunk." He shrugged. "No one else knows. I figured you'd tell mom and dad when you were ready."

He swallowed his guilt. He should have told his family. "I didn't know she was pregnant until a few days before she died." They'd discussed waiting until he got Thorne Enterprises firmly in the black, but he'd been

353

happy when she told him she was almost three months along. Why would she wait?

"What the hell? Listen to this."

"I'm scared. I was so careful! I don't know what he'll do when he finds out. I'm afraid he'll kill Patrick."

"What am I going to do?"

Jack scowled. "This sounds more like paranoia than depression, Patrick. Did you notice any signs her mental state was deteriorating?"

"No. I can't say she was depressed either. It's one of the reasons why I was blindsided by what she did."

"Then who is Robby and why would she think he'd want to kill you?"

An icy shudder rippled under Patrick's skin as Jack flipped through the next couple weeks, looking for more references to the mysterious Robby. "Here. Her final entry, the day she died."

Robby called yesterday while Patrick was at work. He wants to meet outside the World Trade Center on Broadway this afternoon.

Karly was hit by the bus near that corner!

I don't know if I can get there and back before Patrick comes home, but I have no choice. I can't let Robby come to the house. I have to protect Patrick. Robby can never know.

Karly's love for him was heart wrenching. The only thing he'd done that day was argue with her. Suspecting something was wrong that morning at breakfast, he came home early and caught her going out. When he demanded she tell him what was wrong, she burst into tears and said she was worried about the baby, that she was afraid mental illness was hereditary and she couldn't pass that on to their child.

Patrick was so shocked by the implications of what she said he didn't immediately follow her when she dashed out of the house. An hour later, she and the baby were dead. If he'd stopped her, convinced her that everything would be all right, maybe she wouldn't have killed herself. But he didn't stop her, and he'd live with that pain and guilt forever.

"Son-of-a-bitch!"

"What?" He grabbed the diary from his brother's hand and skimmed the entry until he got to the part that had stunned Jack.

I should have run away again, but I just can't do it. Patrick's good to me. I love him. I want our baby to grow up with his father, his grandparents and uncles. I want him to be loved the way they've all loved me.

Somehow, I have to convince Robby to let me go. Finally, and forever. I can't be his Angel anymore.

He glanced at Jack over the top of the diary when a photograph dropped out of the diary to land face up on the table. It was a picture of Karly and Skip. Karly didn't look older than fourteen or fifteen, though she was already curvaceous. Her wavy, chocolate-colored hair was held off her forehead with a headband and fell over her shoulders and breasts. She wore a simple white blouse and a blue skirt that could have doubled as a school uniform.

Just like the skirts and blouses that were nailed to the Southgate wall by his saboteur.

Uneasiness stole through Patrick's bloodstream. Karly's hair was dyed a reddish color when he knew her, but she'd been a natural brunette. The same color as the women who were kidnapped and killed in recent months. They all had similar, girlish looks and curvy body types.

"Christ, Patrick," Jack said, staring at the photograph. "I didn't know Karly was a brunette. Tell me she didn't have a tattoo."

"She had a burn scar where she said she'd fallen against a wood stove."

Jack flipped over the photo to find Karly's distinctive scrawl. *Robby and his 'Angel'.* He leapt to his feet, cursing a blue streak. "Shit! Shit! Shit! Robby is Skip," he said. "Skip's our Angel Killer!"

Patrick remembered the bouquet of flowers tossed in the Kinnikinnick at Karly's gravesite. Not eaten by foraging animals. Ripped to shreds by a raging brother with an unnatural obsession with his little sister. Karly didn't commit suicide. She'd loved Patrick, wanted their baby. She'd met her brother to ask him to let her go, and Skip had killed her. *Jesus.*

Scooping all of the diaries into a box, Jack made for the door. "We've got to get back to Denver. Now," he said harshly. "It's going to take at least an hour to get anywhere near a cell tower and another hour to get to Denver."

He continued to shout orders as they raced for their vehicles in the dark. "Follow me down in your truck. When we get back to the city, go directly to the hospital. I left mom and dad with Rachel and Amanda and a security detail. Tell them what's going on while I get the task force rolling. We have to find Skip before he kills again."

Stopping next to Patrick's truck, Jack gave him a hard stare. "Stay with them. No heroics. If Karly's right, Skip wants to kill you...and Rachel."

Just the thought made his pulse pound. "I'll be damned if I let him hurt any more of our family," he promised. "I'll protect them."

"And, Patrick, be careful driving back to the city. I'm going to be royally pissed if you run your truck off a cliff trying to get to them. They're safe enough under police protection until you get there." Jack turned and ran to his Jeep. "I'll call you the moment we've got him," he called over his shoulder. "Stay in touch!"

They both jumped into their vehicles and began the most nerve-wracking trip down the mountain Patrick had ever experienced.

26

Watching Amanda sleep, Rachel sniffed back a tear of thanksgiving. She was happy when the doctors told her they were cautiously optimistic her little girl had received no further damage to her spleen. They still wanted her to remain in the hospital for a couple of days, but Rachel could live with that.

She was thrilled Amanda continued to talk after the trauma of her father's....

No, *Greg's* attack and arrest. Amanda had a long way to go to be called a chatterbox, but she'd uttered a few single words in answer to Rachel's questions, called her "mama". Rachel had hope the therapist Sam found for her would make progress, helping Amanda become the happy little girl she'd lost.

It would take time. Rachel now knew what had put the shadows in her baby's eyes. At least some of them. Greg's last threat had revealed the sickening truth. He'd killed Amanda's puppy, not a rogue coyote as he'd claimed, and the four-year-old had witnessed it.

She hadn't stopped talking until the night he'd beaten Rachel though. Rachel didn't know for sure—it was something the therapist could help uncover—but she had a feeling he'd used that brutality to traumatize Amanda into silence about the doll, "pwomising" not to hurt Rachel if she didn't let it out of her sight or tell anyone about it. He knew he was going to jail and would do whatever was necessary to protect the information inside the doll. Amanda's odd attachment to the thing finally made sense.

Of course it was all conjecture. Knowing Greg, Rachel wouldn't be surprised he'd done that and more. Thank God, he was now cooling his heels in jail. For the first time in years she didn't have to worry that he'd hurt her or Amanda. This time he wasn't getting out of jail on a technicality.

The FBI caught everything he said on the wire she'd worn under her blouse. His taunt about blowing up the clinic, his attempt to murder Simon. His admission that he'd killed the family pet. He'd kidnapped and endangered Amanda, and at least ten agents witnessed his attack on Rachel. Her ex-husband was going to prison for a long time. To top it all off, the FBI had located the money he'd conned. They'd already frozen his accounts in Dubai and begun the process of getting the funds transferred back to the States. Everyone was happy.

Well, almost everyone. Another tear ran down her face as she rubbed her hand in circles over her flat stomach. Her thoughts weren't on the scars there, but the life she carried deep inside her. Patrick's baby might never know his real father, and that broke her heart.

What was she going to do if Jack didn't find him or, worse, he didn't want to come back? There were no guarantees Patrick's mother and brother were right. They both seemed certain he cared for her. She wished she were as confident.

"Are you okay, Rachel?" Evelyn spoke up from the other chair nestled next to Amanda's bed. Ross was fast asleep on the chair that pulled out into a bed, the pills he'd taken for his damaged knee dragging him under more than an hour ago.

"I'm fine."

Evelyn didn't look like she believed her. "Everything will work out when Patrick comes home and you two talk."

"I hope so," she said with a wan smile.

She still didn't know what she'd say to the man. She'd known it would be difficult to tell him about the baby. She didn't want to force Patrick into marriage for the sake of the child. She was certain, if he felt responsible, he'd be marrying her so fast her head would spin.

At least, she'd been certain until he'd left her behind at the zoo...like he didn't care. She wanted him, but she didn't want him if he didn't love her. What a mess!

A commotion in the corridor beyond the closed door dragged her away from her worry. Using her crutch to push out of the chair, she crossed the room and opened the door a crack to see the policeman stationed outside stiffen belligerently in front of Patrick's brother-in-law.

"Skip!" she said, slipping from the room. "It's okay," she said to the policeman. "Skip's family."

The man relaxed a bit, but not much. "He's not on the approved list of visitors, Ms. James."

Skip shrugged affably. "No problem, Rachel. Patrick wasn't expecting me to stop in so it wasn't necessary to put me on the list. Can I talk to you for a minute though?"

"What about?" She glanced over her shoulder at the closed door. "Amanda might wake up and I don't want her to find me gone."

He shrugged and glanced pointedly at the policeman listening to their conversation. "Um, it's family business. Could we talk in private? Just for a few minutes. The waiting room down the hall is empty." He smiled crookedly. "I'll make it quick. I promise."

If it had been anyone else, she might have put him off. But this was Skip, the man who'd saved Patrick. Surely, she could spare a few minutes to talk to him. She opened her daughter's door and called to Evelyn. "Skip's here. Can you hold down the fort for a few minutes?"

Evelyn nodded sleepily. "Tell him I'll call tomorrow when I'm not so tired."

"I'll tell him," she whispered, shutting the door.

"Ms. James, I don't think—"

"Officer Buson," she interrupted. "I'm just going down the hall for a minute. I'll be right back. I promise."

"I'm not supposed to let you out of my sight."

She understood his dilemma, but didn't want to argue. She could have had her conversation with Skip and been back by now. "How about we stand at the end of the hall where you can still see me?"

He still didn't look happy, but nodded. "Stay where I can see you."

Her left hand wrapped tightly around her crutch, she tucked her right hand through Skip's arm. They walked down the hall. With each step, she felt more and more anxious. Was he here about Patrick? She didn't know where he'd gone after he left the zoo, and it was taking forever for Jack to bring him home.

Pulling Skip to a halt at the end of the hall, she glanced back at the watching policeman. She shot him a smile before turning to Patrick's brother-in-law. "What's wrong? Is Patrick okay?" she asked, giving voice to her worry.

"Geeze, I didn't mean to scare you, Rachel." He shook his head. "I haven't seen Patrick but I'm sure he's fine."

Relief rushed through her. "You scared me."

"I'm sorry. I shouldn't have come. I just—" Distress crossed his face and he turned away around the corner.

Rachel raised an index finger toward the policeman down the hall, a silent request for a minute, and followed Skip out of sight...and looked directly down the barrel of the pistol in his hand. "Skip?"

"No," he sneered. "Skip couldn't make it."

"I-I don't understand."

"You don't have to." He smiled. "Let's go."

"You won't shoot me." The situation was too surreal. "There's a cop right around the corner."

Reaching behind his back, he pulled a knife and waved it at her stomach. "It would be a shame to leave your little girl all alone in the world." His voice was conversational, but there was a glint of madness in his eyes that scared her to death. Where was Patrick's sweet, mild-mannered brother-in-law? "Skip—"

He snarled. "I told you that weakling, Skip, isn't here. If you don't come with me right now, I'll walk around that corner and kill that overprotective cop...and then it will be Amanda's turn."

"Ms. James?" Officer Buson's voice came from the other corridor, was getting closer.

She couldn't allow Skip to make good on his threat. "Don't touch them."

"Don't make me." Skip grinned, grabbed her arm, and tucked the knife behind her back where it couldn't be seen.

Before she knew it, they were walking through the hospital entrance into the warm summer night. Skip led her through the parking lot between the cars until he stopped in front of a battered, black truck. Realization dawned. "It was you that ran me off the road!"

"You're hard to kill," he whispered next to her ear as he covered her face with an awful smelling rag. "We'll do better this time."

The last thing she heard before the darkness overtook her was the crash of her crutch against the pavement and a strange man's laughter.

Patrick had entirely too much time to think on that long trip through the mountains back to Denver. He couldn't get to the hospital fast enough for his peace of mind. He had to see Rachel, Amanda, and his folks, make sure they were all safe. If Skip wanted to hurt him, the people he loved were in grave danger.

He'd missed the signs. It was Skip who pushed Rachel into the elevator shaft. Skip ran her off the road. Skip killed Cook. Wrote the threatening notes.

The first note, the one in his truck, had said, "They are mine." He'd believed *they* referred to Rachel and Amanda, that Bishop had left the note. But he couldn't have left the second one. After reading Karly's diaries, that first message took on a sinister new meaning. Had *they* meant Karly and her baby? Skip met with Karly that day. She must have told him she was pregnant.

Was Skip the mentally ill family member Karly worried about? An insanely jealous brother? The Angel Killer's victims looked nearly identical to the young Karly in the photo. Was Skip obsessively killing Karly over and over again?

The tenor of his thoughts set like seasoned concrete in his gut. Despite all evidence to the contrary, Skip had never struck him as dangerous. The man had shown up on his doorstep freshly released from the service two days after Karly died. Patrick had seen his expression when he was told his sister was gone. He'd been devastated by the news. Was he that good an actor?

He'd been part of the family since then, became Patrick's right hand man. He was conscientious, easy-going, and eager to please. Had he been right under the noses of the cops in the family, and fooled them all, for nearly two years? Patrick's site troubles hadn't started until about eleven months ago. The first woman the Angel Killer took was killed a month later.

How were they related? What could have set Skip off?

Maybe he and Jack had this all wrong. Patrick *wanted* to be wrong. The ramifications of being right didn't bear thinking.

He was half an hour from the hospital when his cell phone beeped a low battery warning. He cursed and plugged in his car charger. He should have checked it before he left Denver but, knowing it wouldn't work once he got to the cabin, he'd blown it off. Jack needed to reach him when he found Skip....

His cell vibrated, almost giving him a heart attack. Expecting it to be Jack, he was surprised Rachel's name popped onto the screen. She'd sent him a photo. His pulse leapt for a much different reason. He wanted to see her so badly he didn't think twice about opening the file.

The air sucked out of his lungs as he took his eyes off the road. It wasn't a picture from Rachel, but a picture *of* her. Her head lolled to one side, the bruise from the truck accident a brilliant mass of purple, green, and yellow on one pale cheek above the duct tape over her mouth. Her hands bound in her lap, some kind of wire was wrapped around her breasts and waist tying her to an exposed metal girder.

That was the space he'd been working before all hell broke loose with Jane's confession and Rachel's accident two days ago! He recognized the exterior wall behind her where he'd made a measurement notation. Right above it, in big red letters that looked too much like blood, one word was scrawled. *Southgate.*

"Son-of-a-bitch!" *Skip had Rachel at Southgate.* Five minutes away.

A horn blared. He swerved the truck across several lanes of highway traffic to another blare of a horn, but caught the exit ramp. "Hang on, sweetheart," he muttered.

Heading south he forwarded Rachel's picture to Jack, tossed the phone on the seat, and hit the gas. He made it to the Southgate gate four minutes later and squealed to a stop. Jumping out of the truck, his heart sank when security didn't come out of the guard shack to investigate.

Reaching under the seat for his Glock, he racked the slide to load the chamber. As an added measure, he grabbed a heavy wrench from the side pocket and tucked it into the back of his jeans under his T-shirt. He eyed the other tools. Wire cutters went into his left boot, a screwdriver in the other. When he dropped his pant legs back into place, they disappeared from view.

Better prepared, he turned toward the gate before Jack's voice resounded through his head. "No heroics." His brother would want him to wait for back up.

To hell with that. Patrick picked up the cell again, called Jack's number, and got voice mail. "Jack, I'm at Southgate. Skip has Rachel on the fourth floor of the unfinished building, west side. Come when you can. I'm not waiting for you."

Tossing the phone back into the truck, Patrick ran for the gate working to calm the fear rolling in his gut, not for himself but for the woman he loved. In the photo, she was unconscious, possibly injured. Patrick refused to believe she was dead. Just thinking about what the Angel Killer did to his victims froze the blood in his veins.

His gun in hand, he ran through the unlocked front gate to the guard shack five feet away, hoping he wouldn't find the guard. If the man was checking the perimeter, Patrick might yet have some backup. He found the guard lying on the shack floor in a pool of blood, his throat cut. The body still felt warm, but the Denver temperatures were hovering in the eighties despite the late hour, so it was hard to tell how long he'd been dead. Looking at the drying blood pool, Patrick was guessing at least an hour. That meant Skip had had enough time to secure his position while he waited for Patrick.

Patrick hunkered adjacent to the interior wall of the guard shack and considered his options. The situation had become all too real. Was he stalking a murderer or was the murderer stalking him?

Adrenaline surged through him. He forced it down and searched the guard's pockets and belt. The man's gun was missing. So was his cell phone.

Patrick closed his eyes and visualized the site, identified where he'd find cover, where he'd be exposed in the open space. The parking lot lights were iffy between the trailer and the first building, which actually helped with cover, but if Skip looked at just the right time he'd spot Patrick.

It didn't matter. Patrick had to get to Rachel.

Keeping to the shadows, he made it to the trailer seventy feet away. Spotting the cut phone line dangling from the pole next to the front door, he didn't bother going inside. "You'd better be on your way, Jack."

At the end of the trailer, he peered across the open space searching the dark windows of the two finished apartment buildings. Nothing stirred. He studied the third, unfinished building where Skip had Rachel. He considered running straight for his destination. Then caution overruled. If Skip had set a trap, Patrick stood a better chance of seeing it before it was sprung if he took his time.

Decision made, he sprinted from building to building until he reached his destination on the far side of the property. So far, so good. But, Jack and his cavalry hadn't arrived yet, so Patrick resigned himself to the knowledge Jack hadn't received either of his messages. He was on his own.

Slipping inside the last building, it took a few moments for his eyes to adjust to lower light. Thankfully, the glow of the city around the site seeped through the open windows allowing him to proceed without his flashlight.

Ignoring the elevator cage on the first floor—it was too noisy even if it wasn't locked down for the night—he ran up the closest stairwell, his gun at the ready. Knowing which room he wanted, he bypassed the first three floors. He didn't slow until he reached the door that opened to the fourth floor.

If Skip had laid a trap, it would be on this floor. They'd barely started closing in the rooms at the other end of the building, working first from the middle where the elevator bisected the building to his position on the stairs. If Patrick was right about what he saw in the photo, he'd find Rachel in the open space beyond the elevator. There were a number of hiding spaces between him and the elevator where Skip could set an ambush, so Patrick had to be on alert.

Opening the stairwell door, he eased into the corridor. One by one, he bypassed the apartment openings where doors remained unhung. He reached the elevator without incident, which worried him. Was Skip behind him? In front of him? Maybe Skip wasn't there. Hell, he could simply be biding his time until Patrick ran out of cover.

When Patrick reached the last completed wall on the floor, he stopped to listen. Nothing. He closed his eyes and ran the layout through his head. The interior studs for the three remaining apartments were completed, but no solid walls were up beyond this point.

Skip had chosen his spot well. It was too damned open. Patrick wasn't sneaking up on him.

Hunkering down, he poked his head around the wall. Peering through the studs, he searched the space. Shock ran through him when he immediately spotted Rachel tied to a girder thirty-five feet away, hunched over in a pool of light from the nearby window, her battered face slack. She looked dead.

No!

Whispering her name, he scanned the area twice before he ran to her side. When he saw her neon green blouse flutter over her breasts, he groaned. She was alive!

Checking again to make sure they were alone, he set his gun on the floor within easy reach next to the folds of her skirt. With one hand under her chin, he raised her head. He peeled off the duct tape as gently as possible with his other hand. "Rachel? Wake up." He patted her unbruised cheek. "Come on, honey. Open your eyes and look at me."

She moaned, tried to roll her head away from his grip.

"Look at me, Rach. That's it." He smiled when her eyes fluttered, opened. Staring into her huge, dilated pupils, his heart sank. Skip had given her something to knock her out. It didn't matter if Patrick could get her to her feet on her ankle cast; she wasn't likely to walk out of here on her own.

He wondered what the drug was doing to her, to the baby she carried. *Their baby.* Worry pounded at his insides.

"Patrick?" Rachel whispered.

"I'm here, sweetheart." Unable to stop himself, he kissed her. "You're going to be okay," he said, speaking as much for his peace of mind as hers. "I need you to stay awake now so I can untie you. Do you understand?"

He waited until she nodded before he let go of her chin and looked at her hands bound by a zip tie in her lap, the electrical wire wrapped twice around her and the girder. Reaching into his left boot, he palmed his wire cutters and made quick work of the zip tie. After chafing her hands, he cut the wire over her breasts and waist. She didn't fall over without the restraints, so he examined her eyes. "Good girl. Head feeling clearer now?"

"Yes." Rachel nodded. She glanced around them. "Where are we?"

"Southgate."

Her gaze darted around them in alarm. "Skip! At the hospital, he—"

"Kidnapped you," Patrick finished for her, his anger and urgency peaking. Setting the wire cutters on the floor, he picked up his gun and tucked it into his waistband. With an arm around Rachel's back and another under her legs, he stood, lifting her. "Let's get you out of here before he comes back."

"Too late, Thorne."

Patrick turned to face his brother-in-law. "You don't want to do this, Skip."

An odd snort of laughter escaped the shadows just before the man stepped into the light. "Skip doesn't, but we do."

We? Patrick stood there frozen, staring at a man who looked like Skip. Yet didn't. This man wore the same work clothes, had the same carefree hairstyle. But he stood taller, with more arrogance and dark purpose. Anger shown from his manic brown eyes. Cruelty. The threat radiating from him was colder than the Beretta 92-F held in his steady hand.

Looking at the sneer on his smiling lips, Patrick knew that he and Jack had it all wrong. Skip wasn't the Angel Killer. It was this man. "Hello, Robby."

"Put her down," Robby ordered. "Slowly."

Patrick needed his hands free if he wanted to keep Rachel alive, but he hesitated. As long as he held her, Robby couldn't see the gun tucked into his waistband. Once he was disarmed, their chances of surviving dropped dramatically.

Rachel squirmed in his arms and his gaze dropped to her face. She glanced to her left, where her right hand rested on the top of his Glock. Her eyelids flickered.

She was out of her mind if she was thinking what he thought she was thinking. He shook his head at her.

"If she tries to shoot me, Thorne," Robby said, "my first bullet goes right through her. She'll die and I'll still get the second shot off before you can drop her to shoot me." He chuckled. "Although I can't see you dropping her then, either. She means too much to you."

The bastard was right. If Patrick set her down, at least he could stand between her and Robby's gun. "I'll set her down."

"Gun first," Robby tsked. "Rachel, reach into his pants. Pull the gun out and throw it away." He chuckled. "Don't worry if you shoot his balls off. He's not going to need them anymore."

Her anxiety clouded her doe-brown eyes. "Patrick?"

"Do as he says, honey," he said.

For a moment, he wasn't sure she heard him. But then, she wrapped her hand around the grip and pulled the Glock free.

Held in Patrick's powerful arms, Skip in range, Rachel wondered if she had the ability to point the gun at him and pull the trigger. She knew how to shoot—her dad had made sure of that—but whatever Skip had used to knock her out was slow to dissipate and she felt weak as a kitten. Her head buzzed angrily.

She didn't want to die. There was too much to live for, her daughter, the baby. Patrick.

The arms under her legs and around her back squeezed a warning. "It's okay," Patrick murmured.

It was not okay! Skip wanted to kill them. *But Skip is sweet and gentle.* He pulled a knife on her, kidnapped her. *He saved Patrick from the gunman.* He was going to kill the man she loved. A sob crawled up her throat.

Patrick repositioned her in his arms like she was getting heavy, and the hand she had behind his back knocked into something hard. Was that another weapon under his shirt? She glanced up at him and, before she could question her own sanity, she tossed Patrick's gun over her shoulder.

Skip didn't look in the direction it fell, somewhere behind her. "Now, Rachel," he said, pointing to the girder where she'd been tied only minutes ago.

Patrick turned and set her down directly on top of the wire cutters he'd used to set her free. He caught her gaze when the cutters poked into her butt and she gasped, but he didn't say anything before he straightened and turned his back to her. He took a wide stance in front of her, blocking her from Skip's view. "Let Rachel go," he said. "She's not part of this."

"Oh, but she is," Skip said conversationally. "The moment you fell in love with her, she became the one thing you can't live without. I thought it was Thorne Enterprises, but I can burn this building down and you'd hardly notice. I burn it down with her in it, that's a different story, isn't it?"

"I won't let you do it."

Their captor snorted. "I'm the one with the gun." He tossed something to the floor at Patrick's feet. "Use the twist tie on her hands."

"No."

A bullet gouged a hole in the floor three inches from Rachel's left thigh. She grunted when a wood splinter jabbed into her leg.

"You bastard!" Patrick's hands clenched, but he stayed where he was, a wall between her and the monster.

"Last chance, Thorne."

With a growl, Patrick picked up the twist tie and came back to her side. The sheer rage in his eyes tore at her heart and told her that what Skip said was true. He loved her and he was prepared to die to protect her.

She watched him kneel in front of her. He slipped his hands under her to scoot her closer to the girder. She felt the wire cutters he'd scooped from beneath her drop into the hidden folds of her skirt over her lap before he put the twist tie over her wrists and drew it closed. She glanced over his shoulder to see if Skip saw him supply her with a means to escape.

"Tighter, Thorne."

Rachel stared at Patrick helplessly as he did as Skip ordered, snugging the twist tie around her wrists. "I love you," she said, suddenly aware this might be her last opportunity to tell Patrick how she felt.

He froze, his hands clenched over hers. He stared at her for one agonizing moment. Then he leaned over, kissed her and, without a word, stood to face Skip.

"Your turn." The man motioned with his gun at another girder ten feet away. There was a heavy duty wire wrapped around the metal post with what looked like a short leash, a twist tie partially closed at the end. "Put the tie on."

Stalking to the pillar, Patrick sat down on the floor and cuffed himself. The rasp of the twist tie clicking inexorably closed in the silent building sounded like a death knell to Rachel. She'd suspected he had a plan. That was before he locked himself in Skip's trap.

An awful thought entered her mind. Dear God, did Patrick expect her to set herself free and leave him behind to be killed? "No, Patrick," she moaned.

Rachel looked at him with such horror, it was all Patrick could do to keep his mind on what he needed to do. Her declaration of love had nearly cut him in two because he knew she was saying goodbye, and this wasn't over. Not by a damn longshot.

He longed to reassure her. Now that he was tied up like a goat ready for slaughter, he wasn't feeling as secure with his plan. Breaking his bonds wasn't the problem. He and Jack had watched a video on how to escape twist ties when they were teens and then practiced for weeks escaping each other in their own version of cops and robbers. There was still a screwdriver in his boot, a wrench at his back. That didn't stop him from wanting his gun, lying in the shadows somewhere behind Rachel. He was taking a big chance Robby wouldn't just shoot them.

If you screw this up or push Robby too far, you and Rachel are both going to die whether you have your gun or not. Concentrate! At least, one part of his plan was working. His brother-in-law was no longer looking at Rachel. "What do you want?"

"I want you to die." Robby lowered his gun and put it on the cross brace of a nearby stud wall. Walking out of sight into the shadows, he came back with a couple of gas cans. He took off the caps, threw them away, and started splashing gasoline all over the surrounding stud walls and sub-floor, more than enough fuel to set the entire building ablaze.

"You don't have to go to all this trouble, Robby," he taunted. "Just kill me, and get it over with." He only needed the bastard to come close enough without his gun to take him out.

Stopping next to Rachel, he looked at Patrick. "That would be too easy," he said, a monstrous light in his eyes. "We want you to suffer before you die. You'll watch her," he soaked Rachel's skirt in gasoline, "die first. Screaming."

"Patrick!" Rachel gasped his name, and then began hacking and coughing as Robby poured gasoline over her head.

Horrified by the unholy look on Robby's face, Patrick realized the true scope of who he was dealing with. His brother-in-law had multiple personalities. It's how Skip had fooled everyone for so long. He was Robby, and this monster, too. The real Angel Killer had just doused the woman Patrick loved in gasoline.

With a roar of rage, Patrick wrenched the twist ties from his wrists and leaped to his feet. He was almost within arm's reach when Robby stood over Rachel with a Zippo lighter poised over her head. "Nuh-uh! One more step and she's extra-crispy, Thorne!" He struck a flame to life.

Patrick froze, his brain working furiously. "Why, Robby? What did I ever do to you?" He knew, but he had to keep Robby talking, from dropping the lighter. If that happened, he'd never save Rachel. He couldn't lose her and the baby, not this way!

Robby stared, and then his expression disintegrated with pain. "You took her from me. She was mine. *Mine!*" He stepped away from Rachel. "You touched my angel. I'll kill you for that."

Patrick showed his disgust, trying to draw him closer. One more step and he'd be within reach. "Karly was your sister, you sick bastard," he grit out. "She could never be yours."

Robby snarled, something feral and vicious in his eyes that startled Patrick, but before he could rush him, Rachel called out. "Skip! Stop!"

The man froze. "Rachel?"

For a moment, Patrick saw Skip look down on her with confusion. He also saw his arm lower, the flame getting closer to her soaked hair and clothes. Out of the corner of his eye, he saw his brother, Jack, sneak up behind Skip with a S.W.A.T. squad at his back, their intent clear.

Patrick threw himself past Skip on top of Rachel. Without stopping, he rolled with her as far as he could as Jack yelled, "Freeze, you bastard!"

Everything happened in slow motion then. Patrick heard Skip shout something, a gunshot, and then a terrifying whoosh that told him Skip's lighter had fallen into the gasoline. A wall of flames rushed up behind them as Patrick rolled with Rachel to a standstill in what he prayed was a gasoline free spot. Jumping to his feet, he pulled her up and ripped off her soaked skirt and blouse, throwing them as far away as possible.

When she was standing there in her bra and panties, he began to pull her into his arms when he realized he'd rolled through gasoline. Stripping himself became problematic when he realized he'd have to sit down to take off his boots to get his jeans off, and there was a wall of flame screaming across the floor toward them. In less than a minute, it would close off their only avenue of escape and they'd be cornered.

"There's no time," he shouted to Rachel, picking her up in his arms. Checking his path in the growing pall of smoke, he dashed along the outside wall toward the last place he'd seen Jack.

Rachel screamed when flames cut off their escape. Seeing a hole, Patrick took a chance and leaped through it. He came down hard on the other side and fell to one knee on the smoking subfloor. Hard hands wrapped around his arms on both sides, yanked him to his feet, and dragged him and Rachel down the corridor toward the exterior stairs. The S.W.A.T. guys didn't let go of them until they'd burst into the fresh night air outside the building and ran them to the parking lot forty feet away.

When they released him, Patrick sank to the pavement and sucked clean air into his lungs, Rachel still cradled in his arms. Hands tried to take her from him, but he wouldn't let go. "No!" he gasped, choking from the smoke and gasoline in his lungs.

"Let us have her, sir," a paramedic said. "She needs oxygen."

Feeling Rachel convulse in his arms in a coughing fit, his arms tightened around her. "She's pregnant," he said shortly. "Been drugged. Gasoline."

The paramedic looked him straight in the eye. "I've got her, sir. Let me help her."

Patrick reluctantly let the man take her from his arms, and then collapsed in his own fit of coughing. Another paramedic helped him strip off his gasoline soaked clothes, wrapped him in a blanket, and tried to make him sit in the EMT truck. He shrugged the help off and walked to where Rachel sat on a gurney with an oxygen mask over her nose and mouth.

He took a seat next to her, picked up her hand, and threaded their fingers. He was never letting this woman go again. "You okay?"

Her eyes filled with tears. She nodded. She lifted the mask from her face to talk. "Were you burned?"

Even raspy with smoke, Rachel's luscious Southern voice wrapped around his heart. His throat was raw and his eyes were burning from the smoke in the air, but he was fine. "I'm good," he said.

"Patrick, I—"

As much as he wanted to hear what she had to say, coughing cut her off. He put his hand over hers atop the mask and put it back over her face. "Keep this on, sweetheart. Okay?"

Two ladder trucks burst onto the scene in a cacophony of noise and firefighters jumped into action to work on the fire eating a hole in the building they'd barely escaped. Looking at the fire rage on, Patrick knew it was a lost cause. He knew he should care, should hope they could keep the fire from spreading to the other two Southgate buildings. At that moment, he just didn't.

The only thing that mattered to him was the way Rachel looked at him with her heart in her eyes. *She loved him.* The words wormed their way deep inside him and, for the first time in forever, he felt calm. At peace. He couldn't wait to get her alone so he could tell her, show her....

A paramedic lifted an oxygen mask over his head. He scowled at the man, but didn't take it off. The cool air felt good on his lungs.

"They tell me you're both going to be okay." Jack walked up to stand in front of them.

Pulling Rachel's hand into his lap, Patrick nodded.

"Good," Jack scowled, "because just as soon as you're completely recovered, I'm kicking your ass."

"I love you, too, bro," he said, coughing into the mask. When he stopped hacking up his lung, he motioned toward the burning building. "Skip? What happened in there?"

Jack's lips pressed into a fine line. "Skip threw the lighter down and ran for a gun he had in one of the stud walls." He glanced at Rachel before he finished. "S.W.A.T had to shoot him."

"Is he dead?" she asked.

"No. Got him through the shoulder. He's been rushed to the hospital for surgery."

Patrick sighed. "So, we won't know everything until he comes out and you can question him."

"We're already taking a look at all of the people who've died suspiciously in his life right back to when his father disappeared. I'm laying odds we're going to be digging up skeletons for a long time. It'll take time to sort it all out. Now that we know who he is, we'll ferret out all of his secrets."

"That might be more complicated than you think." Patrick took his oxygen mask off, waved off the nearby paramedics, and lowered his voice. "I think Skip has multiple personalities, he didn't know what Robby was doing."

"You're joking, right?" Jack stared at him, then at the flaming building for a full minute. "What a clusterbang."

"I gather you got the photo? That's why you rode in with the cavalry?" Patrick asked. He wanted to know what had happened to Jack after they split up at the bottom of the mountain.

"Yeah. I got it." Jack nodded. "Sorry it took me so long to get here."

Patrick tilted his head and studied his hard expression. "What happened?"

Jack ran his hand over his face. "I called the team the moment I came off the mountain and hit the first tower, told them what we'd found. By the time I got to the station, they'd traced Karly's name to a house rental on the outskirts of town and gotten organized." He waved at the S.W.A.T. team milling around their truck twenty yards away. "We hit the house, hoping to find Skip. Good thing the house was close by."

"Guess that was a wasted trip since Skip was planning our demise here," Patrick pointed out dryly.

"It wasn't a wasted trip. We found Jaymie Lindsey, the Angel Killer's most recent kidnap victim. She's alive. Barely." He frowned. "She was locked in a room in the basement, unconscious. I don't know what would have happened to her if we hadn't shown up. When we found her, she hardly had a pulse. The paramedics said Skip overdosed her with whatever drug he was using to knock his victims out."

Patrick felt Rachel jerk. Her hand tightened on his. He kissed her tenderly. He didn't care what his brother thought. "You and the baby are going to be fine," he assured her.

"Yes, she is," Jack cut in, waving the paramedics back. "You two get to the hospital now so I can get to work cleaning up this mess. We can talk later."

Patrick sighed heavily. "The folks are probably going nuts wondering what happened to Rachel. We should call—"

"Already done." His brother waved his phone. "I talked to Dad the moment we got you out of the building. He's spitting mad he was sleeping and didn't protect Rachel." He shrugged. "He'll feel better after he lays eyes on the two of you."

"Is Amanda okay?" Rachel put her arm on Jack's forearm. "Knowing she was safe with your parents was the only thing that got me through."

Jack patted her hand. "She slept through the entire uproar at the hospital. She'll be glad to see her mama in the morning when she wakes up, though."

Two hours later, Patrick watched Rachel sitting in the chair on the other side of Amanda's hospital bed stroking her sleeping daughter's baby fine hair. She yawned, and he felt an answering yawn pull at his mouth. They were both exhausted, yet neither would give up the fight to stay awake.

They'd both been given a clean bill of health. He'd talked his mom into taking his dad home to their own bed. The police office was no longer stationed outside the door. He and Rachel were finally alone and he didn't know what to say to her. He just knew he had to say something. Do something.

Rising from his chair, he walked around the end of the bed to tug her to her feet. "It's time to get some sleep," he said, indicating the chair bed his dad had vacated.

Rachel shook her head. "I can't sleep. My mind's still going around in circles."

"Then, don't sleep...with me." Patrick tugged her toward the converted bed, sat down and pulled her down to lie with him.

"Oh." She snuggled back as he wrapped his arms around her so they wouldn't fall off the narrow bed.

Patrick groaned as her bottom finally stilled against his hard length. "Comfy?" he growled.

"Very."

The humor he heard in her voice was almost his undoing. "You won't be quite so comfortable when I turn you over and have my way with you."

She looked over her shoulder at him. "You still want me?"

Sinking into her doe-brown eyes, he said what was in his heart. "Every day for the rest of my life. I'll never stop wanting you, Rachel."

When she didn't say anything, Patrick searched her expression and wished he knew what she was thinking. They hadn't been alone together since the night they'd made love. When they were together, she'd been distant. They'd argued. "At Southgate, you said you loved me." He paused, suddenly feeling insecure. "Did you mean it?"

Maneuvering around to face him, she nodded. "I meant it."

The tight knot in his check began to unravel. "Then, you'll marry me."

"No."

His heart stopped. "What do you mean, no?"

"I mean, yes, I love you. But no, I won't marry you."

He reared his head back like he'd been struck. "Why not?"

Rachel sighed, her heart cracking. She did love Patrick but she couldn't live with a man who just "wanted" her. Robby had said Patrick loved her, but Patrick hadn't said the words. "I don't need a protector anymore," she said. "You don't have to marry me because of the baby, either. I won't keep you from him, or her, if you want to visit. It's not that far to Dallas and—"

"Shut up," he said. His hands dove into her hair and pulled her into a kiss that started out hard, but quickly evolved into a caress that teased, cajoled...tempted.

She gave into temptation and met him touch for touch, reveled in each stroke of his tongue. There was no doubt he wanted her. It was on his lips, in the power of his arms around her back, and his hands exploring the curves of her bottom. His desire for her was in the hardening length of him against her belly, where his baby grew.

Patrick whispered against her throat. "Stay with me, Rachel. Don't leave me."

Her resolution was wavering. She longed to stay, wanted to marry him. Yearned to bear all of his children and spend the rest of her life loving him. But, she couldn't do it.

Pulling back, she stared into Patrick's eyes. She saw hurt and hesitation and, God help her, love. She grabbed his face in her hands and demanded what she wanted. "Then, tell me you love me."

He looked at her like she was nuts. "Of course, I love you. Didn't I just say that?"

"No." Her lips curved. "But now you have."

Patrick smiled and kissed her tenderly, with so much love that she had to believe him. They were both panting by the time they drew apart. "You'll marry me now, right?" He nibbled on her ear.

She gasped when he nipped it. "Why do you want me to?"

His assault on her neck ended as he lifted his head to look at her. "Are you serious?"

Rachel settled back to rest her head on his arm. "Yeah, I guess I am," she said with a sigh. "You left me behind at the zoo after you heard about the baby."

"The baby scared me, Rach. Hell, loving you scared the hell out of me. But," he snugged her closer when she tried to get up, "I want to marry you. I'd want to marry you even if the baby wasn't mine. I love you."

"You're not just feeling an urge to be the protective rescuer, with me the damsel in distress to fit the bill?"

"What?"

"We've only known each other a couple of weeks. Jack said Karly kicked in your protective instincts, that you married her a few weeks after you met. So I—"

Patrick groaned, understanding her worry. "Jack has a big mouth." And he'd chew his ass out when he saw him. "But, let me clarify something.

"Yes. I married Karly with some vague idea that I could rescue her. She was sweet and helpless and she appealed to my protective instincts," he admitted. "I knew very quickly that I'd made a mistake."

His hand cupped the bruise over her face. "I need to protect you, Rachel. But not because you're weak." His finger traced a line down her jaw. "You're strong and independent and sexy. You're the mother of my child." He settled his hand on her stomach. "I love you for so many reasons, and I promise we'll explore each one for the rest of our lives."

"I want to protect you, too," she said, lifting a hand to his heart. "I love you. You're strong and make me feel like I'm strong, too. You've taught me what real love means and I can't wait to learn how to grow old together."

"Does that mean you will marry me?" His gaze searched hers. "I don't want to misunderstand."

She smiled. "Yes, I'll marry you for all those reasons."

"Good," Patrick said, then tugged her close enough to feel his hardening length. "But, just in case there's still any question of what I want, let me show you a few more reasons."

"Oh! I think I see another one right now." Rachel sighed. "Show me more."

And he did.

One Week....

Three Days....

Ten Hours....

...*after death*.

"He'll be back," Skip whispered the moment the doctor's white coat disappeared from view down the corridor in the psychiatric wing. Through the glass windows of his locked hospital room, he watched the guard scratch at his neck. "That doctor's one of the persistent ones."

A menacing growl reverberated from the depths of his pounding skull where the monster threw himself impotently against his cage.

"I won't tell him Robby's dead...if you don't." He chuckled and looked around, at the restraints that strapped him down despite the fact he was recovering from his bullet wound. "Besides, he wouldn't believe us. He thinks some of us are insane."

He searched the darkness in his mind. Saw the shadow where Robby lay. Poked at it to see if anything stirred. "Nope. Doc's not going to find him."

The monster watched him through the bars inside his mind.

"Robby would be so disappointed to know he's missing the anniversary of Karly's death. He had such plans, was so sure he'd found his Karly this time. Stupid Robby was going to ride off into the sunset with his little tart of a sister."

He plucked at the sheet beneath his fingertips, and considered the isolated corridor outside his viewing window. "I have to say, I'm a little disappointed myself," he said. "I was really looking forward to seeing what he'd do when he realized you didn't kill her. That you didn't kill any of them."

Skip, the Angel Killer, smiled while the monster roared.

EPILOGUE

The moment Evelyn Thorne handed over the ten-day-old baby, Rachel felt her heart swell. Evelyn helped her son, Jack, with his boutonniere in the next room, and left Rachel gently rocking the little girl to sleep in the church nursery. They were all waiting for Jack's wedding to begin. Rachel didn't mind. She could sit with this little one for hours while she remembered how it felt to hold Amanda in her arms, how much she longed to hold Patrick's baby in the spring. This raven-haired child was a stranger's, headed for foster care until she could be adopted, and all Rachel wanted to do was gather up the poor thing and take her home.

Evelyn had broached the idea with her and Patrick the previous evening at Jack's rehearsal dinner, suggesting they take up where his parents left off and foster children after they were married. Apparently, Rachel was the last to know that Patrick had the diamond ring burning a hole in his pocket. Patrick took a knee in front of his entire family, and officially sealed their engagement. Once he put it on her finger, the time for talking was finished. They'd spent the night making love, making it official...again.

Rachel smiled happily at the ring on her left hand, then up at Patrick leaning on one of the low counters that ran the length of the wall of windows. The man was so sexy, as hot in a dark suit and matching tie as he looked in his jeans and work shirt. Although she did prefer him naked.

He watched her rock the baby, a crooked smile on his face. "You're considering it, aren't you?"

She searched his expression, not surprised he'd read her mind. He seemed to do that regularly. "What do you think?"

"It won't be easy with her health issues."

Patrick's comment didn't sound like he was opposed to the idea, just concerned about what they might be taking on. The baby was a preemie taken to a local hospital by the teenaged mother who couldn't take care of her. Baby "Jillian," as she was named by her mother before she signed her over to the state, was born with a heart condition that would demand surgery, maybe more than one, before she was six. No, raising this baby wouldn't be easy. "You're already taking on a wife and two kids," she added. "Jillian should have a permanent home."

"We'll still have four empty bedrooms once I move my exercise equipment into the basement. That's without touching the playroom."

"Last night we were talking about *making* babies." Rachel grinned when desire flared in his eyes at the reminder of how many times he'd made love to her. "You didn't mention a number."

He straightened and approached her. Her heart beat faster and desire settled low in her stomach. He hunkered down next to her chair and leaned over until his lips were a heartbeat away. "I love you so much I can't imagine a limit," he whispered, "for the *making* of babies."

"Oh, Patrick," she said. "I love you so much." Her feelings seemed to intensify every day, and every day she had to pinch herself to prove that it was all real.

Their lips joined and she was lost in sensation. She'd almost forgotten what they were talking about by the time he lifted his head. "Let's take the babies as they come, *however* they come. How does Jillian Thorne sound to you?"

"Like your mother may have to give up planning another of her son's weddings. Jillian isn't going to wait for her mama and daddy until September." They'd planned the wedding in the fall so her father could walk her down the aisle. He'd need the time to recover after his hip surgery.

Patrick tenderly dragged his knuckles over the infant's cheek before wrapping his hand behind Rachel's neck to draw her near again. "Mama and daddy can't wait that long either," he nuzzled her neck. "I told Mom this morning she has two weeks to pull off the wedding she wants or we're running off to Vegas. And your dad's prepared to wheel you down the aisle on his walker if necessary. Although, as well as he's doing in therapy, I'm betting that thing will be gathering dust in the garage before long." He caught her ear in his mouth and suckled it.

When she moaned, Patrick leaned back and looked at her with satisfaction shining in his dark eyes. "Given the impetus of another baby in the family, I can see our family working miracles."

"Hear that, Jillian? Daddy says you can have a whole family to protect and love you," Rachel murmured to the baby.

She picked up Patrick's hand from where it rested on the bundled baby in her arms, and gave his calloused palm a lingering kiss.

Her reward was a deep groan. "Daddy wants to love mama right now," he growled. "If we didn't want Father Sebastian to perform our wedding—" he straightened abruptly and dragged his fingers through his hair. "It will be a miracle if I get through *this* wedding and reception without dragging you into a dark closet."

Rachel sighed when he went back to his previous position, leaning on the counter with his arms crossed. Jillian stirred in her arms and she resumed her rocking, watching the man she loved watch them.

Her life had been filled with miracles lately. A lot had changed in the last three weeks. They'd escaped death. Robby's last victim was returned to her family. It was determined that Patrick's psychologically damaged brother-in-law wasn't going to trial, but he was getting the help he so desperately needed. Patrick's guilt over his part in his wife's death was easing now that he knew she hadn't killed herself and their unborn child.

Greg not only faced charges for kidnapping Amanda and trying to kill Rachel, but for the murder of her friend, Simon. He'd come out of his coma long enough to tell his wife where to find his safe deposit box. The box not only held proof that Amanda was hers, but evidence he'd gathered on several of Greg's cons. Bilking people of their life savings was now an afterthought. Since the FBI had recovered most of the stolen money, Katy wouldn't have to sell off her homestead.

Not that Rachel would have allowed that with the settlement of her Great-Aunt Amanda's estate. Her uncles had withdrawn their objections to the will once they discovered Rachel's desire to fulfill their aunt's commitment to help them build a new children's wing at a Dallas hospital. Rachel's needs were simple and she'd still have plenty left over to invest in her children's futures.

With the help of the specialist Sam found for Amanda, she was working through her PTSD. Rachel cried the day Amanda came home from the hospital and, tucking her into her new bed at Patrick's, Amanda had hugged her and whispered in her ear, "I love you, mama."

Rachel hadn't thought she'd ever hear her little girl speak those words again. Once she started talking, it was like she'd been storing up thoughts the last six months and she couldn't get them out fast enough. Rachel knew there were still tough times in front of them, but for now, she was cherishing each precious word her daughter uttered.

Amanda chose that moment to come into the room. Her frilly, blue party dress was miraculously un-mussed and Rachel was glad of the help of Patrick's foster brother, Ben Zancanelli, who'd flown in from San Francisco yesterday. The poor man had been immediately commandeered by Amanda after he presented her with a Chinese, geisha doll he'd picked up for her in Chinatown. It was clutched in one hand, while her other hand was engulfed in her new hero's much larger one. "Mama, Unca Ben wants cookies."

He nodded. "Yeah, Unca Ben wants one of those pretty, pink sprinkle cookies." He looked down at the little girl tugging on his suit jacket. "Can Amanda have one, too? I gather it's not polite to eat cookies without sharing."

Rachel would have loved to hear the conversation she suspected went on over the reception table because she knew exactly which cookies Amanda had her eye on. "It's true we shouldn't eat in front of others without sharing, but shouldn't you wait for dessert? Eat some sandwiches and salad first?"

Amanda looked at her mother seriously. "S'posed to eat cookies first."

She raised an eyebrow at Patrick's brother, who was every bit as sexy and masculine as the rest of the Thorne brothers. It hadn't taken her long to figure out why they were called Thorne's Thorns growing up. Each one could be as naughty as the next. Put them all in the same room and a girl could get overwhelmed.

Ben grinned, non-repentant. "Life's too short not to eat dessert first."

Patrick, silent until now, laughed. "Bet you can guess who got the first piece of pie or cake whenever Mom baked."

Ben shrugged. "With six of us in the house, pre-emptive strikes were necessary."

"Okay, Amanda," Rachel said, laughing. "You and Uncle Ben can have one cookie each. But then," she waggled a finger at Ben, "you eat a sandwich and salad before you can have another one."

"Yes, Mama," said both the naughty man and little girl.

Before they could leave the room, Evelyn came back into the room. Rachel saw that she did not look as jubilant as when she'd left twenty minutes ago. "Ben, I'll take Amanda to get her cookie. You and Patrick go help Jack."

Both brothers must have picked up on the intensity Rachel heard in Evelyn's voice. "Something wrong?" Patrick asked, straightening from his slouch on the counter.

Evelyn glanced at Amanda, looking up at all of them with that wary look that Rachel hoped to never see again. Evelyn smiled tightly. "Maggie sent a note. She's been...delayed."

Uh-oh. That didn't sound good. You can't have a wedding without a bride.

Ben frowned. "For how long?"

Evelyn reached out with one hand and handed him a wadded piece of paper. "It's all in the note," she said before smiling brightly to Amanda. "Now, let's go get some of those cookies, Miss 'Manda. Grandma thinks we should all have dessert first today."

Rachel watched Ben read the note, his face flush with strong emotion before he handed it to Patrick.

"What does it say?" she asked.

"The wedding's off." Patrick looked at her, pain for his brother in his eyes. "She's run off with the baby's real father."

"Go. Rescue Jack," she said. "Your family needs you now."

He walked to her and pressed his lips over hers. "You're my family, too, Rachel soon-to-be-Mrs. Thorne," he said roughly. "I love you too much to be apart for long. I'll be back." He kissed her again. With a groan, he lifted his head and stared into her eyes. "I can't wait to spend the next fifty or sixty years finding out all of your secrets."

"The only secret you need to know is that I love you." She smiled and ran her palm over his face. "Now, get out of here and help your brother. I'll be waiting."

ABOUT THE AUTHOR

Bestselling and award-winning author K.L. Docter writes romance novels in two genres.

K.L. Docter writes romantic suspense novels with intense dangers for the hero and heroine, usually because a serial killer is bent on ending one or both of their lives. Her Thorne's Thorns series tells the individual stories of six foster brothers with protective streaks a mile wide for their families and the women who capture their hearts.

Karen Docter's romantic comedies and contemporaries are spicy sweet, hometown hero romances. Her True Love in Uniform series is about the men and women that work as first responders in the fictional suburb of Riverton, Colorado, and how their lives change when they meet their love.

When she's not saving her characters from death and destruction or helping them to fall in love, she loves fishing off the dock of her family's lakehouse in coastal South Carolina, gardening, reading, and cooking.

Visit Karen's website: **http://www.karendocter.com**

Sign up for Karen's newsletter: **https://kdocter.substack.com**

Get all of Karen's books: **https://www.amazon.com/author/karen docter**